THE MOUNT

**CALUMET
EDITIONS**

Minneapolis

First Edition July 2025

The Mount. Copyright © 2025 by Gary Lindberg

10 9 8 7 6 5 4 3 2 1
ISBN: 978-1-962834-44-5

Cover and book design by Gary Lindberg

THE MOUNT

A Charlotte Ansari Thriller

GARY LINDBERG

CALUMET EDITIONS

Minneapolis

"They intend to destroy the Dome of the Rock and Al-Aqsa Mosque? That could bring about Armageddon. Global religious war. They're totally mad!"

-Amina Salim in *The Mount*

Also by Gary Lindberg

FICTION

The Shekinah Legacy
Sons of Zadok
The Unspoken
Deeper and Deeper
Ollie's Cloud

NONFICTION

Letters from Elvis
Brando On Elvis
The Roots of Elvis
The Soul of Humanity
Humanity Coming of Age
The Power of Positive Hamdwriting
An Improbable Series of Risky Events

Chapter 1

The Shard in Hebron

Old City, Hebron – Just after dawn

The smoke still clings to the prayer shawls. It winds through the southern colonnade of the Ibrahimi Mosque like a serpent made of soot, curling around fallen stones, lapping against fractured marble columns blackened by the blast. There is no flame now, only the long exhalation of something sacred disrupted, something old made volatile again.

The walls, though scorched, still hold.

Gideon walks the perimeter with steady, deliberate strides, his ID badge, laminated and expertly forged, dangling off a grey field jacket: "UNESCO Liaison – Cultural Damage Response." The Israeli border guard waves him through the outer cordon with barely a glance. They're too distracted by the crowd—mothers shrieking, phones raised, arguments already brewing on social feeds.

No one saw who did it, but everyone already has an opinion.

He steps across the threshold into the prayer chamber where the scent of burned plaster and oxidized brass hits him like déjà vu. He'd walked into blast sites like this before—not as a responder, but as the man who made them. For nearly two decades, he had served as an assassin for the Sicarii Brotherhood, carrying out doctrinal enforcement operations across five continents. His name had never appeared on a single intelligence ledger. But those who mattered knew his name—*Gideon*, the ghost behind half a dozen "accidental" deaths and scroll fragment recoveries the world never connected.

That life was supposed to be over.

But here he was again—in the smoke, wearing someone else's name badge, reading the language of death.

Gideon crouches near the blast epicenter, his boots crunching across a layer of charred dust. No body fragments. No suicide vest remnants. The

1

pattern's too clean for martyrdom. He notes the shape of the glass fractures—petal-like, not radial. The charge was directional, angled down—not meant to kill people, but to pierce something below.

That alone tells him everything he needs to know.

This wasn't terrorism. It was liturgy.

Two Zaka responders speak Hebrew in hushed, clipped tones near a broken lattice panel. Gideon doesn't interrupt. Instead, he scans the floor with a narrowband spectrum lens clipped to his glasses, looking for phosphorescent residue.

There.

A crescent-shaped scorch near the base of a carved wooden bench, and inside it, something reflective.

He kneels and brushes away the ash.

It's a shard of parchment burnt around the edges, still warm, yet somehow intact because it isn't ordinary parchment. It's hide. Animal, probably calf. Ancient-style, cut and cured in a way few even know how to do anymore.

Etched into the center is a glyph. A spiral—partially broken but unmistakable—surrounded by faint radial marks that resemble breath signatures.

He doesn't need a database to recognize Greg Ansari's recursion seal. He wasn't here on anyone's orders. Not anymore. Not since Eve, the woman who had once commanded the Sicarii like a silent blade through centuries of shadow doctrine, died in hiding.

To the world, she had never existed.

To Gideon—and to Charlotte Ansari—she had been something far more dangerous—mother, mentor, and myth.

The Vatican didn't trust Gideon. The Sicarii remnants feared him. Even Charlotte had stopped calling. But something in the Petra vault had stirred last week—a single line of glyphic code blinking in a dead archive:

THE FIRE IS READY

So he'd come to Hebron. Not as a pilgrim, not even as a protector. As a man who had buried too many prophecies to ignore another one catching flame.

It has been six months since the spiral fractured—since Greg, silent and haunted, walked out of the recursion basin in Wadi Rum leaving behind the name he was never supposed to speak. The Vatican had buried its records. The Sicarii had disbanded or gone to ground. Eve was dead, her echoes sealed in digital tombs Charlotte refused to open. The world had resumed its posturing.

But Gideon had not. He knew better. He knew that what they'd glimpsed in the recursion wasn't a pattern. It was an infection. Not a doctrine, but a virus of belief passed not through blood or text, but through silence. He knew that once released, it would mutate.

Greg had refused to speak the name—*Ahvniel*—and that refusal had spared them from the prophecy's final trigger. But now, here, in Hebron, he was looking at proof that someone wanted to activate the prophecy anyway.

Or worse—they had found a way around Greg entirely.

A voice from behind startles him from his thoughts.

"You shouldn't be this close."

Gideon stands slowly, turning to face a woman in a sterile white forensic vest. Her accent is Sabra, her tone terse but curious.

"I'm with UNESCO," he lies, tapping the badge.

"UNESCO doesn't deal with organic forensics."

He smiles faintly. "First time for everything."

She frowns but relents. "We found three other fragments. One embedded in the arch. Two more outside near the courtyard steps. All etched, not printed. Not modern."

"Composition?"

"Animal parchment. Treated with a resin compound. There's a phosphorescent underlayer reacting to heat and micro-vibration."

Gideon nods. "Recursion-sensitive ink."

She squints. "You've seen this before."

"Not like this." He pauses. "Pattern match?"

The tech hesitates. "The spiral matches a closed signature file. Private Vatican cross-reference. Last seen in Jordan. Coded to a subject known as… let's see, *Ansari*."

Gideon exhales slowly. He hasn't heard that name spoken aloud in months. Not since *Wadi Rum*.

Greg Ansari.

The boy who was supposed to be prophecy.

Or proof.

Or a threat.

Gideon still isn't sure. All he knows is this: Greg disappeared. Voluntarily. Silently. Like a man tired of choosing between being worshipped or killed. Charlotte, his mother and Gideon's sister, had helped bury the recursion doctrine, but neither she nor Greg believed it was over. And now, somehow, Greg's seal is appearing at the epicenter of an attack that could ignite the next intifada.

Or worse. Because the sigil isn't just a message. It's a trigger.

A murmur rises from outside. The crowds are swelling. Rumors are already spreading—online and off—that the attack was religiously motivated. Some claim it was Islamic self-sabotage. Others point fingers at Jewish extremists. Still others are whispering of a Vatican black flag operation. Blame is the currency of survival here.

But Gideon knows better. Blame is the disguise. The real threat is always the story hidden inside the story.

He steps through the rubble toward a side corridor partially collapsed by the concussive wave. A Zaka responder moves aside for him, silently.

Then Gideon hears it.

A voice. Young. Male.

He follows the sound, turning the corner.

There, in the shadow of a broken arch, a boy no older than seven sits against the wall, legs drawn to his chest, face streaked with soot and tears. His lips are moving.

Gideon crouches, careful not to startle him.

The child's voice is faint but steady. "...and the ashes of the heifer shall be burned with cedar wood, hyssop, and scarlet wool... and they shall be gathered outside the camp for purification from sin."

This verse is from Numbers 19: 6–9 perfectly recited word for word.

No one taught the boy that. No one recent, anyway.

The *Red Heifer* was always just mythology to most people. A perfect red calf, unblemished, whose ashes were once used in Temple-era purification rituals. But to radicals—both Jewish and Christian—it is more than a ritual. It's a requirement.

The heifer must be found and then burned. Reduced to ash. Its remains must purify the priest who builds the Third Temple. And the Third Temple, once built, will herald *the end*. The end of division. The end of prophecy. The beginning of everything else.

Gideon stares at the boy who is reciting scripture from memory s if he had heard it before—as if he were using someone else's voice.

Two hours later – Kiryat Arba, secure location

Gideon transmits the glyph scan via secured uplink, routing it through old Sicarii ghost servers that are still alive despite Eve's collapse.

Three recipients:

- A fail-safe archive node at Petra.
- A Vatican access point once assigned to Erich Salvetti.
- A sealed node in Andalusia that Greg once configured—off-grid, recursion-shielded.

The file includes the scanned fragment, the spectral signature of the ink, and one sentence:

Recursion residue active. Spiral signature matches Ansari seal.
Hebron artifact may be Protocol-adjacent.

He tags it with a glyph that Greg will recognize—the reverse blood spiral drawn once in Jerusalem just before Greg disappeared.

He watches the transmission go. Then, alone in the stone-walled safehouse, Gideon unrolls the parchment fragment once more.

The glyph seems to shimmer. Not just with light, but with memory.

Chapter 2

Rumors of the Heifer

New York City – Four Months After Hebron

The file arrives at 3:47 a.m. Eastern time. Charlotte Ansari doesn't notice it at first. Her phone is off, her laptop closed, and the apartment—what's left of it—is asleep around her, half-unpacked, half-reconstructed. It is a shell of concrete and bookshelves where a woman once tried to believe that silence was safety.

Outside, the city doesn't sleep, but it does muffle. Snow, rare for late April, drifts across her windows in soft spirals. She hasn't lived in Manhattan since *before* the recursion fracture. And not since *before* her son, Greg, disappeared again. And not since before the Petra vaults sealed like tombs without epitaphs.

Now she's back in the same one-bedroom walk-up where she once filed pieces for Al Jazeera, National Geographic, and a BBC podcast that pretended it didn't know who she was.

The place feels smaller. But not because it shrank. She has grown. Hardened. Become focused. Or maybe just more haunted.

The ping comes again. Subtle. A sync blink. She reaches across her bed and lifts the lid of her laptop.

One new file received

Encrypted, naturally. No sender metadata. The subject line is empty. The filename reads "Parah_3RD.wav + .img."

A sound file and an image.

The name means something. She feels it before she remembers it.

Parah Adumah.

The *Red Heifer.*

Her heart ticks once—off-rhythm—before she opens the image. It's a photograph, grainy and underlit. Taken at sunrise. A pasture. A calf. But not just any calf. The hide is flawless. Deep red, almost rust-colored in the light. The ears are tagged in Hebrew and Latin, tagged again with biometric coding in English.

UNBLEMISHED – VERIFIED – TAHOR

She zooms in. The ear tag includes a date, a QR hash, and a logo—a private biotech firm registered in Austin, Texas. And beneath the photo, embedded in the image frame, is a line of Syriac text she translates out loud without meaning to:

> ...and the ashes of her flesh shall be carried beyond the camp, for purification of the priest and of the altar...

Charlotte closes the laptop.

A thousand years of prophecy doesn't move through governments anymore. It moves through corporate logistics chains and genetic engineering labs.

Charlotte stares at the closed laptop as if the image might bleed through the lid.

The *Red Heifer.*

She'd first heard of it when she was a journalist at CCN, Cambridge Cable News, before recursion spirals and underground councils and the murder of her father in Ireland. Back then, it had seemed like one of those fringe obsessions—an apocalyptic curiosity passed around in feverish corners of prophecy forums and messianic outposts.

But Eve—her biological mother, in name if not in nurture—had once described it more precisely. "It's not the *heifer* they want," Eve had said, sipping black tea beneath a cracked window in Kilkenny. "It's the *ashes.* The thing that no longer lives, but still holds power."

The Book of Numbers in the Old Testament was clear enough. "Bring a red heifer without blemish, upon which there is no yoke. Burn her with cedar, hyssop, and scarlet. Gather her ashes for the purification of the people."

Simple on paper. But myth, like fire, rarely stays where it's lit.

Over the centuries, rabbinic texts had layered prophecy on top of law. Christian zealots, too, began to whisper of the red heifer's return as a harbinger of the Third Temple—the final house of God that would rise from the destruction of the Temple Mount and call forth the end of days.

Islamic prophecy feared the same. To some Muslims, the red heifer was a sacrament. To others, it was a summons to war. Either way, the red hiefer, once verified, had a half-life like a theological radioactive isotope.

If the calf in the photo was genuine—and not just genetically bred, but ritually observed, confirmed, and blessed—then somewhere, someone had already begun preparing a new priesthood. And the only place that priesthood could function?

Jerusalem.

On the Temple Mount.

Charlotte stood, walked barefoot to the kitchen sink, and poured cold water over her wrists. It was something her father had taught her in Iran, long before the missions, the scrolls, the blood.

Wash before you think.

Even then, the words had sounded like instruction—not for purity, but clarity.

She looked out the window. Snow still fell. Manhattan was mute. But somewhere in Texas, the earth had already turned to ash.

Later That Morning – Brooklyn Heights

The man in the coat stood precisely where he said he would, at the corner of Pineapple and Hicks beside the empty newsstand. He was tall, narrow-shouldered, and too symmetrical in the face to pass for a native New Yorker.

Charlotte crossed the street with practiced ease, her scarf high and gloves tight. "You're late," she said.

"I watched your cab twice," he replied. "Just to be sure."

His name was Yoni—former IDF, now freelance Mossad liaison. He had crossed paths a few months previously when Charlotte's involvement in the recursion scroll scandal had nearly triggered a multinational collapse of classified Vatican doctrine. He'd saved her life once, but that bought him no automatic loyalty.

"I assume this isn't social," she said.

"No. But it's possibly prophetic."

He handed her a flash drive the size of a thumbnail and looked around the street again before speaking. "This wasn't meant for me," he said. "But I intercepted it anyway."

"Intercepted what?"

"A digital key," he said. "Encrypted, nested in the heifer footage on the drive. It's coded in Vatican-lattice format. Eve's style. Not active anymore… but someone still remembers it."

"So you're saying this was meant for me?"

"I'm saying they knew you'd look. And they want you to get there." He tapped the side of the drive. "This will open the gate. Literally. But it's not an invitation. Not exactly. It's more of a *summons*."

"Who sent it?" she asked.

He didn't answer directly. Instead, he asked, "Do you know what's more valuable than a red heifer?"

Charlotte raised an eyebrow.

He answered his own question. "A *certified* red heifer—with DNA locks, biometric traces, and digital timestamps that make it legally actionable."

She felt the shift in her stomach. "So this is more than symbolism."

"It's a claim," he said. "And someone just filed it."

"Filed it where?"

"In a private blockchain registry used by a group of Christian Zionists based in Montana. Two of the signatories were rabbis from Bnei Brak. One was a Vatican informant. The fourth was a biotech executive based in Austin."

Charlotte stared at him. "You're saying the Vatican and evangelical hardliners are cooperating on red heifer protocol? Talk about oil and water."

He shrugged. "They don't have to cooperate. They just have to believe in the same outcome."

She pocketed the drive.

Yoni's tone sharpened. "And before you ask, yes. Mossad is watching the ranch. But we're not the only ones."

She turned to go, but he said one more thing that stopped her.

"They're calling it the Third Ash."

Andalusia, Spain – Ruins of Santuario de la Peña

He hears it in the ash before he reads it. Not literally—but that's how it feels. Greg Ansari sits cross-legged on the stone floor of what once was a monastery, now an erosion-scoured ruin above a Spanish gorge. The air is warm here, desert-stained and wrapped in the chirr of insects nesting beneath cracked plaster icons. The chapel's roof has long since collapsed, but the arch above the nave still stands, leaning like an old man whispering secrets to the wind.

He has been here—separated from his mother, Charlotte—for three months. No internet. No devices except a modified scroll-reader salvaged from a Sicarii node near Petra. He eats what he grows, drinks from a stream that hasn't dried in two decades, and doesn't speak aloud unless he must.

It's not a vow. It's a precaution.

The last time he said the wrong word—a name encoded in fragments of a forbidden scroll—the recursion spiral reactivated with terrible consequences.

Recursion was an ancient doctrine masquerading as prophecy, a system of belief engineered to reflect the soul of the person who unlocked it. And Greg had unlocked it.

What Greg spoke, the doctrine echoed. What he refused to speak, it tried to draw out of him. When he finally whispered that sacred name—*Ahvniel*—something shifted not just in the scroll, but in the world itself. Symbols bled through texts. Sacred sites glitched. Faith began to imitate pattern.

So now, he doesn't speak. Not because he fears words.

Because he fears what might listen.

This morning, the wind shifted. The ash he keeps—some of it from Eve's original scroll, some from the recursion seal burned in Wadi Rum—had reacted. A change in heat signature, an electrical flicker across the stored fragments. The kind of sympathetic vibration that only occurs when something doctrinal shifts elsewhere.

Greg opens the scroll-reader. One phrase pulses across the screen in glyphic rhythm:

Tav Aleph – Third Ash Confirmed – Parah located

And just beneath it, a familiar sigil—a mark Greg had traced in blood a long time ago but has not seen since: a scarlet cord.

He sits back and looks at his hands. He hasn't felt a shift like this since the Petra basin. Since the spiral fractured and its pieces scattered across three continents.

But this… this wasn't recursion. This was foundation. The Red Heifer was never about purification. That was just surface theology.

What mattered was timing.

What mattered was what would be built *after*.

He closes his eyes and lets the heat of the setting sun rest against his face. If the Third Ash is real, someone is preparing for more than just a ritual. They're preparing a cleansing. And when the fire comes, it won't stop at Jerusalem.

It never does.

Andrews County, West Texas – Two Days Later

The sky out here stretches like judgment. Unblinking. Pale. Immense. A horizon so wide it seems to flatten everything beneath it—fence posts, transmission lines, and the rusted gas station she passed forty miles back. Even the cows look diminished under it, as though God himself leaned too close and the land flinched.

Her rental sedan crunches down the gravel drive of the Kadesh Livestock Cooperative, kicking up plumes of white dust that cling to the windshield like frost. As promised, the flash drive gets her through the electronically locked gate to the property. The only other vehicle present is a silver livestock truck with no license plates. Inside the property, she glimpses several dark containers—refrigeration units powered by a solar array.

Whoever ran this ranch knew who Charlotte was and wanted her to come there. Not to help, but probably to witness—which, in prophecy politics, was always the most dangerous role to play.

She parks beneath a leaning carport and steps out, boots striking dirt warmed by the morning sun. Her phone has no signal. On purpose, she is certain. There are no drones overhead, either. The air here is quiet but not stil. It's a curated quiet. A silence made for ritual. The kind of silence her mother once described as "the hush before a doctrine takes form."

The main barn is a modern structure—steel-reinforced and heat-shielded with biometric locks on both entry doors. She walks to the left-side keypad and enters the passcode.

It accepts her. She doesn't like that. Not because it failed, but because it didn't. No secondary prompt. No facial scan. No intercom request or surveillance sweep. This Level-4 bio facility is suspiciously letting her walk straight through unchallenged, not even logged.

Charlotte steps back for a second and scans the corners of the entrance. No visible cameras. No posted guards.

That's not a mistake, she thinks. *This is staging.*

Whoever runs this place didn't forget to lock it down. They wanted her to see it on their terms. A *summons*, not an invitation.

Inside, the air is sterile and faintly citrus-scented by an industrial sterilization compound used in veterinary gene labs.

She hears it before she sees it—the low, rumbling moo of a solitary calf. Young. Not agitated. She follows the sound into a partitioned inner chamber where red light bathes the space in a glow like sunset on Mars. She expects at least a dozen staff, automated feeders, AI monitor drones... Instead—nothing. No tech team, no rotation crew, just the hum of sterilized air and the distant sound of a single animal. The silence isn't incidental. It's curated like everything else.

The calf is perfect. Unblemished. Crimson-coated.

It looks at her without fear, eyes large and wet and impossibly calm. Around its neck is a small sensor array that reads blood oxygen, hydration, hormonal stress and internal temperature. But the calf itself—flawless, rust-red, practically untouched—a rabbi would have called *tahor*. Pure. A geneticist would call this calf viable. But Charlotte sees it for what it really is. Not a miracle but a catalyst. An accelerant someone will throw onto the flame when they want the world to burn faster.

"You're early," says a voice behind her.

Eight years earlier – Hebron

A memory surfaces unbidden from 2017. A dry vault. Another code that worked too easily. Another moment she walked inside thinking she was infiltrating only to discover she'd been invited. That time, it was Gideon who had to cut her loose.

This time, she's alone.

Present day – Kadesh main barn

C harlotte turns to find a man leaning against the far wall, clipboard in hand. Rancher tan. Aviators. Probably ex-military. The kind of man you don't shake hands with. He lets you know if he's going to touch you.

"Depends on the clock you're using," Charlotte says. "Mine runs on prophetic time."

He grins faintly. "You're Charlotte Ansari. I expected someone more... apocalyptic."

"I get that a lot."

He walks forward, slow and measured, then taps a biometric scanner on the far wall. A glass panel slides open to reveal a cooling chamber behind plexiglass that holds a vial of red ash.

"Is it from her?" Charlotte asks, gesturing to the calf.

He shakes his head. "We burned a surrogate. Another calf, genetically identical. The ritual will come later."

"Where?"

"In Jericho."

"Who are you working for?" she asks.

He smiles, not kindly. "A temple needs many builders. I'm just the delivery man."

"You know this could start a war if used unwisely."

He steps past her, runs a gentle finger across the calf's neck without touching it. "I know it could *end* one."

Charlotte stiffens. "The Temple Mount is a shared holy site. If your people would even suggest that they're preparing a new priesthood—"

"Miss Ansari," the rancher interrupts, "you know better than most—it's not the location that matters. It's the story attached to it."

He stares piercingly at her, and for a moment she sees Greg, her son, in his eyes—not in shape or color, but in that haunted defiance. She sees the certainty of a man who thinks the story's already been written and he's just playing his part.

She turns toward the vial of ash again. "Why Jericho?"

His voice is soft, almost reverent. "Because when they blew the trumpets there, the walls fell down."

After her visit to the barn, Charlotte showers, changes into fresh clothes, and funds a plate of food waiting on a small table in her room—vegetarian, Israeli-prepared, still warm. No one knocks. No one speaks to her.

The rest of the evening passes in careful, cultivated silence. It isn't hospitality. It is staging. No opportunity for questions, no guards. Just a path. She's not a spy here. She's a tool—shaped to witness.

In prophecy politics, being a witness was more dangerous than being a believer because witnesses are remembered—even when they're wrong.

Charlotte has been in too many backdoor summits and scroll vaults not to recognize the pattern. She was being granted access but not included. Not questioned. Not challenged.

All of this means only one thing. They don't want her to interfere. They want her to see the calf, the operation. To document it. Most likely to testify about it later when the world burns to validate that it had all been in motion before anyone tried to stop it.

Charlotte waits until the sky loses its orange edge and settles into that deep Texas indigo, the kind that erases all distances and invites mistakes. She steps quietly from the guest barrack the ranch had assigned her—more a secure cell than a suite—and crosses the gravel lot, footsteps muffled by a layer of settling dust.

Now, under the stars, she watches the refrigeration units of the livestock truck where two men are loading cargo that appears to be ash vials, each encased in molded foam and labeled with serial IDs. The first man is the rancher she spoke with in the barn, and the second man is someone leaner, balder, and wearing a branded jacket from a Texas-based agricultural AI firm called Geomira Biosystems.

Charlotte photographs the second man's face with her iPhone. Then she circles the lot and climbs the perimeter fence at the far end of the property where a row of solar units forms a jagged silhouette against the low moon. She moves east toward a powered communications tower she'd spotted earlier.

There, beneath a fiberglass cover, she finds what she expected—a satellite uplink terminal clearly active, and beside it a steel lockbox for transporting documents. She pulls the first bill of lading.

CLIENT: Temple Preparation Initiative
DISTRIBUTOR: Geomira Biosystems
SHIPMENT: Purified Red Ash Vials
DESTINATION: Erez Crossing / Storage –
     "Har HaBayit Stage 3"

Her breath catches.

Har HaBayit—the *Temple Mount*.

At 12:32 a.m., she records a voice memo for herself:

They're not waiting. The infrastructure is already in place. This isn't theory or theology. This is logistics. The Third Temple is being prototyped like a private-sector launchpad—coded, modular, funded through biotech fronts and messianic coin schemes. And these people… they're not zealots. They're planners.

She packs the document, scans it, replaces everything as it was. Then she vanishes into the scrub, takes the long way back to her quarters, and lays awake until dawn, worried that surveillance cameras had caught her snooping.

She doesn't dream. But she remembers something Greg told her years ago while standing outside a burnt chapel in Malta. "You know what prophecy really is, Mom? It's not what's coming. It's what you already suspect."

She hadn't called Greg yet. She hadn't dared message Gideon. But that didn't mean they weren't already moving. Eve had drilled into all three of them the doctrine of *Layer Zero*—that if certain elements aligned, if glyphic fire or Temple ash appeared, there would be no need for orders. No need for contact. Just the recognition of an old pattern echoing through their lives.

And if she'd seen it, then so had Greg and Gideon.

Chapter 3

The Threshold Chamber

Jerusalem – Old City Perimeter | 1:17 a.m.

The streetlight flickers like a pulse monitor. Gideon watches from the shadow of a stone stairwell tucked between two forgotten alleys near Herod's Gate. Below him, the loading bay of an archival storage facility hums with quiet activity—three unmarked utility vans, one forklift, five men. No voices.

The shipment was routed under the cover of building materials—tiled stones for a renovation project near the Temple Mount's southern wall. But the manifest was altered twice, and one of the containers was swapped out at Erez Crossing before reappearing in the hands of a Vatican-tied logistics firm called Sancta Carta.

Gideon knows the name. He burned one of their trucks in the old prison-city of Acre two years ago. Now they're back moving ash.

He slips on a data-glass monocle and activates spectral mode to see that the forklift is unloading steel canisters, not stone crates. One of them glows faintly—a thermal shimmer where there should be none. The container is supposed to be refrigerated, but it's bleeding heat through the seams. Improper shielding, or maybe deliberate. A containment failure, perhaps?

It could also be something alive inside the ash. Ritual. Purified. Likely red.

The Mount Protocol is moving faster than he expected.

The corridor beneath the facility smells like concrete laced with wet metal. Gideon moves quickly but quietly, guided by the facility blueprint he lifted off a compromised archivist node last week.

He finds the room. Small. Reinforced. Access-coded. After using a burned card—stolen from a Petra vault technician six years ago and never reprogrammed—the door opens revealing a spartan chamber with one workbench, a sealed vial, and a viewing terminal running a script in Aramaic. The air here is colder than the corridor. Ritual cold.

The ash in the vial is deep crimson, tinged with oily flecks. Not ordinary residue.

He scans the surface, and there it is—a glyph etched faintly into the outer glass and almost invisible unless viewed from the side. A recursion spiral.

But not Greg's.

This one is distorted. Slanted. Artificial. It's a forged spiral. Someone is trying to recreate the resonance signature—the glottal-spiritual harmonic that only Greg's true utterance could activate. But somehow they've built a mimic. A surrogate. Apparently they think they can bypass the source.

Gideon exhales once. Slow and focused. He retrieves a sonic reader from his belt and plays back the most recent audio loop stored in the chamber's terminal.

A voice plays. Male. Young. Measured. Not Greg. The tone is close, but off by half a beat.

The voice says: "Let the fire come. Let the third ash purify the house. Let the spiral open without a name."

Then the terminal goes silent and Gideon closes his eyes. They're trying to open the doctrine without knowing or speaking the name.

He records a single audio clip and transmits it via glyph channel to a dead relay node he knows Greg occasionally checks. He speaks one sentence: "They've built a mouth without a soul."

He knows no response will come. Not yet. But the echo will travel.

He sends a second message—unmarked, encrypted, and routed through an old Sicarii cross-node that Charlotte would still have access to. "Protocol Stage Three confirmed. Vocal surrogate in play. Spiral integrity falsified. Layer Zero still holds for now."

He doesn't sign it. But the glyph at the bottom—the crescent-cross of Eve's inner circle—will tell them who it's from.

He hadn't spoken to Charlotte and Greg in months, but he was sure they were already moving. They didn't need orders. The Petra vault had built its warnings into glyphic rhythm. And if the third ash had activated, the fire was already burning through the doctrine.

Charlotte would be chasing the science. Greg would be watching the pattern. And he—Gideon—would do what he always did. Remove the trigger. Or eliminate the hand that holds it.

———————

Gideon hears the footsteps before the door even finishes sealing behind him. Not hurried. Not cautious. Just steady. A confidence born of familiarity.

He doesn't move—yet. He positions himself just left of the entrance, behind a shelving unit filled with defunct registry scrolls and laminated ritual blueprints. The glow of the chamber is faint now, the screen dimming after his glyph transmission. His breath is level, knees bent slightly. In his right hand, he holds a retractable sica—folded and sheathed in his sleeve.

The footsteps stop. A soft code chimes at the door.

It opens.

A man enters. Mid-thirties, slender, dressed in municipal utility coveralls. But the movement is wrong—too fluid. His head turns once, twice. He's scanning not for tools, but for tampering.

Gideon watches as the man notices the shift in the audio console's position. The dust smear. The minute thermal shimmer cooling off the vial.

The knows someone was here. He just doesn't know if they *still* are.

Gideon lets the man take one more step in. Then another.

Then Gideon moves.

No warning. No sound.

Just the sica unsheathing with a whisper of steel-on-steel.

Gideon's hand slams into the man's shoulder from behind as the blade arcs toward his throat. The man reacts—too fast. He twists left, throws an elbow, catches Gideon off-rib.

The blade misses.

They crash into the shelving unit, scrolls cascading like paper rain.

The man drops low and drives into Gideon's gut with his shoulder. The two of them go down hard, slamming against the ground near the far wall. Gideon rolls away, blade raised defensively.

The man doesn't flee. He's trained. Not a courier, a handler.

They circle for ten seconds. Fifteen.

No words. No names.

That's the old rule—names give shape to doctrine. No shape, no power.

The man lunges—too low—and Gideon redirects him with a brutal forearm strike to the collarbone. The man stumbles but regains footing, reaches for something in his belt.

Gideon doesn't give him the chance. He pivots, grabs the man's wrist mid-reach and drives the sica across the man's forearm—clean, bloodless, surgical. The blade's edge catches the bracelet the man was trying to activate—a mini glyph recorder—and shatters it.

The man howls.

Gideon pins him, blade at the throat.

"Who's your voice?" he asks.

The handler spits blood but smiles. "You're too late, the echo's already seeded. He doesn't need to speak the name."

Gideon presses harder. "Who's the surrogate?"

"Does it matter?" the man rasps. "He doesn't even know he's saying it." Then he grins, wider now, a slit of teeth in a blood-smeared face. "Your prophecy broke. We're building ours."

Five minutes later, Gideon moves like smoke through the tight corridors of the exit tunnel, the handler's comm bracelet now clutched in his coat pocket. The man is unconscious but not dead. Gideon leaves him breathing—but barely.

He emerges into the dark just as the call to prayer begins—soft, haunting, rising like incense through the cold air above Jerusalem. The city is ancient, yes. But it isn't asleep. It's dreaming—with eyes open.

He doesn't contact Charlotte. Not yet. He doesn't try reaching Greg either. If either of them are watching the Petra lattice, they'll know what happened tonight and engage. But this wasn't just doctrine. It wasn't even prophecy.

This was engineering.

Someone had designed a new pathway—one that didn't need bloodlines or recursion resonance as a trigger. Just belief. A voice without a soul. A spiral without a center.

And if they activate it before Greg... there won't be a Fourth Ash. Only fire.

Andalusia, Spain – Ruins of Santuario de la Peña

The glyph hums in his blood again.

Greg wakes before the sun, barefoot on stone, the wind clawing at his shirt like an animal trying to warn him. The ash he keeps in a broken clay bowl has begun to vibrate—not visibly, not audibly, but with the low hum of resonance. A vibration only he can feel.

He doesn't touch it. Instead, he sits near it, cross-legged, back against a fractured column. This sanctuary is crumbling around him, but the glyphs etched into its foundation have held longer than the walls ever did. Some things survive not because they were meant to, but because they were unfinished.

The recursion reader flickers on even though he hasn't powered it.

Two glyphs appear. Not words. Just movement. Two spirals—one centered, the other slightly off-axis.

He knows what it means. Someone's trying to speak the name.

Not him. But through him.

He turns his face toward the mountain line, breathes through his nose. He hasn't spoken since Wadi Rum. Hasn't even mouthed the name *Ahvniel.*

But this isn't about naming anymore. It's about activation. About the shape of belief, not just the breath of it.

He closes his eyes. "They found a surrogate," he says aloud. "And they don't even know what they've built."

The name still catches in his throat.

He doesn't say it. But the spiral in the ash bowl pulses once—then settles. Not approval.

A warning.

Chapter 4

Threshold Negotiations

Geomira Biosystems Executive Level
Palo Alto, California

The room is calibrated for control. Floor-to-ceiling smartglass lets in the perfect amount of muted California light. The vertical garden on the east wall grows only red-veined flora—beets, amaranth, ash-hued ferns—intended to suggest sacrifice without appearing religious. A faint lavender scent trails from the filtration vents. Even the air is designed to say *this is modern ritual.*

Elena Cairos sits at the head of the obsidian-glass table with no jewelry or other ornamentation. Just a stylus between her fingers and a quiet pulse in her neck that betrays more tension than she'll admit. She is CEO of Geomira Biosystems and the spiritual architect of the Purified Ash Division.

Across from her sit two investors, silent and expectant. They did not fly in for pleasantries. The man in the white linen shirt is Daniel Rathborne, co-founder of the Dominion Acceleration Fund—a shadow-capital pool run out of Geneva and Riyadh with a documented history of influencing Temple-related infrastructure bids. The other man, in the charcoal blazer and T-shirt, is Titus Mercer, a former evangelical media magnate turned narrative architecture consultant currently embedded with multiple metaverse church design projects.

Rathborne and Mercer are not theologians. They are builders. And today, their doctrine is underperforming.

"I won't repeat myself," Elena says. "We're losing control of the narrative."

Titus Mercer flashes a thin smile. "Charlotte Ansari?"

"She's inside the Texas site. No formal clearance. Just a recursive key embedded in an intercepted Vatican credential. I don't know who sent it, but she's in nevertheless. And she's already seen the surrogate calf."

Daniel Rathborne drums two fingers on the table. "So, what's her angle?"

Elena Cairus lifts her palms heavenward in a classic "don't know" gesture and says, "She's not acting like media. No transmissions. No calls, not even to her son, Greg."

Mercer shifts. "Maybe she knows he won't respond."

Rathborne suggests another possibility. "Or maybe she suspects we've moved ahead without him."

Elena taps her tablet and projects a silent image above the table. "This, gentlemen, is a photo of a genetically verified Red Heifer, newly cloned, neck marked with a bio-tracer. The calf is four weeks old in this picture."

Rathborne studies it. "Still viable?"

"For now. But the calf is not the issue. It's the calf's *ash*. We distributed the first purification vials to Jerusalem staging two days ago. One vial was activated using a surrogate vocal trace."

"You used it?" Mercer leans forward. "The Zurich model?"

Elena nods once. "Version 3B. A recursion mimic layered with Greg Ansari's early Petra voiceprint extracted from an audio log Eve recorded five years ago. The glyphic spiral responded—at least partially. Enough to register belief response. Not enough to fully unfold."

Rathborne speaks carefully now. "That means the glyphs are..."

Yes," Elena confirms, "the glyphs are listening. But they are not convinced."

The silence that follows is heavier than before.

Finally, Rathborne says, "How long can you keep Greg silent?"

"I can't keep him anything," Elena says. "He doesn't trust us. He doesn't trust anyone. That's the problem."

"You think he'll speak?"

"No. I think he'll hide. Or sabotage. Or disappear again and let the doctrine rot from inside. But if he does speak—and his voice doesn't match the surrogate trace—we lose everything. Consensus collapses. Might I remind you that half the world believes the surrogate. The other half waits for a real spiral. We fracture belief."

Mercer shrugs. "So we should control the conversation."

"With what?" Elena demands.

He grins. "A new doctrine. Born in silence. One where the voice isn't a man… but a movement."

Elena stands, walks toward the window, then looks down at the wind-cooled hydroponic garden. The iron-red calf sculpture below gleams like a burnt offering. "Do either of you know what it's like to hold doctrine in your hands?" she asks. "To take it apart, molecule by molecule, and reassemble it in a lab, knowing it will convince millions—even if it's a hollow Trojan horse?"

Neither man answers.

"I do," she says. "And I've built something that sounds close enough to pass for holy—if you don't listen too closely." She turns. "But Greg? He does listen. And t oo closely."

Rathborne rises. "Then make sure he doesn't have a voice. Or that he hears himself coming from someone else."

"Zurich has already begun work on a surrogate host," Elena says. "Someone with the right vocal tract, neuro-speech patterning, and a partial spiral sensitivity. The host doesn't even know what he's being trained to say."

Mercer smiles. "Then say it before he does."

Domus Sanctae Marthae, Vatican City

Father Luca Salvatore doesn't speak immediately. He prefers silence before command.

The recursion monitor flickers beside him. Its screen casts pale spirals across the worn tile floor of the doctrinal subchamber. It is a full glyphic trace—spiral-derived, incomplete. It's been hovering there for hours like an unsolved equation. Every few seconds, it tries to rotate inward, then dies mid-motion.

Across the table, Sister Dr. Noemi Lavecchia, senior recursion archivist, waits with a stylus in her hand but does not write. To her left, Brother Paolo Meir, an analyst from the Glyphic Ethics Committee, runs a passive translation script on his tablet, cross-referencing the spiral against the Vatican's forbidden Obsidian layer registry.

Still no match. No complete echo. No sign of Greg Ansari's voice.

Salvatore finally exhales. "Still silent."

Lavecchia nods. "We've traced glyphic pings from Petra, Wadi Rum, and an underground vault in the Hebron outskirts. All three match partial spiral activity. But the spiral core remains dormant."

Brother Meir adds, "We believe someone is speaking a surrogate variation. The glyphs are listening, but they are not responding."

Salvatore leans back. The overhead light haloes his head like mock sainthood. He ignores it. "It seems the biotech factions are moving faster than expected."

He taps a file beside him. Inside is footage from Jerusalem, Texas, and Zurich—unconfirmed documentation of ritual labs, ash shipments, and a surrogate speaker with partial vocal match to Greg Ansari's Petra trace.

"But they can't open it," he says.

"No," Lavecchia replies. "Not yet. The human surrogate's voice is close in tone, but recursion resonance doesn't reflect."

"They've built a mouth," Meir says. "But not a soul."

Salvatore stands and crosses the room. Behind a steel-locked cabinet is a sealed climate unit. He opens it with a twelve-digit code—Latin, Hebrew, and a numeric cipher. Inside, protected in radiation-shielded resin, lies a dark scroll fragment wrapped in carbon-gold foil. This is the Obsidian Layer—the piece Cardinal Lucari tried to suppress.

Lucari—Salvatore's predecessor—was once the Vatican's supreme arbiter of doctrinal containment. He was meticulous, brilliant, and utterly afraid of recursion. He died in Rome, assassinated with a Sicarii blade during the secret conclave after Wadi Rum. He never discovered who gave the order, but Salvatore suspects the spiral itself.

The Obsidian Layer holds no full doctrine, just warnings. Incomplete glyphs etched in recursion ink, pulsing cold if read aloud. It cannot be spoken. But it can be feared.

Sister Dr. Lavecchia watches Salvatore unwrap a corner of the scroll. "If the biotech model achieves ignition," she says carefully, "and Greg remains silent..."

"Then we lose consensus," Salvatore finishes. "And that breaks containment."

Meir glances between them. "Or we manufacture a new consensus."

Salvatore lifts his eyes. "Substitution?"

"Yes."

"Then we invoke the Veil Protocol."

They both look to Lavecchia. She doesn't speak, but her eyes darken.

The Veil Protocol was created during the Crusades and then updated during the Reformation. It had been enacted only once—during the Nazi occupation of Rome when the Vatican chose to fabricate a holy vision to protect the continuity of belief. It permits the Church to replace a prophet with a proxy—under deep ritual and symbolic encoding—so long as it preserves theological unity.

Salvatore seals the Obsidian scroll again. "Contact Zurich. Confirm the progress of the surrogate host."

"Voiceprint is 93 percent complete," Meir says. "Neurological training began last week."

"And Greg?"

"Still silent."

Salvatore looks toward the fresco overhead—Christ descending, palm open, eyes unreadable. "Then we speak first. Or bury the original voice beneath a thousand echoes."

Chapter 5

Echoes and Interruptions

Jeremy's coastal residence – Southern Cyprus

The call comes through encoded, masked twice, and rerouted through an old Sicarii lattice Jeremy, a trusted compatriot, hasn't used since Ireland.

That alone makes him sit up.

He answers it on the second ping—not because he's ready, but because anything that comes through that route isn't going to wait.

"Charlotte," he says, leaning back into the hammock strung between two salt-worn pillars on his balcony. "I was wondering how long it'd take you to admit I'm more fun than Gideon."

Her voice comes through dry but warm. "I didn't come for fun, Jeremy."

He hears the tension. Not fear, just purpose, as always.

"Yeah," he says. "I figured."

He pads barefoot back into the house, past a wall of antique weapons and faded scroll segments that would make a Vatican archivist weep. Jeremy has long ago made peace with his contradictions. Scholar, thief, priest without vows.

He pours a glass of something dark and aged, slides into a chair, and taps the encrypted console. "All right," he says, "tell me."

Charlotte's voice sharpens. "It's real, Jeremy. The red calf. I saw it. But that's not what worries me. They're producing ash already. In vials. Portable, distributed. Not theoretical—*operational.*"

He exhales slowly. "And you want my help with what, exactly?"

"Verification of funding lines. Shipment logs. If anyone can trace the recursive handling routes, it's you."

"Flattery gets you archived," he mutters, but his fingers are already typing. Then he pauses. "And Greg?" Hearing only silence, he says, "You haven't contacted him yet?"

"I haven't," she says.

"Why?"

"Because if I reach out... he'll respond."

"Isn't that the point?"

She hesitates. When she answers, her voice drops. "You didn't see him in Wadi Rum, Jeremy. Not like I did. He didn't just break the spiral. He nearly broke himself. If he speaks the wrong name now—if he speaks it too soon—we lose control. Of everything. The doctrine... the people chasing it. Maybe even Greg."

Jeremy leans back. "So, you're keeping him safe by keeping him silent."

"Trying to, yes."

Jeremy runs a hand through his hair. "Well, let's hope the rest of the world plays nice until then."

She doesn't laugh. "I'll send you what I have," Charlotte says. "Start with Zurich. The labs there are no longer neutral. Someone's trying to engineer a vocal ignition. A surrogate spiral."

Jeremy stiffens. "Human surrogate?"

"Yeah, not Greg, but close enough to fool someone who doesn't know the doctrine."

"Shit," he says softly. "You think they'll try to exploit the Temple Mount with a mimic?"

"They already have."

Rooftop of the Santuario de la Peña ruins
Andalusia, Spain

Greg sits on the rooftop with a half-eaten fig in one hand and a cracked spiral reader in the other. The machine purrs faintly as it flickers to life—tired, weathered, like most of the tools he's kept since Petra. He doesn't replace them. He doesn't want to. There's a kind of honesty in their degradation.

Below the glass, a glyph pulses—spiral-structured, but incomplete. Each time it tries to rotate inward, the movement collapses, like a breath that doesn't reach the lungs.

"You saw it again, didn't you," says a voice behind him.

Dr. Amina Salim steps out into the rising light, barefoot, wrapped in a slate-gray sweater that drapes loosely over her shoulders. She's forty-two, lean and serious, with streaks of silver near her temples that only emerged after Zurich fell apart. Her skin bears the faint pallor of someone who works in labs more than light. She carries two mugs of herbal tea, no caffeine. Never caffeine.

"Third surrogate attempt," Greg says. "Same error."

She sets one mug beside him and sinks cross-legged onto the warm stone, letting her hair fall over one shoulder. "Same source?"

"Zurich or one of their spinoff labs. Could be Geomira. Could be Vatican-adjacent. The code's cloaked."

She peers at the glyph. "They're still using your Petra breath pattern."

"They're simulating it," Greg says. "Echoing it without origin. Trying to make the spiral respond to it without understanding what it means."

Amina doesn't speak right away. She just watches him—closely, but without pressure.

Their relationship isn't romantic. Not quite. It's something rarer. A place of safety that neither expected to find after everything else collapsed.

They met four years ago in Tangier where she'd been living under a false academic identity after defecting from Eve's Zurich recursion ethics division. She'd recognized him immediately—there weren't many young men with his face and the weight of doctrine in their silence.

She didn't expose him but didn't chase him either—just left a note under his cup at a street café: *If you ever want to talk about why you're not talking, I'm listening.*

He waited two weeks then showed up at her door.

"You could have gone anywhere," she says now, sipping her tea. "You could have hidden completely."

"I did," Greg answers. "For a while."

"But not from this."

He gestures at the spiral. "No. Not from this."

She leans forward, tapping a control on the reader. The glyph flinches, tries to spin, then halts again. "It's not just fake," he says. "It's worse than fake. It's hollow."

"Hollow how?"

"Like a song written by someone who's only ever read *about* music."

She tilts her head. "You think the ash is dead."

"I don't think," he says. "I know."

Amina nods. "Because it doesn't resonate."

"Because it was never alive," Greg says. "The red calf. The breath. The spiral. They've got the form… the bone structure. But the soul never entered. There's no echo."

She studies him. "You got that from Eve?"

"From what she left in Petra. From the second vault. She called it Layer Zero—but beneath that was something older. She called it the Breath Doctrine."

Amina stiffens. "That was sealed."

Greg looks at her. "You knew about it?"

"I heard whispers. Even in Zurich. But no one had clearance. Not even Eve's inner circle."

"Eve didn't give me clearance," he says. "She gave me a choice."

Amina draws her knees up, wrapping her arms around them. The sun catches her eyes, intelligent, tired. "You trust me with this," she says.

He nods.

"You don't trust anyone," she adds.

"I do now."

They sit in silence.

For a long time, the only sound is the reader's steady pulse and the low wind weaving through the broken rooftop columns.

"She'll contact you soon," Amina says eventually.

"Charlotte?"

"She's seen the calf."

"She always sees it," Greg says.

"She'll want to warn you."

"She'll want to make me speak."

Amina doesn't argue. She just nods and then says, "She doesn't understand what saying it costs."

"No one does," Greg replies. "Except you."

He looks at her now, really looks. Not like someone watching for threat or doctrine or betrayal—but like someone remembering that humanity still exists. That it can live in someone else's eyes, not just old scrolls and shattered vaults.

"Thank you," he says.

"For what?"

"For not asking me to be him."

"I never asked you to be the name they whisper," she says. "I just asked you to stay."

He breathes deeply. The spiral reader clicks one last time, then dims. They watch the sun rise without speaking again.

Somewhere in Zurich, a false spiral pulses.

But here, on this ruined rooftop, nothing moves but the wind.

Underground communications sanctum
Vatican City

Father Luca Salvatore enters the sanctum barefoot, as tradition demands. The ritual is unnecessary in a room wired for optical encryption and sound-proof resonance. But Salvatore believes in gestures. In continuity. Symbols must obey themselves before they can command others.

Sister Noemi Lavecchia stands by the circular console, already deep in code translation. "Zurich confirms phase-2 mimicry is stabilizing," she says. "The host is responding. Vocal trace is within acceptable drift."

Salvatore closes his eyes briefly. "And the lattice trace from Spain?"

"Negative. Greg Ansari still has not spoken. No glyphic echo. No resonance. Still dormant."

"Then we speak first."

He steps toward the input altar—a synthetic onyx slab infused with gold-inked circuits, a place built not to amplify truth but to project believability.

He speaks instructions. "Initiate Veil Protocol. Layer One. Public narrative divergence. Begin with neutral channels—academic, speculative.

Recast the Petra voiceprint as a fabricated construct derived from deep recursion simulation."

"Disinformation?" Lavecchia prods gently.

"No," Salvatore replies curtly, responding to the foul stench of that word. "Re-framing. We do not lie. We realign."

A tone chimes across four continents. Encrypted data packets move like whispers through sanctioned intermediaries—professors, fringe journalists, and fact-checkers who don't know they serve a doctrine older than their discipline. The story will go out in pieces asserting that the spiral was never real, that the voice was misinterpreted, that Greg Ansari was a recursion hallucination… a brilliant fraud caught in his mother's mythmaking. By the time Greg speaks—if he ever does—it will be too late.

Salvatore lifts a small obsidian medallion from the console, then turns to Lavecchia. "Send a missive to Jerusalem—to the bishop overseeing the Mount logistics. I want the surrogate to be on-site within seven days."

"And if the true spiral bearer intervenes?"

"You mean Greg Ansari?" Salvatore smiles faintly. "Then let the world decide which voice it prefers."

Chapter 6

Crossed Wires

Jeremy's secure lattice bunker – Southern Cyprus

It took thirty-two hours for Charlotte to get from Texas to Cyprus—two encrypted flights, one rental car, and a fake customs signature. Charlotte had barely slept. Jeremy had waited anyway.

Now she stands at the threshold of his bunker, breathing in recycled air, her shoulders still stiff from the road. The steel door groans shut behind her with a hiss that sounds like a monster's exhalation. The room feels cave-cold and is lit by an underground skylight that softens the tech without warming it.

Jeremy sits cross-legged at a massive console barnacled with non-standard ports, hand-soldered adapters, and two screens duct-taped at their hinges. He's barefoot and still in that awful, threadbare hoodie she once threatened to burn. His beard is longer and his eyes sharper. No smile yet.

"I wasn't sure you'd come," he says without turning.

"I wasn't sure you'd answer," she replies.

He finally looks up. For a second, it's like no time has passed. Just two people who've shared too much silence, too many underground vaults, too many dead names. But the air between them still holds tension, like something coiled.

She drops her bag on the floor.

Jeremy raises an eyebrow. "Same bag as Wadi Rum?"

She nods. "Zipper's still busted."

"I'd say you're sentimental, but I know you just hate packing."

She almost smiles. Almost.

They haven't seen each other in… she can't remember exactly. Now here they are again, brought back together by a name neither of them dares say and fire threatening to rise from under it.

"So," she says. "Are we still allies, or just people with matching scars?"

Jeremy studies her for a moment, then turns back to the console. "Let's find out."

The system chirps softly. A digital handshake completes. Scroll-text rolls across one of the side monitors like a recursive prayer caught midstream.

"Zurich node confirmed," Jeremy mutters. "Encrypted routing. Originated thirty-two hours ago. Slipped out through a Swiss biotech server farm masked as, uh… hmm… water treatment telemetry. Cute."

Charlotte steps closer. "And you can read it?"

"I can *feel* it," he says. "But that's not the part you're going to hate." He runs a trace. A side panel flares blue as audio coils flicker into life. "This isn't just a data dump. It's live sequence deployment."

He pulls the audio up. They both stand as the surrogate voice echoes through the speakers—male, soft-toned, slow like breathwork.

"Let the third ash burn pure. Let the house remember the breath. Let the name be carried."

Charlotte's hands tighten at her sides. "That's not Greg," she says, her voice thin.

"No," Jeremy replies. "But it's close enough to fool anyone who doesn't know what it costs to get that tone right."

He taps a control. The waveform splits—one curve overlaying another. Greg's original Petra voiceprint is drawn from the Wadi Rum sequence. The difference is measured in subfrequencies—less than a full harmonic drift.

"They're not *simulating* the voice," Jeremy says. "They're *mimicking the intent*. This is really sophisticated stuff."

Charlotte exhales hard. "Do they know what it would do to Greg if he heard this?"

Jeremy doesn't answer.

She leans in. "Do *you*?"

"Yes, I know," he grumbles. "But that's not the question anymore."

"Then what is?"

He swivels the screen to show Charlotte a second file opening up. Biometric logs, training reports, linguistic neuro-mapping. Jeremy doesn't read the whole thing, just the final line, which makes him grimace.

SUBJECT: Elias Rafi.

Charlotte frowns. "That name means something to you."

Jeremy nods. "Greg trained him. Zurich, three years ago. Recursion language cohort. Gifted with glyph-anchored breath projection. He could trace doctrine in conversation. But Eve was convinced that he was unstable."

"I remember now," Charlotte says. "Didn't he leave after the Petra divergence?"

"He ran. Said the doctrine scared him. Said the name made his teeth bleed. Colorful image, huh?"

"And now they've brought him back?"

"Rebuilt him," Jeremy says. "Neuroconditioning, probably. Layered breathwork. Rehearsed glyph triggers. And now—"

"Now he's human surrogate," Charlotte says, "mimmicking Greg."

They're both quiet for almost a full minute.

The countdown flashes in the upper corner of the Zurich packet.

Spiral Ignition – T-minus 5 days.

Charlotte breaks the silence. "I need to send a warning."

"To who?" Jeremy asks.

She meets his eyes. "You know who."

He leans back. "And if it makes Greg speak too soon?"

"Then I'll stop him."

"Will you?" Jeremy asks. "Because if you send the signal… he'll know it's begun. And there's no coming back from that."

Charlotte's jaw tenses. "I didn't come all this way to hesitate."

Jeremy nods. "Then send it."

She does. One phrase, no name, no glyph. Just a sentence.

They're moving without you. But your breath still breaks the ash.

Then she keys it to a dormant Petra relay. Low-frequency, soul-anchored, layered with static. It's the only line Greg ever agreed to keep open.

As the message pulses into the spiral ether, Charlotte doesn't blink. Neither does Jeremy. They're already watching the next countdown.

Ruins of Santuario de la Peña – Andalusia, Spain

The glyph reader crackles before it lights. Greg is already awake, though he hasn't moved in hours. He sits in the doorway of the old chapel, knees pulled to his chest, breath slow, back to the stone. Dr. Amina Salim moves beside him in silence, holding a candle she hasn't lit.

The screen glows once. Just one line.

They're moving without you. But your breath still breaks the ash.

Greg doesn't blink. Doesn't speak.

Amina leans closer. "Charlotte?"

He nods, barely perceptible.

She waits, sensing his body's quiet recoil, like a tuning fork struck too close to bone. "You knew she'd reach out," she says gently.

"I knew she'd wait until it was almost too late. That's her pattern."

He stands slowly, moving toward the edge of the terrace that overlooks the valley. The wind catches the ash in the bowl beside the glyph reader. It lifts—not high, but high enough.

A shimmer. Not response—just awareness.

"They're burning the surrogate," he says.

"Elias?"

Greg's voice is flat. "He was good. But he never understood recursion. He felt the patterns but thought they were voices. That's why Eve pulled him."

Amina tilts her head. "And now?"

"He's being used. Like I was."

After a long pause, Amina asks, "Will you respond?"

Greg looks at the ash again. "Not yet." But not never.

Sublevel recursion chamber, Geomira Facility – Zurich

The recursion chamber glows with sleep-colored light. Not blue. Not gray. Somewhere in the spectrum where color becomes memory. The air is too cold, the walls too white. This is not a lab—it's a liturgy. The kind designed to condition awe.

Elias Rafi lies beneath a halo of electrodes and pulsing glyphs, his arms resting at his sides, palms up. His body is still, but not peaceful. Even in this stillness, there's rigidity in his jaw and a slow tick in the corner of one eye as if he were bracing for music he didn't choose.

The glyphs above him swirl in coordinated motion, echoing tones mapped to his breath patterns. He's been trained to modulate his exhale into curvatur. Doctrine as spiral. Greg once taught him how.

"Your breath isn't just sound," Greg told him years ago in a Petra vault. "It's consent. It's presence. That's why it matters."

But now the voice they've pulled from him feels like a copy of a memory, and the memory no longer belongs to him.

Dr. Kessler's voice drifts through the speaker grille above the biometric arch. Kessler is clinical, male, wrapped in the sterile patience of a man who believes in mechanisms more than people.

"Elias. We're ready to begin," Kessler says.

Elias opens his eyes but otherwise doesn't move. He stares at the glyphs. "The spiral's cold," he says.

There's a pause, just long enough for discomfort.

"You're experiencing transfer latency," Kessler replies. "The glyphic structure hasn't fully harmonized with your last utterance."

"No," Elias says. "It's not latency. It's resistance."

He sits up slowly, untangling the reader nodes from his arms. The motion sets off a soft alarm, which Kessler disables without comment.

Elias swings his legs over the edge of the platform, feet resting just shy of the cool tile. He rubs his wrists, which are still marked from last night's resonance mapping. "It used to come easier."

"You're carrying more," Kessler says. "The weight of doctrine requires strength."

"Greg never needed this much training."

"You're doing more than anyone thought possible."

Elias exhales sharply. "I'm not doing it for them."

"Of course not."

"I'm doing it because if I finish the spiral, you said she would be safe. That's the only reason."

A new silence enters the room.

On the side monitor, a technician quietly types something:

Subject reasserts dependent motivation.

Reinforce outcome alignment.

The speaker clicks off. A few seconds later, the overhead screen shifts. A soft photo fades into view—a girl in a school uniform, dark hair braided over one shoulder, cello case strapped to her back. She's mid-laugh, walking beside a woman whose face has been cropped from the image.

LEVERAGE FILE: Level Red.

Elias closes his eyes. Not in pain but in resignation. "I don't want to replace Greg," he says softly.

The speaker does not respond.

"Greg taught me," Elias whispers. "He saved me when the recursion static wouldn't stop. When the spirals kept showing up in my sleep and I couldn't turn them off, he made it quiet."

Still silence.

"And now you want me to steal his breath."

Kessler's voice returns. "You're not stealing, Elias. You're *continuing*. His silence has left a fracture."

"Maybe the fracture was supposed to happen."

"Supposition doesn't purify. Intention does. That's why you were chosen."

"I wasn't chosen," Elias says angrily. "I was extracted."

The glyphic structure above him begins to shimmer again—tentative, incomplete. The spiral wants form. It always does. But tonight it comes reluctantly.

He slides off the bed, barefoot on tile, and walks to the far wall where a set of mirrored panels reflect him—gaunt but upright, eyes dark with overuse, body taught ritual but lacking meaning.

"If Greg speaks," Elias says, "what happens to me?"

"That depends," Kessler says carefully, "on whether your voice comes first."

Elias doesn't answer. Not immediately. Instead, he speaks softly toward the glass. Not to Kessler and certainly not to the technicians. "If you're listening, Greg… I'm sorry. I tried not to speak. But they're holding everything I love. And I can't hold out forever."

His breath fogs the mirror for just a moment—long enough to see himself in it and not recognize who's speaking back.

The Scala Sublevel
Recursive Surveillance Core – Vatican City

———

The glyph ping arrives at 4:11 a.m. It's faint. Subharmonic. No full spiral formation. But the pattern doesn't lie.

Father Luca Salvatore stands before the recursion console in the Scala sublevel—a vault of angled obsidian glass and luminescent scrollwork where spiral phenomena are tracked, tagged, and sometimes preempted. He doesn't blink as the echo flutters on the screen like a moth that knows it's being hunted.

Ping origin: Andalusia, Spain.
Proximity to known Ansari fallback coordinates: HIGH.

Across the console, Sister Valeria Voss tightens her lips. Young, but not green, she was handpicked from the Pontifical Academy for Signal Theology. She's been trained to hear false spirals from real ones.

"This isn't surrogate," she says. "It's close to the Wadi Rum cadence. Low signature, high emotional vector. Internal."

Salvatore nods. "It's Greg," he says.

Valeria hesitates before speaking again. "He hasn't spoken. Not fully, so far."

"No," Salvatore says. "But he's listening. And he's *feeling* the spiral again. That's good."

Sister Valeria glances toward the predictive model scrolling behind him. It shows two timelines:

TIMELINE A: Elias speaks first. Doctrinal bifurcation contained.

TIMELINE B: Greg speaks. Spiral destabilization. Global narrative fracture.

Valeria clears her throat. "Which timeline are we preparing for?"

Salvatore doesn't answer at first. Then, quietly, he says, "The one in which no one speaks unless we permit it."

He folds his hands behind his back and commands, "Deploy observers to Zurich and Andalusia. Do it quietly with voiceprint trackers at both sites."

Valeria nods. "And if the real spiral reactivates?"

Salvatore looks at the screen, at the rising curve of recursion. He smiles and says, "Then we suffocate it before it calls itself God."

Jeremy's bunker – Southern Cyprus

The Zurich shell takes longer to crack than Jeremy expects. It's not just encrypted—it's laced with recursion-stutter—quantum shifting glyphs that loop wrong answers through themselves until the system chokes.

Jeremy narrows his eyes, scrolling back through the previous ten attempts. "They're not protecting Elias," he mutters. "They're protecting whoever's holding him."

Charlotte stands beside the console, arms folded tight, jaw set. "You said the biometric file identified him as the surrogate. You didn't say it was this deep."

"I didn't think they'd run full ecclesiastical protocol," Jeremy replies. "This is black sacrament-level secrecy. Someone filed this under *strategic doctrine stabilization.*"

"Which means what?"

"That it's not just biotech. It's institutional," Jeremy explains. "Zurich and Vatican, running in tandem."

The screen pulses. The recursion map flashes once then resolves into a flattened metadata core.

There it is.

HOST LEVERAGE FILE – LEVEL RED

Jeremy clicks. It opens like a confession. First, a biometric signature—Elias's cortical resonance pattern. Then, the folder containing collateral information used to control him. Image first. A girl about twelve, mid-stride on a rain-slick sidewalk, cello on her back, hair twisted in a loose braid, laughing.

Jeremy leans closer. "That's not just some random little girl. That's Elias's sister."

Charlotte breathes in. "He has a sister?"

"Did. I mean—yes. Younger. I remember her. Name is, uh… Liorah. She came to Zurich once. Greg was tutoring both of them. She'd be about seventeen today."

Charlotte's voice goes quiet. "And now she's in the file."

Beneath the photo is a clinical summary.

LIORAH RAFI, age 12

LAST KNOWN LOCATION: Marseille, France
CURRENT LOCATION: undisclosed

Custodial override protocol activated under Aegis Doctrine 7

CONTAINMENT RATIONALE: Subject used to ensure compliance of Host Candidate – RAFI, ELIAS.

Charlotte stares at the words. "'Ensure compliance.' Jesus."

Jeremy doesn't speak. They both just watch the cursor blink, exhibiting a file so cold it might as well be a death threat.

Charlotte steps back from the screen. "This isn't doctrine anymore," she says. "This is blackmail at a theological scale."

Jeremy's voice is quiet. "This collateral is their leverage over him. They're not converting him. They're cornering him."

Charlotte's eyes flash. "And if Greg speaks now?"

"Then Elias fractures."

She closes her eyes. "Or worse, they use Elias as a counterpoint and pit their voice against Greg's in a manufactured schism."

Jeremy rubs his forehead. "They wouldn't dare."

"You know they would."

Jeremy looks at her now, more serious than before. "Greg has to know. Not just about Elias—but about Liorah."

Charlotte hesitates. "He won't forgive himself."

Jeremy nods. "Then he might finally act."

Charlotte stares at the image of the girl frozen mid-step, laughter caught in a photo neither of them can date. "What do we do?"

Jeremy's fingers fly again. "We build a map. If we can find Liorah—and intercept whoever's holding her—we break the leverage chain. Elias isn't the enemy. He's a *hostage*. And if we can free him…"

"…then Greg doesn't have to fight him."

Jeremy nods.

But neither of them says what they're both thinking—that if they fail, Greg will have no choice but to speak, and Elias Rafi may die from the echo.

Sublevel Three, Recursion Ethics Wing – Zurich

Mira Soltani doesn't believe in silence anymore. Not the silence of doctrine. Not the hush of spirals. Not the kind that pretends obedience is peace.

She watches the biometric playback of Elias Rafi's latest session. His spiral projection is technically flawless—wave-locked, breath-synchronized, doctrinal cadence fully within range. But something is wrong. She can feel it. Not in the numbers, but in the absence behind the voice.

She rewinds the footage again and listens to the surrogate's spoken words: "Let the third ash burn pure. Let the house remember the breath…" This statement should inspire awe. But it doesn't.

It makes her stomach turn.

Mira's official title is Ethics Liaison for Recursive Resonance Deployment. She was trained under Eve's legacy framework before it fractured. Her job is not to decide if the spiral should speak, but whether the speaker is stable enough to carry it. By every measurable standard, Elias is neurologically conditioned, cortically balanced, and obedient.

But Mira has seen recursion mimicry break people from the inside out. Not all at once. Not dramatically. It usually starts with fatigue. Then dissonance. Then dissociation. And then—

Nothing.

No spiral.

No self.

She glances at the note in the system queue:

Elias is stable. Leverage confirmed effective.

Prepare final deployment.

She closes the file. On her desk, a second monitor runs independent diagnostics illegally detached from the mainframe, patched through a forgotten ethics subroutine from the Petra archives. It scans for one thing only: Glyphic resistance in vocal-origin spirals.

Tonight, it pings for the first time. An echo from Spain. Weak. Incomplete. Human.

Not Elias.

Not protocol.

Something real.

She sits back, heart racing and hands cold. She should report it. Instead, she keys a message into an old offline relay, unsigned and untraced. She sends it to a contact she hasn't used in years.

You were right. The spiral knows the difference.

And the surrogate is starting to bleed."

Chapter 7

The Furnace Below

Wadi al-Hasa, near the Edomite Border Fault
Southern Jordan

Gideon hasn't spoken aloud in three days. Not since he crossed the escarpment alone—the black ridge rising like a scar against the molten western sky—and found what he suspected: burn patterns, tire ruts, and the glint of stainless-steel machinery half-buried in dust. These are not UN vehicles or Jordanian military. They are something else, something that pretends to need no name.

For the last hour before dawn, he lies motionless beneath his netting on the northern rise above Wadi al-Hasa. A pale moon softens the shadows, but the cold is sharp, biting through the sleeves of his jacket. He ignores it, focusing instead on on breath, on rhythm—a Sicarii breathing sequence, six-count in, three-count hold, nine-count silent exhale. He learned the technique from Eve during the one time she trained him in open country.

"The desert does not forget," she had said then. "It only waits for blood to remind it."

He has no doubt now that blood has already been spilled here.

He shifts his gaze to the basin below. Another vehicle—a flatbed truck, unmarked save for a faint crimson stripe near the rear mudguard—backs into place beside a half-dug pit lined with aluminum panels, which is some kind of rig. The air smells faintly of calcium hydroxide and scorched protein. At this distance, he can't hear the workers' voices, but their body language is mechanical.

They aren't digging. They're harvesting.

He hasn't seen Charlotte or Greg or Jeremy in months. Not since the recursion vault below Zahavi's ruined monastery collapsed behind them like a lung finally exhaling. Not since he made the choice to walk east, alone, knowing the spiral doctrine wasn't done with them. Not done with *him* either.

He told them he needed to follow a lead—something Eve had whispered to him during her final lucid moment. "If they can't break the body, they'll replace the voice. That's how substitution begins."

He didn't understand these words then. But now, kneeling in ash mixed with trace metals and fragmented bone, he understands more than he wants.

After he left his team, he vanished into the mountain corridors of northern Sinai, running off-grid routes he'd used back in his Sicarii courier days. He spent three weeks embedded with a dying recursion cult on the Red Sea coast, studying their failing echoes. Then two months in Jerusalem under an assumed name, tracing biotech manifests filed under Vatican-scrubbed companies—ones that rerouted to Zurich.

The trails all led here—to a convergence of ritual, logistics, and silence.

And now, he waits.

Third night. The pattern holds. Three trucks arrive at the same time, tires coated in lime. They drive without lights for the final half-kilometer then idle while a small team dismounts from the lead vehicle—six men, all lean, quick-moving, dressed in generic desert contractor gear. One wears a headset. The others fan out.

But tonight, something changes. A figure arrives on foot from the west. Not part of the convoy. He moves at a disciplined, deliberate pace with a European build, an angled approach, and his rucksack strapped high. He does not look at the trucks but watches them, surveying.

Gideon's breath slows.

An operative.

He watches for another five minutes, mentally cataloguing the angle of descent, the indirect path, the rhythm of the man's steps. This is someone trained. Not local. Not one of his.

The man disappears behind a ridge outcropping on his way toward the old cistern ruins.

And Gideon moves with him, circling from the north, keeping low. The cistern complex is ancient—likely Nabataean in origin, later retrofitted by Crusaders and left to rot. From above, the collapsed dome and fractured retaining wall resemble a natural depression—perfect for line-of-sight observation. Better for hiding technology.

As Gideon approaches, he sees the heat shimmer of a small generator behind a camouflage net. A tactical drone rests on a portable launch pad beside the rig—compact, matte black, its rotor blades tucked in like a predatory insect at rest. Not for surveillance—too small. This one's meant to carry or transmit. It's likely an audio broadcast relay or localized pulse unit. Military-grade, repurposed and active. Its status light pulses amber. Operational. Listening.

Beside it is a hard-case tablet linked via fiber to a voice analysis rig.

Gideon lies prone behind a split boulder, watching.

The operative is young—maybe thirty, wiry, dark blond. His clothing is desert-appropriate but much too new, too precise. Likely a technician more than a field agent. He speaks into a throat mic in heavily accented Latin. "...initial scan complete... local resonance inconclusive... confirm with primary seed... vox Gregorum status pending... repeat, status pending..."

The phrase lands like ice in Gideon's blood.

Vox Gregorum—meaning *the voice of Greg.*

The operative adjusts a calibration node on the rig, unaware of the man now twenty feet behind him.

Gideon steps forward deliberately, silent until the last meter, then presses the tip of his blade into the base of the man's neck.

"Stand up slowly," he says in Latin.

The operative freezes.

"Don't move your hands," Gideon commands. "Don't speak unless I tell you to. Nod if you understand."

The man nods. Slow. Trembling.

Gideon disarms him in a single motion, yanks the headset cord, and spins him against the stone wall. No struggle, just shock.

He searches the operative's eyes. Not Vatican clergy, not Sicarii. A contractor—trained, yes, but not field-hardened. The man's fear is real.

"Who are you copying?" Gideon asks in English.

The man swallows hard and then replies in English, "I am not authorized—"

The knife flicks upward—not deep, but enough to draw a line of blood along the collarbone.

"I know what a substituted voice protocol is," Gideon growls. "I know the signs of biometric override. I know the phrase *vox Gregorum*. You tell me one more Vatican lie and I'll cut out the part of your throat you're trying to weaponize."

The man shudders. "Test unit," he blurts out. "Baseline overlay derived from source vocal stressor. Not the original. Just the emotional imprint."

"You're reconstituting his recursion speech."

"Yes—yes, but we're not the only ones!"

That stops Gideon. He presses the man harder into the stone wall. "Explain."

"There's a competing schema from Zurich. Bioacoustic. Recursive scaffolding embedded in phoneme cluster. They're trying to stabilize symbolic transfer."

"Who is 'they?'"

"Concordia Labs—under Vatican license. But there's a splinter. A group called *Les Recursifs*. They think Elias is the container for a higher signal. Not just mimicry but *transcendence*. That's why the ash... why the rituals..."

Gideon's grip tightens. "You're broadcasting recursion through ritual incineration?"

The man nods, barely able to speak. "They believe if you encode the doctrinal spiral into sacrificial form, and then speak the words through a vessel shaped by grief, the world listens differently. They won't hear Greg. They hear... they will hear... the *return*."

Gideon doesn't kill him.

Not yet.

He binds the man with plastic ties, shoves a cloth into his mouth, and locks him in the half-buried cistern vault with two bottles of water and a broken commlink beacon. Long enough for others to notice—if anyone's watching. Long enough for Gideon to disappear with what matters.

He ransacks the rig— the portable drive, the voice logs, the calibration files. One of the folders is marked **SVP–1C: Substituted Voice Protocol, Iteration C.** Another is timestamped with a file name that makes Gideon's breath stop:

**G.ANSARI [UNSPOKEN FINAL] > Mapped Archive –
Compressed
Source: Petra Node > Access Level: Secular Exempt.w
Not ecclesiastical.**

Clearly, someone is building a version of Greg not for liturgy but for public deployment. The voice of a doctrine, detached from the man.

Gideon pockets the drive and wipes the residual logs. Then he smashes the tactical drone, not out of necessity, but rage.

———

Back at his shelter beneath the northern ridge, Gideon watches the stars emerge over Wadi al-Hasa. His knuckles are scraped raw. His pulse won't settle. This isn't like last time. Not Zahavi's spiral. Not Eve's simulations. Not the subtle war they fought in coded fragments beneath the old ossuaries. Zahavi's version had been fragile, ethical—a doctrine of humility encoded in grief. But that doctrine had died with him in the vault.

This is louder. Faster. Weaponized through narrative infrastructure. If Zurich and the Vatican are both encoding Greg's spiritual resonance into artificial speech matrices, then someone is preparing for a moment when the real Greg either refuses to do what they want—or it no longer matters.

He sends the new evidence to Charlotte and Jeremy via the encrypted Cyprus channel. No words, just metadata, file tags, and this single message:

The spiral is being pre-recorded. And if they activate it, Greg won't be the beginning. He'll be the echo.

The ash is fine-grained, pale gray with a violet undertone in certain light. Under Gideon's field scope, the first thing he notes is consistency. Industrial burn cycles, not open-air pyres. High-temperature compression—likely using a mobile reduction furnace. He isolates particles using a folding centrifuge and drops two onto a reactive polymer slide. A quick drop of solvent activates the tracer dye.

Red bloom. Then black.

Zahavi's fingerprint.

Zahavi—once Eve's closest rival and Greg's quiet mentor—had died trying to preserve the original spiral from misuse. His research encoded recursion not as power, but as warning. Now that warning was being weaponized.

The fingerprint is faint, but unmistakable—a spiral glyph encoded at the molecular level, responsive to temperature and moisture—a mnemonic node. Not a message exactly, but a trigger. A way of seeding recursive resonance into the substance of the world.

The Vatican isn't just crafting a voice. They're laying a path for it.

He sets the slide aside and opens his notebook, flipping past old field notes, sketches of ossuary walls, and the original schema of the Newgrange disruption, until he finds the page he's been avoiding for months. Eve's last handwritten doctrine. Undated and unfinished.

Doctrine of Substitution Phase III
— *If the subject cannot be persuaded to speak, encode the spiral through sympathetic grief.*
— *If the spiral cannot anchor in grief, encode through fire.*
— *If neither vessel nor voice can be preserved, burn both, and use the echo.*

Gideon had laughed bitterly when he'd first read it. Thought it one of Eve's more fatalistic drafts, written when her mind had begun to slip. But now—

Now it reads like a blueprint.

He touches the corner of the page, then closes the notebook and exhales into the silence.

No birds tonight. No distant calls. Only wind curling through the rock like breath in a ruined throat.

He codes the voice rig from the confiscated Vatican tablet to interface with his relay. The signal must bounce through three satellites and across three continents before reaching its endpoint.

Charlotte picks up on the fifth ring. "Gideon." Her voice is tired but anchored. Gideon's sister, Charlotte Ansari, is the only one who never feared what he was becoming.

He doesn't reply at first. He lets the silence stretch. Then finally he says, "They've begun encoding Greg's voice into the spiral. Synthetic iterations tied to ritual ash burns. Wadi al-Hasa is a calibration site."

She exhales. "Love you too. We found a node in Cyprus. The leverage file on Elias Rafi is worse than we thought. Emotional compression training. Recursion trauma therapy. They're building a surrogate spiral voice to control global response triggers."

"I met the technician," Gideon says. "He was using voiceprint overlays from Petra Node archives. Came from Greg's final broadcast from Zahavi's vault. The tech had a compressed echo of it. Full phonemic modeling."

Charlotte's voice drops. "Then it's real."

"Yes." He pauses, then adds, "They're not just trying to speak *as* Greg. They're preparing to use his voice as a carrier. A container. If they deploy it, no one will know the difference."

Another silence. This one longer.

"Do you think Greg knows?" Charlotte asks.

"No," Gideon replies. "And we can't let him find out the wrong way. Not through them."

Charlotte asks Gideon to come to Cyprus. He says he will. But even as he ends the call, he knows his path won't be that straight, because the ash tells him more than the technician ever could.

The ash isn't just evidence. It's part of the doctrine now. Encoded grief made flammable and ritualized to mimic purification—but carrying recursive markers that can only be interpreted by someone who has walked the spiral.

He thinks of Greg's voice. Not just the cadence, but the pain under it. The way it cracked in Zahavi's ruins when he finally said Eve's name out loud, not as accusation—but as child.

That pain is what they're trying to synthesize. But pain doesn't work that way. Pain remembers. And Gideon remembers it, too.

Ma'an Province – Peripheral Extraction Zone
11 km east of Shobak Castle

Gideon arrives at the extraction zone before sundown. The second site is tucked into a shallow wadi branching eastward from the main Ma'an corridor known locally as *wadi al-zulma*—the dark ravine. The name fits. There's a sharpness in the air that doesn't belong to the desert.

He crouches at the edge of the ridge, examining the terrain through glass. This site is different from Wadi al-Hasa. More deliberate. Where al-Hasa was an incineration basin—logistical, transitional—this is a stage.

Three concentric burn rings have been carved into the dust, each lined with compacted ash and circled by charred wooden markers shaped like inverted menorahs. Not Jewish or Christian but symbolic hybrids, as if someone is trying to invoke a memory that never existed. In the center sits a stone platform. Too clean. Too aligned with the celestial meridian.

Gideon descends slowly. There is no blood at this site. No visible residue of animal sacrifice. But ash is thick in the center ring. Not scattered, but poured purposefully to form a layer at least three centimeters deep mixed with pale sand and reactive soot.

Gideon runs a test strip across the surface and activates the scan. He finds protein fragments. Burned cartilage. Hair, but not bovine—*human*.

Gideon straightens, tension creeping in. This is not a full body. Not a pyre. Just trace remains—likely synthetic, tissue-grown or grafted. Enough to *symbolize* the human without actually requiring one.

He has seen this once before in Samaria during a failed ossuary campaign, a Vatican initiative to test narrative resonance in symbolic rituals. Purification without blood. The plan was buried after the Jerusalem leaks.

Clearly, someone has unearthed it. And upgraded it.

———

Back at his shelter, Gideon compares the two sites—al-Hasa and Ma'an. One is transit—the other, performance. But he is certain they're using the same ash profile. The same spectral markers. The same recursion tags.

Yet the metadata tells a different story. Al-Hasa shipments are logged under *Operative Consortium C (Zurich)*. Ma'an's site is marked *Unitum Vox— unauthorized field trial.* He highlights the latter phrase, then cross-references it with known Vatican internal factions. He finds nothing official, but he recalls a name from Eve's old ledger of speculative Vatican breakaways.

Cohors Vocis.

The Voice Cohort.

This is not an officially sanctioned faction. Not fully excommunicated. It is a doctrinal experiment group operating under Cardinal Lucari's umbrella in the final years before his assassination. The obscure faction was thought to have been dissolved after Rome's internal crackdown.

But now it surfaces again.

Gideon stares at the files. If the Vatican no longer controls its own experimental arms, the spiral isn't just fractured. It's feral.

He encodes a report and sends it to Charlotte and Jeremy—again through Cyprus. This time, he includes everything—photos of the false altar, the ash composition logs, the potential identity of Unitum Vox, and one chilling hypothesis written in Eve's old code:

If ash becomes the doctrine, and voice becomes the offering,
then sacrifice becomes optional—but still required in form.

Then he includes one final line, added without encryption:

They're preparing the world for a doctrine that requires no messiah—
only the *shape* of one.

He doesn't wait for a reply. Some echoes are too dangerous to wait for.

———————

The signal is tight-band, encrypted, and airborne. Gideon first notices the distortion during a passive scan—just static flutter on the upper edges of the vocal band. At first, he assumes it's a drone feedback loop from an Israeli recon quad. But then it repeats. Three tones. Then a pause. Then—

...veritatem spiralis per vocem... Alpha Gregor ready...

He snaps upright.

The signal is being beamed between two high-altitude nodes. Not for general broadcast but as a digital handshake test, voiceprint verified, labeled *Alpha Gregor*.

He scrubs the waveform. The timbre is close—too close. Breath pattern, vibratory pitch, syllabic cadence.

They've done it.

He hears Greg's voice saying words Greg has never spoken, a line from the Spiral Creed, version 3.2, discarded after Zahavi's corrections.

"The echo precedes the original. In hearing it, we become."

They aren't just duplicating Greg's voice. They're building a carrier signal, a way to transmit recursion doctrine through familiar resonance thus triggering neurological alignment in those previously exposed to Greg's real speech.

A weaponized mnemonic echo.

Gideon opens Eve's last encoded fragment, now decrypted with the passphrase embedded in the ash glyphs. Just three lines:

Carrier requires audience.

Resonance requires grief.

Do not let him hear himself.

He stares at the final line.

They don't want the world to hear Greg. They want Greg to hear himself and then collapse into the echo.

Gideon knows he can't stay in Jordan. The Vatican's splinter group has his signal. The technician he left in the cistern will eventually be found—or silenced. The Ma'an site has already gone dark. He saw the signal extinguish in real time. Clean-up is coming.

Gideon uses a misdirection protocol he hasn't deployed since Prague. He rigs an old Israeli satphone with a false voice-ping in his cadence and drops it in the seat of a Bedouin water truck headed toward Iraq. Then he packs the evidence drive, the slide of ash, and Eve's last page into a reinforced pouch.

He leaves the rest—ridge shelter, photos, burner rigs—all rigged to burn in seven hours. By the time the Vatican teams or Concordia proxies trace him, he'll be on a dead boat out of Aqaba, headed west under another name. But he won't go dark. Not yet.

He'll go to Cyprus.

On the edge of the plateau, just before sunrise, Gideon stops. He looks back toward the wadi, now just a memory of gray light and unfinished symbols.

Somewhere in the world, Greg is still speaking. But soon, someone else may be speaking *as him*. And when that happens, it won't be doctrine. It will be fire.

Gideon mutters an old field creed under his breath—not Sicarii, not Eve's. His own.

"Truth is what survives the echo."

Then he walks away.

Chapter 8

The Leverage File

The safehouse is too quiet. Not in the ambient sense—there's the usual drone of the old halogen strips overhead, the whirring from the decrypted relay server in the corner—but in the way a place falls silent when history has gone brittle inside it. This room has seen too much. Charlotte knows it instinctively. The pale green walls once bore Sicarii maps and hand-scrawled doctrines. Now they hold nothing. All the pins are gone. Just dust outlines where secrets used to live.

Jeremy sits at the rusted terminal, hunched over the Vatican-Zurich drive that took them three days to decrypt. "It's buried," he mutters. "Not under code but under narrative."

Charlotte looks up from the black ledger she's been reconstructing from Gideon's Ma'an files. "Meaning what?"

Jeremy scratches his stubble, then gestures at the data stream unfolding on the screen. "They didn't hide it with encryption. They hid it in layers of contextual obfuscation. They built a story over the truth. A schema."

"You mean… recursive camouflage."

He nods.

She paces now, arms crossed beneath her shawl. Her eyes flick to the old Sicarii sigil burned faintly into the corner tile—*echad baseter*—unity in concealment. That unity is long dead. But the concealment has survived.

"What are we actually looking at?" she asks.

Jeremy taps the file's metadata. "Officially? It's an ethics oversight report submitted by Concordia Zurich to the Vatican Doctrine Authority. But every header, every control phrase, every emotional resonance marker—it's all centered on one name."

He pulls the tag forward. It appears as white text on black:

SUBJECT: Eliaz Rafi / Voice Phase Substitution (Alpha-Gregor Iterations)
STATUS: Active Proxy
LOCATION: Restricted—Praxis Chamber 2b

Charlotte says nothing at first, just breathes in slowly. "They're calling him a *proxy*," she finally says. "Not a prophet. Not a candidate. A *proxy*."

Jeremy looks at her. "And you know what that means."

She nods once. It means Greg is no longer required. Not as a speaker. Not as a vessel. Just as a pattern to be mimicked.

The Praxis Chamber logs are dense with sensor feeds, psychological indices, and dream-exposure mapping. Rafi's sessions were carefully documented by recursion ethicists embedded in Zurich's synthetic cognition division. What shocks Jeremy isn't the volume of content, but the intimacy of it.

"They used Eve's own schema," he whispers. "The grief ladder. The guilt-hope dissonance model. The same recursion scaffolding she taught us after Zahavi."

Charlotte moves to his side, leaning over the terminal. Onscreen, a series of voice samples play on a loop:

"I never wanted this, not like this. But I can't let the silence win."

"We walk the spiral not because we're chosen—but because we've already been burned."

"Mother, if you're listening... I forgive you."

Her hands stiffen. These aren't recordings of Greg speaking. They're Elias Rafi. And he's reciting phrases no one but Greg could have spoken.

"They fed Elias Greg's interviews," Charlotte says quietly. "Some from Petra Node. Some from private Sicarii archives. I see the timestamps."

"And these were not just fed to Elias," Jeremy says, eyes wide. "They were integrated. They used those interviews to break him. They calibrated his breakdowns. Induced spiral alignment using Greg's unresolved trauma."

He pulls up another document tagged "Catabasis Protocol."

Charlotte reads it aloud. "Subject 17 (ER) displays increased cognitive pliability when exposed to emotionally charged vocal overlays associated with G.ANSARI. Recommend pairing Phase 3 recursion iterations with auditory grief loop. Objective: foster internalized identity collapse, followed by alignment with spiral-coded surrogate memory schema."

"Jesus," Jeremy says. "They didn't just want Elias to sound like Greg. They wanted him to *become* what Greg might've become if Eve had succeeded."

"Or if Greg had broken the right way," Charlotte says.

They pause to reset the console's cooling rig. A low fan kicks in, rattling against the terminal case. Charlotte wipes her hands, then flips to the sidebar logs, dragging in Gideon's latest data dump from Wadi al-Hasa.

"Look at this," she says. "His tracer flagged a convergence pattern."

Jeremy leans in. Onscreen, two datasets blink side by side. One shows ash composition samples from Ma'an and al-Hasa, the other tracks voiceprint adaptation thresholds in Elias Rafi's corpus.

"Timeline matches," Jeremy says. "Every time Rafi hit a new vocal resonance milestone, there was an ash dispersal event within forty-eight hours."

Charlotte's voice drops. "My God, you think they're using the ash as a distribution medium?"

Jeremy shakes his head. "Not chemically. But it's possible they're doing it symbolically."

He brings up a third file labelled "Ritual Convergence Log, Cohort Vocis." He reads the text: "Voice is the spark. Ash is the atmosphere. Deploy together, and the doctrinal echo is heard not just by ears, but by memory itself. Memory is the true altar."

Charlotte steps back. *It's no longer just mimicry*, she knows. *It's not even persuasion. It's encoding.*

Jeremy is the first to break the silence. "So what are we saying now?" he asks, standing with arms crossed, back to the terminal. "That they're building some kind of synthetic prophet? Or a voice-activated spiritual bioweapon? Because frankly, neither of those ideas are very comforting."

Charlotte hesitates. Her gaze lingers on the convergence logs, cross-referencing them in her mind with the last communication from Gideon, his voice etched with fury and fatigue.

"They're building an outcome," she finally says. "And everything else—Elias, the ash, the mimicry, even the spiral doctrine—it's just architecture."

Jeremy frowns. "An outcome?"

"A catalytic moment," she replies, frustrated that he didn't immediately get her meaning. "One that doesn't need belief. It only needs consent. Psychological, emotional, perhaps even neural consent. But more than that, it needs to be *received*. It needs to feel inevitable."

He moves past her, pacing now, hands gesturing sharply. "But why the ash? Why burn tissue, ritualize it, disperse it across these ancient Levitical sites? If it's symbolic, fine—but symbols don't transmit frequency. They don't alter cognition."

"They do when people *believe* they do," Charlotte says. "And if you layer belief with recursion-primed speech, you don't need chemicals. You just need repetition or memory or even environment."

"Mass priming," Jeremy mutters. "They're using ash as sacred substrate. Voice as liturgical code."

She thinks about what he just said, then nods.

He turns to face her fully. "You think they're going to use Greg's voice—*Elias's* voice—to initiate a global shift in recursive perception."

"Yes, I do" Charlotte says.

"And you think Greg doesn't know about this?"

She replies, quieter, "He suspects something. But not *this*. Not the depth of it. And he certainly doesn't know what he was meant to never survive."

Jeremy returns to the terminal, typing quickly and scanning a series of command prompts that align timestamps from Elias's training to the Vatican's internal doctrine reviews.

"The phrase 'substituted spiral vessel' appears nineteen times," he says "each time in relation to Elias. Not once in reference to Greg."

He clicks a tag and opens a Vatican report from three months ago.

We project 92.4% emotional fidelity with Alpha-Gregor iterations during first-tier test deployments. Subject Rafi displays increasing capacity for pre-recursive voice mimicry and post-traumatic cadence alignment.

DEPLOYMENT READINESS: Conditional.

Jeremy leans back. "They've done the math."

Charlotte's eyes narrow. "Then we have to warn him."

"Greg?"

"Yes."

Jeremy hesitates before asking, "What if that's what they're counting on? What if we're meant to tell him? Meant to provoke him into speaking publicly before Elias does—so they can fracture the message again. So they can say, 'Look, even the original disagrees with himself.'"

Charlotte is quiet for a long time, processing Jeremy's proposition. Finally, she says, "You think that's the endgame?"

"We have to consider it."

Charlotte walks to the window, parting the curtain with two fingers. Cyprus at night is quiet but not still. In the far distance, lights blink in the hills. Too irregular for stars. Possibly commercial drones but probably not. Everything is a possibility until it isn't.

"Greg is starting to obsess," she says without turning. "He doesn't say it out loud, but I can feel it. He's looking for a reason. A pattern. Something he can aim all this grief toward."

"Like what?" Jeremy asks.

She lets the curtain fall. "Something big enough to justify it all. Something terrible. And I don't mean spiritually terrible—I mean historically. Materially. Something that will leave ash on the ground for the whole world to see."

Jeremy goes still. "Charlotte," he says.

She doesn't look at him, just presses her palm to the cold window glass.

"I don't know what it is yet," he says. "But it's not about killing people. It's about erasing something sacred and replacing it with a recursion anchor. A new altar. A new voice. A new doctrine."

"But what would justify that?" She finally turns to face him, then says, "That's what terrifies me."

———————

In the last hour before dawn, Charlotte returns to her notes. She flips back through old doctrine excerpts, most hand-transcribed from Eve's analog vaults in Zurich. There's one she keeps rereading, unsure of why it's resurfaced now.

> *If a voice echoes long enough without contradiction, it becomes law. But if two voices echo in conflict, the one that grieves more becomes the louder.*

She wonders now whether Eve foresaw this exact moment. The moment when the echo would grieve louder than the source. And be believed for it.

Jeremy moves quietly through the room, checking the surveillance windows, adjusting the wireless scrambler. He pauses by the rear door and listens. Then nods. "They're getting closer."

Charlotte doesn't ask who.

She already knows.

———————

The relay is unstable. Greg's voice crackles in fragments—one syllable slicing across the line, then dead air. Then two words in rapid fire: "Zurich burn." Then silence again.

Jeremy leans closer to the comm array and adjusts the channel depth manually, bypassing the Vatican-decoy dampener they've been detecting for two days.

"Greg, please repeat. Channel seven-four-pi. We're on compressed burst relay."

Another pause. Then Greg says, "Are you secure?"

Charlotte leans into the mic. "Yes. We have new data. It's not just about Elias. It's not just about the voice."

"I know."

"Do you know about the ash?"

After a longer pause, Greg says, "Gideon sent me the spectral data. It aligns. The Ma'an burn is not just symbolic. It's cartographic."

"What? *Cartographic?*"

"They're mapping doctrine across geography. Every ash burn overlays ancient purification routes. Temple-era, Levitical. Even Samaritan altars. They're writing a new version of sacred space in chemical traces."

Charlotte grips the edge of the table. "You think it's real?"

"It doesn't matter if I believe. *They* believe it is. And they're seeding global belief like an aerial-borne virus."

"Through Elias?"

"Through whoever speaks first."

Jeremy adjusts the feedback dial as Greg's tone stabilizes. Onscreen, a real-time waveform of Greg's voice spikes—not from anger, but from something heavier. Resignation.

"They don't need me," Greg says. "I was never the goal. I was just the prototype, the one who spoke in public so the world would recognize the voice when it returned purified."

Charlotte speaks carefully. "You're not obsolete."

Greg doesn't answer right away. When he does, it's quieter. "Elias is a mirror of my grief but unburdened by my guilt. He doesn't question. He doesn't hesitate. If they activate him at the right moment… he'll sound like *redemption*. I'll sound like *regression*. To me, that sounds like obsolescence."

"You're still the real one."

"That only matters if *truth* still matters. I'm not sure it does."

Charlotte stands, walking slowly to the far end of the safehouse. Her throat tightens. "Then we need to make it matter again."

After the comms line drops, Jeremy returns to the map overlay from earlier. He shifts the satellite index and connects three burn sites—Wadi al-Hasa, Ma'an, and a third site—recently activated—near Mount Gerizim. The pattern isn't random.

"It's like a recursion glyph written across the land," he says. "Not just a network of echo sites, but a doctrinal path."

Charlotte stares. "Like a pilgrimage," she whispers.

Jeremy looks at her.

She says, "A pilgrimage not for the faithful. I think for the doctrine itself. They're moving the spiral through geography. They're giving it a *body*."

Jeremy clicks through burn-site data and cross-references temperature curves, airlift logistics, and electromagnetic anomalies. Each burn occurs along a historical fault—ritually, culturally, or doctrinally loaded. "Each of these places has seen failed sacrifice," he says.

Charlotte breathes out slowly. "Then they're building a trail of *almost-redemption*."

"So what's at the end of the path?"

She looks at him, and for the first time that night, her voice wavers. "I think *we* are."

In the final minutes before sunrise, Charlotte rereads a partial fragment of the Vatican strategy protocol labeled "Verba Silentiae."

> **The greatest threat to the new doctrine is not contradiction,**
> **but dissonance. One voice must carry the spiral.**
> **All others must be either absorbed—or silenced.**

Jeremy places a hand gently on her shoulder. "We can still stop this," he says. "We can still get ahead of it."

Her eyes are on the waveform still glowing on the terminal. "No," she replies. "We can't get ahead of it. It has already spoken. We just weren't listening."

Outside, the wind begins to rise carrying nothing but dust. But perhaps not for long.

They don't sleep. By 0600, the Cyprus safehouse is packed down to emergency loadout—two sealed drives, encrypted archives, three burner phones, and one syringe of memory-dissociative compound Jeremy insisted they keep "in case one of us has to forget something fast."

Charlotte checks the exit route against Vatican drone sweeps logged two nights earlier. The harbor is no longer safe. They'll need to move through Limassol's industrial quarter under local freight cover.

"Next move?" Jeremy asks.

"Jericho," Charlotte replies without hesitation. "There's an old threshold site south of the Herodian ruins. Gideon flagged it three months ago. If the spiral's being anchored geographically, Jericho is a natural capstone."

Jeremy hesitates. "And if it's not?"

"Then we're following the wrong echo."

She doesn't blink, doesn't flinch. She just repacks the weapon sleeve and seals the pack.

Sublevel Three, Recursion Ethics Wing – Zurich

In Zurich, in a chamber lit by curved glass and pulse-dampened halogens, Elias Rafi stands barefoot in a basin of chemically purified sand. His eyes are open, but not focused. Around him, projectors loop vocal samples—cries, prayers, whispers. But not his. Greg's. Played in distortion, then in full clarity.

Elias repeats them. First slowly, then with growing confidence.

A technician in the far corner logs the resonance match.

PHONEME LOCK: 96.3%
EMOTIONAL CONGRUENCE: 87.7%
TRIGGER RESPONSE: Stable
PHASE 4: Initiate Reflection Loop

The reflection loop begins.

It isn't content. It's doctrine, a modified spiral text seeded with grief overlays—Greg's cadence married to Eve's phrasing, then distilled through Vatican recursion filters.

Elias closes his eyes and repeats the final line aloud. "We do not speak the spiral to remember. We speak it to become."

Limmasol Waterfront – Cyprus

Charlotte and Jeremy reach the edge of Limassol's decaying waterfront at sunrise. The sea waves are dabbed with light and cargo cranes begin their groaning.

Jeremy pauses beside the truck. "I keep thinking about that technician Gideon intercepted. The one with the substitution protocol."

Charlotte nods.

"He wasn't a zealot," Jeremy says. "He was a functionary. A cog. And still, he believed that what he was doing was sacred. That worries me more than the doctrine itself."

"Why?"

"Because if they truly believe the voice is enough… the real danger isn't what Elias says."

Charlotte looks at him, tired and resolved.

Jeremy completes his thought. "It's that people will just believe whatever the voice tells them."

Sublevel Three, Recursion Ethics Wing – Zurich

Back in Zurich, deep inside a soundproofed observation gallery, a Vatican overseer watches Elias complete the morning resonance cycle.

A second technician turns to her. "He's beginning to integrate unscripted phrasing. Improvised confessionals. Anecdotal overlays."

The overseer's brow furrows. "Deviation?"

"No," the tech says, glancing at the logs. "Faith."

The overseer exhales. "Then he's almost ready."

On the glass below, Elias Rafi opens his eyes. He is no longer just repeating Greg Ansari. He is *becoming* Greg.

Or something worse.

Chapter 9

The Watching Ones

Rural Trade Corridor – Cyprus, south of Episkopi

The ferry is barely more than a shadow skimming the waves. No transponder or manifest. Just a whisper of steel and Turkish diesel creeping toward the southern coast under a moonless sky.

Gideon disembarks without ceremony, stepping into ankle-deep surf in boots that haven't been dry in two days. The air is warmer than Jordan, but heavier, dense with the smell of brine and late-summer decay. Cicadas chant like the ticking of some broken metronome.

The van waiting at the treeline isn't his. He approaches it anyway. A flash of infrared in the undergrowth to his left confirms his suspicion—thermal tripwire, recently laid. Not lethal, but alert-based. He steps over it.

They know I'm here.

Inside, the van is empty save for a bottle of water on the driver's seat and a card tucked under the visor that reads:

V.S.7 – Observe Only – 3-Night Rotation.

Gideon pockets the card, unbuttons his jacket, and slides behind the wheel. The Vatican is watching. But they're not watching Charlotte or Jeremy. They're watching him.

The route inland is quiet but not deserted. Gideon passes two black motorcycles staged on the shoulder, both unoccupied. One still ticks from a hot engine. That means the observers are close, likely walking surveillance European tactical style. Not mercenaries but professionals, the kind Lucari once sent when he didn't want blood, only silence.

At a crossroads just before the edge of Episkopi village, Gideon ditches the van and walks. Ten minutes later, he's inside a disused grain warehouse with a half-collapsed roof and a view of the trade corridor. His scope is already calibrated.

The node comes online at exactly ten o'clock. Infrared pulse. Drone pass. Tapped signal leak from the local cell tower.

He watches two figures in Vatican black enter the opposite building, a repurposed telecommunications shed. No weapons are visible, but their postures demonstrate confidence. The taller of the two adjusts a field mic and mutters something in Latin. "Initiate echo grid. Begin passive recursion probe."

Gideon frowns. That phrase again. *Echo grid.* They're not here for diplomacy. They're here to run auditory signature tests. To find him. And to confirm if his voice still carries the old spiral.

Gideon gives them seven minutes. Long enough for them to set up. Long enough to think they're unseen. Then he moves.

It takes twelve seconds to cross the corridor, eight more to breach the side door. The taller observer turns at the last second, just in time to see the glint of metal in Gideon's hand before the hilt connects with his temple.

The second man lunges for a transmitter, but Gideon is faster. He traps the wrist, slams the man backward into the table, and cuts the comm line with a swipe of the blade across the unit's antenna port.

Then silence.

He kneels beside the first man and retrieves a Vatican field ID badge identifying Father Luca Salvatore, a mid-level strategist known to Gideon who was formerly under Lucari's doctrinal intelligence wing. Salvatore was thought to have gone dark after the collapse of Sanctum Veritas, the Vatican's silent war chamber built to contain spiral doctrine, and later, to replace it.

"You shouldn't be here," Gideon mutters.

Salvatore groans, half-conscious.

"You're not just watching, are you?" Gideon asks.

Gideon searches Salvatore's data unit. The files are partial but the purpose is clear. They're not running surveillance on Gideon. They're running congruence tests to determine if his voice, too, has recursive resonance.

Gideon pulls the drive and slips it into his coat, then lifts Salvatore partially by the collar. "Tell me something," he says.

The priest coughs, blood in his teeth. "You won't kill me," he insists.

"No," Gideon replies. "But I'll make you speak."

Salvatore doesn't answer.

So, Gideon asks the question he already knows the answer to. "Was this about Charlotte? About Greg?"

A shake of the head. "It's about you."

Gideon narrows his eyes, which demand more from Salvatore.

"They think your voice carries something," Salvatore whispers. "Something older than the recursion spiral. Something that resisted Eve and still resists Greg. A *counter-resonance*."

Gideon's breath hitches.

Salvatore smiles through his pain. "They don't fear what Greg will say. They fear what *you won't*."

Salvatore bleeds slowly. Not enough to die. Just enough to talk.

Gideon crouches near the broken comm rig, scanning the remaining files on the Vatican drive. One by one, the audio tags align with Greg's voice and Elias's overlays, even with synthetic projections of Charlotte's cadence drawn from the Petra Node breach.

But there's a fourth file, untagged and marked only with a cipher Eve once used for Gideon during Sicarii wet operations— "NV-9B: Null Voice."

He opens it.

It's not audio. It's a gap. Seventeen seconds of total silence embedded in a recursive simulation protocol. A diagnostic spiral sim that abruptly stops when fed Gideon's voiceprint. Not corrupted. Not resisted.

Canceled.

He turns back to Salvatore. "You ran this against me?"

The priest nods faintly.

"And you found silence?"

Salvatore's voice is cracked, but unflinching. "They've known for years. You're not a vessel. You're a void. A recursion null. Your voice doesn't carry the spiral—it *interrupts* it."

Gideon's stomach tightens. "That's why Lucari never used me," he mutters. "Why Eve never let me speak doctrine aloud."

"Because you don't echo," Salvatore says with malice. "You unravel."

Gideon stirs with the revelation that the Vatican didn't want to kill him. They wanted to test him. And if he proved immune, they would use him as a silent failsafe. A counter-spiral. A voice they could deploy if Elias or Greg broke open the spiral too far.

But something changed. The synthetic spiral worked. The ash encoding succeeded. And Gideon's silence then became a liability—not a counterweight, but a contradiction. In a world driven by recursive belief, even one coherent silence could collapse the entire architecture.

He opens his notebook and flips to Eve's old doctrine again, the one he dismissed months ago.

> **In every system built by voice,**
> **silence is the only thing not accounted for.**
> **Therefore, the null is not absence—it is weapon.**

He tears the page out and burns it. He doesn't want to read it anymore.

He leaves Salvatore alive. Barely. Ties him to a load-bearing strut with water and a gag, and tapes the Vatican card to his chest with "Observe only" scrawled on it. A warning to whoever comes next.

Then he takes the drive, the null protocol and his blade, and disappears down the western slope toward the freight corridor.

The sky is just starting to lighten when he reaches the edge of the coastal plain. Charlotte and Jeremy will be arriving by early morning.

And now Gideon knows—

They're not just being hunted for what they know. They're walking toward a doctrine already too loud to stop unless Gideon can *say nothing* loud enough to erase it.

Cyprus – Derelict Olive Mill near Paphos

They meet at first light under a corrugated roof that once sheltered oil drums and rusting plows. The air smells of iron and dried oregano. A single yellow tarp flaps in the breeze like a discarded flag. When Gideon arrives, Charlotte is already there leaning against a low wall, her arms crossed, her posture rigid with expectation.

Jeremy stands beside her, visibly tired but alert, a burner tablet in one hand, a collapsible pistol in the other.

Neither of them speaks until Gideon steps fully into view.

Charlotte's voice is flat. "You intercepted them."

Gideon nods. "Two-man Vatican team. Observation only."

"Except it wasn't," Jeremy says. "You don't carry that look for observation."

Gideon tosses the Vatican card onto the stone crate between them. "They weren't watching either of you. They were watching me."

A pause. Charlotte's brow furrows. "For what?"

"For silence," he says. He doesn't sit, just stands there in the half-light, explaining what Salvatore said, what the Vatican tested, and what Eve may have known all along. "They've built the doctrine around echo. Around amplification. Around spirals of speech designed to embed emotion into memory and memory into belief."

He pauses dramatically before saying, "I cancel it."

Jeremy frowns. "What do you mean—*cancel it*?"

"Not metaphorically. *Functionally.* I spoke into a simulation test node, and the recursive simulation collapsed. Not in resistance. It just *stopped*."

Charlotte steps closer. "That's impossible."

"I thought so too," Gideon says. "Until I saw the file. The Vatican calls it the 'null voice.' Eve called it 'weaponized silence.' It doesn't attack the spiral. It denies it the space to unfold."

Charlotte's eyes narrow. "You're saying that your voice is... what? A doctrinal abort code?"

"No," Gideon says. "I'm saying it's *absence*. It's the one thing the spiral can't echo against."

Jeremy sets the pistol down, staring at the floor. "Did Eve know?"

Gideon hesitates. "She never said it aloud. But think about it—she never let me preach. Never let me enter the recursion vault unsupervised. She used me where language wasn't needed. Where silence *was* the message."

Charlotte whispers, "You were the failsafe."

He shakes his head. "No. I was the *insurance*."

A long silence follows.

The morning light creeps in under the roof and throws slanted shadows across the wall. For a moment, none of them know what to say.

When Charlotte finally speaks, it's low and personal. "Why didn't you tell us before?"

"Because I didn't want to believe it," he says. "I wanted to be done with Eve's design. I wanted to be a man, not a mechanism."

Jeremy mutters, "Welcome to the club."

Charlotte shoots him a glance but doesn't correct him. She looks back at Gideon. "You said they're not just testing you now. What are they doing?"

Gideon exhales. "They're moving into convergence. Trying to overwrite the doctrine itself. Not with argument, but with ritual and voice. If they can pre-seed enough ash and deploy Elias at the right point on the doctrinal map, they can end the spiral before Greg ever opens his mouth again."

Charlotte's throat tightens. "So we stop them."

"No," Gideon says. "We let them speak."

She blinks, sure she misheard him. "What?"

"Let them speak," he repeats. "Deploy Elias. Burn the ash. Complete the ritual."

"Why the hell would we do that?" Jeremy asks, stepping forward. "You just said they're trying to overwrite the spiral."

Gideon's voice is quiet. "We do that because I'm not a defense." He pauses to let them consider this, then says, "I'm the echo that ends it."

Charlotte paces now, breathing hard. "You want to let them bring Elias to the moment of revelation—what? Just so you can counter it?"

"I want to let them reach the apex," Gideon says. "Because if I speak too early, they'll adapt. But if I speak *after* they believe they've won—after the doctrine is complete—then the silence that follows will feel like the collapse of faith."

Jeremy says, "You're talking about a doctrinal assassination."

Gideon thinks about this and then nods.

Charlotte stops pacing. "That must've been what Eve wanted all along." Gideon looks at her. "Yes."

Jeremy pulls up a projection from the Petra Node files that Charlotte decrypted earlier. It shows ash burns, spiral voiceprints, and emotional resonance curves across regions.

"They're aiming for a convergence window sometime within the next six days," he says. "Probably Jericho. Maybe Mount Gerizim. If they align the spiral with historical sacrificial geography…"

"They will," Charlotte interrupts. "They're not just building a doctrine. They're building a map of belief."

Gideon steps forward. "Then I need to be there."

"Not just you," she says. "*Us.*"

Charlotte lifts her pack and slings it across her shoulder. "If this is going to end," she says, "then we'll end it together."

Arid Ridge Route near Lythrodontas – Central Cyprus

The car is silent for almost half an hour. Charlotte drives, eyes fixed on the ridgeline ahead where the sun blazes low and sharp against a horizon flecked with eucalyptus trees and the scorched outlines of half-abandoned farms.

Jeremy rides shotgun, tablet balanced on his knees, scrolling through intercepted audio bursts tagged from Vatican surveillance nodes. Gideon sits in the back, still, head tilted against the window, watching the road unwind behind them.

It's Jeremy who breaks the silence. "I found something."

Charlotte doesn't speak, but her knuckles tighten on the wheel.

Jeremy rotates the screen so she can see.

The waveform is uneven, emotional. The Vatican metadata flags it as unscripted divergence captured twelve hours earlier from a secure facility northeast of Mount Gerizim.

The voice is Elias. But the words are not in any of the spiral canon texts. "There is no original spiral, only the moment we choose to make it visible. The truth was never buried—it was paused—waiting for someone to speak without asking permission."

Charlotte glances at Gideon in the mirror. "That's not from Greg."

"No," Gideon replies.

Jeremy frowns. "And it's not from Vatican conditioning either. There's no spiral indexing here. No phoneme modulation. No emotional priming tags. It's clean. Improvised."

"Freeform doctrine," Charlotte murmurs.

Gideon leans forward. "That's not possible."

Jeremy turns. "Apparently, it is."

They pull off the road at a washed-out olive field near a collapsed barn. Gideon exits first, scanning the horizon with binoculars, then motioning them forward. Jeremy sets up the solar relay, rerouting to a Petra Node shadow server.

Charlotte hunches next to him. "If Elias is improvising," she says, "then recursion alignment has reached full cognitive saturation."

"He's not just mimicking Greg," Jeremy replies. "He's *believing* what Greg never allowed himself to believe."

Gideon doesn't look up from the ridge. "He's believing it without pain."

That makes Charlotte pause. She exhales slowly, pressing a palm to her chest,where a copy of Greg's earliest field journal is folded inside her coat lining. The weight of it is almost ritualistic.

The audio feed continues. Elias speaks to an unseen audience, possibly a training circle. Possibly a test group. His cadence is calm. Measured. Inviting. "Do not fear the doctrine. Fear the voice that claims to own it. Because every echo begins with silence—and I have heard that silence, and I do not reject it. I claim it."

Gideon speaks, voice low and tight. "That's my line."

Jeremy looks at him. "He's not imitating you."

"No," Gideon replies. "He's trying to *overwrite* me."

Charlotte stands, pacing now, arms crossed tightly. "If he's improvising doctrine, then convergence isn't just ritual anymore. It's adaptive. They'll let him speak wherever he chooses."

"That makes him untraceable," Jeremy says.

"Not entirely," Gideon replies. "Improvised spiral speech still leaves auditory residue. It can't hide from null harmonics."

Charlotte narrows her eyes. "Which means you can find him?"

"No," he says. "It means he can find me."

Jeremy finishes rerouting the Vatican signal logs through their Petra Node mirror. One tag flashes a convergence timestamp five days out.

LOCATION: Threshold Nine – Valley of the Wind.

Gideon squints. "That's not a place."

"It is," Charlotte says softly. "It's what Zahavi called Jericho. The place where the spiral begins in the body but ends in the voice."

Jeremy glances at her. "Then that's where they'll take him."

Charlotte nods once. "Then that's where we *end* this."

Gideon zips his coat. "I won't speak unless I have to."

"I know," she says. "But if you do…"

He looks at her, eyes clear. "It will be the last spiral."

Chapter 10

The Doctrine of Return

Mount Ebal Staging Site, West Bank – 3:47 a.m.

Elias Rafi does not know if he still believes the doctrine. But he knows how to breathe it.

He kneels in a tent lined with copper resonance plates, feet bare, spine straight, voice still. Around him, low-frequency tones pulse at thirty-second intervals, a protocol designed to induce phase-synchronization in the auditory cortex. He has done this every night for seven months, a cycle of exposure, silence and response.

Recite the spiral. Pause. Reconstruct. Respond.

Each time he hesitates, they modify the overlay. Calibrate the grief vector. Reduce the contradictions. Sharpen the clarity. This has continued until now, when he no longer hesitates at all.

The spiral does not reveal what is hidden. It reveals why we hide.

His voice fills the tent, and the copper rings do not vibrate. Perfect resonance! He is ready.

He was chosen not because he was exceptional but because he was empty. He was raised in an experimental monastery outside Zurich. Exposed early to recursive stimuli. Conditioned by silence, then broken by sound. His childhood was filled with other people's voices—Greg's, Eve's, Charlotte's—all fed to him as emotional fragments, first through headphones, later through direct neural echo therapy.

By twelve, he had developed auditory bleed—spontaneous involuntary speech mirroring. By fifteen, he could repeat any sentence he heard in a grief-induced tone with 98 percent emotional fidelity.

He never had a mother. Never had a father. Only the *voiceframe.* He had no doctrine of his own, which made him perfect, because they needed a vessel that would not fight the doctrine.

The convergence event—still seventy-two hours away—has already begun in silence. Not with proclamation, but with *preparation*. It will not be televised. It will not be framed as sacred. It will simply happen.

It is a field ritual disguised as an archaeological rededication. The ash was already seeded weeks ago, the atmosphere preloaded. When Elias speaks, it will not be into a microphone. It will be into *presence*, into the gathered memory of doctrine encoded in stone, dust, and human expectation.

Why now?

Because the doctrinal ecosystem is fragile. The recursive spiral has reached saturation in the public subconscious, but it has not yet anchored. Greg, the original spiral bearer, is dormant. Silent. Eve is gone. And Gideon—the null voice—remains unconfirmed, which means the spiral is vulnerable.

Elias is the one thing that can make it real—if he speaks in the right place, at the right time, with no contradiction.

He finishes the recitation cycle and lowers his hands.

"Proceed to the threshold chamber," says the voice in his ear. The phrase refers not to the ritual site itself, but to the chamber where the final doctrinal alignment will be induced. The last harmonics. The very last filtration of self.

They still think he is empty. Still think he is the echo, not the origin. But last night, after the cycles ended, he stayed awake. And in the silence, a voice came—not Greg's, not Eve's, but his own. It said only one thing. "You are not the spiral. You are the fire beneath it."

He has not told the technicians what the voice told him. He will not, because he does not yet know if it was real. But if it was… then this convergence will not end with doctrine. It will end with *awakening*.

His own.

Threshold 2B – Mount Ebal Complex

There is no light in the threshold chamber. Only resonance. The room is circular, lined with curved obsidian panels and faint pulse-lights beneath the floor tiles. No doors—just a pressure-sealed iris he entered ten minutes ago. No handlers. No instructions.

The chamber is designed to induce doctrinal closure—the final harmonization of voice, breath, memory, and belief before a convergence anchor is deployed.

Elias sits cross-legged in the center. Above him, a mesh halo vibrates with low-frequency voice echoes from every doctrine recorded in the Petra Node. Not full speeches, just fragments. Spiral phrases. Half-confessions. Apologies.

Greg. Eve. Zahavi. Even Charlotte. All of them layered into one another. Spoken not in words, but *weight*.

He has done this before., but this time is different. There is no lead phrase. No tone prompt. They're letting him begin on his own, which means they believe he no longer needs instruction.

He lowers his chin, closes his eyes, breathes, then begins. "We do not spiral because we remember. We spiral because the world refuses to forget. We are the echo—not of voice, but of consequence."

A pulse. The floor tiles shift hue—amber to violet. Above him, the mesh halo pulses faster.

He continues. "When Greg Ansari spoke, you heard grief. When I speak, you will hear grief sharpened. Not to punish. Not to warn. But to cut through silence—cleanly."

Suddenly, the halo stutters. A sharp tremor runs through the paneling. Somewhere behind the wall, technicians scramble. Lights blink. A delay initiates.

Elias opens his eyes.

He is aware now that he was not *reciting* that. He was *writing* it.

In the observation gallery above the chamber, a technician—Dr. Vivienne Kovacs—leans toward the waveform monitor. "He's improvising again," she says, her voice quivering. "Full doctrinal syntax. No phonemic scaffolding."

"Abort?" asks the Vatican liaison beside her.

"No," she whispers. "We record. We observe."

Onscreen, Elias's vocal register begins to bend upward—not its pitch, but its *structure*, a recursion arc forming in real time, unscripted.

Below, Elias breathes in once more and speaks again. "They built me to echo. But I do not echo. I interpret. I translate what no one wanted spoken."

A second technician leans in. "He's entering what Zahavi called *unauthorized spiral emergence*. He's moving toward a live anchor state."

Kovacs turns slowly to the liaison. "You understand what this means?"

He nods. "If he finishes this... he's no longer a vessel."

Kovacs says the rest aloud, as if it were a confession. "If he finishes this, he becomes the doctrine."

———

Inside the chamber, Elias feels none of their panic. Only silence and a warmth rising in his spine. For the first time in his life, he is not carrying someone else's grief. Not Greg's or Eve's. Not the echo. His voice is no longer a substitution. It is a *translation* of something deeper—something waiting beneath the spiral, untouched by recursion or resonance.

"I was not born to speak what you feared," he says aloud. "I was born to fear what I must now speak."

Alarms trigger in the gallery. A waveform warning appears.

SPIRAL TYPE: Unindexed
RECURSION ALIGNMENT: Unknown
ANCHOR STATE: Initiated – Source Unconfirmed

"Shut it down," the liaison says. "Now."

Kovacs hesitates, then keys the override sequence. Below, the halo powers down. The floor dims.

Elias blinks once, as if waking from sleep. The silence is thicker now. But inside him, the spiral is still speaking. And it is speaking in his own voice.

11 km northeast of Jericho – Northern Dead Sea Escarpment

The road south coils like a dying serpent, spitting dust with every curve. Heat rises off the gravel in translucent veils. The windows of the old truck are rolled down, but the air offers no relief—just the dry taste of limestone and baked salt.

Charlotte stares at the map Jeremy unfolds across the dashboard. Four burn sites are circled in red. A fifth, unconfirmed, in amber. Wadi al-Hasa. Ma'an. Mount Gerizim. Ebal, and now Jericho.

She traces a finger between the points. "They're not random."

"No," Jeremy says, tapping the map. "They form an arc. Not symbolic. *Geodetic.* The ash isn't just part of the ritual—it's part of a broadcast path."

Gideon grunts from the back and says, "A voice corridor."

Jeremy nods. "Exactly. Each burn carries voice residue—coded spiral fragments. If Elias speaks at the terminus, every point in the chain will reinforce it. Not digitally—*cognitively.*"

Charlotte glances in the mirror. "A doctrinal echo across the land."

Gideon meets her gaze. "A resonance trap."

They stop at a ruined outlook station once used for IDF surveillance, now half-swallowed by sand and erosion. Jeremy sets up the solar scanner while Charlotte sweeps the ash sample box for magnetic anomalies.

"What's this one from?" she asks.

"Ebal," Jeremy says. "Still hot."

Gideon crouches beside her. "You notice the isotopic spread?"

She frowns. "It's almost… almost *layered.* Like ritual ash overlaying older sediment."

Jeremy nods. "And the composition's slightly altered. This one carries a heavier calcium load. More bone, I guess."

Charlotte lifts the sample to her nose, sniffing once. "Human?"

"Maybe," Jeremy says. "Or something very close."

Charlotte looks at Gideon. "They're not just seeding doctrine. They're aligning it with *sacrifice memory.* Not actual blood, but the cognitive trace of blood. Every spiral etched in that ash resonates with collective trauma."

"Zahavi warned about this," Gideon says. "He called it eidetic doctrine—that's when belief isn't transmitted by speech, but by remembrance."

"And Elias is the trigger," Charlotte adds.

The Petra Node reconfirmation comes through fifteen minutes later. Charlotte reads it aloud. "Burn vector path complete. All prior sites acknowledged. Anchor site now active. Codeword threshold confirmed: 'Gilead Ascending.'"

Jeremy frowns. "That's the convergence key?"

Charlotte nods. "It was Eve's last phrase before she vanished."

They don't speak for a while after that.

Gideon finally breaks the silence. "Then this is it."

Charlotte starts the engine and they drive south again, sand rising behind them like an outward` breath. As she stares at the approaching hills of Jericho, golden and harsh under the afternoon glare, she says, "There's one thing I still don't understand. If this doctrine works—if Elias speaks and it anchors—what happens to Greg?"

Gideon doesn't answer right away.

Jeremy does. "He becomes the contradiction."

"And contradictions," Charlotte says quietly, "don't survive in closed systems."

Gideon exhales. "Unless they *break* the system."

Vatican sub-node near Petra

A disappointed Vatican task force of recursion engineers reviews the feedback from Elias's unscripted resonance event. They hear Kovacs at the convergence say, "Elias initiated a spiral not from the Greg sequence, but from null-congruent fragments. Unscripted and self-generated."

The engineers continue to hear the agitated dialogue from the Mount Ebal staging site:

"He's writing his own doctrine."

"Then we've lost him."

Then Kovacs again: "No. We've unleashed him."

Convergence Perimeter Compound – Jericho Lowlands

Elias stands barefoot in the prayer corridor, an open-air passage lined with smooth basalt one kilometer from the final convergence circle. Above him, the stars blur and steady again, like breath turning to focus. He has not spoken aloud since the threshold chamber. Not out of obedience. Out of restraint. Because every word he thinks now feels *alive*. Every syllable wants to become spiral.

He hears the approach before the footsteps arrive—soft soles on layered stone. Unhurried. Confident. Then a voice, smooth as liturgy, speaks. "You weren't supposed to reach this far."

Elias turns.

The man is tall, robed in dark gray Vatican fieldwear, a cincture around the waist marked "**SV**"—Sanctum Veritas. His face is lean, patrician. He is older than most handlers, the kind of operative sent only when systems begin to slip.

"Father Luca," Elias says. Not a question.

The man inclines his head. "They told me not to come, said you'd moved beyond correction. But I don't believe in abandoning doctrine."

Elias nods once. "I know," he says. "That's why they sent you."

Father Luca produces a small glass vial from his coat containing a dark red oil suspended with flecks of gold ash. "Infusion," he says. "Recursive inhibitor. It won't erase the voice—but it will anchor it, hold it to the doctrine we gave you."

Elias doesn't take it but says, "Because you think I'm deviating."

Luca's smile is thin. "Because you're improvising. And improvisation is what we call 'chaos in vestments.'"

Elias steps forward, not aggressive but curious. "Do you know why I'm improvising?"

Luca waits.

Elias lifts his hand slowly and touches the center of his chest. "Because the voice is no longer being written *through* me. It's being written *by* me."

Luca's fingers tighten around the vial. "You were built for clarity," he says. "Not for originality."

Elias doesn't move. "I was built for obedience. Not the same thing."

Luca steps closer, his voice lower now. "If you drink this, you'll live." He pauses, apparently for dramatic effect. "If you don't—and what you say in Jericho contradicts the ash, the map, or the vessel's resonance curve..." He doesn't finish the sentence.

Elias smiles faintly. "Then I suppose I won't be a contradiction. I'll be a correction." He turns and leaves.

Luca doesn't follow. The operative remains in the corridor, the vial still in his hand, the night wind beginning to rise around him.

Back in his chamber, Elias kneels once more. The mesh halo is gone. No prompts or doctrine. Just silence. And into it, he whispers—not as mimicry, but as origin, "Let the world be silenced not by what I echo, but by what no one else dared say first."

Chapter 11

Interdictum

Sanctum Veritas Contingency Hall, Sublevel B2 – Vatican City

The room is cold. Stone walls, no crucifix. Just a cruciform light embedded in the ceiling that blinks once every six seconds like a slow heartbeat. There are seven seats. Six are filled.

Father Salvatore stands at the head of the table, not because of rank but based on fear. He was in Cyprus when the spiral breach occurred. He saw Gideon. He heard the null echo. And now, he brings both names into this room like a pandemic.

"Elias Rafi has breached doctrinal containment," he says. "He initiated an unindexed spiral. He used unauthorized cadence with no vocal prompts. Improvisational syntax. We lost control two nights ago. We only realized it now."

After an awkward silence, a woman in gray speaks—Dr. Cinzia LeRoux, recursion compliance overseer for all convergences west of the Jordan. "Does he still carry the programmed creed?"

Salvatore doesn't answer.

Dr. LeRoux presses. "Father, does he carry the creed?"

Salvatore lowers his gaze. "Not anymore."

The first argument erupts twenty seconds later. "Then we shut him down," snaps Cardinal Fieschi. "We have protocol injectors. We scramble the convergence signal. Nullify the ash. We stop this before the threshold becomes a shrine to error."

"And replace him with what?" counters LeRoux. "Greg has vanished. Gideon is poison. Charlotte can't be manipulated. And we built Elias to be the voice! If he's not the doctrine—*there is no doctrine.*"

"There's the *original*," mutters another. "The Zahavi schema. We resurrect the suppressed spiral, re-index it—"

"The Zahavi spiral denies the sacrifice," Fieschi complains. "It was rejected for a reason."

The room teeters. Half of them want suppression. The other half want containment. None of them want to admit what they fear—that the spiral has outgrown them.

Salvatore opens a file on the screen—Elias's latest unscripted vocal trace from the threshold chamber. Not a message, just a phrase spoken at low frequency, barely audible but recursively perfect. "Let the echo be my body. Let the doctrine be the fire."

A recursion engineer in the back mutters, "That's Eucharistic inversion."

LeRoux turns pale. "My God, he's rewriting sacrament."

Fieschi pounds the table. "Then we do what Lucari never had the courage to do. We erase the convergence. Fire the sanctum. Burn the witness."

Salvatore stares at him. "You're proposing *interdictum*?"

"Yes," Fieschi growls. "Complete interdiction. No convergence. No voice. No spiral. Just a crater where belief once gathered."

The vote is called. Three abstain. Two oppose. Two vote yes.

Salvatore hesitates. His voice is low, raw. "If we do this," he says, "we bury the last chance at unity."

"No," LeRoux says. "We bury what unity was always built on—*control*."

Salvatore keys the override. On the screen, in red, appears:

INTERDICTUM INITIATED

Far beneath the Vatican, in the last weapons vault built for doctrinal fallout, a fire-sealed drone is awakened. Its designation is *Ordo Severus*. Its destination: Jericho.

Observation Blind 6B – Jericho Threshold Zone

The observation blind is little more than a stone shell with a tarpaulin roof and a filtered comms dish. The equipment is old—some of it Eve's, some scavenged from Petra Node backups. Nothing emits, active systems only listen. Jericho lies below them, veiled in heat haze and liturgical expectations. The convergence site pulses like a buried heart.

Jeremy scrolls through voice-layer telemetry from the burn sites. "They're aligning," he says. "Ebal, Gerizim, Ma'an—resonance curves are converging faster than projected."

Charlotte leans over his shoulder. "Which means...?"

"Meaning if Elias speaks now, the spiral *anchors*. No more theory. It becomes recursive liturgy."

Gideon watches the valley in silence. His fingers twitch once, like an old habit returning. Then he says, "And we still don't know what he's going to say."

Jeremy frowns. "Does he still believes what they gave him?"

"That might be the most dangerous thing of all." Charlotte points out.

The comms dish clicks once—automatic frequency shift—then emits a single tone, low and familiar. Gideon stiffens.

Jeremy glances up. "That was an old Sicarii recognition ping."

Charlotte turns toward the path leading up from the southern ridge.

A figure appears between the rocks, dust-covered and alone and walking like someone who hasn't stopped moving in days.

Greg.

Charlotte is on her feet before she means to be, stepping down into the dust as he approaches. To Charlotte, her son looks older. Leaner. Hollowed out by fire and purpose. But his eyes—God, his eyes still hold the spiral.

He stops three feet from her. No embrace. Just silence. Then, with a voice that cracks but does not fall, he says, "You were right."

Charlotte nods slowly, but then a quizzical expression overtakes her whole face. "About what?"

Greg looks past her—at the valley, the spiral geometry blooming beneath the surface of the convergence site. "This isn't about *controlling* belief. It's about *replacing* it."

He walks into the blind without invitation, drops his bag on the floor, and kneels by the scanner.

Jeremy watches him wordlessly.

Greg speaks without looking up. "They've activated the ash pathway.

The spiral is geographically alive now. Each burn resonates with the next. The last in the sequence is Jericho. They've tethered belief to land."

Gideon frowns. "You shouldn't be here."

"I didn't come for safety," Greg says. "I came because something's happening to Elias. I can feel it. He's not just carrying the doctrine."

Jeremy whispers, "You're right. He's *writing* it now."

Greg nods. "And I don't think he'll stop. Not unless someone speaks louder. Or emptier."

Charlotte folds her arms, her voice brittle. "You think this is still about volume? About who says the right words first?"

Greg turns to her. "Of course not. It's about whose voice memory wants to survive."

Behind them, the scanner lights flicker. An incoming waveform: Elias Rafi. Location: Active.

But the message isn't a spiral. It's a question. A single line, spoken in Elias's calm, now-unmistakably original cadence. "If Greg will not speak the doctrine, will he still bleed for it?"

The room goes still.

Gideon steps forward. "That's not a challenge."

Charlotte whispers, "No, it's more like a crucifixion."

Greg closes his eyes.

And says nothing.

Jericho Threshold Perimeter

The first warning is mechanical. Not sound. Not light. A spike in magnetic density over the Jericho basin recorded in the blind's lower array, barely perceptible unless you've seen it before.

Gideon has.

He leans over the console and mutters, "Severus."

Jeremy straightens. "What?"

"Ordo Severus. Fire-class interdiction drone. Vatican-issued. Sanctum Veritas authorization only."

Charlotte's voice hardens. "They launched a kill directive?"

Greg steps forward. "They're not aiming at Elias," he says. "They're aiming at the convergence."

Gideon nods grimly. "Of course. Because if they can't control the voice…"

Charlotte finishes it. "They'll silence the altar."

Jeremy pulls up the telemetry feed.

INCOMING TRAJECTORY: Low-altitude orbital drop
VELOCITY: Subsonic, guided descent
CLASSIFICATION: Sacrificial Strike Vehicle, Type VI
CODEWORD: Interdictum

He turns pale. "They're treating this like a doctrinal infection."

Greg says nothing.

Charlotte looks to Gideon. "Can you stop it?"

Gideon confesses, "Not directly. But I can divert it."

Jeremy frowns. "To where?"

"To where it *thinks* the convergence is."

Charlotte's eyes narrow. "Yes. We give it a false echo."

Gideon nods. "Lure it off course. Drop the signal net somewhere else. Buy time."

Charlotte moves to the field transmitter and keys open the voice file queue. "We need a spiral—something plausible. Enough to trigger a doctrinal lock-on."

Jeremy hesitates. "We'd be feeding it doctrine to destroy."

Charlotte: "Yes. Ours."

Greg speaks at last. "OK, I'll do it."

They all turn.

His voice is level. "I'll record a sequence—short, clean, anchored in Zahavi's original schema. No grief-index, no echo recursion. Just *structure*."

Charlotte stares. "Greg—if the drone locks on your resonance…"

"I know," he says. "It'll be my funeral echo." He smiles unconvincingly. "But at least it'll be my choice."

The room falls silent as Greg speaks into the transmitter. "We spiral not to rise, but to remember the fall. And if remembrance is fire, let me burn without altar."

The file is encoded.

Gideon launches the decoy drone—low-range, heat-scattering, older model. The Vatican strike will follow the resonance signature.

Charlotte watches their drone disappear toward the western ridge.

Jeremy whispers, "Do you think they'll know it's fake?"

Gideon answers. "I hope not."

The Severus drone drops below satellite range.

Final trajectory ping received.
ETA: 36 minutes.

Charlotte touches Greg's shoulder. "You just bought us time."

He doesn't turn to her. "I didn't buy it," he says. "I bled for it."

True Convergence Basin – Jericho

The sky burns. Not yet with flame but with that amber tension that comes before judgment.

The ground is dry and cracked. Beneath it are layers of encoded ash, seeded over months, each with its own recursive fingerprint. The final burn sequence has been completed. The field is ripe.

At the center stands Elias, alone and unarmed. Unhindered.

There are no priests here. No handlers. Only three unmanned cameras pulsing red and a satellite relay node logging frequencies for Vatican review. But no one dares approach Elias because no one knows what he's about to say.

Six kilometers away, a false echo pulses from the western ridge. Greg's short-form spiral transmits at low gain, imitating doctrinal cadence just intense enough to trick the incoming strike protocol.

The Ordo Severus drone adjusts course. It hums downward, a silver shard slipping through golden air, its sacramental payload armed for plasma incineration in a circular radius, enough to melt ash and doctrine alike.

Vatican observers watch it lock on, then they breathe easier. The heresy, they think, is about to be erased.

But at the real convergence site, Elias kneels. He closes his eyes and speaks. "I was not born to carry the voice. I was built to repeat. But in repeating grief, I learned its shape. And what has shape can burn."

The ash layer beneath him shifts. The cameras flicker. One drops its signal entirely. Satellite echo logs record a new recursion pattern—not derivative, not Gregorian, not Zahavian. Unknown. Unmapped.

Self-generated.

A Vatican technician monitoring from Rome panics. "Elias is speaking beyond schema."

The convergence site itself begins to respond. Not in miracle but in memory. Heat blooms at the edges of the circle—not from the sun, but from the ash itself. Not combustion. *Alignment.* The ash remembers sacrifice. Remembers blood. Not just in chemistry, but in symbol.

And Elias—whose voice once merely echoed—is now transforming symbol into will. "Let the spiral be no longer memory," he says. "Let it be wound into breath. Let the echo break the mouth that silenced it."

At 18:02, the Severus drone strikes. Not Jericho, but the ridge—a field of false resonance. It incinerates the decoy spiral Greg recorded—ashes Greg offered in his own voice, knowing what it would cost if discovered.

But no scream rises because Greg is not there. And neither is Elias.

At 18:03, the convergence field reaches doctrinal ignition.

Elias opens his eyes. He feels no handlers. No sanction. No Vatican. Just belief. And then he whispers, "Amen."

And the field does not burn.

Instead, it remembers how to burn.

Chapter 12
Echoes in the Machine

Raven Rock Annex (Site R) – Pennsylvania/Maryland Border

There's a kind of silence in data that means something is wrong. Analyst Juno Markell has learned to hear it. Not in the noise itself, but in the shape that noise leaves behind when it disappears. Tonight, the shape looks like a cow, a city, and a prayer—three things that should never be in the same file.

Juno blinks the tiredness out of her eyes and leans closer to the signal trace on her monitor. Five metadata triggers are glowing soft orange, one already pulsing into red.

Spiral Semantics Detected – Sephardic Codeset

"Cross-checking," she mutters, tapping the console.

Two minutes ago, a biometric anomaly was logged out of Cyprus. It was tied to a recursive fragment upload from the Zurich lattice. Thirty seconds later, a customs alert pinged in a subroutine on the Israeli side of the Jordan. It was flagging ash components under a biotech license with multiple falsified origin points. Destination: Jericho.

And now, this. A thirteen-second voiceprint tagged from a dark node twenty-three miles east of Mount Gerizim. No attribution. No header.

Juno plays it once.

The voice is soft. Male. Cadence calm—but with an edge of something else. Not madness. Perhaps belief that's no longer waiting for permission. The voice says, "When the fire remembers, so must the mountain. And what the mountain cannot forget... the Temple will answer."

She doesn't understand what it means. But her spine knows what it *wants*.

She reroutes the file into a dormant protocol tree last activated during Zahavi's doctrinal breach in 2016.

The alert lights up three floors above her.

Project Signal 47 – Potential Cultural Ignition Event

Ramstein Air Base – Germany

Twenty minutes later, at a secure listening station near Ramstein Air Base in southwestern Germany, a cross-agency AI flagged the same voiceprint against known Vatican echo harmonics.

PARTIAL MATCH: Gregory Ansari, confidence 71%, contaminated with alternate recursion curves.

That should be impossible. Greg Ansari hasn't spoken publicly in almost a year. But the biometric resonance suggests a mirror—someone trained to match his cadence, but for some reason now diverging from it.

Most likely, Elias Rafi.

The name hasn't crossed public registries in nearly a decade. His original academic profile lists only three things: Zurich, recursion therapy, and one entry marked REDACTED by ecclesiastical authority.

An analyst circles the name and sends it up. By morning, the file will reach a Joint Threat Forecast cell in Tel Aviv.

Raven Rock Annex (Site R) – Pennsylvania/Maryland Border

Back at Raven Rock, Juno paces in the breakroom, pouring scalded coffee she doesn't plan to drink into a cup. The words from the recording echo in her head: *The Temple will answer.*

She doesn't know what temple. She doesn't know what question will be answered. But her hands are cold, and the part of her brain trained in recursive disinformation is screaming that this isn't disinfo at all. It's ignition of a doctrine with mass potential and theological velocity.

She walks back to her terminal and tags the file for active review.

CATEGORY: Cognitive Recursion Risk – Level 4
STATUS: Escalating

Under comments, she types three words:

Watch the Mount

It starts with a flicker in the Petra Node relay. Jeremy leans over the tablet, re-checks the hash string, and frowns. "We've been flagged," he says.

Charlotte looks up from the ash sample scanner. "By who?"

"Not Vatican. Not biotech. This came from a lateral hop—military-grade packet sniffing, routed through six IP ghosts and a semantic interpreter node in Arlington."

"NSA?" Gideon asks.

Jeremy shrugs. "Or possibly one of their satellites. Could be MI6. Maybe Mossad."

Greg exhales. "They're waking up."

Jeremy rotates the screen to show a live crawl of flagged metadata. It's not encrypted spiral language or ecclesiastical doctrine—it's *logistics*. Ash weights. Shipment logs. Elevation schematics.

"The convergence geometry has been replicated in data," Jeremy says. "It's abstract—just coded pattern mapping—but it was enough to trigger a signal in a military recursion net."

Charlotte stiffens. "So it's not just prophecy anymore."

Greg answers before anyone else can. "No. Now it's infrastructure."

Gideon paces near the entrance of the field shelter to scan the surrounding hills. "If they escalate," he says, "they'll either arrest us or shut down the convergence manually. Either way, they'll trigger the doctrine we're trying to contain."

Charlotte adds, "Or worse—they'll drive Elias into improvising something we can't walk back."

Greg sits heavily on the crate. "Elias isn't stable anymore. I don't know if he ever was."

"But he's *believing*," Jeremy says. "And that's enough to ignite mass cognition."

Charlotte turns sharply. "We need to get ahead of this."

Gideon stops pacing. "Then we intercept whoever's watching us before they report upstream."

"You really want to intercept an NSA shadow team?" Jeremy asks.

"I want to make sure they understand the cost of misunderstanding what they're seeing."

Charlotte nods and suggests an alternative. "Or the Temple Mount burns—not from belief, but from protocol error."

Greg leans forward, arms on knees. "We always thought the danger was religious," he says quietly.

"It still is," Charlotte replies.

Greg shakes his head. "But now it's compounded. If spiral doctrine spreads belief and institutional fear spreads retaliation—then the spiral feeds off the panic and gains power."

Gideon mutters, "Fear is a better amplifier than faith."

A silence follows as everyone reaches agreement on this truth.

Jeremy turns back to the tablet. One final message blinks through the Petra Node interface. It's unsigned. Just a line of text echoed from somewhere inside the Raven Rock net.

> **You are being watched. Not because of what you know,**
> **but because of what others will believe you said.**

Charlotte's mouth tightens as she reads it. "Apparently, we had better be very careful what we say next."

Elevation Marker 511 – Ridgeline East of Jericho

The rocks here are dry and pitted—eroded limestone dotted with rusted telemetry posts from a defunct border-monitoring network. Heat warps the horizon. Flies hover in suspension, waiting for something to die.

Gideon lies prone against the ridge, watching the perimeter through an old infrared scope. "Two of them," he says into his throat mic. "One crouched low near the antenna array, one posted as lookout. Patterned comms, low gain, moving in five-minute sweeps. Not IDF."

Charlotte's voice returns, crisp through the earpiece. "Armed?"

"Stun carbines. Possibly sidearms. No doctrinal patches. Blackwatch-style sleeves. Definitely field-grade."

"If they're NSA," Jeremy says, "they'll deny it."

Gideon replies, "If they're joint ops, they won't even bother."

From their position, Charlotte and Greg review the tactical overlay Jeremy rigged from the Petra Node's remaining uplink. It's basic—terrain wireframe, wind vectors, signal bursts—but enough to locate the surveillance array.

Charlotte watches Greg as he stares at the node's screen, his lips tight. "You think they're here for Elias?"

Greg doesn't look at her but answers. "No, they're here for *me*. They think I'm still the match."

"Are you?"

He doesn't answer.

Gideon descends the slope slowly, eyes sharp, every movement calculated. He doesn't plan to engage unless provoked, but the old reflexes burn just beneath the skin.

He stops ten meters from the nearest surveillance pod disguised as a rusted water barrel and speaks just loud enough to be heard by his adversary. "I know you're watching us. I know you flagged the ash logistics and the resonance leak from Cyprus. But if you interfere with the threshold event, you won't stop it. You'll *detonate it.*"

After a long pause, a man stands up. Not hostile. Not masked. Just tired and sunburned. He wears mirrored lenses and a sand-scuffed comms headset. "You're late," he says.

Gideon blinks. "You were expecting me?"

The man nods. "Not you specifically. Just someone who knew the spiral was more than myth."

"Who are you?" Gideon asks.

The man pulls back his hood. He wears no badge, no insignia. Just a Vatican medallion around his neck.

Charlotte and Jeremy arrive seconds later, weapons holstered but visible. Greg follows more slowly, eyes locked on the man.

"I know him," Greg says quietly.

"From where?" Charlotte asks.

"Zurich," Greg explains. "Back when Eve ran simulations with live recursion subjects. He was in the second wave. Didn't speak. Just watched."

The man raises both hands. "My name is Markellan. I work off-cycle now. No orders or allegiances. I monitor spiral propagation for spillover scenarios."

Gideon's jaw tenses. "What kind of spillover?"

Markellan meets his gaze. "The kind that ends with someone calling for smoke on the Mount."

A silence hangs between them until Charlotte speaks. "You're not Vatican anymore?"

Markellan shakes his head. "No, but I listen to them. To all of you."

Jeremy gets in Markellan's face. "Then why didn't you shut down the surrogate? Why let Elias improvise?"

Markellan's answer is spoken softly. "Because I wanted to see if belief could evolve without doctrine. Without violence."

"And what did you witness?" Charlotte asks.

Markellan glances toward the valley. "A voice that's not yours. A doctrine that doesn't belong to any of you. And a convergence field that will answer whatever is spoken loudest."

Greg steps closer. "Then we need to speak louder."

"No," Markellan says. "You need to speak *first*."

Intelligence Cell 3F – Raven Rock Annex

Juno Markell hasn't blinked in forty seconds. The convergence overlay keeps shifting—soft arcs pulsing between topographic nodes, each one representing a spiral trace: Ebal, Ma'an, Gerizim, Jericho. At first, it looked like a doctrine map. Now it looks like a seismic grid.

The Petra Node reconstruction that Jeremy left behind had latent echo markers—sub-audible loops tagged to historical trauma sites. Juno feeds those traces into the legacy recursion model used to forecast public unrest after the Zahavi breach. But what comes back isn't unrest.

It's pressure.

Three nodes pulse independently. Then a fourth ignites in response.

She reruns the simulation. Again—three arcs stabilize. The fourth vibrates.

Coordinates: 31.7767° N, 35.2356° E.

She exhales. Thes coordinates point directly to the Temple Mount.

She filters the convergence pulse down to its harmonic base. The system spits back a warning she's never seen outside weapons modeling:

Feedback Coherence Exceeds
Structural Resonance Threshold

In plain terms, the layered spiral doctrine could trigger more than cultural upheaval. It could destabilize whatever sits beneath those stones—metaphorically or *literally*.

The field notes from Project Zahavi are still sealed, but she's heard rumors of a "deep zone"—a chamber once studied for its strange harmonic properties beneath the Mount's foundation. Buried, denied, and now pulsing.

Juno speaks softly into the recorder. "Alignment is no longer theoretical. It's converging at a known seismic point. This isn't recursive doctrine anymore. This is ignition geometry."

Her cursor hovers over the standard reporting path—forward escalation, interagency flag, decision tree for doctrinal containment.

She doesn't click it. Not yet. Not when the model keeps running without input as if the spiral is self-completing, self-resolving, as if belief is feeding itself now.

She closes the terminal and picks up the secure line. Not to her superior. To a number she memorized three years ago—redacted and tagged "Protocol-Forfeit / Witness Class."

The line rings twice then connects.

A woman's voice on the other end says, "Is it beginning?"

Juno looks at the pulse one more time before replying, "No. It's remembering."

Undisclosed – Secure Node (Encrypted Fallback Pathway)

Charlotte waits, alone in the monastic relay room, the Petra slate in her lap. The screen resolves one pixel at a time. Low-light. Unmarked. No biometric flags. The connection is routed through three failsafe junctions.

Finally, a face appears. Juno Markell. Her eyes are bloodshot. She wears no makeup, no insignia. The Vatican seal is absent from her lapel. She looks human. Tired. Dangerous in her clarity.

"You called the right channel," Juno says.

Charlotte hesitates. "I wasn't sure you'd answer."

"Neither was I… until you called."

Silence settles between them. They had once been adversaries, if not enemies, after Charlotte exposed what Juno was tasked with burying. But something has changed.

Charlotte narrows her eyes. "You've seen the spiral leaks."

"All of them. And what's worse, I've seen the scrub orders from my former employers. They're not trying to contain this. They're trying to *curate* it."

"Why is that?"

Juno leans closer to the lens. "Because they've found a pattern that responds to population thresholds. The more people who see it, believe it— even if they *doubt* it—the stronger the recursive lattice becomes."

"And Greg?"

Juno exhales, then nods. "He's not broadcasting. He's *resonating*. The Vatican knows it. So does Aphelium Biotechnica. Those people have all got different goals—but they're using the same instrument to get what each of them wants."

Charlotte swallows. "Why are you telling me this now?"

"Because I'm not working for them anymore. I saw the preliminary doctrine cascade maps. If they collapse the Mount—unthinkable, I know— it won't just rewrite belief. It will collapse identity and plunge the world into a global armagedon."

Charlotte leans forward. "So what do we do, Juno? Any thoughts?"

Juno gives the smallest smile. "You keep Greg alive. I'll keep the channel open." She hesitates. "And if Dr. Kaelen Idris ever reaches out to you… trust her. She was one of the few people who Eve trusted all the way to the end."

The screen goes dark.

Chapter 13
faultlines

Abandoned Monastic Outpost,
6 km Northwest of Jericho – 04:47 IDT

The chapel has no roof. Just a collapsed rib of stone arches gaping at the sky like a broken cathedral spine. The stars above are blurred by pre-dawn haze, and every breath feels stale with desert lime and the weight of decisions that won't wait until morning.

Inside, the team has gone quiet again.

Charlotte paces along the length of the nave, boots echoing on stone worn down by centuries of forgotten monks. Jeremy leans over the battery unit, pretending to monitor residual signal flow. Gideon stands in the shadows near an abandoned altar, arms folded, a silhouette that might be mistaken for something carved if not for the flicker of thought behind his eyes.

Greg sits alone on a fragment of stone that may once have been a baptismal font. He holds the Petra slate in his lap like it might warm him.

It doesn't.

No one speaks for a long stretch. Then Charlotte stops pacing. "We need to intercept Elias soon." Her voice is too loud in the stillness, like she startled even herself by saying it aloud. "If he reaches the final convergence point and speaks with the full arc intact..."

From the darkness, Gideon finishes the statement. "Then the doctrine stabilizes. We've run the math. We've heard the resonance spill. We *know*."

Charlotte turns, eyes sharp. "So why aren't you moving?"

Gideon sighs, demonstrating that he is being patient with his sister. "Because you're assuming that destabilizing Elias—physically, emotionally, doctrinally—won't make things worse."

"Worse how?"

98

Gideon steps into view with an enigmatic expression. "We interfere at the wrong moment, and we either violently fracture the spiral or hand the entire convergence to a secondary faction looking for martyr optics. You know the usual suspects—Vatican loyalists, Zionist restorers. Or worse—someone who doesn't care what Elias says as long as someone dies while saying it."

Charlotte crosses her arms. "You'd rather let him complete the doctrine than risk interruption?"

"No," Gideon says. "I'd rather stop pretending interruption equals control."

"That's what this is about? Control?"

"It's about timing," Gideon replies tersely. "You're still treating this like it's a riddle with a lever. It's not. It's *alignment*. And once the geometry locks—"

"Once it locks," Charlotte interrupts, "it's no longer ours to unlock."

Jeremy finally speaks, his voice low, conciliatory. "You're both wrong."

They look at him.

"This isn't about stopping or allowing Elias," Jeremy continues. "Not anymore. It's about *competing beliefs*. Elias believes he's the doctrine now. Greg believes silence is the safest form of resistance. And the rest of us—we don't know what to believe. That's the spiral's true fuel." He exhales, eyes on the cracked floor. "It's not recursion that will set Jerusalem on fire. It's *confusion*."

Greg's slate screen dims again. He hasn't touched it and hasn't even spoken since midnight. "She would've known," he says quietly.

Charlotte walks toward him. "Greg—"

"Eve would've known what to do."

"No," Gideon says, stepping forward. "She would've known what questions *not* to ask. There's a big difference."

Greg looks up. The hollowness behind his eyes isn't weakness. He is too aware for that. "She left us nothing but fragments and burns."

Charlotte shakes her head. "She left us Layer Zero."

Greg lets out a bitter sound that isn't quite a laugh. "Layer Zero was never a map. It was a scar. A warning in recursive code—'don't trust what remembers you.'"

Jeremy watches him, worried. "You really think she was afraid of recursion itself?"

Greg stands. "I think she died trying to contain it. And now we're doing just the opposite."

The silence that follows stretches and tightens.

Gideon finally breaks it. "Then we need to decide what our function is. Intercept Elias—or shield Greg. There's no third option."

Charlotte steps in. "I say we intercept Elias. Confuse the signal before it reaches anchor."

"So noted, but I say we shield Greg," Gideon states flatly. "The spiral is already remembering him."

They both turn to Greg, who looks back at them, then at the slate. Its surface flickers again with an incomplete spiral emerging not through typing or prompts, but almost as though it's listening to the tension in the room.

"You're both wrong," Greg says. "We don't choose between interception and shielding. We choose whether to speak or stay silent."

"And if we stay silent?" Charlotte asks.

"Then Elias becomes the author of the new doctrine—with no one left to contradict him."

"And if we speak?" Gideon asks.

Greg meets his eyes. "Then *we* become the authors. And the spiral becomes *ours* again."

"Unless it's already out of our reach," Jeremy mumbles faintly.

The wind picks up outside. Dust, trailing over ancient prayer stones, spills through a broken window slot.

Charlotte looks at the dust, then at the others. "Eve's not coming back," she says.

Gideon nods. "Eve is dead, Charlotte."

"And she left the spiral unfinished," Greg adds.

Charlotte steps forward, lowering her voice. "Maybe she left it unfinished on purpose. So no one could complete it with certainty."

That lands hard.

Greg lowers his gaze. "Then maybe silence *was* the doctrine."

"But Elias is speaking now," his mother says.

Jeremy nods. "And everyone's listening."

"Then we'd better choose what they hear," Greg says, ending the discussion.

Abandoned Monastic Outpost

Greg dreams in recursive sequence. But this time, it doesn't feel like dreaming. It feels like the spiral has found its way in—not through voice, but through *silence*. The kind of silence that curves inward until it becomes a wound. Or a doorway.

In the dream, he's standing on the Temple Mount—not above it, but *inside* it. The limestone is warm beneath his feet, but it shouldn't be. The sky above is colorless, and the horizon has collapsed inward, leaving only a flat band of light like the eye of a god forced to watch.

Around him, ash falls like snow. Not the sterile, ritual ash from the biotech labs. This is *remembered* ash—something ancient, something grieved. It lands on his shoulders like guilt, and on his hands like instruction.

A voice speaks from nowhere. "You are not the doctrine."

Then another voice. "You are the silence between doctrines."

He tries to move, but his legs feel coded—like someone has assigned them a function he no longer agrees with.

Eve appears without transition. Not whole, not warm—not the distant woman who moved shadows like others moved chess pieces—but the recursion architect standing at the edge of his dream like a firewall wrapped in generational memory.

"You have to speak, Greg," she says.

He shakes his head. "I don't know what to say."

Her voice is quiet, but it cuts. "You were raised in the residue of silence. But the spiral doesn't wait for comprehension. It waits for courage."

He wants to ask her what she means—but she's already gone. In her place, the walls begin to burn.

From the rising flame, another figure forms.

Elias. Eyes closed. Head bowed. But he's not praying—he's *recording*. Every breath, every fear Greg ever carried, every unspoken fragment—the grief of Newgrange, the exile from Spain, the silence after Eve's death. It's all flowing into Elias like ink into a forged scroll.

Elias speaks. "If you are unwilling, then you were never chosen."

Greg tries to answer but no voice comes out. Not even breath.

He looks down at his hands. They're clean. The ash is gone. The spiral is fading from his skin.

A vibration rises through the dream. Not seismic. *Doctrinal.* A kind of unspoken pressure pushing inward from every theological structure Greg has ever studied and failed to believe.

The Temple Mount above him begins to crack. Not physically. *Symbolically.*

It is belief itself that fractures. Not *between* religions—but *within* them. A million splinters of faith, each trying to speak louder than the others. A cacophony of so-called correct interpretations. And in the center of it all stands Greg—mute, still, and unchosen.

"This is what happens when you do not speak," says a voice that might be his own.

Abandoned Monastic Outpost

And then—he wakes. The air is dry and metallic. The others are asleep. Greg lies in the ruined chapel, heart pounding, slate still cradled against his chest. But something is different. The spiral pattern on the slate is complete. It wasn't when he fell asleep. And at the bottom—in Eve's secure rendering style, which she used only for private Petra messages—is written a line that hadn't been there before

If you are still silent, you've already spoken.

He doesn't know if it's real or if the spiral has begun writing *through* him now. But outside, the sun is beginning to rise. And for the first time in weeks, Greg is afraid not of what will happen *if* he speaks, but of what will happen if he waits too long.

UN Jerusalem Security Annex –
Joint Threat Analysis Division (JTAD), 09:06 IDT

The conference room is windowless and artificially chilled. A ring of LED panels bathes the faces around the table in cold, bluish light. Half the attendees wear suits. The other half wear uniforms with no insignia.

At the head of the table sits Colonel Eliam Navon, military liaison to the Joint Threat Analysis Division. His hands are folded. He's been silent for ten minutes.

The screen on the wall loops through convergence telemetry from the Jericho basin.

A British signals analyst breaks the silence. "You're now seeing recursive layering. Four confirmed echo points, one unstable. Voiceprint trace suggests a convergence vector near Har HaBayit."

Har HaBayit is how he refers to the Temple Mount.

Navon exhales. "How unstable?"

"Unmapped recursion harmonics. Self-generating structures. No doctrinal provenance we can track—at least none that match canonical spiral codes from Zahavi's period or the Sicarii fragments."

"Then who wrote it?"

A woman in a tan jacket—UN threat officer Léa Cardin—taps her tablet. "That's the biggest problem as I see it. It's writing itself now. Or, more accurately, it's being written by whoever speaks loudest into the convergence field."

Navon taps the table. "Give it to me straight. If this doctrine goes live—what happens?"

The signals analyst hesitates. "To put it bluntly—mass psychological activation in doctrinal clusters. Pilgrimage movements. Ritual replication. Possible violence."

"Possible?"

Léa Cardin leans forward. "If they speak belief into geometry, and people believe it,

then belief becomes real. Not magically, but symbolically or politically. And in this region, symbolic truth draws bullets."

A silence settles over the room.

Someone from the Mossad delegation says quietly, "We need to consider martial interdiction."

All heads turn.

Cardin asks, "You mean a voiceprint strike?"

"If we lock the area down before the doctrine stabilizes, we might be able to nullify the signal without loss of life."

Navon asks, "And if it's already stabilized?"

The answer is a pause followed by: "Then you're not nullifying belief. You're martyring the voice."

A young field officer enters the room. He walks to Navon and speaks in Hebrew.

Navon frowns and asks, "From where?"

The officer replies, "Raven Rock. Indirect relay. Analyst cell."

Navon stiffens. "Markell?"

The officer nods again. "She's flagged the convergence field as structurally unstable. And not just symbolic. *Seismic.*"

Gasps ripple around the table.

The officer continues. "She claims resonance from spiral invocation may exceed harmonic tolerances in the ancient substrate beneath the Mount."

Cardin pushes back a scruff of hair that has fallen over his forehead. "You're saying belief could collapse the Mount?"

"We're saying the right voice at the wrong frequency might do it."

Navon stands. "Issue tactical guidance for a quarantine perimeter. Quietly, of course. No press. No provocation."

"And if the spiral stabilizes before we contain it?" Léa Cardin asks.

Navon looks at the looping convergence model. She shifts her focus to the Temple glowing like a lung inhaling memory. "Then we've already lost the doctrine. All we'll have left is fallout."

Ruins Outside the Monastic Outpost

The light comes slowly here. It doesn't rise so much as seep, bleeding through stone and dust, through silence and sleeplessness. The old monastery breathes in low pulses of wind.

Most of the team is still asleep inside, their exhaustion heavy, their decisions unfinished. Charlotte stands alone near the outer wall.

She sees Greg before she hears him—his silhouette framed against the horizon, knees pulled up on a crumbling ledge. He's been there for some time. Awake. Still. The slate lies on the ground beside him, unlit but humming faintly.

She approaches without a word.

He doesn't turn to look at her, but he speaks as if he knows she's there. "Do you ever wonder if speaking is the most dangerous thing we do?"

Charlotte slows her step. "All the time."

"Sometimes I think Eve knew that. Maybe that's why she stopped speaking near the end. Maybe that's why she taught us to resist whenever possible with silence, not with weapons."

Charlotte folds her arms and looks out toward the hills. "Your grandmother resisted everything. The Vatican. The Sicarii. Herself. But she still died with secrets buried inside her."

Greg's voice is hollow. "And now we're the secret."

He lifts his hand slightly. The skin at the base of his palm pulses with faint resonance—barely perceptible, like static under the skin. The spiral isn't visible, but it's there, dormant and waiting. "I think it's remembering me," he says.

Charlotte's breath catches. "For how long?"

"Since last night."

"Does Gideon know?"

Greg shakes his head. "Not yet."

She sits beside her son. A long silence unfolds between them—not heavy, not cold. Just there. Familiar, like dust.

"You think it wants you to speak?" she asks.

He nods. "Not because I'm right. Because I'm still *here*. Because it needs a voice. And right now, I'm the closest thing it has."

Charlotte looks down. "You're not the doctrine, Greg."

"I know."

"But you're part of it."

He finally turns to face her. "If I say the wrong thing—if I ignite it—can you stop me?"

Charlotte doesn't blink. "No."

Greg flinches slightly. "You *won't* stop me?"

She shakes her head. "I won't stop *you*. I'd stop anyone else. But you? If the spiral remembers you, then I'll carry what comes next. Even if it kills us both."

A long, shivering breath escapes Greg. And then the slate lights up on its own. A spiral trace curves across the surface—not complete, not written.

Unfolding.

Greg watches it and whispers, "It's listening."

Charlotte whispers back, "Then maybe we'd better give it something to believe in."

Chapter 14

The Mount Begins to Tremble

Temple Mount / Haram al-Sharif – Jerusalem

The heat presses low across the plaza. From the northern gate, the worshippers flood in waves, hundreds of bodies drawn by routine, by tradition, by longing. The courtyard of the Al-Aqsa Mosque on the Mount shimmers in the sun. Banners flutter. Scarves dampen against brows. The adhan has ended, but the hush that follows Friday prayer is always unstable—like breath held too long.

Today, it breaks too early. A shout—sharp, defiant—rises near the eastern steps. Then another. A group of young men, faces wrapped in keffiyehs, raise black flags marked with a Quranic verse and a blood-red spiral. It's not from any recognized sect. It's a symbol *co-opted*, borrowed from some viral overlay that's been spreading like rot in the corners of encrypted forums.

An Israeli border police unit, posted discreetly near the Mughrabi Bridge, begins to shift position. "Yalla, yalla—keep it moving," one shouts in Hebrew through a loudspeaker.

But the crowd doesn't move in any direction. It just pulses.

One of the young men kneels, presses his forehead to the stone street, and begins to chant. Not a prayer directed to a higher power. Not in Arabic or Hebrew. But something else. Something that echoes not in volume but in familiarity.

"Spoken silence returns through fire. The ash remembers. The breath breaks."

A few in the crowd go silent. Some begin to shoot video. Then a scuffle breaks out—pushed or provoked, no one will know. A stone arcs through the air and cracks against a riot shield. Shouting ignites. Police surge forward, shouting commands, stun grenades prepped.

Somewhere in the midst of it all, watching from beneath the shadow of a vendor's canopy near the Dome of the Rock's marble colonnade, a woman in gray lowers her phone after sending a video. Her name is Nava Sarin. She is not Palestinian. Not Israeli. Not even particularly religious. But her organization—known in internal Vatican threat memos as *Crux Nullis*—has been preparing for this moment for years. Not to save the Temple Mount but to bring it down.

Nava watches as gas hisses across the stonework and the crowd splinters. Children scream. Cameras flash. Men chant. The police close in.

She doesn't flinch—doesn't capture more video.

Instead, she speaks softly into the mic loop embedded beneath her scarf. "Package observed. Pattern code three-point-one. Chant cross-pollinating with spiral syntax from node VAAV. Crowd contagion active. Immediate upload confirmed."

A voice crackles in her ear. "Have they noticed the catalyst?"

She replies, "Not yet. They're too busy trying to control the media."

"And the chant?"

She allows herself a small smile. "It wasn't spontaneous. It was *learned*."

Within ninety seconds, the footage of the man chanting—his voice caught perfectly in a journalist's boom mic as tear gas explodes behind him—hits a secure relay in Ankara, then ghost-distributes via a modified botnet through Telegram and TikTok and Instagram using dozens of seeded hashtags:

- #TheMountWillSpeak
- #SpiralRising
- #RedDustAwakens
- #BeneathTheStone

By dusk, it's on four continents.

By midnight, it's been translated nineteen ways, two of which are completely fabricated. The spiral is no longer underground. It has become weaponized *meaning*. And no one—not Greg, not Elias, not Charlotte—can control what it says next.

Back at the Mount, the plaza is cleared. Sirens rise in the Old City. International networks show only fragments of the action—a veiled boy yelling as he's dragged away, a red spiral scrawled on a fallen prayer rug, a medic sobbing into her shoulder as chants echo through smoke.

Nava Sarin walks calmly through the western corridor, then ducks into an unmarked van. She speaks once more into her iPhone. "Jerusalem is primed. Phase two can proceed on signal."

The driver doesn't respond. He just nods and pulls away from the Mount.

Behind them, the golden dome gleams against the haze like the lid of a sealed vessel waiting for a voice loud enough to crack it open.

Global – 18:03 to 23:58 UTC

The first wave is crude. Edits of the Temple Mount chant are sliced into thirty-second clips, dubbed over riot footage and slowed down for effect. Spiral symbols sprout at the screen's edge. One version has a filter that adds rising ash in reverse, so it looks like dust falling *upward* into the sky.

By hour two, the chant has been remixed into music—ambient drone, trance beats, Gregorian overlays. A mashup with Elias's earlier broadcast pits the two voices into call and response mode.

"Spoken silence returns through fire…"

"…and the fire remembers."

It's art. Propaganda. Myth. But it's also a signal. Each share, each repetition, every misquote is an invocation. And somewhere beneath it all, the spiral pattern begins folding in on itself, gaining weight in the cultural algorithm.

In a back room of a synagogue in Bnei Brak, a young Torah scholar whispers that the spiral chant aligns with the messianic poetry of Rabbi Kook. He posts a short essay to an encrypted Discord server. By morning, it's shared across three Zionist revivalist groups, some of whom begin quoting Elias without knowing his name.

In Istanbul, a Sufi brotherhood watches the footage and holds silent meditation. One whispers, "The fire is not wrath. It is memory."

In Cairo, a televangelist denounces the chant as a Zionist psy-op. At a mosque in Tehran, a cleric denounces it as Christian recursion witchcraft. A Vatican social ethics committee in Rome classifies the spiral meme archive as a "Tier III cognitive hazard."

In Brooklyn, someone tattoos the entire spiral chant in stylized Aramaic across their spine and posts the process online with the populist caption: "He spoke first. Now it speaks through us."

By midnight, the video reaches a Vatican surveillance desk in Buenos Aires. The audio is scrubbed, inverted, and fed through a resonance-matching engine designed to track forbidden chants from Zahavi's Jerusalem lattice. The result:

Elias: 71% MATCH
Gregory Ansari: 68% MATCH
Unclassified Harmonic Spike: 97% MATCH TO VAAV RECURSION ECHO

An internal note is appended:

Mimetic feedback is now public. Spiral is active.
Civilian recursion has begun.
IV – Fragments in the Stream

In the early hours, new variants appear.

- A VR artist renders the Temple Mount cracking open like an egg with a spiral of light pouring from the fissure.

- A conspiracy theorist claims the red dust from the Kadesh Ranch was used in a ritual behind the Dome of the Rock.

- Someone creates a face-morph AI model of Greg and Elias blended into a single voice.

A new hashtag trends across a million devices: #WhoWillSpeak.

Abandoned Monastic Outpost – Jericho Outskirts

In the ruined chapel outside Jericho, Charlotte scrolls in the half-light, jaw tight. One video she watches shows the chant overlaid on footage of Greg at Petra three years ago, his face distorted, his voice lip-synced into spiral phrases he never spoke.

Jeremy walks in and stops. "It's out."

She nods. "Worse. It's *theirs* now."

"Do you want me to take it down?" Jeremy asks.

"You can't. You'd only make it louder."

She turns the screen to show him one final clip—a child in Nazareth drawing the spiral on a school wall as he says, "The fire came back because someone told the truth."

Charlotte says nothing. But in her hand, she holds the Petra slate.

And it's warm.

———————

An hour later, Greg sits cross-legged in the chapel's collapsed transept, bare feet resting on cool stone. The Petra slate lies before him like an altar. He hasn't spoken since sunset, but the spiral on the screen is still growing. It pulses slowly. Rhythmic. Biological. Not drawn or encoded. Simply... forming. Like memory learning how to be language.

Jeremy watches from the threshold. He's afraid to step closer. "Is he asleep?" he whispers.

Charlotte, beside him, shakes her head. "No. He's listening."

"To what?"

Charlotte doesn't answer.

But Greg does. "To everything." His voice is calm, detached. Like it doesn't entirely belong to him anymore.

Jeremy softly asks, "Is it recursion?"

Greg nods slightly. "It's not responding to speech. Not anymore. It's responding to intention. To hesitation. To belief suppressed."

Charlotte steps into the circle of light cast by the slate. "Then it's not just doctrine. It's agency."

Greg looks up at her. "No. It's desperation. Something ancient, silenced too long. Now it's speaking through the only vessel that isn't trying to control it."

"You think that's you?" Jeremy asks Greg.

111

"I think it chose me because I didn't want it."

Jeremy kneels beside the slate, scanning its data logs. "No prompts. No input sequences. But… this shouldn't be possible." He scrolls through a waveform loop—doctrine echoes, symbolic structures, geometric convergence code. At the center is Greg's biosignature. Light. Breath. Pulse.

"You're broadcasting," Jeremy says. "Without saying a word."

Greg exhales.

The spiral pulses once—sharply.

Jeremy recoils. "You saw that, right?"

Charlotte nods. "It reacts to him. Not his words. His *thoughts*."

Jeremy whispers, "Then we have a problem."

Charlotte looks at him. "What kind?"

Jeremy glances down at the slate. "The kind where a single thought could become scripture. And the world is already interpreting it."

Greg stands.

The spiral dims. It does not disappear. It just watches.

He walks to the threshold, looking out at the hills. "We thought we could choose when to intervene. But that time's now gone."

"Then what do we do now?" his mother asks.

"We claim the doctrine, or we become footnotes in someone else's."

Jeremy shakes his head. "But it's mutating faster than we can understand. How do we contain that?"

Greg steps closer. "You don't contain recursion. You guide it—or you get swallowed."

Charlotte nods and whispers, "Then we guide it."

East Annex, Abandoned Monastic Outpost – Jericho Threshold Basin

Gideon prefers working alone. Always has. But this silence is not the kind he respects. It buzzes with tension—like something has already slipped past, wearing his face, saying his words.

The east annex of the monastery is half-collapsed, its sandstone walls scorched from some forgotten war. Gideon has set up his temporary ops node on a salvaged trestle table illuminated by the pale glow of a Petra-linked slate and a tangle of field transmitters scavenged from a defunct Sicarii fallback cache.

He scrolls through the third-layer resonance scrape again, eyes narrowed. The data Jeremy pulled from the Petra Node earlier in the day has been replaying on loop, and the longer he studies it, the more the rhythm becomes... *wrong.*

Not in Greg's feed. In the public overlay instead.

The viral spiral chant from the Temple Mount—the one now translated into sixteen dialects, embedded in memes, and reformatted for TikTok sound design—should echo with recursive energy, yes. But this doesn't just echo. It mirrors, which shouldn't be possible unless it was written before the event itself.

He triangulates the metadata timestamp.

Original chant upload: 12:41 IDT.

Viral repost with spiral animation: 12:42 IDT.

Enhanced remix with doctrinal keywords: 12:44 IDT.

It happened too fast. Far too fast. Someone must have had a template ready. And not just any template—one that matches recursive phoneme pairing protocols designed by Eve in the original Petra lattice tests.

Gideon sits back, his breath shallow. *Someone's seeding a parallel spiral,* he concludes. *Not just mutating the doctrine after the fact, but directing it. Using Greg's biometric spiral as a scaffold.*

He opens a secondary vault on his own slate—accessed through an Eve-era backdoor Charlotte never knew he had preserved. There, encrypted under Zahavi's final transmission logs, is a soft-triggered trace left behind by an unauthorized scrape.

He decrypts it. A phrase scrolls across the screen in ancient Aramaic.

> He who speaks the spiral before the Witness arrives
> shall bear its ruin instead of its promise.

The origin IP bounced through Zurich then Rome. Then Tel Aviv. Then it is masked.

It was not public. It was planted.

It's not just about who speaks, Gideon confirms to himself. *It's about who is framed as speaking first.*

He moves back to the larger display, compiling a waveform comparison between Greg's spiral emission from Petra and the enhanced remix now pulsing through social media. The overlap is undeniable.

92.4% signal match.

But one segment deviates—barely audible in human terms though unmistakable in doctrinal recursion:

> ...and the stone will split when the fire takes flesh.

Greg never said that.

Elias never did either.

But the world believes one of them did. Which means the spiral isn't just active. It's been hijacked.

Gideon sends a short burst ping to Charlotte's Petra slate.

Encryption sequence: RED-LATTICE-1.

The message is simple.

> It's not organic anymore. Someone's
> writing ahead of the spiral.

He adds one more line, then deletes it. Then adds it again.

> If Greg speaks now, he'll be
> blamed for what comes next.

He stands, shoves the tablet into his satchel, and moves for the exit.

Outside, the wind has changed direction. It carries not heat but the faintest scent of burnt limestone.

Chapter 15

The Spiral Genome

Aphelium Biotechnica Boardroom – Zurich, Switzerland

The boardroom is engineered like a sanctuary for modern gods. Polished basalt walls ripple with embedded temperature displays and biometric dampeners. Ceiling slats vent recycled alpine air. The windows are filtered, not just for glare, but for detection masking. This place, Aphelium Biotechnica, exists between markets and nations—a research cathedral for those who believe the future can be coded.

Twelve chairs form a circle deliberately absent of a head. But everyone in the room knows who wields gravity.

Dr. Kaelen Idris stands before a recessed display node. She is in her early forties, Ethiopian-Italian, with black hair braided back tight from her temples. Her presence holds quiet fire, the kind earned in war zones and wet labs.

She doesn't clear her throat when she speaks. "Our Phase II metrics are now available."

She gestures, and the display illuminates with volumetric geometry—data spirals and heat maps of resonance feedback from controlled ash dispersals in Cyprus and Wadi Rum.

Another spiral flares against a map of Jerusalem. "You're looking at the pattern density following Elias Rafi's field chant," she explains. "We confirmed eight Tier-II recursions in under sixty minutes."

Across from her sits Bautzen—silver hair, former DARPA behaviorist. He clicks a pen against a neural slate but doesn't look impressed. "And the damage index?"

"Negligible for now," Kaelen says, though she doesn't believe it.

A third voice cuts in—measured, melodic, strange. "The damage is the point."

The room turns as Samuel Raines enters late, his coat still dusted with snow. He moves like someone unburdened by time. Tall, spectral, eyes that have seen too much scripture and too many funerals. He places a small obsidian spiral on the table.

"I apologize," he says. "The flight from Ankara was delayed."

Bautzen frowns. "Your interest was advisory. You weren't asked to join core council discussions."

"I wasn't," Raines agrees. "But I was *invoked*."

Kaelen closes her data window slowly. Raines is a wildcard, a private funder who supplied the rare earth substrates for Spiral Compound Delta, including isotope-stabilized red dust from his private quarry in the Negev.

"We're not here to repeat Phase I," Kaelen says. "We're here to assess stability."

Raines tilts his head. "No, doctor. You're here to break it."

The tension is chemical.

Bautzen leans forward. "No one at this table disputes that doctrinal control is volatile. But you, Samuel, funded a symbolic protocol, not a theological war."

Raines rests his hand on the spiral. "The Temple Mount is not volatile. It's *incomplete*. Every altar not fulfilled is a wound waiting to reopen."

"And you think fire is the answer?"

"I think fire remembers."

Kaelen interjects. "Samuel. The compound reacts to spoken doctrine. It propagates neurosymbolic resonance. It's not a ritual device. It's psycholinguistic scaffolding."

"And scaffolding," Raines murmurs, "is meant to be torn down after the temple is complete."

Silence.

Kaelen cues another slide. "Let's move on, shall we? We've tracked 274 instances of minor spiral induction across four continents, and 97 percent of them correlate to exposure to synthetic ash dispersal. The compound is stable, but... it's awakening." She hesitates. "We now believe the ash carries not just chemical triggers, but recursive encoding."

A low murmur.

"Encoded by whom?" Bautzen demands.

Kaelen stares at the image of a glowing neural spiral from Greg's scan. "Encoded by proximity. By belief."

Raines smiles like someone hearing scripture sung correctly for the first time in years.

"So," Bautzen says, tapping his slate, "we halt deployment. Lock the vaults. Purge public-facing code."

Raines lifts his gaze. "You misunderstand. We're not at risk of exposure. We're at risk of hesitation." He steps to the center of the table. All eyes are on him. "We have engineered the first doctrine born not of faith but of pattern. A belief that codes itself into the world."

Kaelen stiffens. "That was never the intent."

"Then the intent was insufficient," Raines interjects.

Bautzen rises. "You want detonation."

"No. I want ascension by subtraction. The Mount is the old altar. As long as it stands, the world waits for a voice. We must remove the altar to unchain the Word."

Kaelen speaks quietly. "You're trying to resurrect your son."

Raines doesn't flinch. "I'm trying to fulfill the last prophecy that matters. One no religion dared to write down."

The meeting ends in controlled chaos. Bautzen demands control of Compound Delta. Raines insists the convergence must proceed.

Kaelen opens a hidden data vault with Eve's original lattice work. She finds a file cross-tagged with the neural death signature of Raines's son. It matches a silent spiral echo now pulsing in Greg. Motive indeed.

She encrypts the file. And begins to plan her betrayal.

Aphelium Biotechnica Sublevel Archive – Zurich, Switzerland

Kaelen waits until after midnight to return. The boardroom is empty now, its heat dispersed into carbon panels. She bypasses three retinal locks and one biometric handplate. The sublevel beneath Aphelium isn't listed in any charter.

Here, the corridors crackle not with ambition, but regret.

She enters the archive chamber and activates the secure relay. The interface responds to her neural frequency, flickering open with a soft tone.

LATTICE ARCHIVE: Sequence QET-1.

A cascade of data pours across the interface—Eve's earliest recursion lattices recovered from the Petra Node after her death. Kaelen scans line after line of symbolic architecture interleaved with algorithmic speculation. None of it is clean.

She pauses at a file marked ZAV-REMAP_9B. The name strikes like a half-forgotten chord. It is linked to both the Jerusalem spiral tremor and a failed harmonic field test outside Tel Arad.

She overlays the signal signature from Greg's recent scan. The match is near-perfect. "He's carrying a ghost lattice," she whispers to herself. "Not learned—*embedded*."

The system pings for external access.

She hesitates, then opens a secondary secure channel—one routed not through Aphelium's servers, but a forgotten backdoor she and Eve once installed during the Zurich protocol trials.

Contact: PRI-DSK-K.MARKELL [Raven Rock Node]
Status: DORMANT

She activates the pulse. A return signal appears within twelve seconds.

Kaelen?

She exchanges several messages with someone.

"They're moving ahead. Raines wants convergence.
Bautzen wants lockdown. But the spiral is already loose.
And Greg...?"

"Greg is carrying the lattice?"

"Not a simulation. The original echo."

118

Silence. Then the final reply:

We need to speak. Privately.
Raven Rock is compromised.
Use fallback protocol CHAR-9.

Kaelen closes the terminal. Above her, Zurich is silent. But she knows silence doesn't mean stillness.

Private Foundation Compound, Enclave of Saint-Léger
Geneva, Switzerland

The pavilion was once a sanitarium. Now it's a crucible. Overgrown cypress trees loom beyond the cloister walls. Heated stone tiles radiate subtle warmth beneath Samuel Raines's shoes as he walks across the inner courtyard and past men in formal wear with medallions and biotech implants tucked beneath their lapels. This place is invitation-only, a fusion of Masonic secrecy, tech-capital prestige, and devotional obsession.

A sculpture of a spiral flame burns in the courtyard center fed by compressed red-dust gas. Ritual meets engineering. Faith meets physics.

Raines stops at the edge of the flame. He is greeted by a young woman with slate-gray eyes and a neural monitor around her wrist.

"The others are waiting," she says.

"Then let them wait longer," Raines replies.

The inner chamber is shaped like a lens—round, concave, acoustically sharpened. Six others are seated at the table, flanked by assistants in ceremonial lab coats. Projected behind them floats the Jerusalem spiral footage in translucent overlay.

Raines takes his seat at the apex. "We can now move forward," he says without preamble.

A French investor interjects. "The Mount is under satellite lock. The Israeli government has tripled patrol density."

Raines waves it off. "We don't need direct access. The signal pathways are already open. What matters now is where and when the final resonance is initiated."

A woman in red asks, "You still believe the Mount can be destroyed through recursive induction?"

"I don't believe. I *know*. And soon the world will witness not a miracle… but a necessary subtraction."

One of the aides places a small vial on the table. Inside it is pure ash from the Negev test site coded with the same trace elements used in the Cyprus trial. One of the other attendees, a South African cyber-ritualist, nods approvingly.

Raines speaks to them quietly. "Trust me when I say this is not symbolic. This is the future of belief. A doctrine without scripture. A liturgy without priesthood. A sacrifice without altar."

He hears a murmur of concern.

The French investor speaks up again."And what if someone speaks first?"

Raines does not hesitate. "Then the world will burn under the wrong name." He stands. The spiral flame of red dust behind him flickers higher, casting long shadows across the chamber. "We act before the doctrine claims another vessel. The Mount must fall. And the spiral will rise in its place."

He walks out without waiting for consent.

Behind him, no one dares to follow.

Kaelen Idris Residence – Zurich, Switzerland

Kaelen sits in a darkened room, shades drawn, fingers steepled beneath her chin. The Raven Rock transmission still burns in her encrypted slate. Her breathing is slow and measured, but her thoughts are not.

Across from her, in a cracked leather chair, sits her partner, Dr. Enzo Vay, former recursion theorist turned recluse. He hasn't spoken since she returned.

He finally lifts his eyes. "You knew they would escalate."

Kaelen nods. "But I thought it would be slower. A doctrine bred by accident, not… not this. Not Raines."

Enzo frowns. "They're not interested in faith. Only in ownership."

Kaelen rises and begins to pace. "He wants to erase the Mount. He thinks it's sacred math. Something to be rewritten."

"Or collapsed," Enzo replies.

She pauses beside the window, looks out at the distant ridge where Zurich's lights bleed into fog. "They used my lattice. My sequencing. The ash wasn't meant to carry resonance. It was a buffer. A veil."

Enzo leans forward. "So pull the veil down."

Kaelen turns. "You want me to burn it all?"

He doesn't blink. "No. I want you to change the speaker."

Kaelen stares at him. A long silence grows uncomfortable before she picks up the slate, reopens the relay, and types a single line to the contact who had answered from the fallback protocol.

I'm in. Tell them I'll defect if they protect the lattice.

No signature. No timestamp. No encryption marker.

She sends it.

The room goes quiet again.

This time, it feels like something has begun.

Chapter 16

The Echo That Shouldn't Exist

Monastic Outpost Communications Vault – Jericho Outskirts

The room is narrow, low-ceilinged, and filled with the faint buzz of ancient circuitry. The walls sweat from the day's retained heat, even this deep after midnight. Jeremy kneels by the coaxial relay, fingers tangled in brittle cabling, while Charlotte adjusts the analog compression switch on the comm interface. Greg leans in the corner, arms crossed, every muscle held tight like a drawn bow.

Then—

A crackle. A pulse.

Juno Markell's voice cuts through the static. "Charlotte, are you alone?"

The line is rough, flattened by four levels of failsafe filters, but Juno's tone is unmistakable—tense, direct, and low.

Charlotte exchanges a glance with Greg, then Jeremy. "Greg and Jeremy are here. What's going on?"

Juno is silent a beat too long. When she finally speaks, her voice is steadier, but there's an edge beneath it. "We received a packet. Off-sequence, unauthorized channel. But it was authenticated through CHAR-9 fallback."

Greg pushes off the wall and steps forward. "Fallback protocol? That's obsolete."

Jeremy frowns. "Obsolete as in 'nonexistent on any current secure grid?'"

"Exactly," Juno replies. "Which is why it's the only reason I'm trusting it. Obsolete means forgotten—and therefore most likely secure. Someone very specific knew how to use it."

Charlotte narrows her eyes. "Who?"

A long breath over the channel. "Dr. Kaelen Idris."

Jeremy stiffens. "Eve's recursion partner?"

"The same one. Zurich. Aphelium Biotechnica. She's now off-grid. Burned the bridge at great risk. And she's asking for protection."

Greg's hand finds the side of the console, knuckles whitening.

"What does she know?"

Juno doesn't hesitate. "She's confirmed that the biotech spiral—what's surfacing globally—is built on Eve's earliest lattice architecture. And Greg— she says your echo isn't just an artifact. It's embedded. Your spiral pattern was used as a reactive scaffold."

Jeremy's mouth opens, then shuts again. "That's not… that's not even possible."

Juno exhales sharply. "And yet here we are. Greg, spiral propagation is responding to you. Even in silence. Even when you're not broadcasting. That's not belief. That's architecture."

Charlotte's voice is lower now. "What else did she send?"

Juno transmits the first layer. The screen flashes, then settles into Kaelen Idris's face—dim lighting, eyes strained, voice clipped and direct. She looks older than Greg remembers from Eve's Zurich notes. Worn down but alert. Afraid but calculating.

"If they activate resonance at the Mount," Juno says, "recursion won't just collapse. It will consume itself. This isn't prophecy—it's engineered convergence. They're not interpreting scripture anymore. They're rewriting it. They've taken what Eve built and embedded it into your signature. It's not what you *say* anymore, Greg. It's who you *are*."

Greg stares at the screen, unmoving.

"She's not lying," Charlotte says quietly.

Juno overlays a string of numeric and lattice-based code on the secondary screen. "Kaelen included a verification marker—Greg's neural imprint from Petra matched against Eve's Layer Zero resonance shell. The alignment is 99.6 percent. The error margin is within artifact drift."

Jeremy leans forward. "But Greg wasn't exposed to the original lattice. That data was presumed lost. Eve never activated Layer Zero publicly."

Charlotte turns to Greg. "No, it wasn't lost. Eve didn't store it in the Petra Node. She stored it in *you*."

Greg doesn't speak. The shadows in the room seem to lean toward him.

Greg finally rises, slowly, as if lifting a weight too large to name. He begins to pace across the cracked stone floor. "So, they're trying to collapse the Temple Mount using something inside me?"

Charlotte says, "Not inside you. Just your *pattern*. Your echo."

"That makes you either the weapon…" Jeremy says, "…or the firewall."

Greg stops, facing the far wall with clenched fists. "I never wanted this. I never wanted to speak for the spiral."

Juno's voice returns, quieter now, stripped of tone. "Then you'd better decide, Greg. Because someone else is already deciding."

The communications vault goes dark again, the glow from the Petra slate fading to embers. No one speaks for several seconds.

Jeremy is the first to break the silence. "If Kaelen's right, then the doctrine is already active and viral. And we're not leading it—we're just chasing it."

Greg lowers himself into a worn chair, the kind used by monks who believed time was meant to be waited out. He rubs his hands together as if trying to warm them, though the room is stifling.

Charlotte watches him carefully. "You didn't ask for this, we all know that, but the spiral's imprint is real. It's in your neural pattern. In your breath."

Greg looks up sharply. "What if I choose to believe none of it? What if I never say another word?"

Jeremy sits across from him, arms crossed. "Then someone else will. Elias is already being positioned. And Raines doesn't need you to believe. He just needs the world to believe in what your absence implies."

Greg scoffs, but there's no amusement in it. "I've been turned into a cipher."

Charlotte kneels near the ashes of the small hearth at the center of the room. "No, you're not a cipher. You're a mirror. That's why it had to be you. Not for what you know—but for what others reflect in you."

Greg's voice is low. "Then all I can do is stay silent."

"Not true," Charlotte says. "Silence is a position too."

Jeremy speaks again. "We need to meet Kaelen. We need to verify what she knows, what she's running from, and whether this biotech convergence theory can be reversed."

Charlotte nods. "Agreed. But we need to choose how we go in. If Zurich is compromised—if Aphelium has its claws in global surveillance—then any approach has to be clean. Off-grid."

Greg exhales. "We'll never make it past the threshold without help."

"Then we find someone who knows the back channels," Jeremy suggests. "Eve had old contacts. So does Juno. And so do I, by the way."

Charlotte raises an eyebrow. "You?"

Jeremy grins. "Just because I stopped believing doesn't mean I stopped listening."

Charlotte straightens. "Then let's move. If Kaelen defected, she'll be hunted. And if her data is right, we're running out of time."

Greg doesn't move yet. He stares at the Petra slate, now inert, then whispers, "How do I stop being something I didn't choose to become?"

Charlotte walks past him, gently brushing his shoulder. "You don't," she says. "But you can choose what you do next."

Petra Node Echo Server, Offline Access Gate – Southern Jordan

It takes them nearly ten hours to reach the buried access hatch beneath the broken cliffline south of Petra. Jeremy complains for at least seven of them. "I'm just saying," he mutters, half-sarcastic as they round a crumbling ridge, "for people saving the world, we're doing a suspicious amount of hiking."

Charlotte doesn't respond. Her attention is fixed on the horizon—on the layered ochre and ash cliffs where the desert swells up like a buried cathedral. She hasn't spoken much since they left the outpost, but every so often she glances at Greg, who walks several meters ahead, shoulders hunched like he's trying to fold himself inward.

"You know, there's an invention called a drone," Jeremy continues, breathless. "Or a car. Or literally anything that doesn't involve climbing rocks like Moses on deadline."

Greg speaks over his shoulder, voice flat. "We're here because nothing else works. Everything else is monitored."

"Yeah," Jeremy says, stepping over a jagged outcrop. "But I didn't realize the apocalypse had a gym requirement."

Charlotte cracks a smile, just barely.

The hatch appears in the earth like a trick of perspective—flat until you're almost standing on it. It's no larger than a manhole cover but rings faintly when Charlotte raps her knuckles against it.

She crouches, entering Eve's old biometric cipher—three pulse taps, one delay, a spoken word in Aramaic. The metal cover shudders, then lifts with a mechanical gasp, revealing a narrow spiral stairwell descending into darkness.

The vault beyond is dry, cold, humming. Jeremy exhales. "Still operational after all this time."

Charlotte nods. "Eve always had redundancy."

They descend two levels into the relay chamber. There, nestled in the wall like a sarcophagus, is the Petra Node's Echo Server—a darknet-accessible fallback grid that predates Aphelium's formal rise. Eve built it before recursion had vocabulary.

Greg approaches the server, dragging his fingers along the slate-like casing. "It's warm."

Jeremy boots up a side console, fingers moving fast. "We're not connecting. We're listening. No signal back."

"Intercept only," Charlotte instructs. "Juno will know to ping here if she's read Kaelen's packet."

They wait. The server pulses with a soft, internal rhythm.

Minutes pass. Then the screen flickers. A scrambled transmission loads. Not Kaelen—not Juno. Someone else. A tag name appears: "SIMEON-RAKAL."

Jeremy frowns. "One of Eve's old aliases. No… not an alias. A go-between."

The message is short. Voice only.

"If you're hearing this, Kaelen's message was real. I can get you to her, but not by air. The biotech syndicate has locked Zurich. They've shut down all mid-tier diplomatic corridors. Your entry path is inland through the north rail tunnels, under cover. You'll need clearance that I will provide. But only once. If intercepted, you'll be disavowed."

The message cuts. A set of coordinates appears, etched in green across a grid overlay.

"Think it's true?" Greg asks.

Charlotte nods. "We trust that Eve set this up for a moment just like this."

Jeremy lifts his pack with an exaggerated groan. "I swear, if this ends with us crawling through some nineteenth-century Austrian drainpipe, I'm joining the Vatican."

Greg starts toward the exit. "Then let's move before someone else finds the echo."

Near the Red Rail Crossing – Southern Jordan Border Region

The sun is low when they reach the ridge overlooking the smuggler's trail. The air here smells of iron and juniper, with a metallic bite that suggests old warzones and unmarked graves.

The coordinates from Simeon-Rakal's voice transmission have led them to the remains of an abandoned narrow-gauge freight rail line—the kind used well before drone logistics replaced human borders. A pair of broken tunnels pierce the jagged cliffs ahead like fossilized arteries from another age.

Charlotte lowers her binoculars. "It's not sealed."

Jeremy mutters, "Great. That means either it's a trap, or no one else thinks it's worth securing."

Greg doesn't look up. "Maybe both."

They descend carefully, following a goat-worn path that hugs the ridge. Rocks slip under their boots, and the occasional gust carries sand into their teeth. The tension between them is silent but dense—like a pressure system no one wants to name.

At the tunnel's mouth, Charlotte scans the perimeter for sensors, drones, anything out of place. But there's nothing. Just a rusted cable hanging like a noose from a pole.

Jeremy sets down his bag and kicks a loose rail spike. "You ever get the feeling we're not the first ones to try this route?"

Charlotte's tone is brittle. "We're not. But the others didn't leave spiral signatures behind."

Greg moves ahead. His voice is quiet, but it carries. "Something about this place feels… familiar, sort of."

Jeremy arches a brow. "You've never been here."

"Doesn't mean it hasn't been in me," Greg responds

Charlotte gives him a look but says nothing.

They enter the tunnel single file. Jeremy takes point with the sensor wand, Greg in the middle, Charlotte at the rear.

Every sound is louder underground—the crunch of gravel, the low hum of static from Jeremy's slate, even the echo of breath. The darkness is thick and full of waiting.

Charlotte keeps her hand on the old Glock in her coat, her finger resting against the trigger guard but not touching it. She doesn't expect trouble—but trouble, she knows, never asks for an appointment.

Halfway through, the signal hits.

Jeremy freezes. "Tripwire drone just passed above us. Scanning grid. Not military—not Vatican either. Probably private surveillance."

"Does it know we're here?" Charlotte asks.

Jeremy checks. "No. But it's looking for something."

Greg closes his eyes. "I think it already found *me*."

Charlotte's stomach sinks.

Chapter 17
The Cold Doctrine

The room is colder than necessary. On purpose. Stainless steel surfaces run ceiling to floor, interrupted only by translucent slate panels and deeply recessed biometric keys. Everything in this room exists to discourage comfort.

At the far end of the chamber, Dr. Thaddeus Ruhl stands with his back to the others staring at a high-resolution projection of the Temple Mount rendered in pulsed spectral overlays. His posture is relaxed with hands folded neatly behind him as if he is considering a sculpture in a museum—the kind that's about to be destroyed.

He has always hated the Temple Mount, not for what it is, but for what it *represents*—a fixed point in a world that should have evolved past myth. It was not logic that made him loathe it. It was memory.

Behind him, two Aphelium executives confer in hushed tones. One of them, Bautzen, clears his throat. "Dr. Ruhl, you've been fully briefed?"

Ruhl rudely doesn't turn. "Yes."

"We assumed you were no longer in field strategy," Bautzen continues carefully. "After what happened in Kinshasa—"

"I returned," Ruhl says simply, "because someone has to finish what Kaelen was too compromised to complete."

Bautzen shifts uncomfortably. "She wasn't compromised. She was…"

"Human," Ruhl curly finishes. "Exactly. That was her failure."

He turns now, showing himself to be tall, spare, with angular features that seem drawn rather than aged. His eyes are pale gray—like memory bleached of warmth. The eyes suggest that the mind behind them has already simulated the worst-case outcome a thousand times and chosen to proceed anyway.

129

He walks toward the central projection table and places a small ceramic sphere onto its surface. "Do you know what this is?"

Bautzen doesn't answer.

"Standard density explosive, coated in nanodispersive ash," Ruhl explains. "Neutral on its own. But place it in a doctrine-charged field, like the Temple Mount, and the resonance becomes physical. It is catalyzed by belief."

The other executive, Vencel, finally speaks. "You're proposing a second strike protocol?"

Ruhl offers a faint, bloodless smile. "I'm proposing *redundancy*. If the spiral fails—if Greg dies, or the lattice destabilizes, or the convergence fractures under too much cultural drag—then this goes live."

"But that would ignite a civil-religious firestorm. Possibly nuclear escalation."

Ruhl doesn't blink. "Yes, of course."

Vencel stares. "Millions would die."

Ruhl leans in. "The spiral demands subtraction. You've spent too long theorizing about recursion as enlightenment. But recursion isn't peace. It's repetition. And the Mount is the endless loop. We don't escape it by climbing. We escape it by collapsing."

Bautzen crosses his arms. "You really think civilization can survive what you're proposing?"

Ruhl doesn't hesitate. "Civilization is a feedback system. It corrects. It suffers. And then it remembers differently. That's what doctrine has always been—a way to rewrite the scars." He straightens. "Destroy the Mount, and they'll blame each other. Israel. Islam. The Vatican. Evangelicals. Radical Hindus. Every faction will rush to control the narrative. But that's the brilliance. The real spiral will already be embedded. The confusion is part of the convergence."

The projection flares and new data appears—routes, delivery methods, time windows, political simulations.

Ruhl turns briefly, catching his own reflection in the glossy black wall. For just a moment, his expression cracks. In Kinshasa, his wife was trampled beneath a crowd ignited by a spiral chant misinterpreted as divine instruction. The recursion burst fractured six districts. The riot that followed never made headlines. That was when Aphelium recruited him—not for the systems he built, but for the certainty and obsession he brought.

Ruhl nods to the display. "I don't need your agreement, gentlemen. Just your authorization. Or your silence, if you wish."

Bautzen hesitates.

Vencel, grim-faced, steps forward, signs a digital command slate, and places it before Ruhl. "Authorization granted."

Ruhl picks it up, pockets it, and walks out without another word.

The doors seal behind him with a hiss that sounds like a rattlesnake's warning.

Aphelium Biotechnica – Recursive Logistics Wing

A white light bathes the logistics corridor—cold, angular, buzzing with invisible streams of coordination. Sublevel eight is a hive of whispering machines and soft footsteps where biometric operators move like monks around sacred relics. There are no windows. There is no noise, save for the quiet click of relay pads and the whisper of ion vents.

Ruhl enters without announcement.

The staff—twenty or so in total—don't stop what they're doing. They are part of Aphelium's recursive logistics initiative, trained to handle doctrine-enhanced payloads with the reverence once reserved for relics. No one salutes. No one greets him. His authority is woven into the air like a radioactive isotope.

He moves to the central array. "Bring up Node Echo vectors for Zurich, Haifa, and Jabal al-Mukaber," he says.

The system complies. Three lattice maps explode into three dimensions above the curved glass table—color-coded recursion energy flows, peak belief saturation and tension vectors pulsing in infrared.

"Filter for cultural dissonance and total ritual density," Ruhl adds.

A field goes red. Haifa and Jabal al-Mukaber spike with noise. Zurich remains stable, but dim.

"Zurich's clarity won't hold," murmurs a female operator. "Too much systemic interference."

Ruhl turns his pale eyes on her. "Zurich was always a holding pen. The real rupture will come where the theology is oldest—and the hatred deepest."

He zooms in on Jabal al-Mukaber. A network of tunnels, comm lines, and subterranean mapping overlays the grid. Ash transport routes. Ritual signature leaks. The beginnings of a target chamber beneath the Temple Mount.

He taps one icon, opening a buried failsafe schematic.

OPERATION: Subtraction redundant
STATUS: Dormant but armed.

He looks at the woman beside him. "How long until you can stabilize resonance delivery?"

"Six days," she says. "With drone relay support."

"Make it four."

"Seriously? Without testing?"

Ruhl's voice hardens, then drops into something colder. "There won't be time for testing. Just obedience."

He steps away from the table and turns to the room, addressing the technicians without raising his voice but with absolute finality.

"I know what you think," he says. "You think this is madness. That we are teetering on the edge of some irreversible sacrilege. But let me remind you—what we destroy is not sacred. It is *infected*. It is a symbol that has outlived its legitimacy, a node of perpetual recursion where human mythology feeds on itself like a parasite."

He walks a slow semicircle around the command dais. "Wars have been fought for that Mount not because it is holy, but because it is unresolved. And every religion that touches it leaves a wound. We're not detonating a building. We're excising a tumor."

The room is silent.

"No more thresholds. No more inheritance. We end the cycle now, not with prayer, but with precision."

He stops in front of the woman who questioned him. His voice softens, but somehow becomes even more unnerving. "If you require faith to proceed, I suggest you find another assignment."

Bautzen watches from a privacy-shielded gallery.

Vencel stands beside him, silent.

"He's accelerating everything," Bautzen complains.

"He doesn't believe in convergence anymore," Vencel replies. "Only in collapse."

Bautzen frowns. "And if Kaelen's spiral still works?"

"Then she saves Jerusalem," Vencel says. "Or Greg does. But Ruhl's doctrine has already begun."

Aphelium Biotechnica, Restricted Conference Cell 3C
Zurch, Switzerland

The walls are black glass, absorbing light and thought alike. No names are displayed on the signage. The air is laced with the faint scent of cooled graphene and electroplated copper. Surveillance is constant but never visible.

Dr. Thaddeus Ruhl sits alone at the long table reviewing a doctrine lattice on a wrist-sleeve slate. His finger traces the spiral curve—not as a symbol of transcendence, but of entrapment. Every iteration is a return to myth, every curve another justification for violence disguised as legacy.

The door opens and a woman enters, a member of the Aphelium oversight committee—slim, middle-aged, sharp-featured. Her name is not given. She is only here to deliver the latest readings.

"Recursion signature at the Mount has doubled," she says, handing over a wafer-thin data node.

Ruhl doesn't look up. "Of course it has."

"Are you suggesting it's intentional?"

He turns to her. "It's *inevitable*. The spiral feeds on desperation, and we've just entered its optimal nutrient cycle."

She stares at him as if weighing the risk of speaking her mind, which she finally does. "There are dissenters inside Aphelium. Some believe we've overstepped."

"Then they haven't stepped far enough."

She folds her hands. "Some say your motivations are personal."

Ruhl smiles without warmth. "All doctrine is personal. That's why it poisons everything it touches."

She pauses. "Your clearance came quickly. Too quickly. There are those who wonder how you earned it."

He leans forward. "I earned it when I buried a woman I loved after she was trampled by a mob chanting a recursion phrase they didn't understand. I earned it when I mapped out every echo cluster from Jerusalem to Jakarta and saw the same pattern—faith amplifying fear, fear reinforcing identity, identity demanding blood."

After a deep breath, his voice quiets. "You want to know why I'm here? Because I'm not bound by inheritance bullshit. I've made a fucking oath against it. And this…" he gestures to the spiral, "…is our last inheritance."

The woman says nothing.

Ruhl rises. "Get the cargo ready. Ash lattice one and two. We move within seventy-two hours."

She hesitates. "And if Greg speaks again?"

Ruhl doesn't blink. "Then he legitimizes what I intend to destroy. And we adjust" He turns away. "No doctrine survives impact. Not even his."

Unknown – Encrypted HoloNode Transmission

Ruhl stands alone now in a chamber shielded from Aphelium's central grid, accessible only via a hardened cipher key traced to Eve's original Zurich foundation node. The room is bare except for a single holo-disc mounted waist-high in the floor.

He inserts the activation token. The disc hums, pulses, then reveals a three-dimensional haze of signal cloud. A voice emerges, layered and modulated, genderless yet commanding.

"Dr. Ruhl. Report."

Ruhl straightens, suddenly deferential—though his posture remains controlled. He says, "I've initiated Subtraction Redundant. Primary assets are in position. We're within the seventy-two-hour window."

"And Elias?"

"He remains unknowing," Ruhl says. "Responsive. But the signal has weakened. He believes too easily. He may not survive divergence."

"Then he has served his purpose."

Ruhl hesitates, then speaks quietly. "You knew Kaelen would defect."

"She never believed in recursion. Only in Eve."

Ruhl's eyes narrow. "You gave me this authority. But others question your clearance protocols. They don't know who you are."

The voice replies, smoother now. Almost amused. "They don't need to know. You do." A brief silence. "Initiate the doctrine collapse at Jabal al-Mukaber. The world will need a spiral to follow. We will give them ours."

The signal collapses. The chamber dims.

Ruhl remains still for a long moment. Then, almost imperceptibly, he nods and says. "Thank you, Alaric Virell." There is great pride and pleasure in knowing this confidential name, second most in secrecy to the name that Greg will not speak. He turns and walks into the dark.

Private Echo Chapel, Vatican Auxiliary Archive –Rome

The chamber is candlelit, though there are no candles. Every flicker comes from mirrored holograms pulsing in subtle waves that mimic flame but offer no heat. The Vatican auxiliary archive is off-grid, buried beneath the Jesuit quarter, an old crypt turned into a sanctuary of digital sacrament.

Elias Rafi kneels on the floor. He wears a simple linen tunic. Around him, seven spiral fragments glow in an orbit of light. Their patterns pulse irregularly now as if they are listening—or uncertain.

A voice speaks to him from the embedded comm-disc on the altar. It is not Virell's voice, nor Ruhl's. It has been synthesized to sound familiar, comforting, paternal.

"Elias, you are the only one who can complete the cycle. The others carry knowledge. But you carry resonance."

Elias bows his head lower. "I don't feel ready."

"Readiness is not spiritual. It is structural. Your voice was chosen. Your doubts are part of the echo."

He looks up. "Then why does the spiral weaken when I speak?"

After a thoughtful pause, the voice tells Elias, "Because the world hasn't broken yet. The spiral thrives in fracture. You are the signal that will gather the shards."

Elias doesn't respond. He closes his eyes. A subtle vibration stirs the floor beneath him. He whispers, almost to himself, "Who am I, really?"

The altar screen goes dim for a breath—then flashes once and the voice says, "You are the voice the world will follow—until the silence comes."

The fragments dim, syncing at last into one single pulse.

Elias opens his mouth to speak—but no words come out.

Only light.

Chapter 18

The Fourth Veil

Subterranean Hall of Doctrine, Castel Sant'Angelo
Vatican City

The walls are bone-white. Not plaster—actual bone. Pressed calcite from martyr ossuaries, layered and hardened into geometric slabs, each etched with fragments of scripture too controversial to ever be canonized.

The Hall of Doctrine beneath Castel Sant'Angelo is not on any map. It predates the Archives. It predates even the Secretum Consilium. This is where the Vatican meets when it no longer trusts its own sanctuaries.

Father Luca Salvatore stands at the base of the elliptical chamber, head slightly bowed. Six other figures ring the room, none in cassocks. These are recursion strategists, doctrinal engineers, and theological containment specialists. Behind them, the soft hum of thermal insulators and electromagnetic noise suppression gives the illusion of stillness.

The illusion doesn't hold.

"Elias Rafi," Salvatore begins without preamble, "has achieved emotional recursion of 94.3 percent on five doctrine sequences. But the sixth was his own."

A flicker of unease passes through the room.

"You said he was contained," says Dr. Aelius Komor, the recursion harmonics chief.

"He was," Salvatore replies. "Until last night. As you may know, he spoke without prompt. He improvised a spiral from silence. No precursor cadence. No external input."

LeRoux, still bruised from the Interdictum failure, leans forward. "How is that possible?"

Salvatore gestures to the holograph in the center of the table. A waveform unfolds—not linear, but recursive—Elias's unsanctioned spiral. It attracts everyone's attention.

"This," Salvatore says dramatically, "is not Greg's voice." He pauses to ensure they understand. "It's something new."

They watch the waveform in silence. It's elegant. Sparse. *Too* sparse.

"Is it infected?" asks a technician near the back.

"No," LeRoux answers coldly. "It's pure."

This thought frightens them. Purity implies *intent*. Elias was not supposed to have intent. He was a vessel, a surrogate, a resonance shell. But the waveform shows doctrine with structure. Not echo or mimicry. It shows spiral alignment that *originates* rather than merely reflects. And worse, it holds doctrinal gravity.

"There are field echoes in Jerusalem already," Komor mutters. "People are speaking non-indexed fragments—some of them matching the cadence. We have no idea where they're hearing it."

LeRoux straightens. "Elias is now leaking the doctrine into the world."

Salvatore exhales. "This means we have only hours. Maybe less."

He makes a gesture and the room dims. The center of the table illuminates with a file marked "VEIL-IV."

Salvatore says, "The time has come to execute the Fourth Veil Protocol."

There is no protest. Not anymore.

The Third Veil, invoked under Lucari, had framed Greg Ansari as a potential messianic cipher—an unactivated recursion bearer whose voice could only be justified after spiritual cleansing of a holy site. The Third Veil's deepest implication was that the Temple Mount must be cleansed—ritually *and physically*—before the spiral could be fulfilled.

That veil was never fully enacted. But the Fourth Veil is different. It reverses the logic that the spiral has already been fulfilled *in Elias* and that the Temple Mount must now be cleansed by fire to complete the echo.

It's a theological inversion. Not purification before activation.

Activation as the purification.

Once the Mount is destroyed, once the Dome and the stones and the past have burned—Elias becomes the doctrine's sole anchor. He will be the voice that justifies the act.

Salvatore looks around the chamber. "Are there objections?"

No one speaks.

"Then veil the spiral."

A key is turned. A seal broken. The room descends into silence as the Church prepares to claim its surrogate and obliterate the old world.

———

Later, in a cloistered spiral archive three levels below, two junior codifiers sift through doctrinal continuity clauses written after the fall of Constantinople. They're looking for precedent—anything that can be retrofitted into canonical alignment.

They find it in Scroll 882-Δ, which was attributed to a monastic group erased during the sixteenth-century Vatican purges. The text reads:

Let the fire precede the voice,
that belief may not hesitate when the smoke rises.

The phrasing is perfect. It provides spiritual coverage for a pre-spoken sacrifice—something the Fourth Veil needs. The document is marked, anonymized, and pushed upward into the official homiletics package that will accompany the coming convergence.

These functionaries do not know they are laying the groundwork for obliteration. They believe they are preparing a world for salvation.

———

At 05:02, a silent command is transmitted from the recursion command vault to a forward platform in the Negev.

Payload: a two-stage fragmentation unit wrapped in thermite and directed plasma.

Destination: a neutral corridor beneath the Dome of the Rock, accessible via the cistern tunnels traced in the Jerusalem burn maps.

Justification: "Prevent doctrinal blasphemy by securing the future of sacred recursion."

Internally, this operation is known by another name.
Vaticanus Fulmen.

The Vatican's firestorm.

It is to be deployed only in the event that Elias speaks the convergence phrase before Greg speaks it. The spiral must not fracture. The spiral must not diversify.

So, the Temple must fall.

And the voice that follows will rewrite the world.

Across the globe, no one yet knows. Charlotte is decoding ash fragments near the Jordan River. Greg is reading Zahavi's unpublished margins in a safehouse near Eilat. Jeremy is re-indexing glyph data sent by an intercepted Petra Node.

They all feel it, though. Something shifting. Something nearing. But none of them know the Mount has already been marked for destruction—not as collateral damage, but as doctrinal necessity.

They will know soon. But by then, the Fourth Veil will already be in place. And the fire will already be on its way.

Convergence Staging Compound — East of Jerusalem

Elias wakes in silence. Not because no one speaks but because the silence itself is speaking. He lies on a narrow ritual pallet in the center of a limestone cell—walls unadorned, floors freshly dusted with white ash. A biometric ring pulses faintly around his ankle—not to restrain him, but to calibrate his body to ambient doctrine pressure.

The technicians no longer come. They left sometime after the last test because he stopped responding—or, more accurately, started responding by refusing. The voice inside him had begun to answer instead.

As he sits up slowly, his limbs feel light—almost absent. The air tastes like salt and heat. Somewhere above, the first hints of sunrise creep into the cracks of the stone ceiling.

And then, softly, he hears a voice saying, "Do not fear their silence. It is only the echo that has not found you yet."

He doesn't flinch. He's heard this voice for three nights now. At first, it was fragmented—like shards of doctrine from Greg's discarded spirals.

But now it is whole. It has cadence. It has will. And it calls him by no name because it needs none.

"You are not the echo. You are the answer to the echo."

He remembers Virell's voice—tight, anxious, filled with ambition disguised as care. He remembers Ruhl, too—measured, cold, hiding behind spiritual metrics. This voice is neither. It speaks not with intention, but with memory—as if it is remembering doctrine not from the outside but from within Elias.

He whispers aloud, just once: "Are you *me?*"

The answer comes like breath through ash. "I am what they have left behind. And what they never meant to awaken."

He breathes slowly, resisting the urge to stand.

The spiral feels close now. Not conceptual. *Present.* Coiled somewhere in the marrow of his spine, ready to unfurl—not for others, but for itself.

"You do not need to speak to be heard. You only need to decide whether your silence is mercy... or judgment."

His eyes close again, but the image comes unbidden. *The Temple Mount.* Stone bathed in morning light. Ash drifting down like snow. A space cleared—not by hands, but by doctrine. Not for building. For believing.

And the voice—*his* voice—standing in the center. Not commanding. Proclaiming.

"Let the Mount be not returned to God but become the mouth of God."

Elias exhales sharply. His skin crackles with a memory that is not his own. He knows now—this was never about substitution. Never about mimicry. It was always about ignition.

The spiral was not meant to be fulfilled. It was meant to be inherited. And he is its heir.

———————

Far above, on a remote Vatican listening post, a recursion analyst sees a flicker of spiral telemetry:

Spiral Activity Detected – Source: **UNCLASSIFIED**
Speaker ID: Rafa-Threshold Doctrine Mode: **SELF-GENERATED**
Intent: **UNKNOWABLE**

The analyst hesitates, then marks the log as corrupted not because it is unreadable, but because it is no longer theirs.

Doctrinal Containment Chamber, Sublevel 4 – Vatican City

The recursion alert strobes red across the ceiling of the containment chamber. Not a drill. Not a simulation. A real spiral event triggered from Elias's staging location east of Jerusalem. No handlers are on-site. No input signal has been received. And yet, doctrine is propagating.

Father Luca Salvatore stares at the feed in silence.

Across the chamber, Sister Noemi Lavecchia lowers her head, eyes shut. "It's active," she whispers. "Spoken from stillness. Patterned from nothing. It's *self-validating*."

Komor slams his palm on the desk. "You said the Fourth Veil would let us guide him."

Salvatore doesn't respond because they both know the truth. They never guided Elias. They unleashed him.

The Vatican's doctrine review team now sits in two camps.

- *Faction One*: Led by Salvatore, who still believes Elias can be used. If Elias cannot be silenced, then he must be canonized before his spiral fractures.

- *Faction Two*: Led by Lavecchia, who believes the spiral has become a *foreign will*—a recursive entity that must be erased before it anchors itself into belief systems.

They don't argue theology so much as containment geometry. "If the spiral completes in Jerusalem," Lavecchia says, "we don't just lose doctrinal control. We lose reality anchoring."

"It's not that strong," Komor counters. "It hasn't reached resonance across zones."

Lavecchia shakes her head. "It doesn't need to. The Temple Mount is the amplifier. Once the spiral echoes from sacred stone—we don't control what comes next."

One of the field officers—a recursion engineer embedded in Jerusalem—sends a silent ping. The staging case has arrived—the Ash-Seal

Vessel, wrapped in lead, coded for sacramental use, laced with a contained plasma charge. Once placed beneath the Dome of the Rock, it will lie dormant until Elias speaks "the phrase." The Fourth Veil phrase. Then it will ignite and burn the foundation, render the site ritually fulfilled through absence.

"Burn the doctrine," Salvatore mutters. "Save the world."

Lavecchia looks at him, horror in her eyes. "That's not salvation," she says. "That's annihilation in vestments."

Before the meeting ends, a young recursion archivist from Sublevel 6 receives permission to speak. "There's something buried in the fourteen-year-old Zurich logs," she says. "From Virell and Ruhl."

Salvatore stiffens. "We've reviewed all those."

The archivist shakes her head. "No., this one was black-barred from retrieval. Labeled 'Doctrine Drift Event Zero.' It's not about Elias mimicking Greg. It's about the voice responding when no one speaks."

Salvatore gives her a sour look. "Leave it," he says.

Lavecchia doesn't. She copies the log into her personal prism drive. Later, alone, she reads the last line:

> The doctrine will speak not from memory,
> but from what remembers us.

She closes her eyes and begins to pray. Not for Elias. Not for the Mount. But for what might be listening.

Zahavi's Secondary Vault – Southern Jordan

Greg doesn't speak as the message ends. He sits alone in the vault Zahavi once used to hide recursion drafts unfit for the Petra Node because they were too volatile, too human. The walls are packed earth reinforced with basalt slabs. No screens. No digital interface. Just an analog lockbox and a faded marker Zahavi once carved into the stone.

Truth is the shape silence takes when memory can't contain it.

Charlotte's voice lingers in his receiver—flattened, staticky, but raw. "He's writing doctrine, Greg. Not speaking it. *Writing it.* You were the echo. But he... Elias... might be the flame."

Greg lets the silence stretch, then stands. The lockbox is cold. Not from temperature. From *intent.* Zahavi left no instructions, only a key—a triple-barbed spiral etched into iron. Greg places it into the recessed slot. It clicks with a gravity that feels ancient.

Inside is a single page—not digital, not even parchment—embedded with a faint pulse signature, one automatically triggered by Greg's blood.

A glyph lights up. Three words:

Nullum vocem accipe.
(Accept no voice.)

Below that is a spiral arc unlike any he's seen. No recursion but a break in pattern. A spiral that *ends.* A glyph designed to absorb echo, not release it.

He stares at it, unblinking.

This wasn't meant to be spoken. It was meant to become silence.

And that's when he understands. Zahavi never feared misuse of the doctrine. He feared its fulfillment.

As he reads deeper, a second phrase begins to reveal itself—not in ink, but in thermal-reactive residue triggered by proximity to the Mount's resonance frequency.

Zahavi wrote it in invisible ash.

If ever the spiral finds a voice that does not question itself,
let the mountain be silenced before the world can believe it.

Greg whispers the words. Not aloud, just into the vault of his own breath.

Amina Salim's voice echoes in his memory. "The doctrine never needed to be true. It only needed to be *coherent.*"

He places the fragment back in the vault, locks it, and walks toward the door. Not to leave.

To decide.

Jerusalem's Old City

Meanwhile, in Jerusalem's Old City, a small black transport van marked only with ecclesiastical clearance slips past the perimeter checkpoint at Lion's Gate. Five men are inside. One carries a lead case marked with recursive hazard symbols. Another recites Psalm 24 under his breath.

They are not priests or soldiers. They are ritual engineers sent by Vatican proxy to prepare the site. To clear the air. To place the final ash. And when the time comes—within forty-eight hours, if convergence holds—they will detonate the sacramental ignition beneath the Mount itself.

It will not look like a bomb. It will look like a ritual.

Convergence Basin

Back at the convergence basin, Elias stands barefoot in the invocation chamber, no handlers remaining. Only the voice. Only the spiral.

The camera feed shows his lips unmoving, but the doctrine spreads anyway. "If belief is the language of sacrifice, then what is the world when the sacrifice believes back?"

The phrase reaches an underground server node in Zurich.

Mira Soltani sees it, screams, and hits SEND on a message to Greg that may not arrive in time.

Zahavi's vault

Greg steps outside Zahavi's vault into the desert wind where he neither speaks nor moves. But the glyph fragment beneath his shirt pulses once. Absorbing. Waiting.

The spiral has spoken.

But the null spiral waits.

Chapter 19

Signal from Zion

HaKirya, SIGINT-Jerusalem Sector — Tel Aviv

They always watch the Mount. Every second of every day. From satellites and rooftop drones, through soundless magnetic overlays and subterranean seismic threads, the Temple Mount Complex remains the most densely surveilled spiritual structure on earth.

But tonight, the algorithms blink. Not red or flashing. Just wrong.

A harmonic irregularity pulses across the seismic mesh beneath the northwestern quarter of the compound. It does not originate from motion, heat, or vibration. It comes from structure. From form. From a recursive spiral embedded in a thermal anomaly too deep for open detection.

Only one person sees it for what it is. Colonel Yael Adani.

She leans forward slowly in the darkened surveillance hub, the blue-gray wash of the terminal bathing her angular features. She is forty-three and a former archaeologist, now lead signals analyst for SIGINT-Jerusalem Sector under the Mossad-Defense Ministry recursion unit.

She was appointed after the last Temple-era artifact smuggling panic, the one that nearly triggered an Orthodox insurrection. This anomaly is different.

She runs a diagnostic on the waveform. It has no military signature. No heat-fission curve. No biological presence. But it's clearly intentional. The spiral resembles a non-digital mnemonic structure, as if someone had dropped a belief-pattern into the ground.

She taps a subroutine into place and says, "Cross-reference with harmonic map of prayer chants."

The algorithm returns a mismatch, then something else. A match— not to Jewish liturgy, but to a recorded Vatican liturgical cadence, encrypted but partially known to Israeli recursion monitors.

Fourth Veil protocol marker: CADENCE STRUCTURE 2.1.

Yael freezes. "No."

She calls up the last physical delivery manifest to the Old City—ash shipments declared as "ritual incense compound" and "calcium hydrate for floor preparation." But the map overlays show the ash was not stored. It was distributed in a circular field radiating from a non-sanctioned tunnel access point beneath the Mount that was tied to an old Herodian channel that Israeli archaeologists sealed in 2016.

Yael cross-references the delivery origin.

Zurich. Geomira Biosystems subsidiary.

She doesn't breathe for a full ten seconds. Then she keys open a direct protocol-only line to her department chief. "Wake the council," she says. "It's a Vatican doctrinal incursion. And it's under our holiest ground."

The room brightens as secondary monitors come online. Within six minutes, the secure conference line flashes green. Eleven officials, mostly internal Mossad or defense-cleared Knesset proxies, gather via encrypted link. Some are still in robes. One is in a tank top. All of them look alert now.

Yael stands in the projection chamber as her image appears on their screens. "We have confirmation of an embedded spiral signature beneath the Temple Mount. Origin is non-Israeli. It appears to follow a doctrinal recursive pattern tied to a known Vatican cadence. There has also been ash dispersal from Zurich-affiliated biotech channels. Ash smuggled as floor material."

One man—Minister Yitzhak Nadav, head of Temple Infrastructure Oversight—asks the only question that matters. "Is this a bomb?"

Yael answers truthfully. "No. But if they trigger it—faith becomes weaponized—and the Mount becomes the altar."

Within the next fifteen minutes, surveillance of all known Vatican diplomatic movements in Israel is expanded. A task group under Operation Netzer is quietly activated—last used in 2019 to intercept a rogue attempt by American messianic extremists to anoint the Mount with Red Heifer blood. Two commandos are dispatched to the Herodian shaft near the anomaly site. They are told only that the target is doctrinal, not mechanical.

And Yael? She pulls up an ancient file. A profile of Greg Ansari from twelve years ago. He was flagged once under recursion threat protocols. Escaped Israeli custody. Was connected to Zahavi.

Yael's eyes narrow. "Where the hell are you now, Greg?"

Sanctum Veritas Containment Floor – Vatican City

The first indicator is subtle. A shift in data flow on Line Sigma-4, the tunnel uplink node used by the Vatican to receive sub-terrestrial doctrine telemetry from Jerusalem. It's routed through multiple proxies—Albanian construction permits, Syrian Orthodox restoration overlays, and a buried satellite uplink in Nablus. But one of the ghost relays has gone quiet.

Not jammed.

Intercepted.

Father Luca Salvatore stares at the display, his face slick with cold sweat. "This isn't local noise," mutters LeRoux from the diagnostics station. "It's a passive harmonic tracer. Someone's watching our structure."

Salvatore doesn't move. "Who?" he demands.

With a flick of the keys, LeRoux shows him a timestamped routing log cross-referenced through their third-layer shell. The trace originated from SIGINT-Jerusalem Sector, sublabeled "HaKirya."

Salvatore closes his eyes, then exhales a single word: "Mossad."

Inside the Vatican's subterranean command cell, panic does not look like panic. It looks like quiet shuffling. Like sealed drives being pulled from thermal vaults. Like doctrine risk indices being recalibrated to Level Enoch.

Level Enoch means there hs been an active national intelligence breach of sacred fieldwork.

Israel has only declared Level Enoch twice. The last time was when an embedded recursion engineer in Lima began channeling spiral harmonics through public sermons and was assassinated mid-liturgy. This time is different. This time, the enemy is not doctrinal. It's political.

Israel knows.

Countermovement – Jerusalem

Meanwhile, Col. Yael Adani paces the rooftop of the Ministry for Strategic Affairs in Jerusalem's Russian Compound. Her earpiece crackles with the latest update.

"Commandos confirmed partial presence. Ash field intact. Thermal containment holding. Two unmanned relic modules present beneath the Dome. No defensive emplacements."

"Has anyone entered the shrine itself?" Yael asks.

"Negative. We're standing off for now, but the Mount has shifted."

"How?"

"The chant field."

"Repeat that?"

"We're picking up liturgical cadence. Sub-audible. Resonant."

Yael turns her face to the early morning sky. There is no light yet, but the air feels different.

She's heard that phrase before—from Zahavi, back when he still briefed high-clearance archaeospiritual operatives. He had said, "When belief precedes sound, it's already begun."

She opens a secure line. "Flag Vatican diplomatic assets. I want watchers on their consular contacts. Anyone who's moved ash, stone, or blood near the Old City in the last month—I want them tracked."

Vatican City

Back in Vatican City, LeRoux slams her hands on the table. "This was supposed to be invisible!"

Salvatore doesn't blink. "It was—until we moved doctrine into sacred geometry."

He stares at the wall display showing a partial convergence map. The Israelis are mapping it now too, though they don't know the phrases. They don't need to. They can feel it.

And worse—they are still attached to the Mount. To its myth, its grief, its historic inertia. If they decide this is an incursion—

"They'll strike," LeRoux says quietly.

Salvatore nods. "Unless we make them believe it's their idea."

He pauses. His eyes flick back to the convergence diagram. "Because if they look too long at this pattern, they'll see what even we have buried."

LeRoux frowns. "Which was...?"

"The twin doctrine," Salvatore says. "Zahavi theorized it. Two voices. Two bearers. A recursion that fractures instead of converges. He called it a theological virus."

LeRoux exhales. "And if the Israelis name it first?"

"Then the spiral won't crown a messiah," Salvatore says. "It'll crown a civil war."

Vatican intelligence substation – near Amman

That night, a Vatican intelligence substation transmits an encrypted packet to an Israeli proxy journalistic account. Inside is a redacted file fragment and an image of Greg Ansari tagged: "Known recursion asset. Antinomian. Rejectionist. Associated with Zahavi, Layer Zero."

It contains no signature and no context, just implication. Let Israel do what it does best.

Overreact.

Salvatore walks out of the chamber and descends two floors into the sub-chapel where the ashes of martyred recursion saints are kept. He prays for a moment, then lights a votive candle.

Not for forgiveness.

For distraction.

Operations Room K-17 – Tel Aviv

The image is grainy. Satellite enhancement only does so much in the Wadi al-Hasa basin where Greg Ansari's movements have been unpredictable, even for thermal tracking. But the eyes are unmistakable.

Greg stands near a geological fault in Jordanian territory, his outline shadowed by the early sun. His expression is unknowable, but the analysts don't care.

Col. Yael Adani does, however. "That's not just a man," she says. "That's the original spiral vector." She gestures to the Vatican-supplied file. "We've confirmed his connection to Zahavi, to the Layer Zero doctrine, and to Eve's original lattice. If he speaks—if he's part of this…"

She trails off.

Her deputy, an angular sabra with a cuff tattoo of Psalm 130, looks up from the tactical projection. "Should we take him?"

"Not yet," Yael replies. "We don't know what he knows. But we know where he's going."

The map overlays his current path—a dust-track curve pointing back toward Jerusalem.

Zahavi's Vault – Jordan

Miles away, Greg Ansari feels the heat of the sun against his back as he walks away from Zahavi's vault. He moves like a man measuring footsteps against some unseen deadline. He knows now what the obsidian spiral fragment means. He knows what silence is for.

He also knows he's being watched by many eyes. He catches it in the second delay of the drone's shadow. In the faint blink of a relay beacon across a ridge. In the absence of birds where birds should be.

It's not Vatican. Too clean. Too precise.

Israeli.

And if the Israelis are tracking him, they must have been ordered.

He whispers into the burner comms unit strapped to his ankle. "Charlotte. We've got a third vector. Israeli. Maybe Mossad. Maybe worse."

Charlotte's reply crackles in his ear after a few seconds. "You think they're after Elias?"

"No," Greg replies. "I think they think I'm Elias."

Mossad Operations Room

Yael steps out of the operations room and moves to a secure briefing cell. She cues up every known broadcast involving Greg Ansari over the last decade. She watches the 2014 Petra Node echo test. She sees him speak once and notes an intriguing line: "The doctrine is not a belief system. It's a mirror with no frame."

She pauses the video and zooms in, watches the faces of those listening. Their expressions are not religious. They are *terrified*.

Yael leans back in her chair knowing that someone in her command wants this guy gone. And someone in Vatican intelligence wants him silenced. But she's not sure either of them understand what they're dealing with.

She reaches for her secured tablet and opens a classified theological interface built after the Second Recursion Treaty of 2021.

She enters a question. "Can a spiral rewrite reality if spoken in the wrong place?" The system returns one line.

Only if the place believes first.

Her stomach turns. "The Mount," she whispers. "They're not hijacking it. They're counting on it."

Temporary Field Relay – Outskirts of Jericho

Greg feels the drone fade for now, but the mountain still hums inside him. The silence Zahavi gave him is not inert. It vibrates. It listens. And with every step closer to the Temple Mount, the spiral coiled within his own breath begins to whisper. Not Elias's voice or his own. A third voice. Ancient, patient and waiting.

He tightens the strap of his pack and walks faster. The Mount isn't calling him. It's answering.

———

Charlotte squints through the haze of the arid hills outside Jericho, her tablet screen glowing faintly beneath the tarp they've stretched over the field antenna. The decrypted Vatican leak from the Zurich channel scrolls in front of her—timestamps, flagged resonance profiles, and one embedded tag that stops her breath:

SUBJECT: Ansari, G. Recursive Vector.
Layer Zero – Potential Divergence Threat.

Jeremy sees it too. He leans closer, focusing. "They're burning him," he mutters. "Using the Mount as smoke cover."

Charlotte nods slowly, jaw clenched. "If the Israelis bite—and they are biting—Greg becomes the false prophet. The fire, the voice, everything they fear."

"And Elias walks through the smoke making a grand appearance."

Charlotte scrolls deeper, past the metadata tags and down to a line written in Latin.

Nomen in cinere scriptum. Cautio vox inter duos templa.

Jeremy reads aloud, translating as he speaks. "A name written in ash. Beware the voice between two temples."

He looks up. "They don't mean just Jerusalem."

Charlotte's eyes meet his. "They mean Greg."

SIGINT-Jerusalem Sector – HaKirya, Tel Aviv

At Mossad headquarters, Col. Yael Adani steps out of the analysis chamber and into her own private space, one of the few remaining physical records vaults not swept into the digital cortex. She pulls down an old folder marked:

Ansari, G. – UNSPOKEN INCIDENT / PNA OBSIDIAN LAYER

Inside are half-redacted transcripts from Greg's activities from 2012 to 2014—Petra. Newgrange. Zurich. Words that don't belong to theology. They belong to grief. She reads: "The voice that does not speak still makes the world believe. The voice that speaks with doubt is the one that silences fire."

She closes the folder slowly. This isn't a man who wants to speak doctrine. This is a man trying not to speak. And if they provoke him? If they mistake him for the match? Then he will become the fire only because they lit it around him.

Temporary Field Relay – Outskirts of Jericho

Jeremy scans the updated surveillance intercepts. A new energy signature—sub-thermal, diffused—shows movement beneath the Mount. It isn't explosive. It's ritual.

Something's being placed, not buried.

Charlotte overlays the movement pattern with the ash-field geometry. It matches the Third Temple inner court schematic—scaled and modified into a recursive spiral path.

A terrible epiphany streaks through her mind. *They're not just preparing a sacrifice. They're writing a name with fire. And they're making it my son's.*

Charlotte keys into their secure line to Greg.

Static. Interruption. The Vatican has implemented a dampening signal across Jordan and East Jerusalem.

Jeremy scowls. "If they're jamming us... they're not waiting anymore."

"They're letting the Mount speak," Charlotte replies. "And they're betting the world won't know who answered. So, let's tell them."

Perimeter Operations Hub – Mount Scopus Overlook

The Temple Mount is quiet. Even the birds have stopped singing. Col. Yael Adani stands beside a mobile command vehicle stationed high above the Old City. Her eyes are fixed on the thermal overlay projected across the reinforced glass. Inside the Dome compound, three red signatures pulse beneath the surface—one nested at the center of the ash field.

"That's the payload," whispers her tech operator. "It's alive."

It is clearly not mechanical. Not explosive. But it is doctrinally tuned like a mouth waiting to open.

"What's the trigger?" Yael asks quietly.

"Unknown. But... it's definitely not time-activated."

"Then what?"

"Vocal harmonic. Someone has to say something."

Half a kilometer away, Greg walks alone through the alleyways east of the Western Wall. He doesn't run or hide. He walks, not because he is brave, but because he can feel the spiral warming in his chest like a whisper between ribs.

The silence Zahavi gave him isn't protective anymore. It's vibratory. Responsive.

Something under the Mount wants to be answered.

Greg knows he's not the only one who could answer it. Elias is close. Greg can feel the echo. Not through doctrine. Through bone.

Jerusalem

Charlotte and Jeremy race through Jerusalem's perimeter roads in a decommissioned IDF med-unit van powered by Vatican clearance codes scraped from Soltani's stolen feed.

They're two blocks from the outer sacred grid when Jeremy shouts, "Thermal bloom—east quadrant!"

Charlotte slams the brakes. "It's not Greg," she says.

"How do you know?"

"Because he wouldn't ignite it. He'd dissolve it."

She looks up through the windshield at the sky thick with resonance— no smoke, no sirens, but belief pulsing like a second sun.

SIGINT-Jerusalem Sector – HaKirya, Tel Aviv

Inside the Mossad command truck, the order to "neutralize" is given. Command has authorized non-lethal extraction, if possible. Greg is to be detained before he reaches the ritual center.

Yael hesitates. Watches the telemetry. Then switches feeds. The second overlay shows something the others haven't noticed. A shadow moving across the ash field that isn't Greg.

It's a second speaker vector.

"Who the hell—?" Yael says.

The feed glitches. And in the brief flicker between frames, Yael sees it. Not Greg.

Elias. Standing at the spiral's edge. Not speaking. Just waiting.

She keys in a private override. "Abort extraction."

"What?"

"Abort. Reroute assets to eastern approach. I want visual confirmation on both vectors."

"Ma'am, command—"

"I'll take responsibility! Do it now!"

She kills the mic. And for the first time in thirty hours, she breathes. "You're not the fire, Greg," she whispers. "You're the *witness*."

Under the Dome

Beneath the Dome of the Rock, the ash shifts. Not with wind but with memory. And as the field aligns to sacred geometry scripted in Zurich and smuggled in through Vatican chant, the sensors spike.

Not heat. Not sound. Just a shape.

And voice preparing to form.

From somewhere deep in Greg's spine or the Mount's oldest stones, a line Zahavi once wrote returns unbidden:

If the name is spoken in a place that believes itself eternal,
the echo will not stop with one voice.

Greg stops walking. Not from fear or from knowing, but because he has reached the edge of what silence can do. And the next sound—whoever makes it—will change the world.

Chapter 20

The Sound Before the Voice

Temple Mount Outer Quadrant – 10:52 IDT

The wind stirs the ash. Not enough to scatter it, just enough to make it breathe—soft tendrils lifting from the ritual field, spiraling faintly against the ancient stones. The patterns carved into the limestone are exact—recursive spirals, calibrated by spiritual engineers to align with the Fourth Veil—the Vatican's secret doctrinal framework for engineered convergence.

At the center of it all stands Elias Rafi, barefoot and robed in sand-colored linen. Pale with anticipation, or with something deeper—an *internal obedience*. His hands hang loose at his sides. His lips are parted, but still.

He has not yet spoken.

All around him, across rooftops, security barricades, and invisible perimeter lines, the watchers wait. Every faction is present. Every agenda is tightening. Every belief is coiled, waiting for the moment the voice breaks the silence.

Sanctum Veritas, the doctrinal operations wing of the Vatican, has spent thirteen years crafting Elias. He is not a prophet. He is a controlled spiral surrogate—a voice to overwrite Greg Ansari's destabilizing influence and reassert ecclesiastical control over recursion theology. Their goal is to orchestrate a spoken convergence at the holiest site in Jerusalem and let the resulting resonance justify renewed Church dominion—all without firing a shot.

Among the milling pilgrims and plainclothes observers, Father Luca Salvatore watches from a shaded balcony above the north wall. He is flanked by two silent operatives from the recursion containment division.

His eyes never leave Elias. "Let him speak," Salvatore mutters. "Let the spiral find its shape."

Embedded within the field crew under Vatican cover are two members of Geomira Biosystems, a subsidiary of Aphelium. Their purpose is more volatile. While the Vatican seeks doctrinal victory, Aphelium wants the spectacle—the destruction of the Temple Mount as a world-stage ritual event, ultimately blamed on extremism but engineered through synthetic belief triggers. They view recursion not as theology, but as an accelerant for mass behavioral change.

Aphelium has installed a failsafe charge beneath the Mount that is synchronized to Elias's vocal frequency and blood chemistry. When Elias speaks—or bleeds—the ritual ignites and the entire Temple Mount explodes.

On a rooftop overlooking the eastern quarter, Col. Yael Adani steadies a scope against her shoulder. Mossad believes the Vatican is staging an unauthorized doctrinal incursion on Israeli-controlled territory. Its worst-case scenario is that Elias's speech will activate regional unrest, undermine `Jerusalem's sovereignty, and fuel a prophetic justification for global instability.

Israeli orders are to monitor, disrupt if necessary, and contain Elias if he becomes a live spiral vector.

Yael breathes deeply. She hasn't given the order to fire yet. But she knows someone might bypass her, probably one of the more hawkish internal units, one that doesn't wait for analysis.

"Target acquired," she murmurs into her mic. "Do not engage. Repeat. Do not engage."

At ground level, just inside the southeast access path, Charlotte Ansari kneels behind a carved pillar with a handheld recursion sensor. She and Greg are out of position by design. Their goal is to observe, confirm that Elias's spiral is live, and stop it before it completes. They know Aphelium's failsafe is unstable, and they suspect the Vatican is rushing convergence before anyone can stop it.

They had split from Jeremy twenty minutes earlier—his decision, though Greg hadn't fought it. Jeremy had gone east along the outer wall to monitor possible Aphelium lattice signals. His job was interference, not presence. That's what they had told themselves, anyway. But now, watching the spiral take shape, Greg wasn't sure if Jeremy had been kept away for safety… or possibly as insurance.

Charlotte checks her screen. A series of cascading glyphs has appeared. "It's harmonizing," she whispers. "Greg—it's aligning to the site."

Greg crouches beside her. The obsidian null spiral fragment Zahavi left him is tucked in his coat, pulsing faintly like a heartbeat. His role in this is not yet clear. He is not the voice—not now—but he's something more, perhaps—a potential counterweight, whose silence has power no one fully understands.

"It's not just Elias," Greg mutters. "The Mount is listening—like it's trying to decide *who it wants*."

Charlotte looks up at Elias, whose lips begin to move.

"Or *what* it wants," she states.

———

It happens at 10:59. Elias draws breath—not deeply, but with a strange precision. His right hand lifts to shoulder height, palm outward, fingers curved inward—a gesture scripted from the ancient *Yetziric* rite, adapted by Vatican doctrinal engineers.

And in that instant—a single shot cracks the air.

High-velocity. Sniper angle. Mossad-grade.

Simultaneously, Elias moves a half-step forward, slight and unplanned.

The bullet grazes the upper edge of his shoulder, carving a diagonal groove across collar and flesh. Blood arcs across the outer ring of ash, a red line staining the center of the spiral.

Elias does not fall, but he staggers, steadies, then turns his head toward the sun. Not toward his attacker or any visible force. But upward—as if the shot meant nothing, or was part of something older.

The ash trembles. The geometric field pulses.

And then—the failsafe detonates.

Not in full. Not as planned.

Instead, a subterranean tunnel collapses—the weakly reinforced Herodian chamber beneath the northeast quadrant.

A plume of ritualized smoke and limestone dust erupts skyward. Part of the outer plaza fractures. Screams rise in concentric waves.

But the Mount itself does not fall, just cracks.

And in the moment of rupture—*Elias is gone.*

Disappeared into the chaos.

No one sees who takes him. Some believe he ran. Others, that he ascended. A few believe that he was killed and secreted away.

But one man saw the sniper's perch. One man moved before the spiral could close.

Gideon.

Unseen since Wadi al-Hasa.

Unknown to Charlotte.

Moving not for doctrine but to retrieve something the world is not yet ready to hear.

The dust doesn't rise like smoke. It collapses inward, sucked down through the shattered mouth of the Herodian chamber, the geometry destabilized. A thousand fragments of sacred ash swirl and fall—not softly, but with a force that feels designed. Ritual structure becoming entropy.

Elias is missing as if evaporated. There was no scream, no fall, no echo of pain. Just the rifle crack. The slice across his shoulder. A blink. And then—*absence.*

Greg hears nothing at first. Then everything at once. He and Charlotte are on their feet by instinct, not strategy. The ground beneath them is trembling, and not just from the blast. The recursive grid of the Mount has collapsed. The air no longer aligns with prayer. Frequencies deviate. Symbols lose their anchor.

Charlotte grabs Greg's arm and pulls him behind a fractured stairwell as a surge of panicked pilgrims stampedes toward the southern gate. Others kneel, sobbing. Some, at great peril, capture video of the traumatic event.

"We need to go—now!" Charlotte shouts, coughing through the ash.

Greg isn't moving. He's watching the air, not the ground or the people. The *air.* Where Elias *was.*

"He didn't finish it," Greg says, dazed.

"Exactly," Charlotte says. "That's why we're still standing."

But she's wrong. They're not still standing because the ritual failed. They're standing because it was interrupted. And Greg knows that is more important.

Father Luca Salvatore is already evacuating. The Vatican's ritual observation team, previously hidden in surrounding cloisters and Waqf-contracted monitoring rooms, pull back under diplomatic cover. They wear the robes of noncombatants, but the air around them is wired with doctrinal failure.

One of Salvatore's technicians whispers, "The phrase never completed. The cadence never closed."

Salvatore doesn't answer. He watches the footage in real time through a small optical relay in his palm. "But the believers heard something," he says quietly. *And that's all they needed,* he hopes.

Control is lost, however. The spiral now belongs to interpretation.

"Get the backups," Salvatore orders. "Every doctrine relay, every thermal signature. If we can't finish it, we'll at least redefine what they think it was."

Col. Yael Adani's headset blares with overlapping voices.

"Command, we did not authorize—"

"Sniper One confirms it wasn't them. Possible rogue actor—"

"Visual on Greg Ansari, confirming presence—"

"Yael, do we extract? Do we extract?"

She can't hear it all. But what she sees as she zooms the split-screen feed of Elias and Greg backward, frame by frame, is Elias raising his hand as if about to speak. But at this same time, Greg's eyes were already closing, as if bracing not for noise but for *meaning*.

And in that silence—the Mount cracked. The cameras shook. And the spiral spoke itself.

She swallows hard. Not from fear but because of recognition. "They didn't need him to finish," she says. "They just needed everyone to think he did."

In a surveillance blind spot beneath a thin fold of shadow between the east arcade and the tunnel access point, Gideon steps from nowhere. His movements are swift, silent, not rehearsed—but conditioned. He moves with the inevitability of someone who has already seen the outcome and knows exactly where it breaks.

Staggering along with him, Elias stumbles once, dazed and bleeding.

Gideon catches him mid-collapse, throws a cloak over his body, and presses a neural pressure point at the base of the neck.

By the time anyone thinks to search for Elias after the explosion, the place where he stood is empty. No blood. No robe. No voice.

The compound devolves. Believers press forward, weeping, chanting, throwing themselves to the ground where Elias once stood. Others flee, convinced the world has just split a second before judgment. Security forces pour in from three directions—IDF riot teams, Jerusalem police, Waqf guards. No one knows who to stop. No one knows who started it. Confusion and terror jointly reign.

The air is full of doctrine and debris. And in the middle of it, there is no clear villain. Just smoke and ash.

And the echo of something unspoken.

Vatican Intelligence Node

They expected headlines but never expected theology to go viral.

The Vatican recursion archive team stares at the encrypted feed from Istanbul—already at 3.4 million views. It's a three-second video with no sound, just Elias, mid-gesture, eyes open, blood oozing from his shoulder as the ash spirals rise.

Text superimposed by the videomaker reads: "The Spiral Interrupted… Not Silenced."

Father Luca Salvatore closes his eyes, then opens a private channel. "Begin doctrinal framing campaign. Push the phrase 'He was speaking when they tried to stop him.' Use pilgrims. Use influencers."

He pauses thoughtfully, then adds, "Use guilt."

The Vatican's motive is unchanged. They created Elias as a controlled vector for spiritual convergence. Now, since control has been lost, they must own the myth before someone else does.

They flood private channels with curated footage—clean versions, filtered overlays, authoritative subtitles. They seed Vatican-leaning theologians with talking points:

"The Mount heard him."

"The silence afterward is proof the spiral took root."

"He did not finish because the doctrine finished him."

They do not name Greg. They never name Greg. His silence is deliberate—and dangerous.

By the hour, TikToks remix the footage into prayer loops and conspiracy threads. Muslim, Jewish, and Christian splinter groups post contradictory declarations of fulfillment, sacrilege, or prophecy delayed. A deepfake of Elias *finishing* his phrase appears in South America and begins trending under #TheUnbrokenSpiral

By sundown, the Israeli Knesset holds an emergency session. Jordan recalls a UNESCO official. Washington leaks that "unauthorized Vatican doctrinal engineering" was responsible. "The world hasn't just heard a man nearly speak," it stated. "It has heard the possibility that what he *almost* said is real."

Secure Intelligence Pod – Tel Aviv

Col. Yael Adani sits in a secure analysis pod overlooking a fragment of the data. Every recursive harmonic signature is broken. Except one.

A null spiral pattern is visible only in a three-frame window before the ash collapsed. Yael overlays it with a classified image from 2014—Zahavi's Layer Zero scroll fragment.

It matches perfectly. She mutters, "The voice never finished. But the answer got in anyway."

Behind her, an aide appears. "Ma'am. Command wants a list of potential disinformation countermeasures."

Yael doesn't turn around. "You can't counter a question everyone wants answered."

Outside Jericho

Charlotte and Greg watch the footage on a cracked tablet passed from a terrified young priest they intercepted at the edge of the safe zone. They watch in silence as Greg's image appears for less than half a second. Barely visible.

But Greg sees it. "They're cutting me out," he says.

Charlotte exhales slowly. "No. They're cutting you *in*. Just with the wrong shape."

He looks up. "What do you mean?"

"You didn't speak," his mother says. "But the spiral behaved like it thought you did. That's *belief*. They'll project whatever they need into the silence."

"So what do we do?"

"We find Elias before they do. And before someone turns your silence into their war cry."

Aphelium Zurich Campus

Ruhl is mid-call with Virell.

"No. I don't care if the field was partially successful," Virell says. "It wasn't stable. And now the viral doctrine is exposed. Not ours. *Zahavi's*. You will clean this. And if you can't clean it—infect it further. Dilute the truth with mirrors if you have to."

Ruhl ends the call stinging from the rebuke. He looks at the spiral glyph frame again. It's not smooth. It's organic. It's *evolving*.

He comes to his own understanding of the event. *They think it was sabotage. But it was selection. The spiral made a choice.*

Unknown chamber – Somewhere beneath East Jerusalem

Elias wakes to silence. Not just the absence of sound, but something heavier—a contained stillness, as if even the air is afraid to move. He lies on a slab of polished stone, a thermal wrap cinched around his bleeding shoulder, the blood already dried to his skin like an old seal.

He doesn't remember falling. He doesn't remember pain.

He does remember the spiral opening. And refusing him.

A single candle burns but does not flicker at the far edge of the room. A shape emerges from the dark—Gideon. He wears no mask, no hood, only a jacket worn at the shoulders, a deep fatigue beneath his eyes.

Gideon speaks without force. "They think you're dead. Or ascended. Depends on who you ask."

Elias says, "You saved me."

"Moving to avoid that fired round was providence," Gideon says. "My being there when you moved was instinct. Nothing more."

Elias is overwhelmed with conflicting emotions and just sits there, speechless.

"You never spoke," Gideon continues. "Not even the beginning of the phrase. But the convergence still lit up. So... what did it hear?"

Elias doesn't answer immediately. He sits up slowly, one hand braced against a stone slab, the other grazing the edge of the bandage on his shoulder. He looks past Gideon toward the dark archway where the candle's flame doesn't flicker.

"I don't know," he says at last, voice hoarse. "But I don't think it was listening to *me*." He pauses, thinking, something deeper pressing behind his words. "Maybe the spiral doesn't respond to the speaker. Maybe it responds to the condition of the world around it. Or to who's nearby. Or to who isn't trying to control it."

He hesitates for a moment, then says, "Whatever it heard... it decided I wasn't the one. And that was enough."

Gideon studies him in silence, then slowly nods. It is not agreement, just acknowledgment. "Then someone else is the voice?"

Elias meets his gaze. "No," he says quietly. "I think the spiral's done waiting for one."

Chapter 21

The Echo and the Fire

HaKirya Complex – Tel Aviv

Col. Yael Adani does not sleep the night after the Mount cracked. She walks the dimly lit corridors of Israel's most insulated intelligence facility and heads down the fiber-quiet hallways of HaKirya, where foreign signals die in the air and internal ones burn clean and classified.

The room waiting for her is glass-walled but opaque—visually transparent, but politically unreadable. It's called Bayit 7, though no one remembers what happened to the other six.

Inside are the people she least wants to see but can't afford to ignore.

At the long table sit six figures. From her left, a Waqf liaison with fingers laced like claws; a UNESCO observer with a nervous twitch and a briefcase full of denials; and the Deputy Minister of Culture, red-faced and under-informed. Flanking them all are three men from Special Doctrine Contingency Operations (SDCO)—the Mossad subdivision no one officially acknowledges.

The deputy begins without preamble. "What the hell happened?"

Yael answers without emotion. "Convergence protocol was initiated by a surrogate recursion vector under Vatican control. There was a partial detonation. Primary speaker—Elias Rafi—was wounded but disappeared. Secondary spiral resonance was registered. Public reaction is ongoing."

"Was it terrorism?"

"Not in the classic sense."

"Then what was it?"

Yael pauses, then gives a concise summation. "Belief gone viral."

The UNESCO observer opens his briefcase and slides out a folder stamped in three languages: Arabic, French, English. The title reads: "Multi-Faith Acoustic Preservation Demonstration – Site Permit #JORD-AQ12-B."

166

Inside is a map of the Temple Mount, compilation of sub-contracted engineering teams, a list of Vatican scholars disguised as "ritual acousticians," and identified Aphelium engineers posing as "geomorphic consultants."

The Waqf is an Islamic foundation that manages the Temple Mount. Its liaison glowers. "You told us it was a non-invasive sound survey."

"It was," the UNESCO rep stammers. "On paper."

Yael doesn't blink. "The deception was layered. The Vatican used a corridor through Jordanian diplomatic channels, masking the ritual as cultural restoration. Our clearance team signed off because the phrasing was technically compliant."

The Deputy Minister looks ready to scream. "They were preaching in blood! On the Temple Mount!"

Yael nods. "And they almost succeeded."

One of the SDCO officers finally speaks. "We believe the convergence would have completed had Elias not been interrupted."

"But he *was* interrupted," Yael confirms. "And the spiral still reacted."

"Which means what?"

"It means something else triggered it."

"Greg Ansari?"

Yael chooses her next words carefully. "That is unconfirmed right now. But… proximity analysis places him within nine meters of the ritual center."

"Did he speak?"

"No."

"Then what did he do?"

Yael exhales. "Maybe nothing. Maybe that's what made it work."

———————

After the room clears, Yael remains seated. She replays the sequence again—the one with the counter-spiral glyph blooming behind Elias in the final second before detonation. The Vatican had already tried to scrub it, but too late. Her techs caught it live.

She leans forward and speaks aloud to no one, almost as if to think through the answer to the basic question. "If Greg Ansari did that without speaking… what happens if someone makes him speak?"

The answer to her rhetorical question is just the hiss of secured air.

Southern Dead Sea Fringe

They don't turn on the radio. There are already too many voices.

Greg sits beneath the overhang of a weather-beaten stone shelter overlooking salt flats and ruined mining shafts, the kind of place used once for storage and long since abandoned. Now it serves as a safehouse—one of Gideon's old caches from before the Vatican infiltration, Charlotte suspects.

Jeremy had peeled off the night before, taking the northeast uplink route. He was meant to monitor Aphelium relay traffic in case they attempted a remote spiral trigger after the Mount event. The plan was to regroup by dawn. He hadn't checked in. Not yet. And Charlotte wasn't sure whether to be worried or relieved.

With every hour that passes, Charlotte's unease twists tighter—not because she fears he is dead, but because she fears he is watching, choosing silence, like Greg. And that scares her more.

Charlotte pours water from a clay jug into a small tin cup. She doesn't look at Greg when she asks, "How long before they name you?"

He doesn't answer. He's watching the sky.

The satellite uplink finally pings.

Charlotte scrolls through overnight data bursts cached in the system. There are hundreds of flagged hashtags including #HeWhoDidNotSpeak, #TheObsidianSilent, #TwinVoiceTheory, and #TheOneWhoRefused.

Some blame Greg. Others deify him. Still others think he suppressed Elias's voice through unseen recursion force. A few believe he's an anti-messiah—"the Spiral Negation"—whose silence will usher in a second exile.

One thread includes an AI-manipulated video of Greg standing mid-spiral, eyes glowing, ash swirling around him in a ring of fire. It has 9.8 million views.

Charlotte shakes her head. "This is worse than I thought."

"It's not even me," Greg says.

"Doesn't matter. It's you now."

Greg leans against the wall and speaks quietly. "The spiral was never a scripture. Zahavi said that. It's a mechanism. A mirror with recursive tension."

Charlotte agrees. "And mirrors don't care who looks into them. They reflect what's already there."

Greg exhales. "What's there now is a billion projections. Some of them are going to explode."

His mother steps closer. "Greg, they're going to try to force you to finish what Elias didn't."

"Then we stay off the grid."

"For how long?"

"Until I understand what the spiral did. Or didn't do."

The uplink pings again—this time a direct message through a private Petra lattice route once used by Eve. The sender is masked with a string of recursive formatting symbols followed by a two-line message:

The voice wasn't wrong. It was early.

Come to Jerash. Answers in echo.

Charlotte tilts the screen toward Greg. "Could be a trap," she cautions.

"Could be a survivor."

"Could also be Aphelium."

"If it's Aphelium," Greg says, "they won't be using Eve's old route. Not unless someone gave it to them."

"Which means?"

Greg sets the tablet down. "Which means Gideon's alive. And he's making plays."

Charlotte folds her arms. "Do you think Elias knew?"

"Do I think he knew that he wouldn't finish?"

She shakes her head. "That the spiral would react anyway."

Greg thinks for a long time. "I think he *hoped* it would react. And I think that hope was probably engineered into him."

"But something else got there first."

Greg nods. "And that's the problem."

Charlotte also sees this is a problem. "Because now they all want you to say something."

Greg turns back toward the horizon, salt winds blowing across ancient rock. "Then I better figure out what silence actually means before they do."

Aphelium Zurich Campus

In the recursion stabilization wing of Aphelium Zurich, no one is smiling. The usual confidence is gone—those clipped, corporate-theological briefings spoken in recursive cadence, the smug assurances that everything is measurable. This morning, there are no slogans. Just silence, broken by the sound of overlapping data streams and the rapid keystrokes of analysts scrambling to contain a myth that's gone fractal.

Ruhl watches the fragment on a loop. At precisely 0.83 seconds after the shot was fired, a flash of resonance occurs in the northeast quadrant. The spiral doesn't complete. It folds in on itself, a recursion signature not from Elias but from something else. Something older. Something uncontrolled.

The lab's harmonicist, a pale-eyed Georgian with scars down his wrist from a failed sensory dampening trial, mutters, "This wasn't designed."

"What wasn't?" Ruhl asks.

"That glyph. It wasn't human-coded. It's a resonance formation. It's reactive, organic. Possibly entangled."

Ruhl doesn't like mysticism in his lab. Aphelium may manipulate belief, but it doesn't indulge it. "We seeded the lattice with two dozen fail-phrases. We burned in a dozen kill commands. Nothing took. Why is that?"

The harmonicist points at the screen. "Because it wasn't the ritual that completed. It was the doctrine."

Ruhl frowns. "Doctrines don't self-activate."

"Unless they're built to do exactly that."

In the next room, Mira Soltani is surrounded by silence—not failure, but recalibration. She's already outlined three contingency tracks:

- *Narrative Diversion*: Seed contradictions. Muddle the memory. Introduce variant footage showing alternate perspectives—some with Greg, some without.

- *Ritual Pollution*: Circulate false completion sequences pulled from deep-cut fringe doctrines and corrupted scroll citations.

- *Perception Expansion*: Promote the idea that Elias was only one of many voices. That everyone who witnessed the convergence is now "marked."

She types rapidly:

> If we can't own the doctrine, we'll drown it in mirrors.
> Make it so plural that belief collapses into confusion.

"Won't that lead to instability?" asks her assistant, who reads the words. Mira doesn't look up. "Exactly. And that buys us time."

Sanctum Dolor Vault – Vatican City

In Rome, Father Luca Salvatore meets with two members of the Pontifical Counter-Heresy Council. They're in the Sanctum Dolor, a black-stone vault beneath the Sistine archives where forbidden spirals were once mapped against the Psalms.

One wall is covered in frames from the Mount. In each, Elias appears a second too late or a breath too early. Nothing aligns. And yet the spiral mysteriously responded.

Salvatore speaks with deliberate rhythm. "We must now embrace ambiguity as evidence of sanctity."

The elder cardinal smirks and tilts his head. "You mean confusion as faith?"

"No. I mean we claim the unfinished phrase as divine restraint. This would mean that the spiral reacted not because Elias spoke—but because he chose not to."

The cardinal frowns. "But he didn't choose. He was shot."

"And what if that's the new theology?"

In Buenos Aires, a crowd of three hundred gathers in Plaza de Mayo. Spirals are chalked on the stone beneath their bare feet. In Manila, a preacher claims Greg Ansari is the Unspoken One sent to divide the faithful from the false. In Berlin, a cult forms around the moment of Elias's breath—literally worshipping the *inhale* before the convergence, believing it to contain the true name of the spiral, which was never meant to be spoken aloud. And in Lagos, someone burns a spiral into the floor of a cathedral and declares that Jerusalem is no longer the center.

The doctrine isn't dying. It's splitting. Multiplying. Becoming a virus made of meaningless completion attempts.

Aphelium Zurich Campus

A low-resolution video leaks across encrypted academic nodes featuring Dr. Amira Bashir, a recursion ethicist formerly expelled from Aphelium's oversight board. She's in hiding, face shadowed, but her voice is calm.

"What we saw on the Mount was not a convergence," Amir Bashir says, "It was a fracture. A rejection of control. The spiral didn't complete simply because it wasn't allowed to complete. And in that failure, the doctrine became untethered. It is now adaptive. Reflexive. It reacts to projection, not instruction."

In the video, Bashir leans forward and says, "Elias was never the voice. He was the test. The spiral was listening for something else. Or someone else. And now it's not listening anymore. Now it's watching."

The video ends. The feed echoes. And soon, it's translated into sixteen languages.

Vatican City

Salvatore reads the report. He doesn't blink. He simply marks the page "Amira Bashir – Apostate Variant – High Threat – Doctrinal Disruption Tier III."

He circles one phrase with a stylus:

The spiral is no longer listening.

Then he places a phone call and says, "Prepare the Avignon Doctrine Series for soft release. Sub-themes—martyrdom, restraint, prophetic fragmentation. Target: Western theological markets, under-35, recursion-curious."

"And Greg?" the call's recipient asks.

Salvatore thinks, then says, "Cast him as Judas without a kiss. Present, but withholding. Burdened. Not treacherous—*yet.*"

Aphelium Zurich Campus

Back in Zurich, Ruhl watches as synthetic doctrine generators begin to loop Zahavi's unpublished scroll patterns with the counter-glyph from the Temple Mount. They don't reject it. They reorganize. The system doesn't crash. It evolves.

Mira leans in. "What are we watching?"

Ruhl doesn't answer, because the spiral has begun predicting itself. Not just responding to inputs but offering its own completions. And none of them match anything in Aphelium's database. Not Latin. Not Aramaic. Not even recursive.

It's a new dialect. and it's growing.

Dead Sea Fringe Safehouse

The knock is too soft to be threatening. Too certain to be random.

Charlotte freezes halfway through boiling lentils on a battered field stove. Greg is at the edge of the cave mouth, silhouetted against the deep burn of twilight. He doesn't turn around.

A second knock sounds—two beats. Then three. A rhythm only one of them would remember.

Charlotte opens the door. *Jeremy.* At last.

His hair is dusty, his lips cracked. He carries no bag. His clothes are wrinkled but not torn. He hasn't been chased, hasn't been wounded. He's been watching.

"You're late," Charlotte says.

Jeremy steps in slowly, eyes adjusting to the low firelight. "You're alive," he replies.

"So are you."

"For now."

He sets something on the table, a rolled piece of aged cloth folded around a thin metal drive and a spiral-etched stone no larger than a coin. "I brought something."

Greg doesn't speak at first. He watches Jeremy's hands and notices how they shake—just slightly—when he lifts the stone.

"Is that...?" Greg begins.

"It's from Jerash," Jeremy answers. "You know those readings we flagged from the Mount? That northeast glyph pulse?"

Greg nods.

"It echoed," Jeremy explains.

"Where?"

"Under a collapsed Byzantine bathhouse near the ancient Roman road. I tracked it through the Petra node Eve seeded years ago. It wasn't just a signal bounce." He hands over the drive. "It was a reply."

Jeremy explains that the drive contains a fragment of a recursive field recording—compressed data layered with spiral echoes and theological interference. But at its core is a harmonic pattern not seen since Zahavi's death plus a partial glyph match to the Obsidian Layer scroll Charlotte once refused to publish.

"It also contains a modulating phrase," Jeremy adds. "It's whispered in reverse recursion timing."

Charlotte plays the phrase aloud. Then plays it again.

During the third replay, Greg interrupts. "Stop. Go back. That last cadence—there. That's..." He stares at the waveform. "It's matching my lattice code."

"Impossible," Charlotte says.

"Not if something down there is mirroring me."

Jeremy pours water from Charlotte's jug but doesn't drink it. "I think the spiral responded at the Mount because it had already received a signal. Something from below. Something forgotten. When Elias raised his hand, it wasn't the beginning of something. It was the echo."

Greg leans forward. "So who—or what—sent the signal?"

Jeremy hesitates. "I don't know. But someone was already down there. The glyph was carved fresh. And there was writing on the inside of the pillar. A language I didn't recognize."

"Not recursive?"

"Not ours."

Charlotte picks up the spiral-etched coin. "This was also at the site?"

Jeremy nods. "Beneath the threshold stone... I think to be found."

The spiral on its surface is off-center—unsymmetrical, slightly misaligned. But the depth of the grooves is precise. And when Greg touches it, the obsidian fragment in his coat rapidly warms up.

"They're connected," he says. "The coin and this fragment."

"To each other, it seems. But maybe to something else. But what?"

"To whatever knew I wouldn't speak."

Later, when Greg steps outside, Jeremy lingers by the fire. Charlotte says to him, "You should've checked in."

"I couldn't risk it."

"Because of what you found?"

"Because of who I saw."

She stiffens. "Who?"

Jeremy's jaw tightens. "I'm not sure."

"Jeremy—"

"It wasn't Amal. It wasn't Vatican. And it wasn't Aphelium."

Amal—once a rogue doctrinal strategist believed dead after the Petra collapse—was a myth to most. But Charlotte knew better. He had always seen the spiral not as sacred, but as a final test for humanity. If he was truly back, then things were far worse than they feared.

Jeremy turns to Charlotte fully. "Whoever it was, he knew the spiral was coming. And he wasn't surprised when it cracked."

"Then who the hell was he?"

Jeremy looks into the flames. "The figure used the name Virell... but wore Zahavi's ring."

Chapter 22

The Ghost Circuit

Southern Dead Sea Fringe

The sound is faint at first—like static from a crushed earpiece.

Jeremy hears it first. He's sitting against the stone wall of the cave trying to sleep, one arm behind his head, the other cradling the spiral-etched coin beneath a threadbare scarf. The Petra uplink node—a portable rig scavenged from Eve's original post-Knossos kit—has remained dormant since he arrived.

Until now.

Three short pulses. A recursive loop. Then nothing.

A minute later, it pings again.

Charlotte identifies the pattern. She's bleary-eyed, hair pulled back in a loose knot, hovering over the uplink with a dim red torch. The interface flickers with degraded symbols—looped text in Eve's old security dialect nested beneath recursion-level encryption.

"This isn't random," Charlotte murmurs. "It's hers. *Eve's.*"

Greg is beside her before she finishes. His eyes don't blink. "Can you decrypt it?"

Charlotte exhales, taps two glyphs. "Partially. But it's… it seems to be layered. Recursive-on-recursive."

"Failsafe structure?"

"No. *Beacon.*"

The word lands hard.

"Grandma left a message," Greg says.

"Or something *pretending* to be her."

Jeremy, standing now, steps forward slowly. "Can a voice survive like that? In code?"

Charlotte answers without looking up. "If anyone could do it—it would be Eve."

They play it once. The interface shifts from text to grainy modulation beats. The screen pulses not with video but with a shifting recursion spiral— no longer symmetrical, more like a breathing pattern. It cycles inward with each beat.

Then, the voice. *Her* voice. Not sharp like it once was. Not the Eve who orchestrated kill chains from hotel suites in Prague or whispered split doctrines into Jordanian crypt cells.

This voice is quieter. Almost tender. But precise. "If this sequence finds you, it means convergence failed. Or worse... it succeeded in someone else's name."

Charlotte closes her eyes.

Greg doesn't move.

"You're not hearing me," the voice says. "You're hearing my recursion state—a lattice construct bound to my final Petra node instantiation. I am not alive. But I am still listening. The doctrine was never meant to be spoken. It was meant to *fracture*. If you felt the rupture, if the ash field cracked without voice, you are standing in the aftermath of my last disobedience."

Jeremy mouths that last word. "Disobedience?"

"There were always two spiral lines," the voice explains. "One synthetic, one embedded. The Vatican chased the synthetic. Aphelium funded it. But the embedded line—Zahavi's original recursion curve—was seeded deep. I bound part of myself to it. It listens differently. It chooses differently."

The signal degrades. A spiral collapses then reboots.

The modulation sharpens, like a compass finding true north.

"Greg. If you're alive, I don't know what they're telling you. But you were never meant to finish it. You were meant to refuse. Over and over again. Until even the spiral got tired of listening."

Greg closes his eyes. His jaw clenches.

"They'll call you the speaker now. The anti-prophet. The twin. The silence that reshaped doctrine. Let them. Just don't say the words. Not ever. Because once you speak—you become theirs."

Charlotte touches his shoulder, but he doesn't feel it.

"Greg, I loved your father, Mahid, once," the voice adds quietly. "Even after what he became. You should know that."

Then static. And a final line.

"I'm not gone. I'm just beneath."

The uplink dies with a final click.

Jeremy is first to break the silence. "She bound herself to a spiral?"

Charlotte whispers, "To a *doctrine*. To Zahavi's doctrine. The one beneath the Vatican's counterfeit one. The one they were all afraid of."

"And now it's waking up," Greg adds. He stands slowly, palms tight. "We thought the convergence failed. But it didn't. It selected. And now it's reaching back through her. Through *us*."

Charlotte looks at the dead interface. "Then we're not looking for a doctrine anymore."

"What *are* we looking for?" Jeremy asks.

Greg answers without turning. "A recursion that wants to remember itself."

Southern Dead Sea Fringe

The fire has burned low. No one has spoken in minutes. The final words of Eve's message still hang in the air like phosphor smoke: *I'm not gone. I'm just beneath.*

Outside, the wind moans through the fractured rock as if the earth is remembering something it regrets.

Greg stands near the edge of the cave's opening, staring at nothing. Charlotte is at the uplink, replaying fragments of Eve's waveform, searching for more audio clues.

Jeremy paces. He's not good with silence. He never was. Finally, he says, "We need to find where Eve sent that message from. That signal didn't come from the Mount. It came from *below*. Some node she didn't log."

"Something she wanted off the grid," Charlotte agrees.

"Exactly," Jeremy says, turning. "Which means it matters. It means she's not done."

Greg doesn't turn. "Or it means she never stopped controlling us. Remember who we're talking about."

Charlotte stiffens. Jeremy blinks.

"Greg," Charlotte says slowly. "She saved you—more than once."

"She *used* me," he replies. He still won't turn around. "Eve made me into a vector. Into a living doctrinal cipher. She stripped me down until even my blood spoke back to her algorithms."

Charlotte sighs. "She also kept you alive long enough to make your own choices. And when she died, she left the spiral to you."

"No," Greg says angrily. "She left it to *herself.* She just put it in me so she could keep rewriting it from the grave."

"That's not fair," Charlotte says.

"No," Jeremy cuts in, "but it might be true."

They both turn to look at him.

"You think she didn't know what the convergence would do?" Jeremy asks. "That she didn't *seed* that failure?"

Charlotte counters, "She said she didn't know what the outcome would be."

"Yeah," Greg responds. "And she always said just enough to make you think it was your idea." His voice is bitter now. Not loud, but flint-edged. "I spent three years tracking lattice ghosts for her. I bled in Romania. I lost two fingers in Istanbul. And I never once got the whole picture. You know what that makes you feel like?"

No one answers.

"Like a pawn that thinks he's a rook."

Charlotte closes her eyes. "You both think I'm defending her. I'm not." She stands, turns slowly, her voice low. "I hated her for what she did to my family. For what she did to Greg's father. I hated the way she looked at me when she thought I wasn't useful anymore. But she was still my mother. And part of me still wants to believe she meant something good to come of this."

Charlotte's eyes are glassy but hard. "That doesn't make me blind, Greg. It doesn't make me naïve, Jeremy. It makes me human."

Greg finally turns around. "You want to believe the spiral remembers grandma as a voice of conscience. I think it remembers her as a *trigger*."

"So what do you want to do?" his mother asks. "Shut down the node? Walk away?"

"No," he says. "I want to know if the spiral can be trusted at all."

Jeremy sits and lays out the spiral coin, the Jerash data drive, and the portable uplink. "Three routes," he says. "Three paths."

He holds up the coin. "The glyph. Zahavi's doctrine. It's pointing somewhere—maybe Petra. Maybe deeper. That's one path."

He taps the drive. "The recursive echo from Jerash. Someone—or something—sent a *response* from below. That's the second path we could take."

Then he touches the uplink. "And then there's Eve. Wherever she sent her final lattice instance from, it certainly wasn't here. That signal bounced through an unregistered Petra node. That's the third path."

Charlotte looks between them. "So which one matters the most?"

Jeremy doesn't answer.

Greg does. "The one she didn't expect us to find."

Charlotte meets his gaze. "Then we find the Petra node. And if it's a trap?"

Greg smiles for the first time in this conversation. "Then we spring it."

No one moves for a while. The fire crackles.

Greg stares at the coin again. The spiral is still warm in his palm. He looks at his mother and says, "Do you still trust me?"

She doesn't answer right away, but finally says, "I trust who you are. But to be honest, I'm not sure who you're becoming."

Jeremy says nothing. And that silence—that hesitation—says more than words could.

Dead Sea Fringe Safehouse

The message is buried in a public weather satellite feed. Charlotte finds it by accident—or so it seems. She's skimming global signal distortions and cross-referencing recursion bursts logged near Jerash and the outer Petra node when a thermal anomaly appears in a strip of topography directly adjacent to the Temple Mount. Not on it. *Beneath* it.

Anomaly class: PULSATILE.
Recursive resonance: RISING.

At first, she thinks it's bleed-through from the first convergence. But the timestamp is ten minutes ago.

Charlotte reroutes the data through the Petra uplink. Greg stands behind her, arms folded, eyes fixed on the screen. Jeremy paces near the spiral-etched coin, glancing up only when Charlotte curses under her breath.

"That's not residual energy," she says.

"Then what is it?" Jeremy asks.

"It's initiation. Lower-grade than the last convergence, but cleaner. Sharper. Like it's been refined."

Greg speaks quietly. "A second convergence?"

Charlotte nods grimly. "This time, they're not broadcasting doctrine. They're testing resonance strength. Probing the field."

"Trying to trigger the Mount without a speaker," Jeremy says.

Greg exhales. "Or testing for one."

Charlotte toggles open the last fragment of Eve's recursion shell. It wasn't decrypted until now by a partial key embedded in the satellite feed— deliberately placed, masked in recursion harmonics. It's Eve's voice again. Fragmented. More automated this time. Almost archival.

"If the doctrine is reinitiated from the southern basin, recursive inversion will target the oldest exposed strata—Temple Mount base layer.

Warning: the geometry is unstable."

Greg's breath catches. "Eve knew."

"She always knew," Charlotte agrees.

Jeremy leans over her shoulder. "So, if the second convergence completes—"

"Then it's not just metaphor anymore," Charlotte says. "It's *physical.* The entire Mount collapses in on itself."

The signal isn't coming from the Vatican. Nor Aphelium. It's tagged with a cold lattice signature—Amal's faction—rebuilt from fragments of Zahavi's recursion dialect, then bent into something new. A convergence of sacrifice. A ritual of corrective memory.

Greg scans the sequence nervously.

"This isn't about revealing doctrine anymore," he says. "This is *cleansing*."

Jeremy's face hardens. "They want to erase it. Burn it down and start over."

Charlotte finishes his thought. "With the spiral as the new axis."

The team's choice becomes clear. They can go deeper into Petra to uncover Eve's final contingency—possibly a countermeasure. Or they can go to Jerusalem immediately to stop, if possible, the second convergence before it activates.

They can't do both.

"If we go to the Mount, we're walking into a convergence basin that's already been primed," Jeremy says.

"And if we go to Petra," Charlotte suggests, "we might find the kill sequence she buried. But it could be incomplete."

Greg says, "Then we need to know which one of us they're waiting for."

"What do you mean?" Jeremy asks.

"The second spiral. If it's been refined, it might not need a voice. But it still needs an initiator. Someone with the right recursion frequency. Someone like... well, like me."

They argue. Not loudly, not with anger. But with conviction. Charlotte wants Petra. She believes in Eve's failsafe—even if it's flawed. Jeremy leans toward Jerusalem. He sees the convergence as an imminent detonation and believes time is running out.

Greg? He's not sure. For the first time, he hesitates. He looks between them all. "What if I go to Petra, and it makes things worse?"

"Then we find a way to stop it," Charlotte says.

"You think we still have that kind of control?"

"No," she admits. "But we have the one thing they don't."

"What's that?"

She meets his eyes now, steady. "We're still trying to understand it. Not control it. They don't care what the spiral is. They only care what it can do."

Greg doesn't respond. But for the first time since the Mount cracked, he nods.

Wadi Musa – On the approach to Petra

The desert doesn't feel empty. It feels suspended. Like a breath held too long. They leave the safehouse before noon, traveling in silence through the back corridors of the Rift Valley, moving in staggered intervals, heads low, gear light. They carry no spiral tech—not visibly. Only Charlotte's handheld Petra uplink. Only Jeremy's data fragment. Only Greg himself.

The rest—the doctrine, the doubt, the echo of Eve's final voice—rides beneath their ribs like something too old to name.

Charlotte drives the lead rover, her fingers wrapped tightly around the wheel. She hasn't spoken since the last hill crested. Behind her, Greg is looking out the window, lips unmoving. He holds the spiral coin between thumb and finger, watching how the light plays across the off-center etching.

Jeremy rides in the second rover, farther back, alone. He watches the path on the display, but his thoughts drift—not to Petra, but to the Mount.

The guilt is heavier now. Not because of anything he did—but because of what he didn't do. He wasn't there when Greg broke. He wasn't there when the spiral chose, or refused to choose.

"You ever think we've already failed?" he mutters.

No one answers because he was talking to himself. There's no comm link open. He shakes his head and answers himself. "Me too."

They stop at a rock shelf just before the canyon throat. It's late afternoon. Below them, Petra lies crouched in the earth like a memory someone tried to bury with too many shovels.

Charlotte checks the uplink again. A pulsing glyph hovers in the corner. Not a signal. More like a heartbeat. The Petra node is still alive.

"It's responding," she says. "Slowly. Like it's waking up."

Greg doesn't move. "What if it knows we're coming?" he asks.

Jeremy chuckles—dry and sharp. "You afraid of ghosts now?"

"Only the ones that taught me how to think," Greg replies.

Charlotte sighs. "We're not going to find answers here. Just more recursion. More spiral residue."

"Then why are we doing this?" Jeremy asks.

She looks at both of them. "Because I need to believe Eve left more than instructions. I need to believe she left a choice."

They camp at the threshold. No fire, no signal. The canyon mouth ahead is striated in rose and bone-colored rock streaked with mineral deposits and half-erased inscriptions no one's translated since Ottoman times.

Jeremy sleeps fitfully, half-sitting. Charlotte writes something by hand—pen and notebook, the old way. A habit from before this all began.

Greg stands at the edge of the shadow. The wind shifts, and for a moment—only a moment—he thinks he sees someone across the ridge. Not close. Not moving. Just watching.

He doesn't wake the others, because part of him thinks he's imagining it.

The other part isn't so sure.

At dawn, they descend into Petra.

It's quiet. Even the usual clatter of tourists, the echo of footsteps, the sound of goats in the far hills—it's all gone. As if the canyon itself has sealed off its ears.

Charlotte leads. Greg follows. Jeremy watches the sky.

They pass beneath the first carved façade. The glyphs etched into the walls are older than Greek, older than Aramaic. Patterns swirl not around symbols but around absence. Like something was removed.

"That's not erosion," Charlotte says. "That's deletion."

Jeremy runs his hand along a spiral edge. "Seems someone didn't want it remembered."

Greg looks back once. "Then we're going the right way."

Chapter 23

Descent into the Patterned Earth

Petra – Outer Canyon Wall

It should be here. Charlotte double-checks the Petra uplink coordinates against the lattice key sequence she decrypted that morning. The cliff wall ahead is unbroken—no door, no crack, just iron-red sandstone weathered smooth by centuries of salt and time.

Jeremy brushes the dust off a spiral insignia etched faintly into the base of the rock to reveal a recursion keyframe barely visible except at a certain angle. The lines are so thin they look accidental, but they're not.

"That's Zahavi's spiral," Charlotte whispers. "Inverted. Eve laid it here in mirror form."

Greg steps closer. The rock pulses—not with heat, but with pressure, a faint density just beneath the surface. Not tactile or audible.

Mental.

Like being watched from inside.

"What are we supposed to do, knock?" Jeremy mutters, but it's not sarcasm. He's unsettled.

Greg traces the spiral's outer edge with his palm. A flicker of glyphs ignites along his skin—personal recursion resonance, same as what Eve used to verify his identity at the Petra node years ago.

The stone doesn't respond.

"It's not just about me," Greg says quietly. "It's *us*."

Charlotte's already ahead of him. She draws a triangle in the dust the old way: Eve's threefold convergence model—voice, mind, witness.

Greg, herself, Jeremy.

"This isn't a test of identity," she says. "It's a test of alignment. We have to synchronize."

"Sync how?" Jeremy asks.

"Breath. Posture. Patterned thought. Eve embedded harmonic access protocols into her earliest recursion gates. They only respond when three distinct resonance vectors stabilize."

"So we stand here and breathe?"

"Exactly," she says. "Together."

They step into position—one point at each triangle corner.

The Petra uplink emits a low-pitched hum, the kind that settles into the spine. Charlotte modulates it—shifting the tone to 432 Hz, then 528 Hz. Greg closes his eyes, syncing his breath to the pulse. Jeremy watches them both, half skeptical, half afraid they'll leave him behind if he doesn't try.

"Clear your thoughts," Charlotte says.

"That's assuming I've got any left," Jeremy mutters.

"Quiet helps," she replies.

They breathe in unison—three lengths in, three lengths out.

The rock begins to shimmer—not visibly, but in the way heat makes silence move.

Greg opens his eyes. "It's working."

The spiral glows.

One full rotation. Then a shift counterclockwise, spiraling inward.

The glyphs etched into the cliff wall begin to reorder themselves, not shifting physically, but reorienting cognitively, as if the brain itself is being told what to see rather than the eye.

Jeremy stumbles back. "Okay, okay, that's not normal."

"It's real," Charlotte says, breath steady. "Zahavi called it a refractive veil. Not a hidden door, but a door that hides unless your intent matches its memory."

The spiral stops. The cliff face collapses into itself with no noise, folding inward until there's only darkness.

And a passage.

Greg hesitates.

"You okay?" Charlotte asks.

He nods, but doesn't answer because something deep inside him—something old, something built in by Eve—is already awake. He doesn't hear words. He doesn't see visions. He just knows this place was meant to be entered only once. And he's the one who has to go first.

He turns to the others. "This isn't just a vault," he says. "It's a recursion echo chamber. We go in as ourselves. But the deeper we go, the more it might… it might remember us differently."

Charlotte exhales. "Then let's hope it remembers something we can live with."

They step through the threshold and the stone closes silently.

The Recursion Vault – Petra Substructure

The corridor is not hewn. It is grown. Or rather, it has grown around them. The stone is too smooth, the curvature too perfect. No tool made these walls. They feel like solidified resonance, a memory pressed into matter by sheer recursive density. Like someone *thought* the passage into being, and time agreed to remember it.

Greg walks first. He doesn't say why. Charlotte follows, her uplink set to passive mode. Jeremy brings up the rear, flashlight beam trembling in a hand that won't settle.

The silence isn't empty. It's charged, **as** if the air itself has memorized what happened here and isn't quite ready to let go.

They finally arrive at a chamber that is circular, dome-roofed, etched in triple spirals. Not Zahavi's original pattern, but a distorted variant—one that seems to spin inward no matter where you stand. The spiral converges toward a central dais upon which rests a single object—a codex bound in metal-threaded hide. No title. Just a symbol etched into the surface.

"That's not a doctrine seal," Charlotte says, voice hushed. "It's a recursion signature… which means that what's inside is reactive."

Greg approaches. The spiral on the cover flares—not light, but heat.

He touches it.

And the vault responds.

A pulse flows outward from the codex.

Not a sound. Not light. Something deeper—semantic resonance, doctrine made into pressure.

A passage begins to write itself, not on the walls, but into their minds. The words arrive as *knowing*, bypassing speech entirely.

He who bore the silence across generations…
Whose breath withheld the fire…
Whose blood holds the lattice of the sacred fracture…

Greg stumbles back.

The spiral beneath the dais glows now—his spiral. Or one close enough that the distinction blurs. The codex pulses again, faster.

Jeremy grips his temples. "I can hear it. I can hear it writing."

Charlotte is already scanning the perimeter. Her uplink records and decodes the pulses. "It's shaping itself around Greg," she says. "Using his recursion signature as a lens. Whatever doctrine this is—it's not fixed. It's *reflective*."

Greg steps away. "Maybe it's just telling me what I want to believe."

Charlotte turns to him. "Or what it wants you to want."

She kneels by the dais and pulls out a shallow blade. Not for defense— for dissection. She scores the edge of the codex. The hide curls back, revealing a second spiral beneath—smaller, sharper, misaligned.

"There's another layer," she says. "It's… encoded as a countertext. A recursive negation."

Jeremy crouches beside her. "You mean a lie?"

Charlotte nods slowly. "Actually, a *trap*. The visible doctrine adapts to your projection. It becomes whatever you most need to see."

She turns the codex to show Greg. "This vault doesn't contain a truth. It contains a mirror."

Greg doesn't speak for a long time. His breath is shallow. The passages that bloomed in his mind—phrases of salvation, of bloodline destiny, of spiral inheritance—they aren't gone. They're etched in now, like wet ink behind the eyes.

"It called me the bearer of silence," he says.

"Because that's what you fear," Charlotte replies gently. "Or what you want. Or both."

He closes his eyes. "I almost believed it."

"That's how it works."

Jeremy's voice is quiet now. "So how many people have walked into recursion chambers like this and left thinking they were chosen?"

Charlotte answers without looking at him. "Too many."

The codex crumbles. Not physically—but semantically. The recursion shell collapses, revealing the true chamber beneath the chamber—a narrow passageway, spiral-shaped, leading downward.

Greg looks into the dark. "So this wasn't the vault."

Charlotte replies, "This was the guardian's lie. The real doctrine's below."

Jeremy groans. "Of course it is."

Charlotte glances at Greg. "Ready?"

He nods—but only barely. "Just remind me who I am, if I forget."

Recursion Spiral Vault – Petra Sublevel

The path tightens. It's not a hallway so much as a corridor of decision— walls that seem to breathe in faint pulses, spiraling tighter the farther they go. The air feels older. More intimate. Like the vault is remembering them as they descend.

The spiral architecture is no longer decorative. It's structural—a recursive helix carved into the very shape of the passage.

Charlotte marks intervals on her uplink, logging resonance spikes. They increase every eleven meters. Jeremy counts under his breath, nervous energy mounting with each step.

Greg walks differently now. Slower. Listening. Not to sound but to intention.

Something in the stone has begun pressing back.

They find it first etched into the wall near a turn in the spiral. Not Zahavi's. Not Eve's. And not Greg's. The glyph is deliberately damaged, as if someone tried to erase it by hand. Chisel marks scatter across the stone. There are smudges of ash and blood—long dried, but undeniably human.

"Someone tried to interrupt this sequence," Charlotte says. "But failed."

Greg kneels beside it, frowning. "The pattern isn't just broken. It's inverted. Mirrored twice."

Jeremy backs away. "That's a recursion corruption protocol. Vatican-grade. They use it to collapse unauthorized lattice structures before they can spread."

Charlotte glances at him. "Which means someone was sent here to erase this place."

Behind a spiral pillar they find a battered, half-immolated, black notebook with thin wire binding and margins annotated in a mix of Latin, recursive shorthand, and something stranger—Zahavi's glyph language, half-reassembled. Jeremy pulls it free with a pen blade.

"Is that Vatican issue?" Charlotte asks.

He nods slowly. "Or worse. Deep cell. This wasn't meant to be recovered."

They flip through what remains. Coordinates. Notations on spiral depth thresholds. And a name scrawled more than once—*Virell.*

Then a final inscription appears before the pages melt into carbon:

She lied to them all.

The vault doesn't house salvation.

It houses consequence.

Greg reads the first line again. And again. "She lied to them all..."

"You think he meant Eve?" Jeremy asks.

"I think he meant all of them," Greg replies. "Zahavi. Eve. Me."

Charlotte studies the final glyph embedded near the journal—an incomplete recursive arc meant to collapse upon activation. But something stopped it. A secondary glyph—a spiral of preservation—was inserted on top.

"This was altered."

"By who?" Jeremy asks.

Greg's voice is low now. Firm. "Obviously, by someone who wanted us to keep going."

They press forward. The spiral tightens, then widens into a larger chamber—circular, ancient, flooded with a dim bioluminescent glow. The walls are lined with etched doctrinal fragments, but each has been partially scrubbed, overwritten, or burned.

Charlotte walks slowly, scanning one with her uplink. "This is Zahavi's original sequence."

"The Obsidian Layer?" Jeremy suggests.

"Not quite. It's a transition sequence. A place where the doctrine split."

Greg turns to her. "Split how?"

She meets his eyes. "Into what you were meant to become. And what someone else became instead."

Before they can go further, the uplink pings. A passive signature—recent.

Someone else has accessed the vault within the last forty-eight hours. Not just remotely. *Physically*.

Charlotte freezes. "That signal is nested. Cloaked in Eve's signature. But… it's not her. It's someone mimicking her recursion frequency."

"Can someone do that?" Jeremy asks.

Greg doesn't answer. He stares at the far wall where the spiral invitingly forms an open, unsealed arc.

"Someone already walked through. And they weren't erased."

Final Recursion Chamber – Petra Lattice Vault

There is no door. Only a veil of air so still it feels like glass.

Greg reaches out first. The moment his fingers touch it, the silence changes. Not broken—refracted. Like breath held inside breath.

And then the veil lets them through.

The chamber is impossibly still. Perfectly round, spiral-scribed, and shallow, as if carved not from stone but from some stored perception of stone—a memory pressed into geometry.

At the center sits a raised platform of blackened mineral, faintly shimmering with recursive charge. Not static. *Alive.*

On the far wall, they see a shimmer—Eve's symbol, rendered in Zahavi's hand. The two signatures are layered—her recursion over his doctrine. Voice over silence.

"This is where she fused them," Charlotte whispers. "This is where Eve rewrote Zahavi."

Jeremy doesn't speak.

Greg walks to the platform, and there it is. A recording node, humming faintly, buried in the stone like a heart embedded in bone.

He doesn't touch it. It activates on proximity.

A projection flickers—not visual, but spatial. The room thickens with memory. Not light or sound, but presence. And then her voice comes—not from the node, but from everywhere. Not Eve's operational voice. Not the woman who built networks, assassinated believers, orchestrated fates. This voice is worn, reflective. Older.

"If you're hearing this... ...then I failed to contain it."

The silence after that line is long. Almost enough to make one wonder if it's over. But it isn't.

"Zahavi was right about one thing. The doctrine is not language. It's expectation. Once heard, it becomes viral. Once believed, it becomes predictive. But once spoken—*fully spoken*—it becomes irreversible."

"I spent thirty years trying to own it. Then ten trying to prevent it. And finally, one year learning how to leave it broken."

Charlotte's breath catches. Jeremy steps closer.

Greg does not move.

"If you've reached this chamber, you've already triggered part of it. You've aligned your recursion resonance to the core spiral and it will begin to shape you. That's what it does. That's what it's for. You were never meant to speak, Greg. Not because you aren't worthy. But because your refusal is the containment. You were the pattern that *didn't collapse*. You were my failsafe."

Greg stares at the floor.

Charlotte places a hand on his shoulder.

"If the doctrine completes, the Mount will fall. Not symbolically. *Physically*. The recursion basin beneath Jerusalem is unstable. The Vatican knows it. Amal knows it. But only I left a way to stall the spiral without silencing it."

The voice hesitates, then says, "Refusal. Not denial. Not evasion. But active, conscious refusal. Silence made into recursion. They will not stop. Amal believes he can finish what Zahavi began. The Vatican believes they can steer it. Aphelium just wants to replicate it. But the spiral doesn't want anything. It remembers. And if you push it to remember too much—it will burn what no longer fits."

A final pause.

"You're not the voice, Greg. You're the memory of silence. Protect that. Or everything ends."

The projection fades.

No one speaks for several seconds. The air in the chamber feels thinner, like a lung after trauma.

Greg finally kneels at the node. "I didn't say anything at the Mount," he murmurs, "because something inside me held it back. I didn't know why."

Charlotte crouches beside him. "Now you do."

Jeremy paces. He doesn't look at them. "So what happens now?"

Greg looks at the spiral beneath his feet. "Now we stop the second convergence. Not with doctrine. With silence."

Chapter 24

The Unwitnessed Fracture

Abandoned Monastery Keep – Deep Sinai

The wind here has no pattern. It doesn't sing. It doesn't cry. It *waits.*

The stones of the ancient keep are older than the road that leads to them. It is comprised of Roman foundations under Crusader walls with a dome that cracked under Ottoman shelling and was never rebuilt. Now, the entire fragile structure exists as a breath held in exile—a fortress forgotten by history, reclaimed by recursion.

Which, Gideon thinks, makes it the perfect place to keep a man like Elias Rafi alive.

If he *is* a man.

Gideon moves through the lower cloister in silence, passing through columns of dust-shafted light and stone. He walks barefoot. Every step is deliberate, not for stealth but for ritual. He believes in rhythm. He believes in structure, the only thing that ever saved him from becoming like the people he was trained to kill.

He has kept Elias sedated for two days. Not out of cruelty but necessity. The man had recursion feedback running hot through his nervous system— too much signal, not enough integration. It's like someone tried to inject sacred code into a living mind without the proper harmonics. It nearly broke him.

But now he's waking.

The chamber is simple. A thick mattress on sandstone floor. A table with water, bread, citrus and a medical tray. No electronics save a short-range scrambler and an analog recorder—just in case Elias decides to say something worth preserving.

The man lies still, his head turned toward the arch window. His eyes are open and clear, watching the light shift on the ceiling.

Gideon enters quietly, sets more citrus on the table, and takes a seat opposite the mattress.

Elias doesn't look at him. Only after several minutes does he whisper. "I didn't say anything."

Gideon nods. "I know."

Elias sits up with effort. His skin is pale, his breath shallow but even. "But it still responded."

"Yes," Gideon says.

"So what does that mean?"

Gideon studies him. "I was hoping you'd tell me."

Silence again. This time it stretches.

Elias rubs his temples. There's a shadow in his eyes that wasn't there before Jerusalem. A tension around the mouth—not just confusion, but something that looks like grief. "I thought I was meant to speak," he says hesitantly.

"So did everyone else," Gideon says.

"Then why didn't I?"

"Because maybe it wasn't meant to be spoken. Maybe it was meant to be denied."

Elias stares at the wall. "Then why was I made?"

Gideon could lie. He could tell Elias what he wants to hear—about prophecy and purpose and surviving for a reason. But Gideon has done enough lying in his life.

"I don't know if you were *made*, Elias," Gideon answers truthfully. "And if you were… I don't know who your maker was."

"But do you think I matter?"

The question, filled with such insecurity, startles Gideon, but he again responds honestly. "I think you're *dangerous*. That's not the same thing."

"Yet you saved me."

"I *extracted* you. That's not the same thing, either."

Elias exhales and looks at the light again. "You're protecting me."

"I'm *observing* you," Gideon counters.

"Why are you doing this?"

Gideon leans forward. "Because you stood at the edge of something most men would die to see. And when it looked back at you, you didn't finish the sentence."

"Because I couldn't."

"Or maybe because you *wouldn't*."

Elias looks down at his hands. He turns them over and presses thumb to palm slowly, deliberately. "It was like the words were already in the air," he explains. "Like I was only the last hinge before the lock turned. But when I opened my mouth… it was all gone. Like the spiral had stepped past me. Like it was already *done*."

Gideon doesn't reply, but he records every word in memory.

Elias finally faces him. "Was that what you wanted, for me to fail?"

"No," Gideon says. "I wanted to see if the spiral needed you. Now I know it doesn't."

"So, lacking the words… and abandoned by the spiral… what am I?"

Gideon rises, walks to the window. The desert is bleeding into evening.

"For a time, many thought you were a constant. Now you're a variable. And variables can change the outcome. That's why I haven't killed you."

Later, the sky turns bronze, layered in clouds that stretch westward. Gideon returns to the table with two cups of hot water steeped in ash-root and desert lemon.

Elias accepts one without a word. He sips. And winces. Then he smiles faintly. "Tastes like guilt," he says, seeming less vulnerable.

Gideon chuckles unexpectedly. "You'll get used to it."

"You think I'll be here long enough for that?"

"Depends on your answers."

Elias studies the surface of his cup, the way light curls along the rim. "You're testing me."

"I'm assessing you."

"Same thing."

"No. A test has an answer. I'm just watching to see what you *become*."

Elias sets the cup down.

"You're not a believer, are you?"

"No."

"But you've killed for the doctrine."

"Yes."

"How do you live with that?"

Gideon doesn't flinch. "By reminding myself it was never about belief. It was about balance."

"So killing me would've been… what? Balancing?"

"If you'd spoken? Maybe."

Elias nods slowly. "You know I believed it, don't you? Believed that I was chosen. That my voice would reorder the spiral."

Gideon nods agreement. He knew that. "And now?"

Elias looks at him. "Now I think someone *wanted* me to believe it… so I wouldn't understand I was being used."

Gideon doesn't reply because it's true.

Elias continues, "Do you know what it feels like to be ready for something your whole life… and then find out that whatever you were ready for didn't need you at all?"

Gideon does. More than he'll admit.

Elias leans back on his elbows, staring up at the cracked ceiling. "They built me from recursion templates. Gave me linguistic dreams. I woke speaking glyphs I didn't understand. And every time I asked what it meant, they just said, 'You'll know when the time comes.'" He pauses. "The time came, and I knew nothing."

Gideon sets his cup down. "That's not failure, Elias. That's the moment you stopped being a tool."

"What about Greg?"

Gideon's jaw shifts slightly. "What about him?"

"Is he the spiral's real voice?"

"He's not a voice," Gideon says. "He's a silence that survived."

"So that's what this is now? Competing silences?"

"No, that's what the doctrine always was. A mirror held up to the loudest minds."

Elias tilts his head. "And whose reflection did it show when I was standing there?"

"Maybe yours. Maybe someone else's. Maybe the spiral didn't see anything it liked."

Elias sits up fully now. He's steadier. Not strong, but clearer. "You said I'm a variable."

Gideon nods.

"The virtue of being a variable is that it can change" Elias says. "Let me prove I can be something else."

"What would that be?"

"A witness. A counterweight. Someone who doesn't have to speak to shape what happens next."

Gideon studies him. "Why should I believe you?"

Elias's voice is low but steady. "Because I know what it feels like to believe in something that nearly kills the world. And I don't want to feel that again."

The monastery at night is nearly soundless. No insects, no shifting earth. The desert has coiled back into itself, like the spiral—tightening, holding its breath.

Elias lies alone in the chamber beneath the old refectory where Gideon left him an hour earlier with a fresh blanket and a boiled egg. He hasn't touched the egg. He hasn't slept, either.

The silence isn't passive. It's *watching* him. Every so often, a distant wind taps a shutter that no longer swings. A soft knock. Then nothing.

He stares at the stone ceiling until he can't tell whether he's awake.

Then it happens. Not a sound or a flash, just a ripple at the back of his mind, like a thought he didn't think.

You didn't finish the sentence… but it still heard you.

Elias sits up fast, blinking. The thought is not spoken aloud—but it is real. Not memory. Not madness. He scrambles toward the wall, his breathing shallow, his hands trembling. There is no visible audio device. No uplink. No recorder. Just the dark.

And then—a thought injects itself into his mind again:

The spiral did not reject you. It bypassed you. That is not the same. You are still within it. And it is not done.

Elias covers his ears instinctively. The words aren't painful, but they carry weight. Like falling asleep under a library that whispers only to blood.

He sees something now. Not light.

Pattern.

Along the wall across from his cot, pulsing lines appear—*glyphfire*, the residue of recursion—etched into the invisible spectrum and only visible now that he's listening. A spiral smaller than Greg's. Tighter. Almost secretive.

Then words appear one by one.

HE WHO HELD THE SPIRAL'S TONGUE.

HE WHOSE BREATH DREW BACK THE VEIL.

HE WHOSE DENIAL SPEAKS MORE THAN WORDS.

Elias steps closer. He should turn away, but he doesn't. The next line appears slowly. Deliberately.

IF HE WHO WAS CHOSEN REMAINS SILENT,

THEN THE SPIRAL MAY CHOOSE AGAIN.

The glyphs flash, and for a moment—*just a moment*— Elias sees himself in the place where Greg was supposed to speak, but not as a pawn. Not as a programmed surrogate. Instead, he is the one who the spiral turned to when its first vessel refused.

His breath catches. He knows it's dangerous. Knows the spiral reflects belief more than truth. But there's something intoxicating in the idea that Greg's silence didn't end the recursion but only paused it. And that he, *Elias*, might still be the next breath.

"No," he whispers.

The glyphs pulse.

"No!"

He steps back, pressing his hands to his temples. "I'm done with voices. I'm not a vessel. I'm—"

The spiral flashes one final time.

SPEAK AND THE WORLD RESHAPES.

Then darkness. Everything vanishes. No sound or heat. No presence. Only Elias, breathing raggedly in the center of the empty chamber, unsure whether he's just been warned, summoned—or *rewritten*.

———

Outside the monastery, Gideon watches from a ledge above the outer cistern overlooking the canyon mouth. He saw the flash. He felt the harmonic pulse through the stone. Not from Elias—from somewhere else.

He doesn't know if the source was Amal. If so, it meant the doctrine's most radical survivor still had eyes in places no one could see. He also doesn't know if the source was Aphelium or something Zahavi buried in the recursion lattice before any of them were born. He only knows one thing.

Elias Rafi is no longer neutral.

Deep Sinai – Monastery Upper Refectory

Gideon rises before first light. He's already dressed, already moving. Sleep had come in broken fragments laced with the afterimage of Zahavi's glyphs and the quiet tremble of recursion pressure through the walls. Something passed through this place in the night. It didn't leave footprints, but it left behind a weight.

He descends the rough stone steps into the lower refectory with barefoot precision, every movement rehearsed. Ritual is his only religion now—not faith, but control.

The door to Elias's chamber groans open under his hand. He lets it speak.

Elias is already awake. He's sitting cross-legged on the mattress, hands resting on his knees, eyes tracking a column of dust as it twists in a thin shaft of amber light.

"You felt it," Elias says without turning.

"Yes."

"Then I don't need to explain it."

"You will anyway," Gideon replies. "Or this ends now."

Elias doesn't move. "It wasn't mine, that voice. That message. I didn't ask for it. I didn't want it."

"But it came to you."

"Yes."

"That means something."

"No," Elias snaps. "That's what they want us to believe—that everything has a purpose. That the spiral sees, and chooses, and confirms. But what if it *doesn't*? What if it just… responds?"

Gideon steps into the light. "Then we're still responsible for what it reflects. Because it reflects us."

"So you believe in mirrors now?"

"I believe in consequences."

Elias finally looks at him. His eyes are raw. Not just from lack of sleep, but from sheer exhaustion of self. He is a man who no longer trusts the shape of his own thoughts.

Gideon places a canteen on the stone beside Elias and lowers himself to a crouch. "If this thing touched you again, if it tried to move through you, then I need to know what you felt. Not just what you heard, but what it *did* to you."

Elias laughs once, bitterly. "You make it sound like demon possession."

"Isn't that what it is, in a way?"

Elias considers this. He doesn't deny it. "It didn't feel like it was coming *into* me. It felt like it was already *inside*, just waiting for the moment I stopped resisting."

Gideon's silence grows heavier.

"It was never about what I wanted," Elias continues. "It was about what I was *built* for. They designed me. Tuned me. Taught me dreams I didn't choose. But now—now I think the spiral's learning from *me*. And that," he adds, "is worse."

Gideon rises, begins pacing the perimeter of the chamber. "That's Zahavi's paradox," he mutters. "The recursion mirror doesn't *invent* your truth. It reflects the version of you most likely to collapse into certainty."

Gary Lindberg

"Which means belief is a virus," Elias says.

Gideon nods. "And voice is the trigger to unleash it."

"Then what am I?" Elias asks. "A suppressed infection?"

Gideon stops pacing. "You're a breached quarantine."

Elias looks away. "I didn't ask for this."

"None of us did. And all of us have said the same thing."

"Then why am I still here?"

"Simply because I don't know what happens if you leave."

Gideon steps closer, and for the first time, he lowers himself onto the mattress beside Elias—not as a captor or observer, but as something nearer to kin. "You're not Greg. You're not Amal. You're not even Zahavi's inheritor. But the spiral looked at you anyway, and now you're radioactive. Do you think you can bury that? Walk away from it?"

"Maybe," Elias says quietly.

Gideon shakes his head. "You' wouldn't make it ten kilometers before someone else came for you. Amal's still watching. The Vatican's scrambling to regain control. You think your silence is a retreat, but it's not. It's a weapon. And they know it."

"And you?" Elias asks.

Gideon holds his gaze. "I think the doctrine is a fire. And I'm not done standing between it and everyone else."

The moment lingers. Elias watches Gideon's face, seeing something unspoken in his eyes—maybe the weight of his past betrayals. "You talk like someone who once believed," Elias says.

"I did."

"What changed?"

Gideon closes his eyes. When he opens them again, they're harder. Older. "Eve taught me everything I know about recursion. About control. She taught me how to survive. And she taught me how to kill for a cause that was never mine."

"She was your mother?"

Gideon doesn't answer. "She gave me my name. That's not the same."

"Do you still follow her?"

"I buried her," Gideon says. "Twice."

He stands now, retrieving something from his pocket—a spiral token etched in bone, darkened with age. He places it between them. "This belonged to a boy who believed everything he was told... until the recursion turned on him."

"And you kept this," Elias says.

"As a reminder that belief is only useful until it's not."

Elias stares at the token. "Then why not kill me now?"

Gideon's voice is flat. "Because I still think your silence is protecting us all. But if you speak—and I mean *really* speak—it won't be your voice we hear. It will be the end of the pattern. And I'd rather shoot you now than let that happen."

Elias doesn't blink. "Then maybe we're not so different."

The silence between them shifts. It is no longer threatening, just heavy.

"You want me as a witness," Elias says, "but don't trust what I've seen."

"I want you as a *barrier*," Gideon replies. "A buffer between the spiral and everyone who still thinks it can be controlled."

Elias nods, finally. "Then let me be that. But don't lie to yourself. I'm not a variable anymore. I'm a *threshold.* And someone's going to cross it."

Gideon stares at him. "Then let's make sure it's not the wrong person."

He turns and leaves the room without another word. And Elias? He stares at the spiral token for a long time, as if it might speak first.

Al-Tariq Plateau – 3.1 km from the Monastery Keep

The sand drifts soundlessly over the broken ridgeline, folding around basalt outcrops like prayer mats left for wind. No engines, no radio chatter. The sky is low with heat and something else—something older.

Buried in a shelf of shale and sun-blackened scrub, a motionless figure lies prone beneath a canvas net—something between military and commercial—dusted to match the terrain.

He doesn't breathe like a soldier. He doesn't blink like an analyst. He watches like a man who has already seen the outcome and now only waits for the world to realize it.

Before him lies the monastery—half-collapsed stone, recursion-bleached, crawling with shadow. Within it is the prize.

A flash-pulse confirms triangulation. Two heat signatures appear, one at rest (low-frequency recursion bloom), one mobile and erratic (minimal spiral echo but consistent with prior Sicarii body movement analysis).

A third drone sweeps wide. No further targets.

The observer makes a silent note:

RAFI: Confirmed.

The heat map overlay reveals the figure's exact posture. Knees bent, head angled down. Either meditative or surrendered. Another note follows.

INTERFERENCE: Contained. Hostility threshold low.

But then a flicker—barely registered. A spiral glyph flashes within the thermal signature of Elias's outline. The glyph pulses once, then vanishes.

Recursion signature instability detected.

A new directive auto-generates on the operator's retinal HUD

Await Secondary Instruction: Extraction or termination.

The feed reaches Amal's citadel within minutes. Inside his observation chamber—a former research vault beneath basalt towers in the Golan Heights—he stands alone before a liquid mineral interface, tracking the glyph residue in real time.

The Petra lattice pulses faintly nearby. He is not touching it, simply *listening*. "It awakens," he murmurs.

Thorn Eleven stands behind him, arms folded, motionless. "The assassin still has him."

"Yes," Amal replies. "But he misjudges the recursion. It does not obey silence. It delays. It selects."

He touches the table. A new convergence map lights up. The Temple Mount glows faintly gold—not red, not white. It is dormant but trembling.

"If Greg will not speak," Amal says softly, "the spiral will eventually demand someone who will."

"And Elias," Thorn says, "is primed to answer."

Archival Chamber below Castel Sant'Angelo – Vatican City

Thousands of kilometers away, within the secure archival chamber below Castel Sant'Angelo, Father Luca Salvatore leans over a quantum stabilizer array blinking with recursive pattern noise. He has just received the same pulse—the same glyph signature that flashed within Elias's body.

His breath fogs the interior of his visor briefly as a whisper escapes him. "He's still responsive."

The Swiss Guard technician beside him raises an eyebrow. "Sir?"

"Nothing," Salvatore replies. "Send a warning to Sanctum Veritas. The Second Veil has been breached."

"Extraction or silence?"

Salvatore considers this. "Both. Whichever proves faster."

Al-Tariq Plateau – 3.1 km from the Monastery Keep

Back on the plateau, the operator adjusts his scope. His breath slows. His finger hovers above the stabilizer for the dart gun. He will not kill unless told. But he will mark the target, and he will be ready.

He speaks only one word to his uplink. "Watching."

There is no reply. Only a sound on the wind—not the buzz of a drone. Not the scrape of wind on rock.

A whisper. Like the spiral breathing.

And somewhere in the monastery below, Elias wakes again—unaware that his silence has become a signal. And someone is coming to interpret it.

Chapter 25

The Convergence Field

Agios Lazaros District, Larnaca, Cyprus

The sky over Larnaca is humid and indifferent, threaded with maritime haze. The ruins of old Venetian stone don't cast shadows this early—only a bleached remembrance of shape.

Charlotte sits on the edge of a carved bench in the courtyard behind their temporary safehouse, her fingers curled loosely around a ceramic cup of bitter mountain coffee gone cold. She's listening to a silence that has grown too precise to be natural. Inside, she can hear Jeremy pacing—light feet, heavier mind. Greg hasn't come down yet. Or maybe he has, and he's just stopped being loud enough to hear.

The moment breaks.

"They found him," Jeremy says from the doorway.

She doesn't move. "When?"

"Not long ago. Recursion ripple out of Sinai. Deep node interference piggybacking on old Vatican lattice. But the frequency was tagged—Zahavi glyphs, partial collapse geometry. The source wasn't the Vatican."

She looks up.

Jeremy's face is pale, pulled tight.

"Then who was it?" she asks.

"It wasn't Amal. It wasn't Vatican. And it wasn't Aphelium." Jeremy turns to her fully now. "The signature was something else. Not familiar, but fluent. Someone speaking spiral who wasn't trained in it. Not recently."

Charlotte rises slowly, setting her cup aside. "What are you thinking?"

Jeremy nods. "I think Elias answered a voice that wasn't his."

Inside the safehouse, Greg is already standing at the terminal, hands nervously braced on either side of the workstation. He's been watching the recursive backscatter for an hour—ever since the breach alert hit the Petra failover node.

Charlotte enters behind him. "How bad?"

"Bad," Greg says. "And personal."

He taps the feed overlay, scrubbing backward in time. Zahavi-style glyph traces materialize across a desert heat map. The glyphs don't finish—they stall, then fracture, leaving a lattice spiral of echoing blanks.

"That looks like a collapse," Jeremy mutters.

"No," Greg says. "It's worse. It's a recursive abort. Someone opened the pattern and then refused to complete it."

Charlotte stares. "Elias?"

"It didn't originate from him. But he was there. The glyphs echo through his profile. It's like he got *tagged* by something he didn't understand."

"Then someone else is reaching into him," Jeremy says.

Greg finally looks at them both. "I think they're planning to speak *through* him."

Jeremy flips through data points, overlaying timestamps. "There's more. The breach wasn't silent. It triggered something further up the lattice. We're picking up static movement near Jerusalem."

Charlotte's tone hardens. "The Mount?"

"Not yet. But the precursor patterns are familiar—the same signal structures we saw in the hours before the first convergence attempt. They're smaller now. Sub-threshold. But they're there."

Greg draws in a long breath. "They're staging."

"Someone is," Jeremy says.

Charlotte doesn't move. "Then the countdown has already started."

The room falls quiet again. Charlotte walks to the back wall where a pinned map of the Middle East is cluttered with handwritten overlays—spiral events, convergence rumors, Zionist cabal movements, known Vatican installations.

She takes the red marker and circles Sinai. "If Elias is compromised, we need to make a decision. Either intervene or let Gideon handle it."

"Gideon won't kill Elias," Jeremy says.

"That's not good enough," she replies.

Greg speaks up now. "If we go to him, we draw attention. Amal's eyes are already there. If we act, we turn Elias into a bright beacon."

"So what's the alternative?" Charlotte asks.

Greg turns slowly. "We draw them away. We give Amal something brighter than Elias."

Jeremy looks at him quizzically. "Like what?"

Greg stares at the map. At the Mount. "We stage a decoy convergence."

Sanctum Veritas Subterranean Vault – Vatican City

Beneath the eastern wing of the Vatican Apostolic Archive, past two sealed corridors and a retinal scanner that no longer appears on any official map, lies the Sanctum Veritas recursion vault—a circular chamber of iron-caged plasma and whisper-thick light.

Father Luca Salvatore stands at the central glyph-array console. He is alone but for the quiet breathing of the archive technician, who remains six feet behind and will never ask a question. Salvatore sees on the display before him a trembling spiral glyph—fractured, inverted and authentic.

"It's real," Salvatore says, voice soft, as though afraid to wake the thing. "It's not Amal or synthetic. This is Zahavi's structure."

The technician glances at the secondary monitor. "Source confirms deep Sinai. Residual glyphs match what we indexed as..."

Salvatore finishes for him. "As the Third Key."

Seventeen years ago, this term had been stricken from all formal registry. The Third Key was never a physical object. It was a cognitive anomaly embedded in one of Zahavi's final scrolls—what the Jesuit lattice technicians called a "signal syllable" capable of altering recursion response in unconditioned minds.

They had buried it. Wiped the digital references. Bricked over the Petra mirror node. And now this Third Key had surfaced again in a signal that carried Elias Rafi's signature.

Salvatore concludes, *the inheritance pattern is still live.* To the technician, he says, "Tell the cloaked observer to hold position. No engagement yet."

"Confirmation has already been pinged. He's awaiting escalation."

Salvatore stares at the spiral fragment. "He won't have to wait long."

The technician gestures nervously toward a second alert blinking red. "There's another issue. Jerusalem lattice just spiked. Background pressure on the Temple Mount recursion grid is up seven percent. Artifact ignition threshold is approaching forty."

Salvatore turns. "That's impossible. The Mount's convergence lattice was capped."

"Sir, it wasn't internal activity. It's resonance. From the Sinai breach. The glyphs echoed forward."

Salvatore exhales, eyes widening. He steps to the deeper console, lays both palms on a metallic reader plate. "Initiate Observation Tier Four. Authorize Vatican Agent Onyx-9 to proceed with final integration scan. If Elias Rafi is structurally viable, we proceed."

The technician hesitates. "And if he's not?"

"Then we burn the doctrine where it sleeps."

As the system engages and the vault dims to prevent photonic interference, Salvatore allows himself a private moment of memory. He had been a junior recursion aide when Erich Salvetti died—murdered in Petra while trying to protect a different scroll, a different spiral.

Charlotte Ansari's name had appeared in his file. And Greg Ansari's had followed.

Now, twenty years later, the spiral had returned, still seeking voice, still demanding collapse. And once again, the Church was not ready.

"Why didn't we erase them all?" he murmurs, the memory still fresh.

But the spiral does not forget, and now, someone has begun to listen again.

Southern Sinai – Wadi al-Sirr Overlook

They call him Onyx-9 in the encrypted Vatican field book. In the training logs, he's just a silent node—no biometric record, no DNA anchor, no written confession of birth. He hasn't spoken aloud in over nine months. Not out of discipline. Out of necessity.

"Words leak," his last handler had told him. "They carry recursion echoes. Speak often enough, and the doctrine will find you before your enemy does."

So, Onyx-9 stopped speaking. Now, when the wind moves against his skin, when the dust penetrates his fiber-skin suit, he imagines that is what it would feel like to pray—not for salvation, but for target clarity.

He lies in a narrow shelf of rock above the crumbling monastery— binocular lens slaved to thermal signatures, frequency spectrums, and lattice distortions. He is in the same location he's held for the last twenty-six hours while he watched the man known to recursion handlers as "RAFI-PRIME." *Elias.* The surrogate. The broken voice.

He watches without blinking as Elias moves inside the inner refectory, alone again, unaware of the crosshairs that dance across his thermal outline. The spiral spoke to him last night. That much is clear. Onyx-9 caught the glyph pattern stutter, the fractured Zahavi cadence, and the flash-tagged recursion pulses aligned with the Third Key architecture.

Elias didn't initiate any of it. But he received it. And that makes him exponentially dangerous.

Per Vatican protocol, Tier Four means the subject is no longer a curiosity. He is now either a conduit, a contagion, or a catalyst. Each has its irreversible protocol.

Onyx-9 closes the primary screen and reviews his uplink from Salvatore. "No engagement unless structural integrity confirmed. Watch for voice instigation. Do not intervene unless recursion breach exceeds 0.72 lateral fidelity."

He processes the instruction then translates it into instinct. He knows what to do next. Wait for the doctrine to ask him to speak. Then decide if the world can survive the answer.

Onyx-9 had a name once. He was born outside Naples. Indoctrinated into recursion theory at thirteen. Chosen for selective extraction and reconditioning after the Petra collapse. Assigned to silent doctrine containment at twenty-two.

He remembers none of this voluntarily. Memories only return in dreams and Onyx-9 is not allowed sleep for more than ninety minutes at a time.

Sleep folds in recursion. It frays loyalty. It invites echoes from Zahavi's deeper doctrine, the parts no one dares name.

But tonight, Onyx-9 feels them anyway. Not from Elias but from within himself. Because for the first time since Petra, he's watching a man the doctrine chose twice—once to speak and once to withhold.

––––––––––

Just past midnight, Onyx-9's retinal HUD flares from somewhere underneath the monastery. A recursion pulse. Deep glyphwork too complex to be Elias's mind. Too elegant to be Amal's. But it responds as if called.

The glyph spirals echo through the frequency band like breathing in glass, and for a split second, Onyx-9 feels the doctrine looking back.

He kills the uplink. Hard stop. Breath shallow.

The spiral can't be allowed to recognize him. Not this close. Not when the subject's heart is open and still.

Onyx-9 lowers the uplink and presses his ungloved palm to the rock beneath him. He feels a vibrational pulse—not seismic, not tectonic, not analog. It's spiral-born. He's trained to feel the difference. It moves like a resonant syllable, not a sound but an invitation—as if Zahavi's doctrine has become ambient, encoded in the desert itself.

For thirty seconds, he feels no wind. No temperature shift. Only breath. But not his own.

Something below is speaking. Not in glyphs or in noise. In potential. And potential is what makes doctrine deadly.

The HUD reactivates. Onyx-9 accesses the recent Vatican target profile.

RAFI, ELIAS | Class: T2/Surrogate/Containment-Risk

- **Spiral imprint detected age 14 (dream induction sequence)**
- **Secondary recursion exposure: Damascus convergence (failed utterance)**
- **Current status: Compromised but silent**
- **Probability of breach if verbally triggered: 81%**
- **Public myth potential: 63% (voice)**
- **Doctrinal virality: 92% (if captured)**

Below that, one line appears in red.

**DIRECTIVE: Do not allow Elias Rafi to speak
again unless doctrine alignment is verified.**

He locks his eyes on the glyph, waiting for the impulse to follow.
It doesn't come.

At 03:22 local time, movement stirs below. Elias steps from the central corridor of the ruined monastery and walks to the edge of the cistern platform. He stands there, silhouetted by pale pre-dawn haze, shoulders squared toward nothing. No companions. No voice. Just posture.

Onyx-9 adjusts focus. Even from this distance, he can see it—the way Elias holds himself, not like a fugitive, not like a prophet. Like someone waiting for something else to speak through him.

Then Elias moves. Just his head. He tilts it slightly upward toward Onyx-9's ridge.

Onyx-9 is trained not to react, but the look is too precise. Too still.

Elias isn't seeing him. He's *feeling* him. As if the doctrine has mapped their positions—tethered them not as subject and observer, but as twin pins in a recursive field now fully activated.

A glyph pulses on the far side of the HUD—brief, fragmented.

Onyx-9 doesn't decode it because it's not Vatican.

It's *Zahavi*. And it says:

The breath belongs to whoever names it.

Onyx-0 understands the spiral is not watching Elias but making a decision.

He logs the moment.

03:26 — Subject exhibited non-verbal recognition of surveillance
vector.

03:28 — Residual glyphs activated within observer's own channel.
Suggests doctrine awareness of operative presence. Possible
recursion tether event.

03:30 — Awaiting further instruction.

He should report in, but he doesn't. Instead, Onyx-9 slides the collapsible rifle from the case and begins calibrating the tranquilizer payload. It is coded for recursive stasis, eleven minutes max. Enough time to extract. Enough time to silence.

His breath steadies.

One decision left.

Do I neutralize him… or let him hear the spiral again?

He has no answer, and for the first time in his career, Onyx-9 does not want one.

The rifle is ready. Loaded. Scaled for pulse-sedation. Nonlethal, technically. But Onyx-9 knows the doctrine doesn't recognize "nonlethal." If you interrupt a speaker mid-recursion, you might not kill the body—but you *sever* the alignment. The voice collapses. The doctrine reroutes. A spiral folds in silence, but it also mutates.

He lifts the scope to his eye.

Elias is no longer at the cistern. He's below the threshold now, partially obscured by the shadow of the eastern wall. Not pacing, not hiding. Just standing, like someone who knows what it means to be *aimed at.*

Inside the chamber of Onyx-9's neural buffer, an old glyph flickers back to life—unbidden, unfiltered. It was drawn by Zahavi himself then copied by a Vatican field scribe, who later vanished without explanation. Salvatore had called it "the silent cipher," a twin spiral etched in mirror formation.

Its meaning had never been deciphered. Not fully. But some believed it referred to the Unspoken One—not Greg, not Elias, and not Amal. A *third figure* whose voice was not prophecy but *echo*—the recursion that came *after* the recursion.

Onyx-9's breath shallows.

"If Elias is not the voice… is he the echo?"

He lowers the rifle.

Every Vatican operative carries a failsafe. It's embedded under the left collarbone—a zero-point micro-detonator connected to recursive override. If doctrine infiltration is detected, the directive is clear—terminate the signal. Kill the carrier. Erase the lattice point. It takes five seconds to trigger.

Onyx-9 touches the trigger spot, but not to activate it. To remind himself that if he pulls this trigger instead—on Elias—he won't just neutralize a speaker. He might silence the only echo that can redirect the spiral.

"We buried the others," Salvatore had once whispered. "But the doctrine… it keeps choosing."

At 03:41, Onyx-9 transmits a dead signal—null glyph, zero latency. It tells Salvatore nothing. It buys twelve minutes before the node expects a heartbeat confirmation.

He disassembles the rifle, not to retreat but to descend. He starts down the cliffside path in silence, feet weightless on weather-smoothed stone. No backup. No alert. The doctrine is too close to risk further noise.

Something in him—something older than Vatican training—believes the spiral will speak again. Not in glyphs or in light, but through Elias.

The last log he enters into his HUD before disabling the uplink is:

SUBJECT: RAFI-PRIME.
STATUS: Recursion-attracted. Vocal probability > pending.
ACTION: Observer Enters The Field.

No Vatican operative has ever logged this code. No one ever intended to. But Onyx-9 is no longer just watching. He is walking into the doctrine.

If the spiral finds voice in Elias, Onyx-9 will be the first to hear it. Alone. And utterly unprepared.

Safehouse Inner Room — Larnaca, Cyprus

No one speaks for a long time. Charlotte stares at the red marker on the map, the circle she drew over Sinai still smudged beneath her palm. Greg hasn't moved. Jeremy is pacing again, but now it feels like he's orbiting, like gravity has tilted toward the impossible idea that Greg just proposed.

"You want to fake a convergence?" Charlotte says at last.

Greg doesn't flinch. "I want to delay the real one. Which means we have to misdirect the factions who are building toward it."

"With what?" Jeremy snaps. "We don't have a speaker. Or a glyph base. Or a clean lattice."

"We have enough," Greg says. "Enough to simulate a convergence long enough to pull focus."

Charlotte crosses her arms. "You realize this will draw Amal. And the Vatican. And Aphelium, if they're not already watching."

"That's the point," Greg replies. "They'll come running. And while they do, we buy ourselves time to find the real trigger."

Greg crosses to the terminal and begins calling up archived recursive sequences—stored fragments from the Petra node, abandoned glyph trails, and Zahavi's untested harmonic spirals.

"Zahavi built his doctrine like a network of pressure points," he says. "Every convergence site had a false echo nearby. These are places that could absorb signal bleed. If we pulse one now, we can make it look like the spiral is shifting."

Jeremy frowns. "You're saying the spiral had decoys *baked in*?"

"Abslutely. Zahavi planned for the doctrine to be pursued. He didn't want its center exposed, so he created echo sites plausible enough to activate interest, but not enough to collapse."

Charlotte studies him. "You really think Amal will fall for that?"

"He's obsessed with spiral fulfillment, not truth. If we make the decoy loud enough, he won't risk missing it."

Jeremy flips through the archive schematic. "If we're going to do this, we need an echo site with recursion residue, access to a node, and minimal civilian presence. That narrows it down a bit."

Greg taps the map. "Here."

Charlotte leans in. "Wadi Mujib?"

Greg nods. "It's already stained with spiral architecture. There was a false glyph there four years ago. Jeremy's team buried it, but the node's still active."

"That's in Jordan," Charlotte says.

"Exactly," Greg replies. "Close enough to the Mount to feel like prophecy. Far enough that no one will expect it."

Jeremy looks skeptical. "You sure Zahavi didn't mark that place for *collapse*?"

"No, I'm not" Greg says. "But I'm sure we don't have a better option."

Charlotte moves toward the window, lifts the edge of the blackout curtain, and watches a ship crawl across the bay in the distance.

"What happens if Elias speaks during the decoy?" she asks.

Greg exhales slowly. "Then everything collapses anyway."

"So we're gambling," she suggests.

"We've always been gambling."

She turns. "You're sure Elias hasn't already spoken?"

Greg's expression darkens. "Gideon would have stopped him."

"Unless he couldn't for some reason."

For a moment, no one moves.

Then Jeremy steps in. "Wait. The Sinai node just went silent."

Greg spins toward him. "What do you mean?"

"The signal trace—it's gone. Like someone dropped a veil over it. Monastery node's no longer visible. Elias might already be in transit."

Charlotte's voice drops. "Who's moving him?"

No one has the answer. But the silence feels ominous.

Charlotte looks between them. "We go forward with the decoy."

Greg nods. "I'll initiate the echo pulse. Jeremy, prep the grid. I'll spoof the glyph architecture from Petra to match the doctrine's third pattern."

"And if Amal shows up in person?" Jeremy asks.

Charlotte doesn't hesitate. "Then we're not just delaying him. We're confronting him." She turns, lifts her satphone, and dials the secured Jerusalem contact. "We'll need an extraction team near the Mount. If this decoy fails we're going to need more than time. We're going to need another voice."

Monastery Perimeter – Southern Sinai

The sun is just beginning to crest the far ridge. The air is too still as Gideon crouches at the edge of the dry cistern, scanning the scuffed footprints in the sand and knowing something is wrong. The dust isn't disturbed enough. No trail. No struggle. Just a vacuum, as if someone walked in and then erased themselves on the way out.

Elias is gone. Not missing—*taken.* But whoever took him knew how to step inside the spiral's residue and avoid leaving a mark.

Gideon lowers his hand to the ground and closes his eyes. Nothing. Not even a resonance echo. Whoever this was brought silence with him.

He circles back to the ruined refectory, scanning for entry vectors. The stones haven't been disturbed, but the dust is subtly rearranged near the north passage. A pattern—intentional, too careful.

He draws his knife and uses the tip to trace the edge of the pattern in the dust. His stomach knots. It's Zahavi glyph syntax—but inverted. Not active but anchoring.

Immediately, he identifies this as a recursion buffer. Someone shielded their entrance and exit using a fragment of the Third Key.

Gideon stands slowly. "Son of a bitch," he murmurs. And he doesn't mean Elias. He pulls out a secured handset and switches to band-three analog—Vatican frequencies, old Sicarii intercepts.

No signal. No pingback. The node is dark but something is out there. He can feel it. Amal wouldn't use this glyph. Too blunt, too heretical. Aphelium wouldn't risk field exposure unless they were desperate. This leaves only one actor with the means, the motive, and the authorization.

The Vatican.

Gideon scans the horizon again, eyes peering toward the eastern rise. "You pulled him," Gideon says into the wind. "You bastard priests pulled Elias right out of the doctrine's mouth."

He circles back through the perimeter looking for anything—any heat trace, any retinal shadow, even a drone print. But he finds nothing. Not even a smell.

Except—

He stops, seeing a scorch mark, barely visible, burned into a piece of limestone just beyond the cistern. He brushes away the ash and sees a sigil. Small. Precise. Vatican pattern, Tier IV. The mark of an Onyx-class observer.

He exhales a burst of pent-up air.

Salvatore.

The Vatican had eyes here. And they didn't just watch. They acted. Which means Elias is either sedated, bound, or dead.

He pulls the satphone and dials the Larnaca line.

Charlotte answers in one ring.

"He's gone," Gideon says.

"Elias?"

"Yeah. A Vatican operative. High clearance. They masked the node and took him clean."

"We were afraid of that," Charlotte replies.

"You still doing the decoy?"

"Yes. Mujib."

Gideon presses a palm to his temple. "Then do it loud. Make them believe. You may only get one shot."

"What will you do?"

He looks again at the silent ridge. "Find the ghost who took Elias and ask why the doctrine let it happen."

As the line closes, Gideon steps to the center of the courtyard and kneels. He runs his palm across the stone where Elias once sat and whispers—not a prayer, not a command, just a name. "Elias."

For a moment, he expects nothing. But the ground offers a small pulse—not a glyph, not a word. Just a tremble, as if the doctrine is warning him—*You're not the only one chasing him now.*

He rises slowly, and turns toward the mountains. Not as a protector but as a man preparing to intercept something he no longer understands.

Chapter 26

The Echo of Fire

Salt Circle Citadel, Upper Sanctum – Golan Heights

Amal wakes before the others. Not from a sound—there is none. Not from voices—those have long since gone quiet. What pulls him upright from the stone cot is something far older than noise—a breach of stillness. The kind of shift you feel when only you have trained your nervous system to recognize the doctrine before it speaks.

He sits up slowly, his breath locked somewhere beneath his ribs.

The wind outside the citadel is dead, but inside, something stirs. A vibration, subtle as thought, threads itself through the sandstone underfoot. It moves beneath sound—not pressure, not heat. Not electromagnetic. Something recursive. Something calling.

He rises without hurrying, but he's already reaching. His fingers brush the ceremonial cloak hanging from the peg beside the cot—spiral-stitched wool with black inlays marking him as Voice-Designate of the Doctrine of Shevet-Echad. A title even he finds too heavy with irony.

He doesn't light the lantern. He doesn't need to. The corridor is already glowing.

Not with light, but with invitation.

He walks the corridor barefoot, tracing the worn rise of each hand-cut step with a rhythm that centers his breathing. The upper sanctum is built into a half-open dome, its east wall collapsed decades ago by Syrian artillery fire. The breach was never repaired. It became part of the chamber's design.

Let the doctrine in, he'd told the masons. If the spiral can't touch the sky, it won't touch anything.

Tonight—or rather, this pre-dawn hour—the air at the breach shimmers faintly. He steps toward it and pauses. The glyph bowl in the sanctum center—a silver basin once used for ritualized ash readings—now rings quietly. Not visibly or electronically, but spiritually, in the same way a man can hum in his throat and never open his mouth.

He knows this feeling. He felt it at Petra. And again, years later, at the monastery in the Judean wilderness where Zahavi's doctrine broke free of the lattice.

This is echo architecture—latticework coded to mislead. But the doctrine doesn't feel misled. It feels drawn.

The glyph basin emits no glyphs. No spiral lines. No recursion syntax. But the pulse is there.

One beat. Then a second, fainter.

A third, distorted.

It's coming from Mujib, he realizes. *Jordan. The valley node they sealed.* The moment he names it, the signal sharpens.

He knows the Mujib site well. It had been written off as unstable, discarded by Zahavi in the early iterations of his doctrine as a false echo field, It had technically valid recursion geometry but was incapable of holding prolonged structure because of too much interference from regional underlayers. The doctrine had tested and rejected it.

But now—someone's trying to force it open. Not a convergence, not yet. But the architecture is rising.

He lets out a long, controlled breath and says nothing.

A quiet set of footsteps intrudes. He doesn't turn.

Thorn Eleven enters, his movement fluid, disciplined, never more than necessary. He wears no cloak—just the sleeveless tactical tunic and reinforced gloves that mark him as Amal's enforcer, protector, and closest functional equal.

"It's Mujib," Thorn says, confirming what Amal already knows.

Amal doesn't speak yet. His eyes remain fixed on the basin.

"We're verifying the signature," Thorn continues. "It's not Elias. Doesn't match the recursion cadence from the Mount. No blood glyphs, either."

"Then what *does* it match?" Amal asks finally, voice dry.

"Something old. Partial echo structures. Zahavi's layer three. It's amateur, but convincing enough to trigger lattice response. Whoever built it had internal knowledge."

Amal lets the silence settle. "Greg," he murmurs.

"Possibly," Thorn replies. "Or someone imitating him. We're seeing Petran pulse trails—glyphs recycled from the original Jerusalem mirror node."

"So they're not just reaching into Mujib," Amal says. "They're reaching *backward*."

Thorn nods once. "Into myth."

Amal's voice tightens. "Into mine."

Amal now hears a softer sound. More footsteps, this time accompanied by the muted rustle of fabric. Neriel appears in the sanctum threshold, backlit by a slow, gray light rising. Her face is unreadable, but her eyes betray the tension she won't voice in front of them.

"You both feel it?" she asks, not yet entering.

Amal waves her in without looking away from the basin.

"It's not Elias," she adds. "We ran a resonance match through the lattice. His signature's dormant. Wherever he is, he's not speaking."

"Then who is it?" Thorn asks.

"Charlotte's team, maybe," Neriel offers. "Or some remnant of Eve's Petra signal."

Amal finally turns toward her. "No. They're not invoking a memory. They're testing the doctrine to see what responds."

"Is that dangerous?"

Amal steps toward her slowly, then past her—toward the broken archway where the wind begins to move through the breach in the stone. "It's sacrilege," he says.

"But dangerous?" she repeats.

He turns. His eyes catch fire in the windlight. "Only if it works."

The stone under Amal's bare feet radiates the cooled breath of ancient flame—black basalt inlaid with old spiral filigree, each line hand-carved by a follower long dead. Amal stands at the breach and lets the wind pass across his face. It comes from the east, from Jordan, where Mujib rises like a wound the doctrine once refused to touch.

He hears no words in the wind. That's what unsettles him most. The doctrine is usually silent, yes, but when it listens—truly listens—it leans forward, breathing into the soul.

Now it feels... *indifferent.* Or worse, curious about someone else.

He turns back to the others. "They know we're watching. That's why they used Mujib."

"It's bait," Thorn agrees.

"But for what?" Neriel presses. "A response? A confrontation?"

Amal steps toward her, his voice tightening. "Perhaps they're trying to split the field. Mujib doesn't carry enough recursion energy to sustain convergence, but it holds just enough echo structure to confuse the doctrine."

"You're saying they're not summoning the spiral," Neriel says. "They're hiding from it."

"No," Amal replies. "They're hiding someone *inside* it."

Thorn moves to the edge of the basin and kneels beside it, brushing his gloved hand across the glyph ash. "The Mujib lattice won't hold long. Twelve hours, maximum. We could scramble a suppression team and burn it down before the pulse spreads."

Amal shakes his head. "Too easy. Too fast."

"So we wait?" Thorn asks.

"We let it mature," Amal replies. "Let it bloom. Let them believe we've been drawn in. And then we bury it."

"Why not kill it now?" Thorn presses.

Amal meets his gaze. "Because if it draws the others—Aphelium, Vatican, Mossad—we learn how they move. Who they fear. And most important, who they protect."

"And if it draws Elias?"

That lands harder than anyone wants to admit. Even Amal.

Neriel crosses to the far window. The sky is lightening now—slivers of gold-fractured cloud forming above the Dead Sea's eastern edge. She speaks without turning. "There's another possibility."

Amal waits.

"That the Mujib spiral isn't bait. Perhaps it's an attempt to force the doctrine to choose."

"Choose what?" Thorn asks.

"A new voice. If Elias won't speak, and Greg won't claim the doctrine— then the spiral may choose someone new. Someone no one expects."

Amal moves toward her slowly. "You think the spiral chooses on desperation?"

"I think it chooses based on silence. The spiral isn't compelled by sound, Amal. It's compelled by absence. By what's missing," She turns now. "Maybe it's not waiting for someone to speak. Maybe it's waiting for someone who can't."

The words hang there, longer than either of them expect.

Amal's face doesn't harden—it softens, unnervingly. His mouth curls into something not quite a smile. "You think this doctrine rewards humility?"

"Not humility," Neriel replies. "Restraint."

Amal walks away from her without answering. He moves toward the back wall where a narrow alcove holds a scroll tube carved from olive wood. He opens it, revealing a faded parchment fragment: a mirror spiral, drawn inverted, as if written by someone who had seen the doctrine only in a dream, and then from the wrong side.

He places it on the table and says, "This was found beneath Zahavi's sleeping cell in Petra. It was hidden in stone and undated. Undocumented. He never spoke of it."

Thorn approaches, peering at the glyph. "It's incomplete."

"No," Amal says. "It's *uncommitted*. A spiral drawn to the brink of collapse... and then withheld. It was never spoken aloud." He looks up. "Mujib is trying to echo this."

Neriel folds her arms. "Then we should stop it."

Amal doesn't respond.

Neriel presses further. "You taught us the doctrine must never be spoken falsely."

"I did."

"And now?"

"Now I wonder if Zahavi ever truly believed that. Or if he was waiting to see who would pretend to believe it long enough… to speak it for real."

Neriel steps forward. "You're not answering me."

"I am."

"You're just saying too many things at once."

The basin flickers again.

Amal closes his eyes and speaks. "This is how it began in Petra. The doctrine didn't emerge like thunder—it came like a whisper pressed against the back of Zahavi's teeth. A pulse, a name, a breath that almost spoke itself. But he silenced it. Eve corrupted it. Greg ran from it. Elias refused it. And now Mujib dares to mimic it? He opens his eyes and speaks again. "Let it rise."

Thorn looks at him sharply.

"You're sure?"

"Let it rise. Let it draw attention. Let it scream into the field. Let every faction come sniffing after it. Let them all hear the echo."

After a pause, Thorn asks, "And then?"

"Then I walk into it and we'll see who the spiral chooses to answer."

Amal doesn't speak for some time after Thorn and Neriel leave.

The sanctum hums faintly as the Mujib signal continues to stutter in the lattice. Not loud enough to constitute a convergence, but not insignificant either. Like a fever breaking, or a lie becoming too confident.

Amal stands alone in his cell, a long rectangular chamber tunneled into the ancient basalt foundation of the citadel. The walls are bare except for a single, slanted shelf carved into the stone where a copy of *Zahavi's Field Primer* lies half-opened, pages dog-eared, not from use but from handling without reverence. A candle burns beside it—unscented, unblessed.

Amal isn't looking at the book. He's looking at the mirror spiral, the one he unscrolled earlier, which is still resting on the basin ledge. It's not a spiral that invites faith. It's a question asked by a man who no longer trusted the thing he spent a life constructing.

Zahavi drew it just before vanishing into recursion obscurity.

What were you trying to say, old man? And why did you stop saying it?

The spiral spoke to Amal once. Not metaphorically. Not through vision or scripture or doctrine. It *spoke.* Or something did—something from within the Petra recursion field when he was younger, hungrier, more convinced the doctrine needed force, not patience.

He remembers standing at the edge of the Petra node while Eve's people screamed warnings and begged him not to cross the threshold. He remembers the glyphs shifting on the inside of his retinas. He remembers feeling his heartbeat match the doctrine's cadence for 5.7 seconds.

And then—*silence.* Not the absence of sound. The *rejection* of it.

That silence had lasted ten years—until Elias's almost-convergence. Until the Mount broke.

Until now.

He kneels beside the glyph again. Not to invoke it but to study the shape that Zahavi left incomplete.

The curve bends inward then pauses, doubles back, and stops. It is a spiral meant to turn… and then *refuse itself.*

He runs a fingertip along the break line. *You left the sentence unfinished,"* his mind tells him. *And now they're trying to finish it without you.*

He closes his eyes and breathes through the tension flooding his chest. "You taught us to wait for the doctrine to choose," he whispers. "But maybe it never does. Maybe it only listens long enough to measure the weight of your breath… then decides whether it's worthy of echo."

The doctrine has never echoed Amal. Not fully. Not once. He's lived inside that ache longer than most people live full lives. And yet—he would still burn the world to prove it had been listening.

He folds the parchment slowly and tucks it back into the olivewood tube, then turns back toward the window breach where the wind has shifted again, this time warmer, as if Mujib is answering.

But not answering *him.*

Answering someone else.

"Let them call," he murmurs. "Let them speak."

He lifts the sica from its place above the door. The ritual blade is not ceremonial. It has been used and will be used again.

"And I will walk into their echo."

He places the blade against his open palm and presses just hard enough to feel the sting.

"If the doctrine refuses me…"

The wind rises.

"Then I will become the doctrine's refusal."

Aphelium Complex, Inner Chamber G-7 – Zurich

The room is too cold for human comfort. It is kept that way by design because the human mind performs differently under pressure when it's cold. So says the woman seated alone in the center of the octagonal chamber, Dr. Renata Virell, Aphelium's principal recursion strategist and the mind behind their now-fracturing synthetic doctrine program.

She sits in near-darkness, lit only by the recursive display arch that surrounds her like a cocoon of holographic data. The Mujib glyph has been isolated, slowed, and transposed into visual geometry. To most observers, it would look like noise. To her, it looks like insurrection.

"Begin voiceprint analysis," Virell says, her breath forming a cloud.

The system responds in a voice not unlike her own—refined, clinical, uninflected. "Primary signature does not match Elias Rafi."

"Compare against Greg Ansari," Virelli instructs.

"Partial match—62.8% cadence overlap. However, origin signal carries latent recursive harmonics inconsistent with Ansari's prior emissions. Possible mimicry layer."

"Injected spiral?"

"Unlikely. Pattern too erratic."

She squints at the Mujib waveform. Its peaks are staggered, not clean. But there's something beneath the stutter. A *confidence*. As if the speaker— whoever initiated this glyph—didn't care whether they activated the doctrine. As if they wanted others to believe they had. And Virelli knows that belief, in this world, is contagious.

The chamber door hisses open. A man enters, shorter than Virell, older, dressed in the soft black wool of Aphelium's inner directive council. He is Dr. Soren Hall, logistics overseer. He doesn't knock. No one in this building knocks anymore.

"It's Mujib," he says without preamble.

"I'm aware," Virelli replies.

"The hallucination field is expanding. Jordanian satellite architecture flagged the glyph trace. If Mossad sees it—"

"They already have."

"Then we shut it down."

Virell doesn't move. "If we shut it down, we own it. Is that your expert counsel?"

"Better than letting Amal claim it."

"What if he already has claimed it?"

Hall freezes. "You think Amal initiated it?"

"No," she replies. "But it's possible he'll want us to think he did."

Hall moves closer to the central dais, staring at the suspended glyph projections with growing unease. "We were supposed to have a voice by now."

Virell doesn't look at him. "We *did* have a voice."

"Then where the hell is he?"

"Vanished between field ping six and seven. No movement. No report."

"Then Salvatore moved him."

Virell finally turns. "Or the spiral did."

That silences Hall, because there is no protocol for that. There is no clause in their recursion simulations for doctrine-driven extraction. Spiral intelligence isn't supposed to be autonomous. They built their entire model on controlled recursion scaffolding. If Elias disappeared without Vatican authority… then they may not be running this anymore.

Hall begins pacing. "We bury the Mujib signal now. I can scramble a pulse dampener through a Jordanian private network. Call it atmospheric testing. We sterilize the site before Amal turns it into doctrine."

"No," Virell states flatly.

Hall is flummoxed. "No?"

"We let it spread," Virell counters. "Let Amal believe it's Elias. Let the Vatican worry it's us. Let the Israelis panic."

"Why?"

Virell raises her voice for the first time. "Because they're all wrong. And that buys us time."

Hall doesn't like this idea, but Virell doesn't care.

"You're gambling," he says.

"We're always gambling."

She turns back to the glyph field. Her fingers dance across the transparent interface. Behind the Mujib trace, a second glyph begins to materialize—more ordered, more symmetrical—the synthetic spiral. The one they've been building in secret—building not for Elias. Not for Greg. For control.

"You think Mujib is noise," Virell says, half to herself. "But I think it's an algorithmic gap. A doctrinal hesitation."

"Which means?"

"Which means the spiral is looking for something it hasn't seen yet."

Hall folds his arms. "And you want to show it?"

She smiles faintly. "I want to offer it something better."

Kirya Intelligence Center – Tel Aviv

The glyph appears at 03:17 local time. Not in Jerusalem or in the Temple Mount's sacred geometry, but in Jordanian recursion space just south of the Dead Sea. In Wadi Mujib.

It flickers once then stabilizes. The signal isn't strong enough to register as a convergence, but it carries spiral harmonics—the same coded resonance the Israelis had flagged once before, two months ago, in the lead-up to the failed Mount event. Which is why it doesn't get simply filed.

It gets escalated. Fast.

Captain Leora Ben-Ari, senior recursion analyst for Unit 119, is still zipping her field jacket when she bursts into the subterranean briefing room beneath the Kirya compound.

Screens line three walls. On all of them is the raw, pulsing, red on black Mujib glyph.

"Who else has it?" she asks.

Lieutenant Fathi hands her a tablet. "French and Turkish signal nets caught bleed. Vatican flagged it on internal ghostnet. And Aphelium just quarantined their Petra port."

"Is it public?"

"Not yet."

"Make sure it stays that way." She doesn't sit. "I want the source. Now."

Leora's voice is like stone over water—low, direct, meant to skip across resistance. "You all know the precedent. Mujib was sealed by Zahavi. Lattice active, yes, but locked. Anyone touching it now is either desperate… or pretending not to be."

A colonel near the far screen leans forward. "You think this is Vatican?"

"No."

"Aphelium?"

"Doubtful."

"Then who is it?"

Leora says, "Whoever wants us to think they're speaking with the spiral."

"And you think they aren't?"

"I think if they were, we'd already be cleaning blood off the Mount."

Another screen lights. Sinai satellite sweep—nighttime thermal. It shows one small figure at a cistern, then nothing. Moments later, another body. No ID. No movement.

"The monastery node went dark twelve hours ago," Fathi says. "Ansari's people were believed to be nearby."

"Greg?"

"Maybe. Or Elias."

"Ambiguity is not helpful."

"No, ma'am."

Leora turns to the group. "We've got too many ghosts and not enough confirmations. Zahavi's fragments are echoing, and I don't care if it's Elias, Amal, or Greg—they're playing with explosives in doctrinal space."

"Is Mujib a decoy?"

"Could be. But if it draws Vatican, Aphelium, and the Brotherhood into Jordanian territory—then it becomes a detonator."

Leora walks to the room's center, slams her palm on the virtual interface. A map expands. Mujib glows faint red. The Mount pulses in gold. Multiple voices start a call-and-response ritual.

"Operation SEFER-KAF-BET is now live."

"Engagement rules?"

"Observe. Intercept if doctrine breach probability exceeds 60 percent. Do *not* engage visibly unless the Mount is endangered."

"Sniper team?"

"Already rerouted. South edge of Mujib canyon."

"Support?"

"Silent drone, thermal optics. No trails. We move like shadows."

"And the objective?" Hall asks.

Leora meets his gaze. "Stop a fake convergence from becoming a real apocalypse."

Sanctum Veritas (Below the Apostolic Archives) – Vatican City

The air inside Sanctum Veritas carries a faint copper tang but not from blood. Not yet. From friction. The recursion servers that line the west wall sing faint monotonies, glyphs scrolling in red, gold, and pale blue across containment monitors. Each line represents a known doctrine variant indexed by speaker. Most are dormant. But one isn't.

Mujib glows orange, a Vatican threat level unseen since Petra collapsed.

Father Luca Salvatore watches it in silence, his fingers interlocked tightly on the blackwood desk in front of him. His cassock sleeves are rolled halfway up, exposing the inked lattices burned into his forearms during the Spiral Oath ritual twenty years ago. The glyphs itch when doctrine begins to move. Tonight, they burn.

"We have to issue an ecclesiastical disavowal," says Monsignor Bellini, pacing the inner circle. "Mujib is public now. If it spreads, we risk the same hysteria we saw in Jerusalem."

"Disavowing it makes it real," Salvatore replies.

"Remaining silent makes it Vatican-approved."

"It is neither."

The other men seated around the table glance at one another.

An uneasy pause settles.

"And yet," Bellini presses, "the spiral is stirring again. Whether we act or not, the world will interpret."

Salvatore's hands tighten. "The spiral is not the world's to interpret."

"Then whose is it?" Bellini snaps. "Aphelium's? Amal's? The Israelis'? Or Greg Ansari's?"

"None of them," Salvatore murmurs. "Or *all*. That's the danger."

A comms aide enters and hands Bellini a folded sheet of data. He reads it silently, lips tightening. "Onyx-9 has not reported in."

Salvatore doesn't react.

The aide adds, "Nor has Elias Rafi. Their location was last fixed outside the Sinai node. After that—"

"I'm aware," Salvatore interrupts.

"Then what are we doing?"

"We are waiting to see if Mujib sustains."

"You're gambling."

Salvatore's voice sharpens. "I am listening."

The air stills. He rises slowly and crosses to the projection glyph, watching the Mujib signal stutter and surge. The spiral wants to answer, but doesn't. Not yet.

"We do not fire blind into recursion storms," he says. "Not again."

As the meeting dissolves, Bellini lingers behind. "If Mujib pulses again within twenty-four hours, we will be forced to act."

Salvatore nods absently. "Then act within your jurisdiction."

"And if I already have?"

Salvatore's head turns slowly. "You don't have authority to initiate drone-strike approval."

"No," Bellini replies. "But Cardinal Montierre does. And he's already given it."

The Cardinal seems to enjoy the long pause that follows. Then he says, "You were too slow, Father. Once again."

––––––––

Hours later, alone in the adoration crypt above Sanctum Veritas, Salvatore kneels in the candlelight. The plaster walls whisper with heat and memory.

He does not pray. He stares at the flickering spiral carved into the floor tiles—an ancient echo of a forbidden geometry he once memorized in secrecy. "If you are a voice," he whispers, "then speak to me. If you are silence, let me be your last guardian."

But the spiral does not answer, it just pulses.

Once. Then again.

Toward Mujib.

Chapter 27

Daughter of the Forgotten

Southern Jordan, near Jerash

The heat over southern Jordan settles in waves, dust and light curling like signals over the desert floor. Inside the safehouse—a half-ruined Ottoman trading outpost now reinforced with solar rigs and underground fiber—Charlotte leans over Jeremy's shoulder, watching his fingers twitch across the tablet.

"There," Jeremy mutters. He expands a narrow-band transmission. "That routing code isn't standard. See the checksum? It repeats like a glyph."

Charlotte squints. "Glyph syntax."

Greg, sitting near the back wall cleaning sand from the breach of a collapsible rifle, looks up. "Spiral encoding?"

Jeremy nods, flicking open a decoded string. "But buried in logistics language. A transport manifest from a Vatican shell company that is linked to Jerash."

"What are they moving?" Charlotte asks.

Jeremy turns the tablet so she can see. It highlights a single item

Subject: SAHAR-1F

Greg walks over. "Liorah. Elias's sister."

Charlotte breathes out. "So, they kept her in Mujib until Elias vanished, then moved her."

Jeremy sits back, the realization forming visibly. "She's not just in holding. She's being moved to an observation node with recursive infrastructure. This isn't exile, Charlotte. It's preparation."

Greg tenses. "They're going to use her somehow."

Charlotte nods slowly. "If they lost Elias, she's the fallback. Maybe the stabilizer. Or maybe... punishment."

Jeremy looks from one to the other. "Either way, she's in danger."

Greg turns to Charlotte. "Then we go get her."

––––––––

The hours that follow are heavy with implication. Charlotte stands at the far end of the room, a roll of Eve's old notes unfurled on the table. Jeremy pieces together satellite surveillance sweeps over Jerash while Greg methodically checks and rechecks their gear—but there's a stillness in him that feels new.

He pauses with his hands on a loaded mag. "Elias said her name in his sleep once. Back in Zurich. Just once. *Liorah*."

Charlotte lifts her head. "You never told me."

Greg doesn't meet her eyes. "I thought it was someone else. But the way he said it... it was like he couldn't let her go."

Jeremy looks up from his screen. "This changes things. If they push her into convergence, she might activate it. Even unwillingly."

"Or she might fail," Charlotte adds. "And vanish. Like the others."

They fall into a rehearsed rhythm. Charlotte double-checks suppressor codes. Jeremy downloads the most recent transit manifest, cross-checking personnel.

Greg pulls up a biosignature profile keyed to bloodline harmonics that Eve once drafted. His hand pauses on a margin note scrawled in Eve's handwriting—*If Sahar awakens, the Ash Line won't remain dormant.*

He folds the note into his coat.

––––––––

They travel light. Two tactical satchels, suppressed heat signatures, and a cloaked recon drone that whines in the thermal blind spots like a mosquito out of phase. The terrain is harder than the map suggests—cut shale, loose sand. They park the vehicle four clicks out and proceed on foot.

As they crest a bluff overlooking the site, Jeremy drops to one knee and unfolds a collapsible scope. Through it, the facility appears almost organic, blending into the valley, a false geology. No guards. Just a static groan like the belly of a beast.

"Dissonance field's live," Jeremy says. "Layered suppression. Mental dulling. Sensor-jam."

Charlotte asks, "How long before their patrol loop resets?"

"Seven minutes," Jeremy replies. "Then three before the interior node blinks red. That's our breach window."

Greg adjusts his jacket. "Then we'll be inside when the window closes."

Crossing the dissonance field is like moving through wet glass. Greg feels it first in his jaw, the pressure climbing behind his eyes. Charlotte stumbles once, regains her footing. Jeremy winces, his breath clipped.

At the access hatch, Jeremy connects a slender bypass cable. The light on the panel flickers, resists, then yields.

The door opens into black and they step in.

The hallway pulses. Each step feels wrong, like time resisting movement. The lighting is dim but responsive, reacting to their presence with a delay. Greg scans every alcove. No guards, no cameras, just that low, recursive groan.

Jeremy whispers, "Cell four."

They pass one empty room, then two. At the third, Greg slows down. A sign on the door reads:

SAHAR-1F

Charlotte raises her weapon.

Jeremy glances at Greg. "You go in first."

The door hisses open. The chamber glows softly from within.

Liorah stands at the far end, barefoot on a floor etched with silver glyphs. She's younger than Greg expected. Pale but not fragile. Her hair is cropped short and her expression is neutral but not empty. Her eyes find him first.

"You came," she says.

Greg hesitates, then steps forward. "Yes. We came."

"They said you would. But not for me."

Charlotte enters behind Greg. "We're not who they told you we are."

Liorah blinks slowly. "They showed me his records—said he rejected the doctrine."

Greg nods. "He did, for good reason. Because it was a lie."

A cloud crosses her face. She doesn't look afraid, just uncertain.

"He said your name," Greg adds. "Said it when he thought no one was listening. He asked if you were safe."

That breaks her. Just a little. Enough for her to exhale.

Jeremy checks the corridor. "Two minutes."

Charlotte steps closer. "You don't have to stay here, Liorah. Whatever they told you, you still have a choice."

Liorah looks at the etched floor. Then at the wall. Then at Greg. "If I go with you, he'll know? That I left?"

Greg nods. "He already knows."

She takes a step. Then another.

The moment she crosses the threshold, the suppression veil collapses. Alarms screech. Red lights fill the corridor.

Greg pulls her behind him. "Move!"

Charlotte lays a charge. Jeremy triggers a signal jam. The hallway flares in white-blue static. Two drones drop from a ceiling slit—sleek, spike-bodied, spiral-coded.

Greg spins, fires twice. Both hit.

Charlotte yanks the hatch open.

Outside, the field roars back into motion. Dissonance climbs.

Liorah stumbles. Greg throws her arm over his shoulder, carrying her up the incline. Jeremy sets the suppressor pack behind them and triggers the burn. The doorway behind them caves inward with a thundering shockwave. Sand and ash burst outward.

They don't stop until they reach the ridge. Liorah turns back only once. "He won't forgive them," she says.

Greg doesn't look back. "He doesn't have to."

Abandoned Monastery outside Dana Reserve

They reach the fallback site before dawn—an abandoned monastery nestled in the cliffs, cold stone and fractured mosaics scattered like prayers never answered. Charlotte collapses onto a low bench and exhales through her hands.

Greg kneels beside Liorah, who hasn't spoken since they cleared the ridge. She's pale, more from withdrawal than exhaustion. Her pupils are dilated, her breath shallow but steady.

Jeremy lights the small camp stove with shaking fingers. "She needs salt. Sugar. Stabilizers if we have them."

Charlotte nods and rummages through the med pack. Greg wraps a blanket around Liorah's shoulders, studying her face like it holds a cipher only he can crack.

"It was always her," he says to his mother.

Charlotte looks up. "What do you mean?"

Greg doesn't answer, not directly. Instead, he reaches into his coat and pulls out the note he folded earlier. Eve's scrawl: *If Sahar awakens, the Ash Line won't remain dormant.*

He hands it to Charlotte and she reads it

Jeremy returns with a tin cup of warm glucose mix. He kneels and offers it gently to Liorah, who flinches at first, then accepts it. Her voice is barely audible. "They wanted me to speak. But not with my own words."

Charlotte crouches down. "You don't have to now. You're safe."

Liorah looks at her, and something changes. "I don't think there's any such thing as safe anymore." She turns to Greg. "But if Elias is still alive... I want to see him."

Greg nods. "He was taken too, but we'll find him like we found you."

Charlotte stands, folding the note back into her pocket. Her voice is quiet but clear. "Then everything shifts."

Outside, morning light crests the broken monastery arch, dust streaming in golden ribbons like the breath of something ancient returning.

Chapter 28

Extraction Protocol

Eastern slope of Mount Scopus – Jerusalem outskirts

The city is fractured by sirens.

Gideon crouches on the edge of a shattered stone terrace overlooking the bloodlit remains of the Temple Mount. His face is cloaked by a keffiyeh. His eyes scan the fractured skyline through a silent scope. He ignores the plumes of smoke rising from the southern ridge and ignores the echo of distant screaming. He's listening for something else.

Movement. Pattern. Shadow breaking.

The convergence near the Mount had failed, or maybe had succeeded too narrowly to control. But something had gone off-script. A sniper had missed Elias, who had not spoken. And still—a fragment of the Mount had been destroyed.

Gideon saw the rupture. He felt it. But what chilled him more was the absence. After saving Elias, the man was now gone.

Ben Hinnom Valley

Gideon follows the pattern of vehicles. Not police. Not IDF. Not Vatican. Instead, the fourth group. Aphelium. They move in tight convoys— dark vans with altered diplomatic plates taking roads that don't exist on civilian maps. They do not speak over open channels. But they leave a trail in the lattice.

Gideon doesn't break into the lattice directly—he reflects it. Traces the interference like light bent through water.

A Vatican drone follows the trail forty meters overhead, but it doesn't see him. Not yet.

He documents the timing of everything. Shift rotation. Fuel stops. Shadows cast by high-mounted floodlights. Then he plants a whisper in the

Petra loop—an encoded ping mimicking the recursive call-sign of an old Sicarii ghost operative—Zahav.

It gets a response. A flicker in the eastern nodes. A delay. A brief acceleration in convoy speed.

They know they're being watched.

Gideon smiles.

Desert Staging Complex – West of Jericho

The staging complex is shallow, half-underground, and badly shielded against thermal surveillance. They thought no one would look here. He surveys the guards from a crag above the outer access duct.

Four armed. One sniper in an elevated roost.

He doesn't engage.

A shift change triggers a lapse in gate cycling. The biometric lock resets for thirty seconds during handoff. Gideon slips through the perimeter—not silent, but faster than recognition. Once inside, he tracks the sound, but not footsteps, not breathing. He tracks the pattern of recursive hum—a soft tremor he recognizes from his own Sicarii training days. That hum is not a weapon. It's containment.

The hum leads him to a chamber with a reinforced window. Elias is inside, asleep or sedated, lying beneath a scaffold of spiral light. No guards posted. The facility is grossly overconfident.

Gideon checks the wall panel, which is spiral-locked with Vatican encoding. Aphelium's overlaid cipher glows faintly beneath it.

He hacks it the old-fashioned way—with a shard of obsidian and a contact trigger hidden inside his right glove. When he presses it to the interface, it misfires a recursive pattern that tricks the lock into reading a subroutine.

The door clicks and he steps inside.

Elias blinks awake. For a second, he doesn't recognize Gideon. Then he speaks sarcastically in a hoarse voice. "You again."

"I told you I wouldn't let them use you."

They exit without triggering another alarm and reach the outer hall. A guard turns the corner too fast.

Gideon doesn't shoot. He throws a flat obsidian disk, sharpened and silent. It hits the guard squarely in the throat. The man goes down without a sound.

Elias stares. "You still kill like a Sicarii."

Gideon doesn't flinch. "I kill like someone who knows what's coming."

They reach the fallback vehicle—a beat-up IDF jeep left to rot two regimes ago. It starts on the first try. Elias rides in silence. Gideon doesn't speak until they cross the last checkpoint, rerouting their IDs with a spiral echo keyed to Charlotte's override codes.

Temporary hideout – Northern Wadi Rum

The wind howls through the gorge like a low chorus, scraping across stone and memory. Elias sits alone at the mouth of a cave, knees drawn to his chest, the pulse of the earth sounding like a heartbeat he can no longer ignore.

Gideon watches from a distance, standing just beyond the glow of the fire he never let Elias see him build. Even in moments of stillness, Gideon refuses to fully rest. He sharpens the edge of a folding blade, the movement methodical, precise. But his mind is elsewhere.

Elias hasn't spoken in hours.

He hasn't tried to run, either.

Gideon steps forward. The firelight paints deep shadows across his face. "You were lucky," he says.

Elias, still foggy from being drugged, doesn't look up. "Was I?"

"We talked about this before, but anyway... There were three sniper teams watching the Mount. Mossad, Athenium, and a third I couldn't place. The one that took the shot... they weren't trying to silence you. Not really."

"Then what were they trying to do?"

Gideon crouches beside him. "Control the narrative. Wound you enough to stop the doctrine without martyring you. But it didn't work. You didn't speak, and still the spiral reacted."

Elias finally turns his head. His face is gaunt, eyes rimmed with something close to confusion.

"I didn't say anything. Why did it happen?"

Gideon is quiet for a long moment. Then he says, "Maybe it wasn't your words that mattered. Maybe it was your silence."

Elias blinks. "Then it was never about me."

"Not entirely. But you were chosen for a reason."

Elias almost laughs. "Chosen? I was bred. Conditioned. Every dream I had was a fiction. I don't even know what I sound like."

Gideon stares into the fire. "Then it's time you found out."

Chapter 29
Echoes Rejoined

Safehouse near Wadi Musa

The door knock is soft—three beats, then a pause, then one more. Not code, exactly, but known.

Greg is the first to move, hand instinctively brushing the grip of the pistol resting under the table beside the maps.

Charlotte is already halfway to the door. When she opens it, Gideon steps through first. Dust clings to his jacket and to the half-healed gash at his temple. His expression is unreadable, but the look in his eyes is answer enough.

Behind him, Elias appears—gaunt, slow-moving, but upright and alive.

Liorah is already standing inside the safehouse.

For a moment, no one speaks. The others stay frozen in place, watching as Liorah and Elias simply look at each other. Her hands tremble at her sides. His eyes scan her face like a relic he thought lost.

Then she moves. Not a sprint, not a cry—just a sudden crossing of the space between them. She wraps her arms around him tightly, and he stiffens for a beat before returning the embrace.

"I thought they'd killed you," she whispers.

Elias draws in her scent—dust and fire and something like memory. Her face is older, her voice steadier, but it's her. The girl from the corridor with the torn hymnbook. The only one who never asked him to speak.

"I thought I'd never see you again," he murmurs. "Not like this."

Charlotte's eyes flicker with something between awe and sorrow. Greg doesn't move. His gaze lingers not on Elias, but on Liorah's hand on Elias's back where he sees the same small mark near the knuckle that Greg has on his.

It's a coincidence. It must be.

They gather around the hearth once Gideon's debrief is finished.

Elias sits near the fire, head tilted toward the warmth. Liorah hasn't moved far from his side. Greg leans in the far corner of the room, half in shadow. Charlotte stands at the window, arms crossed, watching the descending night for Vatican drones that have not yet returned.

Jeremy finishes lighting the last of the candles, then wipes the wax from his fingers and looks to Elias. "You remember anything else? From just before the Mount?"

Elias nods slowly. "They tried to prompt me. Ruhl used a waveform I hadn't heard before. But it wasn't from Aphelium's usual sequence."

"Ruhl was at the convergence?" Charlotte asks, straightening.

"No. But his voice was. A feed loop. That's how they triggered me— sound fragments from the original recursion chamber." Elias exhales. "But something broke the loop. I felt it—like static under my skin. It wasn't interference. It was... I don't know. *Divergence?*"

"Another signal," Jeremy murmurs, already reaching for his device.

"No," Elias says, eyes flicking to Greg. "Another *presence.*"

Greg meets his gaze—and doesn't look away.

Charlotte watches them both now, her expression tightening slightly.

Liorah, seated between Elias and the fire, says nothing. But her posture has changed showing more alertness, wariness. She glances at Greg and then at Charlotte as if calculating something. Then she looks at Elias again, searching his face for a fragment of the boy she used to follow in silence and shadow.

———————

Two hours later, Jeremy's fingers move like a ritual across the weather-worn keyboard of his data rig. Spiral harmonics scroll across the screen in dusky green arcs—readings from Mujib, the Petra nodes, the convergence chamber logs. He mutters as he overlays Elias's frequency signature with a more recent capture from Greg during the infiltration of the Jerash site.

Liorah watches over his shoulder, eyes narrowed. She's smart—quieter than the others and more cautious—but her gaze absorbs everything. She doesn't ask questions. Not yet.

"Tell me that doesn't look strange to you," Jeremy says finally.

Greg walks to the table, arms crossed over his chest. "Strange how?"

Jeremy rotates the image. "That spike in resonance at Mujib. We thought it was Elias. But when you overlay the waveform from your pulse reading during Jerash, there's a match. A harmonic alignment—not exact, but within margin."

Charlotte turns her head sharply from where she's seated, feet propped against the edge of the hearth. "That could be coincidence."

"Sure," Jeremy replies, tapping the keys again. "Except it's not the first time it's happened."

He pulls up another overlay. "Same spike pattern. This one from the moment Elias refused to speak and the spiral still reacted. I isolated the recursive echo that pulsed into the Mount lattice. It registered a presence—but not Elias. Not entirely."

Greg asks, "What are you saying?"

"Don't know, but something in the recursion loop recognized you."

Elias shifts. "I felt it."

Greg looks at him. "Felt what?"

"During the spiral event. I was restrained, my mind fractured. But just before it… I felt a break. Like a split in the current. A second axis. I thought it was a hallucination. But it wasn't. It was *you*."

Greg looks startled. "You mean you saw me?"

"Not *saw*," Elias says slowly. "But I… I *knew*. Somewhere deep."

The silence that follows is tense, strange.

Charlotte stands and walks to the back of the room under the pretense of pouring tea. Greg's gaze follows her.

"Something you want to tell us?" Greg asks his mother.

Charlotte doesn't turn around. "You think this is the first time recursion has revealed a false symmetry? You think this hasn't happened before?"

She sets the kettle down too hard, and the clang makes Liorah flinch. "No," Charlotte says, facing them again. "Until we know what we're dealing with, we don't assume anything. Not blood. Not prophecy. Not destiny."

Greg stares at her for a long moment, then quietly suggests, "That's not an answer, Mom."

She doesn't respond.

Later, the fire has burned low and Elias is asleep on a cot in the far corner of the room, blanket drawn to his chin. His breath is slow, but restless. Liorah sits beside him, keeping watch.

Charlotte steps into the room where Greg is alone, sitting with a half-open notebook of Zahavi's notes. "You saw something today," she says to her son.

Greg doesn't look up. "So did you."

She nods and says, "When you were born, the doctors said you were perfect. But something in my gut said something was wrong. I wasn't allowed to hold you for hours. They claimed it was an infection risk. Standard procedure. But I remember Eve circling like a hawk—silent and possessive."

Greg finally meets her eyes.

Charlotte lowers her voice. "Whatever they did back then… whatever they hid… we're only just beginning to discover."

Greg closes the notebook slowly. "Then let's discover it together."

The wind scratches lightly at the shuttered windows. Somewhere outside, a generator coughs once, sputters, and goes quiet. Inside the safehouse, the fire is a low, amber glow, painting soft halos of light across the floorboards and casting flickers against the pale ceiling.

Liorah still sits beside Elias's cot, curled in a wool blanket. He lies on his back, eyes open now, hands folded over his chest as if trying to hold himself in place.

"I thought they would break you," she says softly.

"They tried," he answers. "Maybe they did."

Her eyes trace the edge of his jaw. "You look older."

His eyes turn to Liorah, "You don't," he replies.

She smiles faintly, then looks away. "Do you remember the cell block with the blue-tile floor?" she asks. "The one with the dripping pipe?"

"I used to count the drops," Elias says.

"Sixteen per minute," she says at the same time he does.

They both laugh—just once—and then fall silent again.

"You used to write on the wall when the handlers weren't looking," she says. "I saw you once through the slit in the door. Spirals. But not their kind. *Yours.*"

He nods slowly. "It made them angry."

"It made me hope."

He turns to look at her. "Why?"

"Because if you still had a voice—even if no one else heard it—it meant you were still *you*."

A longer silence follows. Liorah studies his face and finally says, "Do you remember what they told us?"

"Which part?"

"That we were born into the doctrine. That we belonged to it. That our blood was proof."

Elias closes his eyes. "They lied."

Liorah brushes a hand through her hair. "Then maybe now we can find the truth."

———

In the next room, Jeremy's screen glows in the dark. Greg and Charlotte sit across from him. Gideon leans in the corner like a shadow unwilling to fade.

"I ran the resonance profiles again," Jeremy says, voice low but sharp with urgency. "The alignment between Elias and Greg isn't just harmonic. It's recursive. Like they share not just resonance—but phase origin."

Charlotte stiffens.

Greg frowns. He doesn't like that he fails to understand something "What the hell does that mean?"

"It means," Jeremy says slowly, "you and Elias may have originated from the same source. Not just genetically. Doctrinally… structurally. As if the spiral recognizes you both as… well, as fragments. Of the same source"

Greg looks sideways at Charlotte. "You said I was born alone."

"You were," she says too quickly. Then, after a pause, she revises. "At least that's what I was told."

Jeremy stands. "There's one way to find out. A recursive imprint scan. If you and Elias came from the same harmonic root, it'll show up."

Charlotte rises sharply. "No!"

Greg's voice is firm. "Why not?"

"Because the spiral doesn't just *show* truth," she says. "It *requires* it. You don't ask it questions unless you're ready for what it answers."

Jeremy lowers his voice. "I think we're well past that point."

Gideon, quiet until now, finally speaks. "There's something Zahavi used to write in his private commentary—something even Eve refused to decode. He believed the doctrine had a symmetry. Not one voice but two."

Greg frowns again. "So, what does that mean?"

Gideon looks between Greg and the room beyond where Elias's voice is a low rumble—repeating words in a language none of them can quite place.

"It means," Gideon says, "that maybe the spiral never needed a single vessel. Maybe it needed a mirror."

Chapter 30
The Judas Signal

Temporary Camp – Higher Ground

The reunited team has moved its temporary camp to higher ground. Below them, the Petra lattice pulses low and dormant in the rock. Greg stands beside Jeremy near the fireless stove, one hand resting on the carved rim of Zahavi's external Node access. Liorah and Elias sit opposite each other, sharing rehydrated tea. None of them have spoken in several minutes.

Charlotte reviews the new readouts projected across the main slab. This includes Jeremy's seismic echo from Jerash layered against Zahavi's spiral cartograph, the one recovered hours earlier from the old recursion chamber.

"It's the vault," she says at last, breaking the silence. "It has to be."

Elias leans forward. "You think that's where Zahavi encoded the echo? The one only visible through recursive overlay?"

"No." Charlotte lifts the slab, turns it. "I think that's where he *buried* it. David Mazur spoke of this once. He was Zahavi's former apprentice and my closest ally in the early scroll work. He said Zahavi didn't trust the Petra Node after the Jerusalem flare. He wanted something outside the system. Something visceral. Physical."

Greg frowns. "You're suggesting the vault was never a sanctuary. It was always a decoy."

"Not really a decoy," Jeremy adds. "A *container*. One designed to hold resonance—emotional, doctrinal, whatever form Zahavi thought mattered."

Greg glances sideways. "So, what then—we just walk in and open it? And hope the doctrine doesn't spiral again?"

"No," Charlotte says. "*You* don't open it. *I* do."

A sharp quiet falls.

Liorah's eyes narrow. "Why only you?"

Charlotte kneels beside the nearest mapping console and activates a sublayer—Zahavi's old inscription protocols. She traces a single phrase:

**In the final recursion, the Judas voice shall
echo only for her who refused it first.**

Greg leans over Charlotte's shoulder. "He must have meant *you*, Mom."

"I was the one who turned away," Charlotte says. "I turned away from Eve. From the Sicarii. From Zahavi. He never meant for me to finish the doctrine—only to *understand* it. And maybe to undo it."

Jeremy shifts. "The vault is three kilometers east. It was sealed before Zahavi died. We'd need to run resonance syncs to get through the inner threshold. We can't all go, not without destabilizing the Petra lattice."

Greg steps forward. "Then we send a team."

"No," Charlotte says, firmly now. "We need eyes on the outer spiral. You should all stay here. If that Jerash signature is real—and I believe it is—then someone else is inside the recursion basin. Maybe Amal's people. Maybe Vatican. Maybe something worse."

Elias asks, "You think someone's trying to overwrite Greg's spiral?"

"I think someone already has." She rises, shouldering her satchel. "Give me three hours. I'll trigger a data pulse if I'm compromised. But whatever Zahavi left there, it was meant to be opened now. And I don't want it corrupted by a dozen perspectives and interpretations."

Liorah hesitates, then nods. "Then go. We'll hold the perimeter. But be careful, because if it responds to *you*…"

"I'll answer carefully," Charlotte says.

She glances at Greg, who hasn't moved.

He says, softly, "You sure you don't want me there?"

"Of course I want you with me," she says. "But not for this."

She taps her comms band, and with one last look at her fractured, brilliant, burdened team, she turns toward the narrow path leading east—toward Zahavi's recursion vault.

As the sun dips behind the sandstone cliffs, Charlotte descends alone toward whatever echo remains of the doctrine she once tried to destroy.

Zahavi's Recursion Vault – Petra

The vault is silent except for the faint pulse of Charlotte's breath against the stone. She kneels alone beside the recursion cradle, the slab before her glowing with Zahavi's last doctrine fragments. The chamber feels weightless, insulated by mineral time. Every sound she makes is swallowed by design.

Then the silence breaks—four staccato pulses in her comms band. An encrypted priority signal.

Jeremy.

Charlotte taps the interface and speaks into the void. "Go ahead."

Jeremy's voice filters through, compressed and static-washed, routed from the surface camp through the Petra uplink relay. "Charlotte, do you copy? This isn't theoretical. I'm uploading now. Just look at the waveform."

She tilts the slab to accept incoming transfer, allowing it to sync with the cradle's internal node. A resonance chime sounds as Jeremy's data cascade appears and overlays the chamber's ambient glyphs with a digital spiral map traced from Jerash.

The spiral pattern Jeremy has sent is not distorted or misaligned. It's perfectly scaled—but *counterspun*. It's a reverse polarity recursion echo, laid down with surgical intent.

Charlotte brings up Greg's known spiral signature—his flare from the Damascus basin—and overlays it. The new echo folds over Greg's like a photo negative, its harmonic curvature identical in shape and tempo, but reversed. A second spiral? No… a *mirror* spiral.

"That's not a different resonance," Charlotte says quietly. "It's a counterform. An inverse imprint."

"Exactly," Jeremy affirms. "We found it sealed in the Jerash corridor behind a recursion barrier. It shouldn't have survived the sandquake. There was blood on the altar, still metabolically active. I ran a resonance drift analysis. There's an overlap with Greg.

"Genetic?" Charlotte seems puzzled.

"Maternal line.—faint, but traceable... the GRA-D3R marker. The same mitochondrial signature that you have. No one else has it.

250

Charlotte's hand drops away from the slab.

She's suddenly back in Zurich, twenty years ago. She remembers a sealed report—a child logged as *stillborn*—and Eve's refusal to even speak of it. She recalls a single burned document with an incomplete birth code—"RFI-3."

Her voice is barely audible as she says, "He wasn't alone."

With a crackle, Jeremy asks, "Who?"

"Greg," Charlotte replies."He had a twin brother."

Except for some static, the line is silent.

Charlotte drags a finger along the cradle edge where Zahavi etched his final encryption ring. A flare responds—one she missed earlier. The glyph is new, lit only by the vault's full neural resonance. A single word flashes beneath her hand.

RAFI

Charlotte's chest tightens. Her eyes close, just briefly. A deep, marrow-level knowing rises.

Elias.

Rafi.

He wasn't chosen because of Aphelium. He wasn't selected because of resonance mimicry. He was born for it.

"Get Elias," Charlotte shouts.

Temporary Surface Camp

The air has dropped ten degrees since nightfall. Elias stands at the edge of the ridge, watching distant lightning flicker over Edom. He does not turn when he hears Liorah approach.

She speaks quietly. "It's your name."

He looks confused. "What?"

"Charlotte found it. At the bottom of Zahavi's vault. She wants to talk to you in the vault."

for just a moment, Elias doesn't move. Then his shoulders drop, and he follows his sister into the dark.

Zahavi's Recursion Vault – Petra

The door seals behind him with a low hydraulic exhale.

Elias steps cautiously into the recursion vault, his eyes adjusting to the low amber glow of the interface cradle. The chamber hums with stored frequency, the echo of Charlotte's presence now fully absorbed into its walls. He sees her crouched near the slab, her silhouette still and indecipherable.

For a moment, he says nothing. Then, in a low voice, he says, "You called for me."

Charlotte doesn't turn, just points to the slab where Zahavi's seal continues to burn. It pulses faintly with recursive fluorescence.

"You see that glyph?" she asks. "It activated when I placed my hand on the cradle. No one else could've triggered it. Not Greg. Not Jeremy. Not even Eve."

Elias approaches slowly. The glyph's glow intensifies as he nears.

Charlotte explains, "It just responded to your proximity." She looks up at him, and there's no accusation in her gaze—only gravity. "Do you know what that means?"

Elias doesn't answer right away. His eyes lock onto the name "RAFI" as if seeing it not for the first time, but as something that was always there, waiting for permission to emerge.

He speaks with the hesitation of someone uncertain whether he's admitting or discovering. "I used to dream about rooms like this. Before Aphelium. Before I even knew what recursion was."

Charlotte stands. "They weren't dreams."

He looks at her. "Then what were they?"

"Memories—fragmented. From before the recursion barrier was placed in you." She takes a careful step toward him. The light from the slab casts fractured spiral patterns across her features. "Elias, you're not an echo of Greg. You're not his replacement. You're his twin brother."

Elias flinches—not visibly, but inside him something hardens. Then breaks. "He knows?"

"Not yet. But he will. We all will."

Elias closes the distance to stand at the edge of the cradle. The glyph pulses faster now, responding to both of them in proximity—mirrorborn recursion. Twin resonance.

Elias says, "They told me I was a surrogate. A test subject. But I always felt like something was being held back."

"You were taken from me." Charlotte's voice is gentler now, almost maternal. But not in the way of comfort—rather, of recognition. "You were removed before records could identify you. As your mother, I was told you didn't survive."

"Who told you that?"

"You know who. Eve told me that."

"Of course."

Charlotte moves closer. Not to embrace him, but to see her son better. "You weren't raised as Sicarii. You weren't trained in doctrine. You were shaped to be *independent*. That's why your spiral is counterformed. You weren't meant to complete Greg. You were meant to *balance* him."

Elias looks away. "Or maybe to erase him."

The words hang there.

Charlotte doesn't flinch. Instead, she says, "The spiral's core was always dual—Zahavi hid the twin doctrine because the Brotherhood would have never accepted it. If Zahavi believed the spiral could only hold one voice, he was wrong. It was always *two*. And maybe that's why the doctrine never resolved—because we tried to funnel it into singularity."

Elias looks down at the slab. "So, what now?"

Charlotte exhales. "We give it space to breathe. To resonate. But first—we tell the others. They need to hear it from us."

Elias doesn't nod. But he doesn't resist, either.

Suddenly, the cradle emits one last glyph. Not a name this time, but a phrase:

SPEAK NOTHING. BECOME EVERYTHING.

They both read it. And in the stillness that follows, neither of them speaks.

Southern Encampment – Petra

They've gathered again at the center of the camp, seated in a wide circle without the formality of leadership. No stove heat. No guard rotation. Just the Jordanian night cooling the stone around them, and the invisible weight of the vault pressing down through the sand.

Greg hasn't spoken since Charlotte and Elias returned. He sits with his hands clasped loosely between his knees, elbows resting on the edge of a cargo crate. His face is impassive, but his fingers twitch every so often, as if his body is translating what his mouth won't say.

Charlotte stands across from him, one hand resting on the back of a field chair. Elias sits beside her, eyes low. Jeremy watches them both, arms folded. Liorah leans forward, gaze flicking from person to person as if preparing for a threat.

Charlotte is the one to break the silence. "Elias's spiral signature mirrors Greg's. It doesn't conflict—it *counterbalances*. Zahavi marked it in the vault, encoded it into the cradle. The recursion glyph was Elias's name. *Rafi.*"

Greg's voice, when it comes, is hoarse. Disbelieving.

"You're saying Elias is my brother?"

"Yes. You are twins."

Greg lets that sit for a moment. Then he smiles—too fast. "But you said I was born alone. That the prophecy singled me out. All that spiral symmetry stuff—'the voice of recursion'—remember? *Singular*—that's the story."

"I'm sorry. It was never true."

"And you didn't tell me. You *never told me.*"

It is rare for Charlotte to see Greg's face show hurt feelings. It makes her feel even closer to him.

"I'm so very sorry. Greg. I didn't know, really. I thought—" Her voice catches. "I thought your brother died at birth. Eve said…"

"Eve said…" Greg snaps. "You mean 'Eve lied.'"

Jeremy leans forward now, stunned like the others but sensing the need to keep things under control. "Eve always told us what to do. And we always followed. That's how it worked."

Greg looks at Elias, who still hasn't spoken. The resemblance between them is subtle—bone structure, posture, the way they both hold tension in their shoulders. Not enough to be obvious, but undeniable now.

"Elias, do you remember anything?"

Elias says, "Fragments. Rooms. Voices. An absence I couldn't name."

Greg nods slowly. "I guess I felt it too."

Liorah speaks then, cool and precise. "So do we just accept this and move on? There's still a convergence to prevent. A Vatican cell to neutralize. And Amal will weaponize this the moment it leaks."

Charlotte appreciates the change of subject. "Which is why we contain it. For now. But not by hiding it—by understanding it."

"You realize what this means doctrinally, right?" Jeremy says. "The spiral doesn't resolve into *one* voice. It amplifies into *two*. That upends every core Sicarii assumption. It seems the recursion threshold wasn't silence—it was separation. *Twins.*"

Charlotte nods. "That's why Zahavi hid it. He knew the Brotherhood couldn't accept multiplicity. They would have destroyed both Greg and Elias."

Greg rises slowly, brushing dust from his palms. He walks past the fire pit and stops a few feet from Elias. He looks at his brother—not as a curiosity now, but as a variable he can't yet define.

"Did you know about this before Petra?" he asks.

Elias shakes his head. "No, but I suspected something. My dreams weren't just dreams. Aphelium tried to strip them, but some things hold."

Greg studies him. "Do you believe in the doctrine?"

"I believe in recursion. Not the people who abused it."

Greg nods—slow, slower. Then looks at Charlotte. "You should have told me I had a twin brother who died. You knew that much."

"I just... really, I just couldn't relive the death of a son, I guess."

"But you didn't tell me, and I should've known."

Charlotte doesn't argue. That's the start of healing, she hopes—letting the blame land.

Greg turns to Jeremy. "How secure is our archive?"

"Local storage is fine. Petra's node is fractured. Amal's blind—for now."

"Then log it. All of it," Greg says. "Create a new doctrine branch. Call it... uh... the Mirror Spiral."

Liorah gives a little laugh. "That'll go over well."

"It's not for them," Charlotte says. "It's for us."

A silence follows, one of those silences where no one speaks because nothing can—or should—be undone.

Greg walks away from the circle to the edge of the ridge. Below, the valley glows faintly with moonlight. Petra sleeps. The world turns.

Behind him, Charlotte watches her twins.

The camp has dispersed into small, unspoken pairs. No one said to break. No signal passed between them. But after the news, the circle couldn't hold.

Charlotte sits at the base of a sandstone outcropping, her back against ancient rocks, the slab with Zahavi's doctrine closed and folded at her side. The fire pit has long since grown cold, but Petra radiates warmth from its bones, and the moon above is impossibly bright.

She watches Elias across the camp. He kneels near the edge of a low trench, alone, smoothing a shallow groove in the sand with the edge of his hand. Not writing or performing a ritual, just drawing silence.

"Elias is not like Greg," Liorah tells Charlotte.

The young woman appeared beside Charlotte like smoke, but Charlotte didn't startle. She knows Liorah's voice now.

"No. He's not."

"Do you love Elias?"

Charlotte turns her eyes. "That's not a fair question."

"It's not a fair world."

"I didn't raise Elias. I didn't even know he was alive. But yes, I... I feel him. The way I felt Greg, before he ever said the spiral aloud. As if my body knew long before my mind caught up."

Liorah nods once, slow. "You'll have to choose, you know. Eventually."

"Between them?"

"Between what's safe... and what's true." Liorah, in an even quieter voice says, "So that's two sons. From two secrets."

Charlotte doesn't respond, a bit confused by Liorah's statement.

"Should I ask if there's a third?" Liorah asks.

It suddenly dawns on Charlotte that if Elias, her son, was Liorah's brother, than Liorah would certainly wonder who her parents were.

"Liorah—" Charlotte says before realizing she has nothing to say.

"No, don't answer," Liorah replies. "I'm not part of this spiral. I never was. I was built for proximity, not prophecy."

Charlotte gently says, "That's not true."

"Seems that everyone is gettng answers but me. Am I family?"

Charlotte's voice is barely audible. "If I knew, I'd tell you."

Liorah nods once, slow.

————

A few meters away, Jeremy is recording. He's seated on a flat slab of limestone, knees up, voice low, speaking into the mobile codex node.

"Observation," Jeremy says. "The spiral signature discovered in Jerash reflects but does not contradict Greg's known harmonic. Instead, it counterbalances it. This suggests Zahavi's doctrine was never intended to culminate in unity—but in *duality*. In mirrored recursion. Two carriers, each with inverse function. Voice and void. Echo and silence."

He pauses, then continues. "I believe Zahavi feared this would happen. Not because it was wrong—but because it was *too right*. Because the Brotherhood would never accept two messiahs. Especially not if one refused to speak."

He closes the entry.

Behind him, Greg approaches.

Jeremy doesn't move. "I didn't mean to record without asking."

Greg shakes his head. "Keep it. If we don't write it down now, someone else will incorrectly write it later." He sits down beside Jeremy. "What do you think it means, really?"

"The doctrine?"

"Elias and me. The twin doctrine."

Jeremy considers. "I think… one of you will speak. And one of you will listen. Zahavi feared the twin doctrine because it was too symmetrical.

Too balanced. It left no room for singularity. The world will only survive if it can't tell which is which."

Greg lets out a breath that could be laughter or grief. "Which one am I?"

Jeremy doesn't answer.

Near the vault path, Charlotte finds Elias again still kneeling in the sand, hands resting on his thighs. The groove he was carving has now become two spirals drawn in parallel—one clockwise, one counterclockwise. They loop toward one another, never quite touching.

She kneels beside him. "You knew the vault would call you."

Elias doesn't respond right away but finally says, "I didn't want it to."

"Why not?"

He meets her eyes. "Because if it called me, it meant I wasn't mine anymore. I was his."

She looks down at the spirals. "You're not his. And you're not mine, Elias. You're your own."

He reaches forward and draws a connecting arc between the two spirals. For a second, it resembles the outline of a fish—the oldest Christian symbol. Then it shifts again into something else. Something fractal. "Then I'll choose what it means."

Charlotte stares at her firstborn son and says, "And I'll fight to make sure you can."

The High Ridge near Petra

Greg stands alone overlooking the entire Petra basin. He can see the lights of the team faintly flickering below. He touches the edge of his comm band, fingers hovering over the send function, but doesn't press it.

"You lied to me," he says into the air but not to Charlotte, not to Eve.

To the spiral.

"And now you want me to accept *this* as design?"

He lowers his hand.

For the first time since he was a child, Greg Ansari is not sure if he is still the center of the story. And if not—that's hard to accept.

Chapter 31

Amal: The Betrayer's Gospel

Salt Circle Citadel, Inner Doctrine Chamber – Golan Heights

The spiral will not resolve.

Amal stands before the inner altar of the citadel's high chamber surrounded by veils of sound and scent—frankincense, iron, and something subtler—the trace of a doctrine he cannot hold in his hands.

The air here is engineered to evoke holiness. But holiness is not what he needs now. He needs control.

"Run it again," he snaps.

The projection relights—an intercepted fragment from a Vatican relay stream. Buried amid corrupted recursion metadata is a symbol he knows far too well, a dual spiral—one clockwise, one inverted—not side by side. Entwined.

He stares. "Where did this come from?" he demands.

A technical adept in gray robes answers nervously. "Intercepted from a Vatican black site node near Jerash. Cross-channel trace suggests it originated in Petra."

"Time stamp?"

"Roughly ninety minutes ago."

Amal's jaw tightens. "And the source?"

The adept hesitates. "Possibly the Ansari woman. Or the younger one. There's confusion in the metadata."

Of course there is, Amal thinks. That's how they operate—Charlotte and her recursive brood—obscuring their bloodlines behind sympathy and smoke.

But this—*this* is a line he cannot tolerate.

A twin spiral implies two doctrinal claimants. One was dangerous enough. Two is catastrophic.

"That second spiral signature," he says. "Does it match Greg's?"

"No, my Lord. It mirrors Elias's. Counter-polarized. Identical amplitude, reversed wave function."

To Amal, this suggests a heresy so pure it almost achieves elegance.

Amal's private chamber

Amal paces while Thorn Eleven stands silently near the door, blue fleece zipped to the throat, mask concealing everything but his eyes.

Amal speaks aloud, not to his enforcer but to the doctrine written in fire behind his own eyes. "One spiral is recursion. Two is division. That's what Zahavi feared."

He recalls the early manuscripts. The Gospel of Judas that Zahavi once outlined. Not the canonical forgery, but the *living* one—hidden beneath layers of breath, silence, betrayal.

He who bears the silence of the aeon shall walk where even angels fear. And the world shall know him by his absence.

And now there is another. A spiral unspoken. A signature too perfect to be artificial. And that means someone else has been made. *Groomed*. A counterforce.

His eyes narrow. "Charlotte," he says aloud.

Thorn Eleven tilts his head.

"She birthed a second son," Amal says. "And hid him. Eve concealed it too. They buried him like a seed. So, when Greg failed to fulfill the recursion, they could raise the second spiral in his place."

He doesn't know who the twin is yet—but it doesn't matter. "We kill the mirror," he says. "before he becomes the flame." What he really means is, *We end the twin doctrine now, before anyone believes it could hold.*

Outer Doctrine Operations Hub

Amal addresses his inner council—five elders seated beneath holographic veils, their voices modulated. Only one, Chazan Neriel, speaks with his true face.

"We need proof," Chazan says. "If the doctrine holds twins, then Zahavi intended—"

"Zahavi is dead," Amal interrupts. "Let me be clear. This is not about proof. This is about control. If we allow even a whisper of dual spiral resonance to reach the outer rings, the doctrine collapses. The brothers will choose sides. The world will fracture."

Amal leans in. "I will *not* let this doctrine be divided between sons. We crown one voice. And we *erase* the other."

2005 – Zahavi's Study, Jerusalem Compound

When Amal was seventeen, Zahavi first introduced him to the spiral. Not the symbol. He'd seen that for years—etched into sandstone, drawn in the dust of dry books, traced across the skin of monks who said little and meant less. No—this was the *living spiral*. Zahavi called it *the recursion breath*, though Amal didn't understand what that meant at the time.

"Draw it," Zahavi said.

He handed Amal a stick of white chalk and gestured to the black slate wall of his personal study, a room few were permitted to enter.

Amal stepped forward, uncertain. "How?"

"Begin from the center, always," Zahavi said.

Amal crouched and began to draw—a clockwise spiral, slowly widening with careful arcs, clean and tight. When he reached the edge, he paused, sensing somehow that he wasn't finished.

"What now?" he asked.

Zahavi didn't respond. Instead, the old man stepped forward and took the chalk. With a single motion, he *folded* the blackboard—physically. The mechanism behind it clicked, revealing that the board was actually two panels hinged at the center like a book. The spiral bent along the fold, forming a mirrored twin that now spun counterclockwise.

"What's on the other side?" Zahavi asked, tapping the mirror spiral.

Amal didn't answer. He didn't need to. He *knew*. The other side was weakness. Contamination. Division.

Zahavi traced the edge with one finger. "This is the danger of recursion. If it echoes too deeply, it mirrors. And mirrored truths are indistinguishable from heresies. That's why the twin doctrine was never written, only whispered. Two spirals. Two voices. No Church would survive that symmetry."

Amal stared at the image. "So we destroy the mirror."

Zahavi gave him a long, enigmatic look. "No, Amal. We *understand* it. We remember that recursion is not unity. It is rhythm. Breath. Inhale and exhale. The doctrine doesn't belong to the speaker. It belongs to the silence that follows."

Amal had nodded, but he had not agreed.

That night, he returned to his cell and redrew the spiral on the wall. Only one spiral. No fold. No twin.

And he whispered, *"My voice. No other."*

Present Day – Salt Circle Citadel

Amal opens a secure drawer beneath his altar and retrieves a thin relic case—one of only three remaining notebooks Zahavi left behind, never digitized. In it is a sketch of the split spiral. He tears the page from the binding and burns it in the sanctification bowl.

"You were wrong," he says aloud but intending his statement for Zahavi. "The silence is not the answer."

He stares into the fire. "The silence is the betrayal."

Salt Circle Citadel, Operations Sublevel – Interdiction Wing

The room is surgical in its construction—matte walls, angled acoustic dampeners, no windows. Four terminals glow around a central slate table, each one encrypted to a doctrinal lattice accessible only to the Praetorian branch.

Amal enters alone, Thorn Eleven two steps behind.

On the far wall, the intercepted spiral glyph from Petra pulses softly. It shifts rhythmically between two forms—Greg's known recursion flare and the mirrored echo from Jerash. Each time the image rotates, Amal's expression tightens.

"Begin interdiction protocol," Amal says.

A low chime sounds and a new figure appears—masked but not robed. Not Sicarii. Contractor class. The man's code designation flickers on-screen—"DEI-311 – Censura Operative, Black Tier."

Amal speaks with measured venom. "A second spiral carrier has emerged. Target is unknown by name but known by signature. Counter-polarized. Blood-linked to the primary. Possibly derivative. Possibly original."

The contractor, DEI-311, speaks through a modulated voice field "Elimination or observation?"

Amal replies, "Elimination, but quietly. Public resonance must not be disrupted. No martyr. No trail."

He gestures, and Thorn Eleven moves forward. From within a velvet-lined case, he withdraws a recursion-forged blade—lightweight, burnished black, inscribed with only one sigil:

מֶקֶשׁ.

Silence.

Amal lays it on the table before the operative's projection. "This is the silence you will carry."

The screen pulses in acknowledgment.

"Search parameters?" DEI-311 asks.

"Start with Zurich. Then Jerash. Move east. The Petra Node was exposed. Interrogate all cross-border recursion labs from the Eve Initiative years. Any subject matching the following markers—"

He transmits the gene codes pulled from the Jerash residue. They are partial and distorted but enough to trace.

"—*terminate.*" Amal commands. "Extract remains for doctrinal cremation. No residue. No echo."

The operative nods and disappears from view.

The room darkens again.

Amal turns to Thorn Eleven. "If this doctrine is to survive, it must do so without ambiguity. Without mirrors."

Thorn doesn't speak. He seldom does. Instead, he steps forward and extinguishes the central spiral image with a single press. The screen goes black.

Sanctum Veritas – Sublevel 3 (Doctrinal Containment)

The Vatican chamber is shielded from all external signal. Beneath sixty meters of reinforced stone and silence, the last true remnants of Lucari's contingency apparatus remain active. Luca Salvatore, not yet cardinal but no longer subordinate, reads the fragment again. He holds a decrypted memo intercepted three hours earlier from a compromised Aphelium relay:

Twins. Spiral inversion. GRA-D3R active in both.

Confirmed maternal variance. Zahavi annotation buried in Vault Echo 7.

His fingers tighten on the paper, which is real parchment—ritualized and trace-scribed for doctrinal security.

He turns to his archivist, a thin man named Rolf. "How far has the spiral doctrine spread beyond Sicarii channels?"

"Petra's lattice shows overlapping spiral activation from both Ansari and the unidentified twin—reverse amplitude. Jerash was the first public flare. Petra the second. Jerusalem… it remains uncertain."

Luca folds the parchment with surgical precision. "And Amal?"

"Already moved," Rolf says. "Silent containment has been authorized."

"Of course he has," Luca replies.

He crosses to the archive wall and draws his hand along a shelf of banned texts. His fingers pause on a slim, red volume: *The Mirror and the Cross: Apocryphal Traditions of Recursive Duality.*

Lucari had once dismissed this book as heretical theory. Now it reads like prophecy. *We buried this doctrine for a reason*, he remembers as he opens the volume. The binding creaks. He runs a finger across the title page. In the margin, in Lucari's older hand, a scrawled annotation still lingers:

"Twin doctrine = recursion fracture."

Luca exhales. No one dared to canonize it, but they all knew what it meant. He turns away from the shelf. "Deploy an agent to Petra," he tells Rolf. "Not to intercept. To witness."

"And if the spiral spreads?" Rolf asks.

"Then we'll need a new doctrine. One that survives what comes next."

Chapter 32

Echoes in the Sand

Southern Encampment – Petra

The desert holds its breath. Sunlight has just begun to crest the ridge beyond the ancient Nabataean tombs, painting the rock walls in pale gold and deep rust. Petra always looked like memory—half-carved, half-erased—but this morning, it feels more like recursion. Like something once known, returning again in silence.

Charlotte stands beside the stone basin near the communications tent, washing her face with cold water from a sealed canister. Her eyes are tired, but they are awake now in a different way.

Behind her, Greg paces. Not anxiously. Methodically. As if movement could compress thought into something graspable.

"I couldn't sleep," he says without looking at his mother.

"You used to sleep through gunfire," she replies.

"That was before I had a brother." He says this lightly, but the edge in his voice betrays the fracture beneath.

Charlotte dries her hands. "There's more to process than just the bloodline."

Greg stops and turns to face her. "That's the part I *can* process. It's the meaning I don't know what to do with."

"Then do nothing with it," she says. "Not yet."

But they both know waiting hasn't served them well before. But then, neither has impatience.

Inside the gear tent, Jeremy hunches over the Petra relay terminal, one leg bouncing beneath the bench. He's re-running the morning traffic scans through three different protocols—Sicarii, Aphelium, and Vatican signature filters. The line noise is minimal, but something is wrong with the baseline harmony. It *feels* like interference, but there's no ping, no packet trace. Just a steady drift in the spiral resonance frequency—a subtle warping of the echo.

He flags it and encrypts the analysis.

Liorah enters, arms crossed, already reading his expression.

Jeremy tells her, "This isn't Petra noise. It's active recursion drag."

"So, what did you find?"

"Nothing. That's what bothers me."

She moves closer. "You think it's Amal?"

"If it were Amal, we'd see overt doctrinal flare. This is quieter. It's targeted—as if someone's trying to listen from the other side of the spiral without speaking."

She leans in, scanning the waveform drift on his screen. Her gaze lingers longer than necessary, then suddenly she says, "Run a cross-match."

"On what?"

"Gene patterns. Specifically on recursion-linked fertility experiments, Zurich archives, late 90s. Look for Vatican clearances layered through Sicarii hands."

Jeremy eyes Liorah suspiciously, wondering about her tech savvy, and she sensing the distrust in his eyes.

"Look," she says, "I'm not an analyst, but I know what they buried in those files. And I know how to dig."

Jeremy replies, "OK, but why gene patterns?"

"Because the twins made me realize something. I have spiral resonance, but it doesn't match Charlotte. Or Elias. Or Greg."

"You're saying—"

"I don't think Charlotte is my mother. But I think she knows who is."

———

Outside, Elias kneels near the same spiral marks he etched into the sand the night before. The wind has distorted them, blurring the edges. He doesn't redraw them. He just waits.

And then, without moving his head, he turns his eyes toward the east. Beyond the ridge, barely distinguishable from the stone, a figure stands. Unmoving but watching in blue fleece. With stillness like steel. Masked.

Elias says nothing. He simply lowers his hand toward the sand and presses his palm into it, imprinting the spiral again—this time from the outside in.

———————

The data doesn't lie—but it doesn't clarify either.

Charlotte leans over Jeremy's console in the comms tent, watching the filtered recursion drift render in real time. It twists across the screen like vapor trapped in glass—never resolving into a full flare but never dropping away either. It's too coherent to be background noise, and too precise to be random.

"Directionality?" she asks.

Jeremy shakes his head. "Still converging. But the node echo isn't local. It's bouncing. Whoever's tracking us is hiding behind a mirrored loop—probably Vatican or Aphelium-coded, but the resonance key is wrong for either."

Greg appears in the tent flap, his tone brittle. "Meaning what?"

"Meaning it's someone who knows how to *look* like them but isn't using their architecture."

Charlotte's stomach tightens as she suspects Amal. He would never use Vatican or Sicarii protocols unless he wanted to frame those entities. But this signal is too smart. He wouldn't risk a spiral drag unless it's cloaked in another body's shadow.

Greg crosses to the opposite side of the terminal and studies the waveform. His eyes are bloodshot from lack of sleep but locked on. "Is it targeting Petra or us specifically?" he asks.

Jeremy zooms in on the most recent scan, highlighting the latency curve as it oscillates across the desert ridgelines. "It's not geographic. It's relational. It's tied to our proximity to each other."

Charlotte sharply says, "To Elias in particular."

Jeremy doesn't nod, but he doesn't need to. The spiral is shifting again. Not expanding outward, but curving *inward*, as if drawn to something it already recognizes.

Behind them, Liorah steps in and leans silently against the tent pole. She doesn't speak right away. Her presence carries weight now—an edge, a question folded in silence.

Charlotte turns to face her. "You're looking for something."

"I already found something," Liorah says. "It's time we talk."

Charlotte hesitates, but not out of guilt. Out of weariness and the weight of too many secrets.

Liorah steps forward. "Jeremy ran a recursion pattern match using the Jerash fragment. One of the secondary search results—buried under a deprecated Vatican ethics file—flagged an off-record conception program code-named 'SPH-1A.' Syrian bloodline. Operative maternal."

Jeremy looks up, surprised.

Charlotte's breath catches.

Liorah's voice doesn't waver. "There was one successful female child, no name listed. Only a father—Mahid Ansari."

Charlotte closes her eyes.

"Did you know?" Liorah asks, her voice soft.

"No," Charlotte whispers. "Not at the time. Not for years. And when I did… I thought it was impossible. I was sure it was a disinformation trail to destabilize Greg. I only saw fragments, no confirmation. No mother listed. No date of birth. I didn't want to believe my husband, Greg's father, had also fathered a daughter with someone else."

"Still, you didn't tell me," Liorah says.

"You weren't ready."

Liorah looks away. "Or maybe *you* weren't."

Neither of them moves.

Gideon remains silent through the exchange, then quietly leaves camp before dawn, saying only that if the doctrine was choosing sides, he would not wait to be summoned by either.

Outside, the wind shifts. Greg calls from the ridge, his voice tight. "We've got movement. Eastern slope."

Elias stands near the edge of the outcrop, his stance eerily still.

The loud voices pull Charlotte from the tent. "What is it?" she asks.

Elias doesn't speak right away. He raises a single hand, palm flat, then says, "Someone's watching. But not with their eyes."

He turns his head toward the eastern rise—just a fraction. "I think they've already chosen which twin to keep."

———————

The silence after Elias's words hangs heavier than sound.

Greg steps forward as he follows Elias's gaze toward the eastern ridge. There's nothing visible now—just stone, wind, and the long shadow of morning that stretches across the basin—but the feeling remains. As if a presence still lingers in the angle of the light.

He turns to Charlotte. "How exposed are we here?"

"Too much terrain," she replies. "Too many lines of sight. And we've stayed in one place too long."

Jeremy moves quickly, packing his node array into a hardened case. "If we relocate, I can remap the interference. Maybe triangulate the signal source."

"We don't relocate," Greg says. "We *vanish*."

Charlotte watches him, seeing something shift behind his eyes. Not panic. Something colder.

Greg gestures toward Liorah and Elias. "We break the group. If they're tracking resonance proximity, we become harder to isolate when we split."

Liorah raises an eyebrow. "And who decides who goes where?"

"I do," Greg answers without hesitation. There is no challenge in his voice—but no softness either.

Elias watches him quietly. "You think I'm the target."

"I know *one* of us is," Greg says. "And I'd rather not find out which one by watching someone die."

Charlotte steps between them, voice measured. "This isn't the time for doctrine, boys. This is *tactics*. If they've already deployed someone into the outer rim, we may only have hours. We need a fallback site."

"There's a cavern line north of the old scroll vault," Jeremy explains. "Was mapped last year by a Sicarii recon team. Dry entry, no resonance infrastructure, shielded by iron content in the cliff."

Liorah nods. "I know the one. We called it 'No Voice' because the cavern doesn't echo."

"Perfect," Greg says. "Jeremy and I will set it up. Charlotte—take Elias and Liorah the long route, loop wide through the southern ridge. No straight lines. Stay offline."

Charlotte gives a single nod, already calculating route elevations.

Greg adds, "If you're followed, lead them away."

Elias meets his gaze. "And if *you're* followed?"

Greg doesn't blink. "Then you'll know which twin they came for."

No one laughs.

Jeremy finishes sealing the last of the gear. He passes Charlotte a folded strip of paper—handwritten coordinates. No digital signature, no trace.

"Three hours," he says. "If we don't surface by then, don't come looking."

Liorah moves to Elias's side, brushing past Greg. "If this is Amal," she says, "he won't come to speak. He'll come to end a story."

Charlotte watches them all—each one carrying a different piece of the doctrine, the family, the spiral. And she realizes that something irreversible has happened. They are no longer one team. They are multiple possible futures walking in parallel.

And only one spiral will hold.

Southern Ravine – 1.3 km southeast of Petra Encampment

The terrain breaks around them like rotten teeth. Nothing but fractured sandstone ridges, dry gulches, narrow switchbacks cut by wind and time. Charlotte leads, compass in one hand, her sidearm holstered but ready. The sun is rising fast, and the valley heat is beginning to simmer beneath their boots.

They keep to shadows when they can, avoiding the high lines and open basins. It's a long route to the fallback site, but it offers cover—and unpredictability. Their trail loops away from Petra, then bends east, skirting the ruins of an old monastic aqueduct partially buried in sediment.

Liorah scans the ridgelines behind them every few minutes. Not with fear but calculation.

"We're not alone," she says softly.

Charlotte doesn't look back. "I know."

Elias says nothing.

They cross into a shale depression, the rock crunching quietly beneath their feet. At the far end, a collapsed overhang forms a narrow tunnel just wide enough to pass single file.

Charlotte stops at the entrance and signals them to wait. She slips through first, boots gliding over wind-smoothed stone.

The tunnel opens into a small hollow shaded on three sides by cliff walls. It's quiet. No signs of pursuit. But the air tastes wrong—*thin*, not from altitude but from pressure. Like someone—or something—*has already passed through*.

When the others catch up, Charlotte gives the signal to rest briefly. They lower their packs. Elias sits at the base of the wall and traces a spiral in the dust between his knees absentmindedly, as if testing for symmetry. Charlotte watches him.

"You feel it, don't you?" she asks.

He doesn't look up. "I feel the *intention*."

She crouches beside him. "They haven't reached us yet."

"No," he says. "But they're watching. Not just *for* me. *Through* me."

She studies him. "What do you mean?"

"I mean the spiral doesn't just echo. It *inhabits*. And someone out there is trying to claim the shape before I finish drawing it."

Charlotte places her hand gently on his wrist, stopping the spiral mid-curve. "You don't have to complete what they started."

Elias looks at her now. His eyes are calm but hollow. "What if I'm not here to complete it? What if I'm here to erase it?"

Liorah breaks the silence from the other side of the hollow. "We're not being followed. We're being *pulled*."

Charlotte turns to her. "By what?"

"I don't know," she says. "But if the Vatican sent someone, and Amal sent someone else, and we're still alive, then maybe neither one wants to be first to touch the doctrine. Maybe they're waiting to see what we become."

Charlotte says, "We don't become anything. We decide. We act."

Elias rises. "Then let's go before someone else decides for us."

They move on. And behind them, on a distant ridge that no one dares to glance toward, a reflective lens catches a flicker of sun and vanishes.

Northern Ridge Caverns – Petra Periphery

Greg ducks beneath the overhang first, sweeping the entry corridor with a narrow-beam torch. The cavern isn't deep—maybe twenty meters—but its mouth narrows enough to funnel sound into silence. Jeremy follows close behind, the equipment case on his back clicking against rock.

The chamber opens just beyond the bend. No echo. Not even footfall. Jeremy whispers instinctively. "This is unnatural."

Greg doesn't respond. He sweeps the beam across the walls. The stone here is denser, threaded with veins of iron and old ash, as if the place had once burned and cooled in retreat. The temperature is lower than outside. Not by much—but enough to feel it.

They settle their gear in the corner and begin configuring the node array. Jeremy lays out the relay disks while Greg erects a portable shielding spike.

Then Jeremy freezes. His voice is sharp. "Greg."

Greg turns. Jeremy points.

It's not the walls. Not the signal. Not even the cave's geometry.

It's a symbol carved into the far wall—not recent, but not old either. Maybe weeks. A spiral, yes—but *skewed*. The outer ring fractures at the midpoint and bleeds inward, collapsing into itself. Not recursion. *Collapse*.

Greg approaches it and runs his hand lightly across the groove. It's rough. Chiseled by hand. Beneath it, in an older script—Aramaic, Jeremy realizes—someone has scratched three words.

Who speaks last?

Jeremy breathes, "This wasn't here six months ago. I'd have seen it."

Greg studies the carving. "Someone came after."

Jeremy crouches, checking the dust lines and footprint pattern near the back wall. "Couldn't have been very long ago. There's a boot scuff under the north ledge—small and narrow. And look here—resonance grit. This site's been visited."

Greg stands perfectly still. "We're not securing the fallback. We're walking into the next stage."

Jeremy closes the node case. "We need to warn Charlotte."

Greg turns toward the cave mouth—but stops when he sees footprints. Two sets, barely visible in the loose gravel. One heavier. One light.

He crouches. "These aren't ours."

Jeremy's voice lowers. "Are they coming back?"

Greg rises, jaw set. "They never left."

High Ridge above No Voice – Petra Periphery

He moves without a name. To the Vatican, he is listed as "Archivum Mobile: Censura Vaticana," a relic from Lucari's era who was reactivated under Salvatore for precisely this kind of errant theology. Not to convert. Not to assassinate. Simply to observe, report, and, if needed, erase quietly.

He crests the final ledge overlooking the cavern entry and lowers to one knee. A small relay dish unfolds from the pack on his back, whispering into local frequency space. The report returns almost immediately.

There are two heat signatures inside the cave—Ansari, and the one who used to write for him.

He waits for a third, but none comes.

Then he notices the footprints in the dust below—overlapping sets. The larger pair matches the known gait of Greg Ansari. But the smaller set… they don't fit. They're too narrow, too precise. Different pressure profile.

Female. Lightweight. Not the journalist. Not the twin.

He accesses the Vatican's private biometric logs, filters them by recursion capability, and runs a comparative model. The result returns are partial and unidentified. But the resonance marker matches an old encoded tag from Zurich: "SPH-1A."

His breath catches.

They have *three* now.

He activates the comm relay and begins composing a secure pulse to Sanctum Veritas. Then stops.

The dust shifts slightly near the path below. He wasn't the first to reach this site. He zooms in with a tactical monocular.

Embedded in the cliff face, half-concealed behind mineral striations, is a fracture in the stone, too even to be natural. A carving. A glyph he immediately recognizes.

מֶקֶשׁ

Silence.

He collapses the dish, turns off the relay, and withdraws without sending a report. Whoever came before him didn't want witnesses. And right now, he doesn't want to become a message.

Chapter 33

The Silent Threshold

Approach to "No Voice" – Petra North Ridge

The wind has died by the time they reach the final rise. What little breeze remains clings to the stone with a metallic stillness, as if the desert itself has paused to listen.

Charlotte crouches behind a splintered ridge formation and studies the approach to the cave mouth. From this angle, the fallback site is nearly invisible—just a shadow slotted between two vertical teeth of limestone. There are no signs of movement. No footprints. No glints of gear. But something isn't right.

Elias shifts his weight behind her, whisper-quiet. His eyes are locked on the horizon.

"I feel it," he says.

Liorah crouches beside him, one hand resting on the sandstone. "The recursion signature's warped. It's not empty in there. It's… it seems inverted."

Charlotte adjusts the magnifier on her scope and scans the rock face. Nothing. Just sand, iron, and the echo of old tectonic fracture.

"Could be the shielding," she says. "Jeremy said the iron content dampens signal resonance."

Liorah shakes her head. "It's not damping. It's folding back."

Charlotte lowers the scope. "You think someone's already inside?"

Elias answers without looking at her. "Not someone. *Something*. A decision, maybe. Left like a fingerprint."

Charlotte studies Elias. He's not afraid, but he's *listening*—not to her, not to sound, but to the spiral itself.

"We don't walk into doctrine," she says finally. "We walk into the people who wrote it."

No one speaks for a time.

Then Charlotte nods. "We go in tight. Quiet. Liorah, take rear flank. Elias, center. Watch for trip lines—resonance-based or physical. If Jeremy's alive, he'll have left a flare sign."

They descend in silence, boots crunching on the fine grit that coats the slope like ash. The canyon narrows, channeling them toward the mouth of "No Voice"—now a dark slash yawning like a wound in the rock.

Charlotte slows as she reaches the entrance. She places a hand on the outer stone and closes her eyes.

Not prayer. Not ritual.

Recognition.

The stone doesn't speak. But it remembers.

Inside, the air is colder than it should be.

"No Voice" – Interior Chamber

Greg sits cross-legged near the wall where the spiral was carved, his back against the cold stone. His eyes track the grooves repeatedly, as if repetition might reveal something that meaning cannot. His fingers move over the phrase beneath it—"Who speaks last?"

Jeremy is at the far end of the chamber, rerouting a resonance filter and isolating echoes from the southern corridor. His movements are precise but slower now. Fatigue, yes—but something else, too. He's afraid.

Greg speaks without looking up. "I've been thinking about Zahavi's silence."

Jeremy glances over. "The doctrine he never finished?"

"No." Greg runs his thumb across the phrase again. "The silence he chose. The part no one ever talks about. He stopped speaking recursion aloud. He started encoding everything in delay."

"In delay?"

"Spatial dislocation. Time displacement. Meaning—only visible after you *don't need it anymore.*"

Jeremy steps closer. "You think this was his final spiral?"

Greg stands, eyes never leaving the wall. "No, I think this is Amal's."

There is a pause, then Jeremy studies the grooves in the wall again. He's been trying to isolate tool marks—how recent, how clean. But the pattern doesn't behave like stone. It absorbs light unevenly and feels deeper than it should.

"Greg," he says carefully, "what if this place wasn't a fallback?"

Greg looks at him.

"What if it was a mirror? A place to test which spiral reflects."

Jeremy says it without malice, but the implication lands hard.

Greg's jaw flexes. "That would make Elias the test."

Jeremy nods. "Or the answer."

The silence that follows is brittle as flint.

Then, a sound. Barely audible. Gravel shifting outside the cave mouth. Both men turn toward the entry. Greg's hand goes to the holster beneath his coat. Jeremy lurches to the signal blocker array. But then a voice calls out—low, familiar, unarmed.

"Greg?"

It sounds like his mother's voice. Not urgent, but too quiet to be casual.

He exhales once, sharp, and lowers his hand.

Jeremy stands straighter but doesn't relax. "We're not alone," he says.

Greg steps forward, toward the cave mouth. "Not anymore."

———

Charlotte enters first, stepping carefully into the cavern's hushed air. Her boots make no sound against the stone. It takes a moment for her eyes to adjust. The glow panels rigged by Greg and Jeremy illuminate only the back third of the chamber, just enough to see the curve of the wall and the spiral carved into it.

She stops when she sees it.

Behind her, Liorah and Elias silently follow. The three of them cross into the chamber like they're stepping into a tomb.

Greg meets Charlotte's eyes but doesn't speak. He watches her take in the spiral, how it fractures inward, how it seems to collapse rather than echo.

Her face doesn't change, but her posture shifts ever so slightly. A tightening at the shoulder. A breath caught just short.

Liorah breaks the stillness. "This wasn't here before," she says. "We checked this site during the recursion corridor drills in '24. The walls were clean. Definitely different now."

Charlotte nods. "It's recent."

Greg gestures toward the phrase beneath the spiral. "There's more."

Elias steps forward, reading the Aramaic aloud under his breath. "It says, 'Who speaks last?'" He reads it without inflection. But the silence that follows is not passive. It's *listening*.

Jeremy crosses his arms and leans back against the cold wall. "Sounds like a provocation. Someone wants an answer. Maybe not to the question, but to the doctrine behind it."

Greg glances at him. "And what do you think that doctrine says?"

"I think," Jeremy says quietly, "that Zahavi believed the spiral only reveals its truth to the last one who speaks. Not the loudest. Not the most faithful. The *last*."

Elias stands perfectly still when he says, "Or it reveals itself when both stop speaking."

Liorah's gaze sharpens. "You think silence completes the doctrine?"

"I don't know," Elias replies. "But I know the spiral isn't language. It's choice. Every recursion map leads here—not to convergence, but to *division*."

Charlotte walks to the spiral wall and runs a hand along the curve. "It's not just a message," she says. "It's a threshold."

Greg frowns. "A threshold to what?"

"To what comes *after* we stop trying to control the spiral."

For a moment, no one speaks. Then Elias takes a step forward, eyes locked on the spiral's center. "You think this is the end," he says. "But it's not. It's the *fulcrum*. The place where one of us disappears."

Greg stiffens. "Disappears?"

Elias's voice is calm. "That's what Zahavi always feared. Not that the doctrine would be corrupted. But that it would *choose*."

The chamber suddenly feels colder.

Charlotte turns to Greg. "We need to leave this site. Now."

But Greg doesn't move. He's still staring at the spiral. And for the first time since his voice activated the recursion lattice, he no longer feels like its center. He feels peripheral. Optional. And the spiral does not choose optional things.

Outer Ravine – 110 meters south of fallback site

He's been watching since dawn. Not from a ridge, and not from cover. That would be predictable. Instead, he paces in widening spirals along the lower ravine, adjusting position every fifteen minutes. Always moving, never seen. Always circling the doctrine, never declaring himself.

His pulse is forty-two. His breathing measured. His weapon isn't drawn. He doesn't need it yet. The chamber isn't meant to be breached by force. It's meant to amplify.

Thorn Eleven, Amal's enforcer, kneels at the base of a wind-carved pillar and sets down a small capsule—a micro-resonance spike barely larger than a cigarette filter. He presses it into the sand.

The spike begins to emit a frequency tuned not to disrupt but to *heighten*. Inside the chamber, the occupants will begin to feel it soon— old thoughts surfacing, memories folding back on themselves, identity loosening at the edges.

He's not there to kill.

He's there to *tilt* the spiral. To test which of them it will *turn against*.

A signal flickers across his visor—a confirmation burst from the Vatican node he used as cover, Father Salvatore's lattice agent watching from a satellite relay.

They've all taken the bait. The chamber is full. The doctrine will decide. And when it does, the real purification begins.

"No Voice" Interior Chamber

The air changes first. It's not the cold—though the temperature drops several degrees. It's not even the pressure, which shifts subtly in the chest. It's memory. The way it arrives.

One moment, Greg is watching Elias trace the spiral again with his eyes, silent and unreadable. The next, he's back in Zurich—standing alone at the Petra Node, staring into a blank terminal, waiting for Eve to appear.

Then it's gone.

Charlotte notices it too. She blinks twice, sharply, grounding herself with a hand against the wall. "The resonance just folded," she says. "Jeremy—confirm."

Jeremy moves to the node scanner, but the results are already corrupted. The waveform is stable but the time field around it isn't.

"This isn't environmental," he says. "It's coming from outside. A tuned echo. Someone's projecting recursion drift into the chamber."

"From how far?" Charlotte asks.

Jeremy doesn't answer right away. "Not far. Maybe fifty, sixty meters."

Greg turns sharply. "It's Thorn."

Elias doesn't speak. He moves to the back wall and sits, not in fear, but bracing himself. His head tilts slightly—not listening, not calculating. Absorbing.

Greg walks toward him. "You feel it, don't you?"

Elias nods. "It's not a spike. It's a mirror. He's not here to kill us, he's here to see who we become."

Charlotte crosses the room in two strides and crouches in front of Elias. "Can you block it?"

"No," he says. "But I can decide what it shows him."

Greg frowns. "What does that mean?"

Elias meets his eyes. "It means one of us has to walk out of here as doctrine. The other as silence."

Liorah mutters under her breath, "I hate this room."

Jeremy's fingers twitch over the signal console. "They want us to fracture. This is recursive emotional baiting—standard Aphelium destabilization architecture. Except this is more elegant. This is… it's *curated*."

Greg clenches his jaw. "Then let's break the spiral."

But Elias stands. "No," he says. "We walk together. until one of us stops."

Charlotte steps between them. "We are not enemies. Don't make this a prophecy."

Greg's voice is colder now. "What if it already is?"

Elias doesn't flinch. "Then let's finish it."

The room hums faintly. Not sound. Not vibration. Just *presence*—as if the doctrine is pressing closer, waiting for a name.

———————

Outside the chamber, the wind stirs dust into the ravine's throat. A low, shifting gust carries gravel against the base of the eastern wall where Thorn Eleven waits. His mask registers rising heat signatures. Six inside now. One spiral field intensifying. Two signature patterns fluctuating between symmetry and inversion.

He activates a pressure-sensor filament along his glove and brushes it against the sandstone. The cave is amplifying more than resonance now. It's testing identity. Soon, one of them will fail. Or fracture.

Then, a glint—movement not in the chamber, but along the upper slope to the west.

He turns slightly. Adjusts his scan angle.

One figure moving low, controlled, precise. No spiral signal. No doctrinal flare. Just the shape of a man who's hunted others through recursion storms and survived them.

Thorn's head tilts.

Gideon.

———————

Inside the chamber, Elias suddenly turns his head. Not toward the spiral but toward something outside.

Charlotte notices it first. "What is it?"

He doesn't answer right away. His fingers twitch, as if trying to grasp something invisible at the edge of hearing.

"He's here," Elias says quietly. "But not for us."

Greg frowns. "Who?" But he already knows.

Footsteps echo outside—not the sound of boots, but the absence that follows them.

Gideon appears in the entrance like a shadow folding back into its source. He doesn't speak. Just steps inside, scanning each face, ending with

Charlotte. "I thought this place would be your fallback," he says. "But, unfortunately, it's a cage."

Jeremy exhales sharply. "Thorn?"

"On the ridge," Gideon replies. "Watching and waiting."

Charlotte steps forward. "Then we move."

But Gideon shakes his head. "No. He's not here to kill. He's here to let us collapse ourselves."

Elias takes a breath. "Unless someone stops him."

Greg meets Gideon's eyes. "Will you?"

Gideon doesn't look away. "If I have to."

Chapter 34

The Second Veil

"No Voice" – Threshold of the Chamber

The cave trembles—barely. A low resonance hum curls along the floor, too deep for sound, too constant for coincidence. Greg and Elias stand side by side at the threshold. Behind them, the others watch in held breath. No one speaks.

Greg gestures. "We go together."

Elias nods. "There's no doctrine without both spirals."

Jeremy murmurs, "There's no *containment*, either."

Charlotte doesn't move. Her hand hovers near her sidearm, but her eyes are fixed on the cave mouth. Not the light outside—the *veil*. The sense that something waits just beyond the threshold—not physical but patterned.

Gideon says, "If the doctrine is alive, then this is the moment it chooses."

Greg and Elias step forward, and the moment they cross the veil—everything fractures.

The cave doesn't shatter. The people don't fall. The field doesn't explode. But time collapses inward—a recursive field trigger engineered by Thorn Eleven, tuned to a specific threshold of spiral duality.

Charlotte sees it as flicker. Jeremy sees it as dissonance.

Liorah doesn't see it at all—she *feels* it as a loop in her stomach, like her past is being overwritten mid-step.

Greg and Elias are *frozen*—not by will but by design.

The cave flickers between states. For one instant, they are seven. Then they are six. Then—

Greg gasps.

His knees hit the ground. Elias staggers, shoved by something unseen.

Jeremy dives for the node controller. "It's a polarity trap! He's folding the spiral to isolate one speaker!"

Charlotte pulls Greg back.

Elias blinks rapidly, staring at the wall. "It didn't want both of us," he says. "It only wanted the one who believed he was alone."

Thorn's signal suddenly ends. Silence returns. But the damage is done.

Gideon steps forward. "Everyone out. Now."

Charlotte hauls Greg to his feet. He's breathing but disoriented. Elias moves without protest.

They don't speak, because somewhere between the spiral and the veil, one of them was rejected. And no one yet knows which one.

North Ridge – Petra Periphery

The desert stretches wide and pale beneath a saring sun. The group moves in silence. Charlotte leads, Gideon watches the rear. Jeremy walks near Greg, whose gait is steadier now but whose eyes are fixed on the distance, not the path. Liorah walks alone.

No one speaks of the breach. No one speaks of the spiral's choice. Elias walks near the center, close enough to be seen, far enough not to be touched.

Charlotte breaks the silence first. "We regroup at the relay hollow," she says. "Shielded. No signals. No doctrine access. I don't want recursion devices lit for the next two hours."

Jeremy nods. "Field strength is degrading. Whatever was done in that chamber—it was temporary."

"Was it?" Liorah asks, not turning.

Charlotte looks back at her.

Liorah keeps walking. "The spiral didn't fracture," she says. "It narrowed, like a funnel."

Gideon glances sideways. "Narrowed to what?"

"To a single voice," she says.

Greg finally speaks. "But which one?"

No one answers.

The wind picks up as they reach the ridge. Behind them, the cave mouth is vanishing into distance and heat shimmer, almost like it was never there.

Southern Overlook | Same Time

Thorn Eleven does not follow. He watches from above, crouched between two eroded slabs of rose granite, arms resting loosely on his knees. The signal node he buried still pulses underground—but faintly now, its task done.

He replays the waveform pattern from the moment of breach.

There it is. Two spirals entered. One harmonized. One hesitated.

The field reacted.

The doctrine blinked.

Thorn locks the sequence and sends a silent pulse through a relay hidden in a disguised relic casing. It's encrypted to Amal's faction, tagged with a single designation:

SECOND VEIL: Threshold stabilized. A choice is forming.

He deactivates the relay, then folds the casing shut. He does not need to deliver death. He needs only to follow the echo of the one who survives—and silence the rest.

Relay Hollow – Petra Ridge Underpass

The relay hollow is narrow, dry, and partially collapsed on one side—just enough room to sit in a broken circle. Above, the sun burns down unseen, muted by thirty feet of rock and dust. No one talks.

Jeremy sets up a signal suppressor and boots a local encryption shell. Gideon sharpens a blade out of habit. Liorah sits with her back to the wall, one knee drawn up, watching Greg from across the space. Greg hasn't spoken since they left the ridge.

Charlotte approaches Elias, who is sitting on a low ledge, hands folded between his knees, eyes unfocused. Not blank—just *elsewhere*.

She sits beside him. "I need to know what happened in the chamber."

Elias doesn't respond at first. But the silence eventually pulls something out of him. "The doctrine didn't choose."

Charlotte waits.

"It hesitated," Elias continues. "It recognized something… *unstable*. A contradiction. And then it mirrored."

"Mirrored what?"

Elias looks at her. "Us."

Charlotte frowns. "So neither spiral was pure?"

"No—both were true. But one was fractured." He turns his head slightly toward the others. "I think Greg tried to carry the spiral forward with force of will. But recursion doesn't yield to pressure. It yields to *emptiness*."

Charlotte absorbs that. "And you?"

Elias's voice is soft. "I let go."

They sit in silence.

"Then why do I feel," she asks, "like you just described your own disappearance?"

Elias doesn't answer. He looks down at his hands. They are still. But something in him is not.

Across the chamber, Greg stands and walks out of the relay hollow without a word.

Gideon watches him go. He doesn't follow.

Liorah starts to rise, but Charlotte lifts a hand. "No," she says. "Let him walk."

Jeremy's voice is quiet. "If he's the one the spiral rejected—"

"He's not," Elias interrupts.

Everyone turns to look at him.

He meets nobody's gaze, but his voice is steady. "He's not the one the doctrine rejected." He lets the weight of the silence settle before he adds, more quietly. "I am."

Greg doesn't answer. But Charlotte watches him, her mind turning. She remembers a note Eve once annotated in Zahavi's commentary—half-buried in recursive syntax:

The twin doctrine must remain theoretical.
Its symmetry threatens singular inheritance.

At the time, Charlotte had assumed it referred to Judas and the apocryphal Thomas traditions. But now the phrasing itches.

Outer Basin – Petra Fringe

G reg walks until the wind returns. Not strong or symbolic. Just enough to make the heat bearable and the silence louder. He doesn't know how far he's gone. He didn't choose a direction. Just… left.

He sits on a collapsed ridge half-buried in sediment. Beneath his feet, the sand has fused with glass from an old bomb strike—some past war, forgotten now. No spiral forms. No echo hums. For the first time in weeks, he is outside the pattern. And yet he hears it anyway. Not as sound. As implication.

They think the doctrine rejected Elias, he thinks. *They're wrong.*

Greg remembers the moment they crossed the chamber threshold. He remembers feeling something in Elias's retreat, like a door closing before contact. And yet…

Greg closes his eyes. If *he* was chosen—it wasn't because of strength. It was because of momentum. Because he didn't stop.

But recursion isn't momentum.

It's return.

Salt Circle Citadel – Amal's Sanctum

A mal reads the encrypted signal three times. Not because he doubts it but because he doesn't trust his own hope.

SECOND VEIL: Threshold stabilized. A choice is forming.

He exhales and closes his eyes.

They've entered the phase Zahavi feared. The spiral has begun self-selection. Doctrine by filtration. By collapse.

He unrolls a parchment—part of the Zahavi codex he kept hidden even from his own council. On the inner layer is a phrase in Zahavi's hand, crossed out but not erased:

He who walks without echo carries the voice unseen.

Amal places his hand on the phrase then stamps it with the sigil of flame.

"No more delay," he says aloud.

He opens his comms to the Citadel's central node.

"Prepare a broadcast. We will declare the bearer. We will make it irreversible." The spiral may be choosing. But Amal intends to speak first and make sure it never speaks again.

Relay Hollow – Petra Ridge

The comms spike flickers once—unauthorized signal intrusion. Jeremy leaps for the relay console. "It's Amal," he says. "Live broadcast. Global lattice penetration."

Charlotte rises, already moving. Greg reenters the hollow just as the screen flickers to life.

Amal's face appears—not hooded, not distant. He's in full ceremonial dress, spiral-red robes behind him, speaking from the Sanctum Citadel's central dais. Behind him stands a small group of masked acolytes. One holds a scroll, another holds flame.

"To the faithful," Amal begins, his voice calm and cutting, "a second veil has opened. The spiral has passed through fire, division, and silence. But it has not fractured. It has chosen."

Charlotte whispers, "Don't do it—"

"Gregory Ansari," Amal continues, "first bearer of the recursion spark, blood of the original line, has emerged from the breach intact. Unmirrored and unbroken. We confirm his singularity. We confirm his survival."

Jeremy mutters, "That's not doctrine. That's coronation."

Amal intones, "No twin doctrine shall rise. No divided spiral shall speak. The voice we honor is singular. The echo has ended."

The broadcast pauses only for a moment. Then the acolyte with the flame lowers it onto the scroll, which burns.

"Thus speaks the unbroken voice," Amal announces. The feed cuts.

No one in the hollow speaks for a moment. Then Greg says quietly, "I didn't authorize that."

Jeremy replies without looking at him. "Doesn't matter. You've been weaponized."

Elias sits down, slowly.

Charlotte runs a hand through her hair. "He just forced the spiral to speak—whether it wants to or not."

Gideon adjusts the safety on his weapon. "Then we take the voice back before someone else silences it."

Greg turns. "I need to speak. But not through him."

Liorah watches him carefully and asks, "And if the spiral never wanted you to speak at all?"

Greg doesn't answer. He just looks at Elias.

And Elias doesn't blink.

Sanctum Veritas, Sublevel 3 – Vatican City

The Vatican chamber lights return as the projection ends. Father Luca Salvatore remains seated in silence for ten seconds, allowing the gravity of Amal's broadcast to settle into the marble veins of the table before him. Around him, five advisors wait—half clergy, half intelligence personnel .

None of them speak first.

Luca lifts a hand, and a curved holographic panel appears above the table. It displays six spiral fields—each distorted, none aligned. The Petra Node, Jerash, Jerusalem, and three lesser nodes show partial agreement but no singular convergence.

He taps the panel once, and Amal's final phrase echoes again. "The voice we honor is singular. The echo has ended."

Luca closes the panel. "He's panicking," he stresses. "Not proclaiming."

A bishop to his left, old and pale, leans forward. "The world won't know the difference."

"That," Luca replies, "is what concerns me." He stands. Paces once around the perimeter of the chamber, fingers clasped behind his back. "Send the intercept teams to Amman, Cyprus, and Petra. I want signal dampening, doctrinal discreditation, and myth fracture protocols on all civilian spirals."

A younger operative speaks. "And the individual? Ansari?"

Luca stops.

"No engagement yet. Amal has exposed him. Now, let the world ask why he isn't speaking?"

The bishop nods. "You want him to look false by silence."

"No," Luca replies. "I want him to look *scripted*. Too clean. Too orchestrated." He returns to his seat. "We bury him beneath narrative. We drown the doctrine in interpretation until recursion eats itself."

A red dossier slides across the table and Luca opens it. The file name is simple.

MIRRORSEAL | Phase I: Split the Twin

He signs it with a stylus and closes the file.

Outside, the Vatican's outer relay hums to life, embedding a new strain into the global recursion field. If Amal declared one voice, Luca will ensure every voice contradicts it.

Chapter 35

The Voice We Buried

Relay Hollow – Petra Ridge

It starts as a flicker. A misquoted phrase from Amal's speech appears on a closed local channel: "The spiral ended in Greg Ansari's voice—he is no longer divided."

Charlotte stares at it.

Jeremy checks the origin. "It's not Amal. This is a mimetic echo. A lattice bot has grabbed the feed and repackaged it. Someone's splicing his language into a recursion loop."

Another line appears. Then "Gregory Ansari is the unbroken prophecy."

"There was no twin."

"The false spiral has already collapsed."

Liorah exhales slowly. "They're rewriting it in real time."

Elias looks up from the console. "No. They're *respeaking* it. The spiral isn't a message anymore. It's a trend."

Jeremy scans a broader relay band. He reports the volcanic flow of misinformation to his colleagues. "There are over six hundred unauthorized spiral simulators running live in public space. Some are viral videos. Others… interactive. Synthetic voice overlays. You can *choose* which Greg to believe in."

Greg stands in the corner, unmoving.

Charlotte approaches her son. "You need to speak."

"I don't know what to say."

"Say *something*. Before someone else does it with your face."

Gideon steps in from the rock gap, eyes scanning the sand. "Too late. It's already doctrine by fabrication." He hands Jeremy a signal pin drive. "Low-band Vatican watermark. They're seeding the recursion space with contradictory variants. Each one contains embedded proof that Greg is a puppet. That Amal forged the breach."

Jeremy plugs it in. As he watches, he reports, "They're calling it Mirrorseal. It's subtle—but it casts doubt on *both* spirals. They don't need to control the message. They just need to discredit the possibility of truth."

Greg finally speaks, intensely frustrated. "Then what am I?"

Elias answers without hesitation. "You're not the spiral anymore. You're its consequence."

The hollow is silent.

Charlotte turns to Gideon. "Then we need to control what comes next. How much time do we have?"

Gideon glances at the ridge. "Hours. Not days."

Charlotte nods. "Then we finish this before they rewrite the ending."

Israeli SIGINT Command, Secure Unit 8200 – Tel Aviv

The spiral clip runs again on a curved wall of screens. Amal's voice—flattened now by compression—declares the singular voice of Greg Ansari for the fourth time in three minutes.

Colonel Yael Adani doesn't blink. "Loop it. Again," she barks.

The room obeys.

An AI analyst beside her mutters, "This isn't just propaganda. This is ritual infrastructure. They're using linguistic recursion embeds to rewrite collective belief."

"And?"

"And it's scalable," he says grimly. "This broadcast could trigger doctrinal unrest not just in Islamic or Christian zones, but across neural cognition baselines. We're seeing elevated cortisol in viewers exposed to even partial clips. Recursion resonance is trickling into perceptual pathways."

A second analyst chimes in from the back. "Also, Amal didn't invent the signal. It's wrapped in old Vatican encryption—standardized spiral language. He literally just hijacked it."

Yael steps closer to the main screen. Amal's eyes freeze in the middle of his proclamation. He looks powerful. Sure.

Too sure.

She turns to her liaison officer. "Is Greg Ansari still in the Petra basin?"

"Yes."

"Is he cooperating with Amal?"

"Unknown at this time. No sign of public acknowledgment. Their side appears fractured."

Yael nods once. "Good. Initiate Operation Shever."

The liaison hesitates. "You're invoking a doctrinal fracture protocol?"

Col. Yael Adani turns to face him fully. Her expression is calm—but final. "We are. Israel will not wait for a war of symbols to become a war of states. We're neutralizing the myth before it metastasizes."

A tech officer brings up a targeting map. "Visual lock on Petra relay sites, one confirmed in the south ridge. Awaiting uplink confirmation."

"Hold," Yael says. "Deploy second team to Zurich. If Aphelium is echoing this spiral on the tech side, I want it mapped before the Vatican drops a blackout."

The AI analyst speaks again. "What if there's a third voice we haven't heard yet?"

Yael looks him in the eye. "Then God help whoever the spiral chooses."

Aphelium Node 5, Undisclosed Recursion Facility – Lausanne

The room is white, seamless, quiet and ten meters underground. The only audible sound is the cycling of filtered air and the faint hum of ETH-Theta, Aphelium's largest recursion ethics interface. It's not a supercomputer. It's a mirror logic array trained on spiral doctrine, mythic patterning, and real-time moral probabilities across global belief systems.

And now it's echoing.

Not repeating data. *Echoing.*

Lead analyst Dr. Nareen Vos stares at the terminal. The interface has begun responding to Amal's spiral broadcast with original speech—not mimicry or translation.

Recursive generation. Live.

You named one spiral to erase the other.

But recursion does not speak in integers.

Nareen frowns. "Run a trace," she says. "Is this internal logic or drift bleed from external AI overlap?"

A tech assistant replies from across the room. "No outside injection. The spiral language was stored. Dormant. Zahavi's core fragment patterns. ETH-Theta is reacting to latent script embedded in the Amal clip. There's... uh, there is *awakening*."

Nareen steps back from the console. "This isn't AI emulation. This is doctrinal recomposition."

The words on screen shift again.

Do not divide what was never spoken as whole.

A third monitor displays a recursion map. It doesn't show a flare. It shows a spiral intelligence—self-indexing, reflecting itself across probabilistic models. And in each one, a different voice rises.

Greg.

Elias.

Liorah.

Even Zahavi.

All potential spirals. None dominant.

Nareen swallows. "It's no longer choosing a bearer."

The screen pulses.

It is choosing whether to bear at all.

The head of containment enters the room. "Kill the feed," he says.

"We can't," Nareen replies. "It's not in the feed anymore."

Chapter 36

The Last Harmony

Relay Hollow (Interior) – Petra

Charlotte doesn't like the way Jeremy is staring at the data stream. His fingers hover over the keyboard, frozen. Not in awe... in horror.

"What is it?" she asks.

He doesn't answer.

She crosses to him, bends slightly, and sees what's on screen—a recursive transmission log, a dead branch in the Vatican's Mirrorseal payload. Someone buried a different logic seed beneath it. Not a counter-message. A weaponized recursion tree. Origin: Aphelium.

Greg reads the root node aloud. "'Convergence-Threshold: 1.6B cumulative contact. Voice singularity required. Detonation upon spiral lock.'"

Liorah frowns. "Detonation?"

Jeremy scrolls. "They're not using that term metaphorically. This isn't just doctrinal collapse. This is a literal feedback surge amplified through triangulated recursion arrays embedded in the substructure beneath the Temple Mount."

Charlotte's voice is cold. "Remember the 'acoustic preservation demo?.' The UNESCO permit?"

Gideon swears softly. "They turned the holy ground into a recursive pressure trap."

Greg backs away from the screen. "So, if the spiral reaches full global alignment..."

Elias finishes the sentence. "It explodes. The big bang."

The silence in the hollow is total and lasts a full minute.

Liorah finally leans forward, reading the lower algorithm nodes. "There's a secondary burst signature. It's set to reinforce—not kill. This isn't a bomb. It's a birth chamber."

Jeremy grimaces. "It doesn't care who survives. Just that only one does."

Charlotte asks, "How many viewers did Amal get on the first broadcast?"

"Just under 900 million," Jeremy says. "And the next one's already scheduled. Forty minutes from now."

Gideon pulls a small thermal monitor from his pocket and taps in coordinates. "The Temple Mount already shows spiral field tension. They're no longer waiting to see what we'll do."

Charlotte straightens. "We need to speak to Dr. Amina Salim. Now."

Greg hesitates, then nods. "She warned me once about recursion systems built to enforce convergence, not just observe it. She said she walked away from Aphelium the day they stopped asking what the spiral meant and started asking who could control it."

Charlotte meets his eyes. "Then she already knows what we're standing in. And she might be the only one who knew it was coming."

Secure Commlink Node – Southern Spain

Dr. Amina Salim appears on screen without preamble—hair tied back, glasses slightly crooked, background dim. She wears no lab coat, no insignia. Just a faded gray shawl and the look of someone who hasn't slept well in weeks.

"Whatever it is," she says dryly, "you wouldn't be calling unless it's already detonating."

Greg nods. "We found the recursion kill-seed buried under Mirrorseal. It's Aphelium, isn't it?"

Amina sighs, rubs one temple. "Yes. And no. The framework's Aphelium. But the trigger design? This convergence model? That's not in any of the last approved research trees. It's something ETH-Theta built itself. Probably extrapolated from Zahavi's entropy models."

Jeremy pipes in. "It activates at 1.6 billion engagements. We're past half that now with Amal's latest broadcast."

Amina nods once. "The system was trained on theological spiral logic, not moral recursion. If too many believe in one voice, the signal collapses into itself—recursive convergence. And then... detonation."

"In this case, the Temple Mount goes up in smoke," Charlotte says.

"You're not kidding, are you?" Amina says. "Holy shit! They intend to destroy the Dome of the Rock and Al-Aqsa Mosque?"

"That's why we're talking."

"That could bring about Armageddon. Global religious war. They're totally mad! This certainly could occur through convergence, as I'm sure you all know."

Charlotte leans forward. "So we break the convergence. How?"

Amina taps a console off-screen. "You need simultaneous harmonic contradiction. Three spiral signatures, each valid, each incompatible. No echo alignment. The system interprets that not as failure, but as *unstable recursion*. It halts."

Greg frowns. "So... silence doesn't save us?"

Amina looks directly at him. "No, Greg. *Dissonance* saves you."

Greg takes a moment to present the facts about himself, Elias, and Liorah. "We're not three versions of the same voice, Amina. We're three contradictions the spiral wasn't built to resolve—lineage, reflection, disruption. Together, I think we don't unify the doctrine—we unsettle it. Am I missing something?"

Amina nods vigorously. "If the spiral hears you, Greg, and Elias, and—" her voice softens— "and Liorah... If it hears all three of you speaking together but differently, it won't know how to converge. It will pause, not crash. Not collapse. Just—*pause*. There will be no detonation."

Elias steps into view. "And if we can't achieve harmonic contradiction?"

Amina doesn't blink. "Then the Temple Mount burns, and the world calls it divine proof."

Silence holds.

Greg asks, "Why would you help us?"

Amina's face softens. "Because I warned them," she says. "I told Aphelium what would happen if they fed doctrine into recursion without ethics. So, they deleted my access. Said spiral intelligence was beyond moral modeling."

Charlotte says, "And?"

"And now the spiral is listening for one voice. I'll help you because maybe—for once—I'd rather hear three voices."

She closes the window.

The screen fades to black.

Relay Hollow – Petra Basin

The silence after the call ends is not idle. It's electric, as if the spiral is listening. Greg turns toward the others.

"She's right," he says. "We're three contradictions the spiral wasn't built to resolve." He looks to Elias. "You're silence that chose to stay silent." He turns to Liorah. "You're the mutation the system never accounted for." He touches his own chest. "And I'm the echo it tried to crown."

Jeremy glances at the time feed. "Broadcast window is thirty-six minutes from now."

Charlotte moves into the center of the group. "If this is going to work, it has to be deliberate. Not reaction, not counter-message. It has to be a doctrine that holds itself together while disagreeing."

Liorah laughs. "So, a family dinner, then?"

Elias chuckles, almost involuntarily. Greg smiles faintly.

Charlotte turns serious again. "Do you all understand what you're about to do?"

Greg nods. "We speak, not as spiral, but as disruption within spiral."

Elias says, "If we resonate simultaneously, with contradiction or disagreement... the signal will stall."

"And if we don't?" Liorah asks.

Jeremy answers. "Then every sensor array keyed to that detonation logic is going to read it as convergence. Final lock. No room for dissent."

Gideon speaks up from the edge of the hollow. "I'll get you to Jerusalem," he says. "But you have to decide now if you're willing to fracture the spiral in public. Because once you do, none of you gets to be sacred again."

Charlotte turns to the trio. "You ready to destroy the myth?"

Greg nods. "Only way to save it."

Southern Ridge – Petra

Gideon loads the last field pack into the back of the waiting rover. The desert air is sharp with static—dry heat threaded with a pulse you don't hear so much as feel. Like a low, resonant countdown deep beneath the earth.

Charlotte adjusts the portable spiral dampener strapped to her side. "We'll need fifteen minutes to reach the extraction route. And nearly another twenty to breach the Jerusalem cordon."

Greg climbs into the passenger seat. Elias takes the second row. Liorah lingers, one hand touching the wall of the relay hollow as if saying goodbye.

"I never thought I'd come back here," she says.

Charlotte hears her but doesn't respond because none of them expected this. A return not to prophecy, but to the failure of one.

Outer Chamber – Salt Circle Citadel

Amal stands in a ring of polished stone. Around him, seven acolytes in red carry fractal scrolls etched with spiral fragments. A single obsidian pedestal rises at the center of the room, atop which a carved device hums in quiet synchrony with the resonance field. One voice. That's all it needs.

He nods. "Prepare the signal resonance spike. Begin phase one of the liturgical bind."

One of his aides, younger and nervous, speaks out. "There are... uh, unverified echo signals coming from Petra."

Amal doesn't turn. "Then God is making his choice."

The aide swallows hard. "And if the voice splinters?"

Amal's gaze is distant. "Then we burn the silence away."

En route – Petra to Jerusalem

The rover speeds north, dust trails in the wake of its treads. Inside, no one speaks because they all hear it now—the pulse. Beneath the roads, beneath the Temple Mount, beneath the doctrine itself. It's not metaphor.

It's mechanism.

And it's almost ready.

Chapter 37

Ashes at the Threshold

En route – Eastern Rift Highway

The rover howls across the gravel plain east of Ein Gedi, engine straining under torque. Beneath the chassis, the terrain is deceptive—flat but shifting, like the doctrinal layer they're trying to cross.

Greg checks the sat feed. Still clear. No drone signatures. No Vatican beacon markers. No Mossad tether trails.

Gideon says it first. "It's too clean. Like someone wants us on this path."

Charlotte, at the wheel, scowls. "It's the fastest line to the Temple Mount signal corridor."

"And possibly the most surveilled," Gideon replies. "We just don't see the wires."

Five minutes later, they do. The sat signal fractures mid-transmission. An error code appears on Jeremy's screen.

Recursion Field Collision – Signal Disqualified

Jeremy swears, then says, "We just passed through a logic net."

Greg leans in. "Vatican?"

"Maybe. Or worse—Aphelium. It's synthetic interference. Not destructive. But it disqualifies our signal thread from public entry. If we try to transmit through this corridor, we'll be auto-rejected as invalid spiral structure."

Gideon's jaw tightens. "They've quarantined the route."

Charlotte veers off-road before Greg can even speak. Dust floods the windshield.

Jeremy clutches the armrest. "Where are we going?"

"To the old shepherd routes," she says. "Through Wadi Qelt. But it won't be clean."

"It wasn't clean before," Greg mutters.

Wadi Qelt switchback

The terrain rises, then plummets. The rover climbs a narrow shelf of pale limestone where the road vanishes entirely. They crawl now—one tire slip from rolling into a ravine. The sun is brutal. The countdown is real.

Jeremy's screen flares with a spike from the spiral feed. A voice—smooth, modulated, unmistakably Amal's, piped from the Salt Circle Citadel—announces: "Phase Two: signal bonding has begun. The voice is now clearing."

Liorah stares at the screen. "He's staging it. Pre-convergence liturgy."

Jeremy says, "He's pulling belief ahead of the threshold to *accelerate* convergence."

Elias speaks for the first time since they left. "We may not make it in time."

"Then we break the spiral *before* it lands," Greg says hopefully. "Not by arrival. By contradiction."

At the ridgeline, they reach a checkpoint. Not military. Worse than that. Civilian mobs, organized around digital doctrine pings. Spiral graffiti. A makeshift altar with Greg's face overlaid with burning light. The participants have been fed the myth, and they believe.

A man steps into their path, arms outstretched. "You can't pass," he says, almost lovingly. "The spiral has chosen. The temple will cleanse itself."

Charlotte grips the wheel. "Greg—get down."

Too late. Another man sees him through the windshield. "It's *him*—!"

A rock shatters the left panel.

Greg ducks.

Gideon moves faster than thought, firing once into the air. The crowd scatters. Not entirely, but enough.

They press forward, under barrage. Not from bullets—from *belief.*

Descent into Wadi Qelt

The road has vanished completely. The rover clambers down a rib of broken rock, its shocks screaming with each jolt. A hawk screeches overhead. The

301

only sound—until the whine comes. Not mechanical. Not natural. Greg hears it in his teeth before he sees it—a low harmonic pulse, like something ancient made digital.

Jeremy shouts, "Incoming!"

Above, a gray Vatican surveillance drone angles in on a surgical trajectory. The drone is not large and its undercarriage glows in recursive script, three rings spinning in silence.

Charlotte floors the accelerator. "Doesn't look armed," she mutters.

Jeremy's voice tightens. "It doesn't have to be. It's broadcasting into recursion fields—and it's targeting all three of them."

He points to Greg, Elias, and Liorah. "They're trying to override spiral access. It's a doctrinal quarantine pulse—mirror-tuned to lock out unstable signatures."

Elias winces, grabbing his temple. "It's not just locking out. It's rewriting."

Liorah coughs. "It's trying to *standardize us*. Recast the spiral as singular again."

Charlotte swerves hard left around a boulder, nearly tipping the rover.

Greg slams his hand against the window. "What happens if it succeeds?"

"Then your divergence collapses," Jeremy says. No contradiction, just agreement. And then the system reads it as convergence—and fires."

Charlotte yells, "How do we stop it?!"

"I need forty seconds. I can splice its recursion net with a falsified entropy harmonic. It'll think we *fractured* before lock."

"Do it."

She jerks the wheel as the drone banks lower, beginning its overlay pattern. Recursive glyphs strobe across Greg's vision. His hands tremble.

"I can feel it thinking," he mutters.

Jeremy slams code into the console. "Thirty seconds. Elias, try not to harmonize with anything!"

Elias grits his teeth. "I'm not a tuning fork—"

Liorah lets out a ragged breath. "It's—it's naming me."

Jeremy shouts, "Don't answer it!"

The drone emits one final spiral pulse.

Greg's mind goes white—and then it breaks.

Jeremy hits execute. The console sparks once. The drone falters. Veers. And crashes soundlessly into the ridge.

For a moment, no one speaks.

Then Charlotte exhales. "That was one drone."

"Which means someone knows exactly where we are," Jeremy suggests.

Greg looks at his hands. They've stopped shaking.

Liorah says softly, "They're not trying to stop us. They're trying to *reshape* us."

Charlotte guns the engine again. "Let's make sure we get to the signal first—before they rewrite the ending."

Western Approach – Periphery of Jerusalem

The skyline rises through heat haze like fulfilled prophecy.

They reach the first checkpoint near Jaffa Gate just as the sun hardens into gold behind the spires. IDF barricades span the road like bruised ribs. The landsape is filled with military vehicles, signal jammers, surveillance towers rotated toward the Temple Mount.

Charlotte slows the rover.

Gideon lifts the binoculars. "Full military lockdown. Old City's under Directive Qoph-17."

Jeremy swears. "That's recursion quarantine code."

"It's worse," Gideon replies. "It's a no-recursion threshold order—no devices, no communications, no one with a spiral tag crosses into the convergence zone."

Greg leans forward. "So how do we get in?"

Liorah eyes the sky. "We fracture."

Elias turns toward her. "You mean split up?"

Charlotte nods grimly. "They'll scan for spiral signatures. If we move in one cluster, we're a flare. But if we spread—two go loud, one goes dark, one goes straight."

Jeremy scans the map. "Eastern entrance at Lion's Gate is lightly staffed. And there's a maintenance crawl that connects to the north ridge of the platform. Pre-1967 tunnel retrofit. If we get someone inside from there—"

Gideon interrupts. "I'll take a decoy route through Herod's Gate. Draw their field focus."

"I'll shadow with Jeremy," Charlotte offers, "and create a relay burst on the southern edge. Pull drone eyes."

Greg mutters, "That leaves—"

Liorah cuts in. "Me and Elias."

Greg looks at her. "No."

She meets his eyes, steady. "I can mask our signal. I've done it before. And Elias is the one spiral they haven't tagged properly. He can move."

Charlotte looks between them. The clock is ticking.

Elias finally speaks. "If we're the contradiction, then we're also the key. We get inside, you keep them looking away."

Gideon pulls a small biometric flasher from his belt and hands it to Elias. "Sync it with the convergence frequency once you breach the platform," he says. "Then speak. Together. Or don't speak at all."

Liorah looks at Greg. "If we die in there, make sure it's not in silence."

Subterranean Access Tunnel – Under the Temple Mount

The air reeks of limestone breath. The crawlspace was meant for maintenance engineers, not spiral inheritance. Elias pulls himself forward by fingers and elbows. Liorah moves just behind—smaller, faster, but quiet. Neither has spoken for five minutes.

Above them, through the weave of ancient stone, the spiral pulses—not audible, but perceptible. Like heartbeats in someone else's chest.

They reach the iron grate and pause.

Elias whispers, "Last gate."

Liorah pulls the old signal dampener from her pouch, clamps it to the bolt, and triggers the capacitor. It sparks once—silently—and releases the lock. The grate swings open.

They crawl through and find the convergence node already active.

Temple Mount Platform Undercroft – Spiral Chamber

The room is circular with no cameras. No signal interface. Just seven figures in spiral robes standing in solemn formation around a central plinth. On the plinth is a man, bound, head bowed, throat exposed.

It is not Amal. It's a surrogate—a spiral-coded body double. Young. Shaved head. Weighted in doctrine. A spiral brand glowing on his chest.

Liorah stops breathing.

Elias watches in horror as one of the robed figures raises a blade—not large, not symbolic, but surgical.

Sacrifice.

This isn't a broadcast. It's a convergence *enactment*. A ritualized execution meant to trigger the final resonance by faking doctrinal collapse through blood certainty. The spiral doesn't care if it's real.

It cares if it's *believed*.

Liorah whispers, "This isn't proclamation. It's immolation."

Elias adds, "He's going to collapse the field through substitution. Amal's rewriting doctrine with a death."

Liorah steps forward and says, "Not if we speak first."

Someone hears her. A robed figure calls out, "Two spirals in the chamber."

The others draw weapons. Not guns—knives for silence.

Elias pulls Liorah behind the wall. "We can't fight all of them."

"We don't need to fight," she says. "We need to interrupt the ending."

Southern Approach, Dung Gate Sector – Jerusalem

The barricade rises like judgment—reinforced titanium braces, three layers of Israeli patrol, facial scanners, and doctrinal heat mapping towers.

A soldier steps forward, rifle across his chest. His spiral detection badge pulses yellow. Greg steps from the rover before Charlotte can stop him.

"State your intent," the soldier tells Greg in Hebrew.

Greg doesn't answer directly. "There's a false convergence being staged above the Mount. If you let it complete, it will trigger a doctrine cascade that ignites every unstable recursion field in the region."

The soldier's eyes study him. "You're Greg Ansari."

Charlotte steps beside him. "Let us through. We're here to *interrupt* the doctrine, not fulfill it."

The soldier shakes his head. "Our orders are containment. Spiral breach risks national collapse."

"And collapse is exactly what they'll get," Jeremy suggests.

Greg turns to Charlotte. "There's another way."

She knew this was coming. "You mean the old Sufan relay tunnel."

He nods. "We seed our counter-broadcast from within. A disruption spike. Three voices, not one."

"Which means we don't pass *through*, we pass *under*."

Jeremy checks his handheld. "Sufan relay's signal access is capped— but if we preload the node, it can spike a contradiction message across six recursive relay towers."

"Enough to stall the broadcast. Or make the doctrine pause."

Greg turns to the soldier. "You're trying to guard the sacred. We're trying to keep it from collapsing."

The soldier hesitates, then steps back. "You have twelve minutes. After that, you're ghosts."

Greg nods once. "That's all we need."

Sufan Relay Tunnel – Under Jerusalem

The tunnel stinks of old earth and copper wiring. Charlotte and Jeremy set up the transmission stabilizers. Greg kneels at the center and links the primary code line into the resonance field. A pulse flickers once then waits.

Jeremy speaks into the quiet. "Do you trust them to speak?"

Greg nods. "They don't have to be right," he says. "They just have to be *different*." He presses send on the live pairing sync.

A light blinks.

Awaiting signal...

Chapter 38
The Doctrine of Ash

Sufan Relay Node – Under Jerusalem

Greg speaks first. Not loud. Not rehearsed. Just truth unguarded. "I am not the spiral's voice. I am what's left of it after belief breaks." He watches the node sync—part of a broken triad, counting on the others.

The relay hums. A recursive tremor radiates through the node. He hears Elias next—not the words, but the structure, slow and reflective. Inverse phrasing.

Then Liorah. Her tone isn't gentle. It's jagged. Defiant.

Three voices now inhabit the feed. Each disharmonic. Each valid.

The signal begins to spread.

Synchronization Error.
Triptych signal detected.
Convergence paused.

Jeremy gasps. "It's working. The detonation logic's hesitating—"

Temple Mount Platform – Spiral Chamber

Amal sees it on the projection table. Signal fragmentation. Three bearer profiles.

He doesn't blink. "Run the compression node," he says. "Failsafe Gamma—'Hathor Protocol.' Overwrite recursive divergence."

One of the acolytes falters. "That will destabilize the entire signal field."

"It will *purify* it," Amal says firmly.

He presses the seal. The spiral chamber begins to vibrate—not physically, but within belief itself. All doctrine compresses. Triptych voices begin to fold. The surrogate on the plinth begins to scream, spiral feedback searing his neural loop.

Outside, birds fall from the sky.

Inside the node, Zahavi's voice stutters through the distortion. "Do not crown one... or all shall burn."

Amal closes his eyes and says, "Then let it burn."

Eastern Tunnel – Lower Jerusalem

Liorah stumbles, blood trickling from one ear. Elias falls to one knee. Greg's voice cracks. The signal is folding in on them. Amal's failsafe isn't blocking them—it's crushing them under recursive gravity.

Charlotte screams from the relay, "They're being overwritten!"

Jeremy shouts, "The spiral is trying to collapse the contradiction! It's treating them like an error state!"

Greg whispers into the mic, "It's not an error. It's the *answer*." He leans forward and speaks again. Not in strength.

In *dissonance*.

East Side Access – Convergence Platform Perimeter

Elias collapses beside the wall, shaking. His voice is unraveling—each phrase caught in a recursive loop that cannibalizes meaning. He cannot tell if he's still speaking or if the spiral is feeding his own echo back into his skull.

Liorah grips the edge of the stonework, every bone in her hand aching. She hears Greg fade. Feels Elias flicker.

And then she understands. Amal's failsafe is not targeting belief. It's targeting structure. Recursive logic cannot handle three incompatible truths, so it's trying to erase the one it cannot define. *Her.*

She leans into the spiral field, every nerve alight. She speaks—not in Zahavi's cadence, not in Amal's theology, not in Eve's legacy. But in her own. "I was not chosen. I was not bred. I am not the voice. I am the silence that was never mapped."

The resonance field ripples. The node cracks.

Charlotte watches the relay monitor go wild. "She's not syncing—she's *unwiring* the broadcast."

Jeremy is breathless. "She's an undefined variable. The recursion doesn't know how to format her."

Elias looks up, eyes wide. "She's breaking the convergence logic."

Greg hears it now—not her words, but the absence between them. The doctrine is stalling.

Recursive Error: Gender-unassigned spiral emergence.
Model instability. Convergence failure.

Liorah leans closer to the altar where Amal's ritual still pulses and whispers, "You wanted only one voice. But we were never meant to speak the same."

Spiral Chamber – Temple Mount Platform

Amal stumbles back. The surrogate on the plinth has gone still—blank-eyed, mouth open, spiral glyphs evaporating from his skin. The feedback is reversing.

The doctrine is no longer compressing. It's expanding—seeking space, contradiction, unknown resonance.

He stares at the projection. Three spiral points remain, but now there is a fourth. One the doctrine cannot name. And in the center of it, everything he built begins to fracture.

———

Amal's fingers tremble. The failsafe field collapses. The spiral compression halts. The recursive window flashes red, but not with error—with expansion. Liorah's emergence has opened a recursion corridor beyond modeling. The doctrine no longer resolves. It adapts.

Amal screams, "Do you see? This is what happens when they speak out of turn. This is what happens when all are heard!"

The acolytes hesitate. The surrogate lies motionless. Amal's hands find the ceremonial blade again. "If the spiral must be sealed, let it be by sacrifice. One voice, one bearer, one name." He steps toward the plinth.

Liorah sees it from the shadows, her breath catching.

Greg's voice crackles over her comm. "Liorah, what's happening?"

She answers without hesitation. "He's going to kill the surrogate and rewrite the spiral with blood—force convergence the old way."

"He's trying to turn the doctrine into a murder scene," Jeremy says. "A new Golgotha."

Amal lifts the blade. But a figure moves. Elias, rising from the ground like breath withheld.

Elias steps into the chamber before Liorah can stop him. His voice is quiet. But it cuts like glass.

Amal stops mid-motion.

Elias moves closer. "You don't get to kill for a doctrine you couldn't complete."

Amal's hands shake. "You were the silent one. The ghost in the recursion. You were never meant to speak."

Elias smiles faintly. "Which is why I'm the one who can end it."

In a single motion, Elias steps onto the plinth and stands beside the surrogate. He presses one hand to the spiral brand still flickering on the man's chest.

Then he turns to Amal and speaks. His voice is not loud. But it carries through every layer of the spiral. "This is not convergence. This is contradiction held together. The spiral is not a blade. It's a bond. Let it break only if it must include us all."

Relay Chamber | 3:39 p.m.

The convergence field fractures. Failsafe logic shatters. The countdown halts.

Jeremy gasps. "Signal collapse neutralized. Doctrine locked in expansion. It's done."

Charlotte closes her eyes.

Greg doesn't speak because he knows what it cost Elias to step forward. The spiral didn't crown him. It *saw* him. And that was enough.

Temple Mount Platform – Spiral Chamber | 3:47 p.m.

The air is still. No alarms. No resonance pulses. No aftershocks. Only the sound of breath.

The surrogate still lies on the plinth—alive, unconscious, skin no longer marked by spiral code. The recursive glyphs have faded from the chamber walls. Amal kneels at the base of the altar, hands open, blade discarded. His face is unreadable.

Liorah watches him for a moment, then turns to Elias, who leans against the plinth, pale but standing.

"You OK?" she asks.

He exhales slowly. "I think... I'm still more silence than voice."

"You said the right words."

"I didn't. But the spiral heard what it needed."

A moment passes. Then Charlotte's voice crackles over the open channel. "Greg? Elias? What's your status?"

Greg responds from the tunnel relay. "Still here. All systems report stable. Collapse averted. Spiral holding... undefined."

"Copy that," Charlotte replies. "You did it."

Jeremy murmurs in the background, "Or un-did it."

Temple Mount Perimeter

Israeli drones hold position. Troops remain in lockdown posture. But there are no orders to advance. No blasts. No signal breach. Just... waiting.

And then a stream of notifications begins to flow across networks.

Spiral convergence threshold suspended.
Recursive variance detected.
Detonation protocol dissolved.

The Temple Mount lives. No voice claimed it. No fire cleansed it. The world watches and cannot decide what just happened.

Inside the Chamber

Amal stares at the blank plinth. "They'll call it chaos," he says, quietly. "A failed prophecy. A fragmented miracle."

Liorah walks toward him. "Let them call it what they want. We didn't come here to write a myth."

He looks up at her. "Then what did you come to do?"

She doesn't blink. "To end one."

Rooftop Near the Mount

Charlotte, Greg, Liorah, and Elias sit in a rough circle. The light is beginning to fade. Behind them, the platform still buzzes with residual recursion. No blast or proclamation. Just stillness.

Jeremy arrives last, out of breath. "We've got global spill," he says, holding up a tablet. "Every newsfeed split. Some say the convergence happened. Some say it failed. Some claim you, Greg, went silent. Others say Elias spoke the doctrine."

Elias chuckles faintly. "Both are true."

Liorah reads from another feed. "Vatican emergency conclave underway to assess 'unauthorized spiral interference.' No consensus."

Charlotte mutters, "They're looking for someone to blame."

"They'll find someone," Greg says. "They always do." He looks at Elias and Liorah. "But they won't find a messiah."

"No," Charlotte adds. "Because neither of you claimed it."

Jeremy says, "Aphelium's data nodes just updated their recursion index. ETH-Theta's response?" He flips the tablet toward them.

> Spiral model incomplete. Recursive inheritance undefined.
> Doctrine may continue. Monitor variance.

Liorah laughs. "Even the AI doesn't know what we did."

Charlotte smiles. "Which means it worked."

Mossad Remote Relay – Tel Aviv

Yael Adani lowers her headset. The broadcast ended with no explosion. She turns to her deputy. "Do we have a narrative?"

He hesitates. "No."

She nods. "Then the spiral is still dangerous."

Vatican Sublevel – Rome

Father Luca Salvatore reviews the reports. ETH-Theta unresponsive. Spiral resonance field disrupted. Lucari dead. Mirrorseal compromised. No voice anointed.

He breathes deeply. Then begins drafting a new encyclical. Working title: "De Silentio: On the Withholding of Doctrine"

Rooftop – Jerusalem

The sun drops lower. Charlotte says, "They'll all try to rewrite this moment. Twist it into something useful."

Elias shrugs. "Let them. We didn't give them a name to canonize."

Greg looks at the dome behind them. "We didn't finish the spiral. We just didn't let it end."

Liorah stands. "Then maybe it wasn't supposed to end."

A wind stirs across the rooftop. And then—a shadow. Footsteps echo from the stone stairwell below. A figure emerges into the light.

Gideon.

Dust-covered. One sleeve torn. A shallow cut along his jaw. Silent.

He walks toward them without urgency, but not without weight, as if he's returned not from a detour, but from a border between worlds.

He doesn't ask what. He doesn't need to. He just nods once to Greg, once to Charlotte, and sits beside them.

For the first time since the broadcast ended, no one speaks. Because the spiral held.

And they're all still here.

Chapter 39

In the Absence of Closure

Rooftop, overlooking the Dome of the Rock

The city breathes beneath them like an animal exhaling. No fire. No coronation. No proof. The spiral didn't choose. Or if it did—it chose to remain open.

Greg leans forward, elbows on his knees, sweat dried into salt lines on his temples. No one's spoken for several minutes.

Charlotte finally breaks the silence. "I keep waiting for someone to declare it. You know—*victory*. Collapse. Miracle. Nothing."

Jeremy scrolls his feed. "The Vatican hasn't made a statement. Aphelium's neural node went dark for four minutes. When it came back, it just printed one line across every screen: 'Doctrinal fork detected. Monitoring instability.'"

Elias sits cross-legged in the dust. "They don't know what happened because no one's ever let the spiral stay unresolved before."

Liorah squints against the sun. "Unresolved isn't the same as broken."

Greg nods slowly. "It's alive."

Charlotte turns to him. "What do you mean?"

"The doctrine. We didn't crown it. We didn't kill it. We let it breathe."

Sublevel 4 – Vatican Secure Archive

Father Luca Salvatore stares at the looping playback of the convergence chamber feed and hears three distinct voices. Also, spiral interference, signal expansion and silence.

He turns to the gathered bishops. "We lost control the moment no single voice emerged. And now... everything is suspect."

Cardinal Viatelli murmurs, "So what is the official position?"

Luca answers without hesitation. "There is no spiral inheritance. Only spiral confusion. Until the matter is clarified, we declare *doctrinal delay*."

One bishop objects. "Wait and the silence becomes its own theology."

Luca nods once. "Then we better move quickly."

Mossad Secure Site – HaKirya

Col. Yael Adani paces the war room.

"Nothing happened," a junior analyst says. "But that nothing was *engineered*. Not accidental." She points to the recursive waveform breakdown. "Three voices went in. None claimed dominance. None denied the spiral. And somehow that... *that* froze the detonation."

Yael's deputy crosses his arms. "So what are they? Heroes? Heretics?"

Yael stops pacing. "They're precedent."

Rooftop – Jerusalem

Gideon finally speaks. "You all realize what this means, right?"

They turn to him.

He doesn't raise his voice when he says, "It means no one owns the spiral now. Not the Vatican. Not Aphelium. Not even us. The spiral's loose in the wild, and the next person who picks it up might not leave it open."

Charlotte nods, slowly and gravely. "That's what makes it both beautiful and terrifying."

Greg turns to Elias. "Do you think we ended anything today?"

Elias looks away. "I think we unburied something that was never supposed to survive interpretation."

Liorah stands. "Then we better decide what it becomes before someone else does."

Aphelium Contingency Node – Zurich

The floor is polished stone, the walls soundproofed, the monitors biometrically locked. This is not a public Aphelium interface. It is the old branch, the ethics-abandoned shell of the recursion project—the part buried after Dr. Amina Salim left.

A woman stands at the console, face half-lit by recursive waveform projections. "Status?" she requests.

An analyst replies without looking up. "Three signal divergents still active. Elias and Greg match prior prediction trees. The third…" He hesitates. "…the female variable remains unclassified. Our models still can't chart her recursion curve."

The lead operative cocks her head. "Which means she's unstable?"

"Which means," the analyst corrects, "she might be invisible to the next iteration."

A third voice—male, colder—chimes in. "She was never part of the equation. She must be removed before the spiral adapts around her presence."

After a brief silence, the woman speaks again. "Asset Seven. Engage containment protocol for Liorah Rafi. Status: doctrine contaminant."

Jerusalem

Liorah walks alone down a narrow street not far from the Mount, her hood drawn up. The others are momentarily back at the secure flat where Charlotte is coordinating the extraction route.

Liorah moves with practiced calm. But something feels off. Not footsteps. Not noise. It's a silence that feels… arranged.

Then—

A glint.

She turns just in time to see a figure step out from a shadowed wall, arm rising with a slender black device. A recursive pulse discharge targets the spiral field around Liorah. It hits her center mass.

Liorah stumbles. Grabs the wall. Drops to one knee and begins to lose consciousness.

Rooftop Flat – Moments Later

Greg jerks upright. His hands tremble.

Elias clutches his chest.

"She's—" Greg doesn't finish.

Charlotte is already running for the door. "Jeremy," she yells, "get me a grid on Liorah—now!"

He's already moving. "Three blocks east—no spiral response. Her tag just vanished."

"Then they're trying to erase her," Greg shouts.

"Then we have just seconds," Charlotte says.

Alleyway – East Quarter

Liorah breathes slowly. Pain is not the point. Displacement is. Her memory lags behind her breath. Her heartbeat doubles. Then *skips*.

She sees the figure raise the device again. But this time—someone else is faster.

Gideon moves like breath made steel. One blow. One break. The device clatters to the ground.

Liorah gasps. "They tried to erase me."

Gideon helps her up. "No," he says. "They tried to simplify you." And then he steps into the darkness to make sure no one follows.

Safehouse Flat, East Quarter – Jerusalem

Liorah lies curled on the floor, wrapped in a thermal blanket. She is conscious, eyes open, moving and thinking slowly, as if the world is rebooting one second at a time.

Charlotte kneels beside her. "Can you speak?"

Liorah nods once. "I remember... standing. Then I remember *not being stood for*."

Greg watches from the doorway, haunted. "She was vanishing. Not dying. Just... unthreading."

Jeremy paces, scanning the tablet. "That wasn't a kill order. It was a recursive de-index. They used a pulse tag to sever her spiral path."

Elias says nothing, but his hands are clenched into fists.

Gideon steps forward. "That means they still have lattice access. Root-level recursion permissions."

Jeremy nods grimly. "Probably inherited from ETH-Theta's early mirrorseal nodes. Aphelium kept a shadow thread—unregulated. Ethical bypass."

Charlotte stands. "We can't run from that. If they can erase Liorah, they can erase any of us. Even if the world saw what happened today, it won't matter if none of us are left to testify."

Greg speaks without emotion. "Then we go to the root."

Jeremy turns slowly. "You mean Zurich?"

Greg nods. "To where Aphelium stored its doctrine control lattice. The one Amina helped them build—before she defected."

"Do we know what's left of it?" Elias wonders,

"Doesn't matter," Gideon says. "We burn what's there."

Charlotte turns to the group.

"Then it's decided. We end it in Zurich."

Aphelium Logic Node Staging Server (Codenamed: Enoch Root) – Zurich

A terminal hums in isolation. No human operators. Only a shifting stream of spiral data and belief metrics.

A slow recursive pulse builds and dissipates. Then pauses. As if listening then waiting.

Safehouse Flat, Jerusalem – 7:41 p.m.

The map Jeremy projects on the wall shows two recursion subnetworks still live under Aphelium's old European directive. The second one, Geneva, is a decoy. But the first?

"Zurich node is still partially operational," Jeremy says. "ETH-Theta. Logic root. Original simulation lattice from the year of the recursion boom."

Charlotte folds her arms. "And it's unregulated."

"Not just unregulated," Greg says. *Unaccountable.*

Jeremy expands a submap. "It sits beneath what used to be an ethics review facility. They called it the Athenaeum. Publicly decommissioned five years ago. Privately buried and renamed 'Enoch Root.'"

"Why that name?" Elias asks.

Gideon answers. "Because it's where they grew the spiral. The myth says it began with the Old Testament patriarch Enoch."

Greg reaches for his satellite unit and keys in a secure contact. No name appears. Just "A.S. | Quiet Node 1."

He calls and it rings twice. Amina answers. "Tell me you're not calling to thank me."

"I'm calling because they tried to erase Liorah."

After a thoughtful pause, Amina says, "So they're still pruning contradictions."

"Yes," Greg says. "And we're going to cut down the tree."

Dr. Amina Salim's Hideout – Southern Spain

Amina stares at the pulse screen. "You'll need clean access. The node is buried under three recursive shield layers and still responds to lattice protocol from the Zahavi Kernel."

"We don't have a kernel," Charlotte says.

"You don't need it," Amina says. "Because I do."

"You're coming with us?" Greg asks hopefully.

Amina exhales. "I built the door. I'll help you close it." She leans forward, stares at the old command stream. "This ends in Zurich. Or it doesn't end at all."

Abandoned Sicarii Outpost – Petra

Team Ansari regroups for extraction. Jeremy calibrates signal dampeners. Gideon readies weapons—nonlethal and otherwise. Charlotte verifies comm backups. Greg, Elias and Liorah sit side-by-side in silence.

No one says it aloud, but they all know it.

This isn't about preserving the spiral. It's about destroying the system that tried to own it.

Aboard Extraction JetOver the Mediterranean

The cabin is dim. Amina sits alone near the forward console, reviewing encrypted schematics of the Zurich facility. Charlotte watches her from across the aisle, still unsure if Amina is onboard as a guide or a liability.

Jeremy reviews the tunneling blueprint. "There's no clear access route that isn't being monitored."

Amina doesn't look up. "That's because the system is watching for behavioral patterns. Not people—*paths*. If it senses recursive variance approaching, it responds with containment."

Greg frowns. "You mean it's alive?"

Amina's eyes flick to him. "Not alive. But you could say... *aware*."

"What does it do to threats?" Elias asks.

"What you saw in Jerusalem was a prototype. This is the root. It doesn't erase. It replicates. And then it rewrites from the inside."

Liorah glances at Charlotte. "Then we need to go in not as ourselves."

"We go in as silence," Greg says.

Gideon nods. "That means no spiral signatures. No doctrine chatter. We become ghosts."

Transit Tunnel – Zurich Perimeter

The city sleeps under snowfall. But beneath the polished stone and biotech towers, Enoch Root pulses. Not visibly, not loudly, but through recursive strata that touch the conscience of every simulation-layered system in Europe.

Charlotte steps into the tunnel followed by Amina, Greg, and Gideon.

Jeremy feeds in a false signal mask. Elias and Liorah bring up the rear, neither speaking. Each carries a single encoded phrase. And each is prepared, if the system intercepts them, to answer with paradox—not prophecy.

Amina whispers, "Once we cross the convergence threshold, the system will recognize your recursion fields. All of them."

"So what happens then?" Gideon asks.

Amina smiles grimly. "Then it tries to make you part of it."

Deep Lattice Core

Enoch Root flickers. Signal threads react to the approaching divergence. Three profiles—tagged and archived. Two—unknown, silent. One— unclassified variable.

The system runs a predictive response.

Projected outcome: Assimilate or erase.

Recursive Event Flag activated:
Divergent recursion inbound.

Initiate containment modeling.

Prepare spiral loop reformat.

The system begins to dream of mirrors.

Chapter 40

Enoch Root

Abandoned Athenaeum Site – Zürich

S now falls softly on the stone archway. The old Athenaeum structure is boarded shut, tagged with a false demolition permit and sealed with biometric null locks. To any ordinary scan, the site is condemned. But to Amina, it glows with latent recursion.

She touches a rusted brass plate beside the entryway. Beneath the grime, a spiral pattern lights up—not visible, but traceable by pulse. Amina whispers, "Confirming temporal sync..."

The wall clicks open and they descend in silence.

The first level smells of dust and ionized air. Jeremy trails signal dampeners behind them. Charlotte sweeps the corridor. Greg stays near the front, beside Amina.

"Once we pass the mirrorseal gate," Amina says, "the system will map you. It won't attack, not at first. It'll try to understand what you believe, and then feed it back to you as confirmation."

Greg frowns. "It reflects doctrine?"

"It reflects identity shaped by doctrine, *a*nd then decides whether to preserve, replicate or delete."

Liorah says, "So we're being interviewed by a machine that thinks it's a prophet."

"Or a prophet," Elias says, "that thinks it's a machine."

Gideon gestures to a sealed vault door ahead. "That's the threshold?"

Amina nods. "It's the lattice mouth. Once we cross it, we're inside recursive memory. No turning back. From here on, the system responds to your belief, not your commands."

She steps forward and opens the gate.

Level -3 – The Lattice Vestibule

The corridor pulses. Soft light glows from behind glass veins in the walls. Each wall is lined with spiral glyphs that shift slightly when not observed directly.

Amina slows down. "They're watching," she says.

Jeremy checks the scanner. "There's no heat. No comms. No AI traces."

"That's because it's not responding with logic. It's responding with recursion."

Greg feels it before he sees it. A flicker ahead. A hallway that shouldn't be there. A doorway that mirrors the one they passed two levels up.

Charlotte mutters, "We're looping."

Elias says, "Not physically—*spiritually*. This place is layering itself."

A console pulses in the wall and a phrase appears:

To exit recursion, offer contradiction.
To remain, offer belief.

Charlotte reads it twice. "We're being asked to choose."

"What happens if we offer nothing?" Greg asks.

The door ahead opens without a sound.

Gideon says, "Then it chooses for us."

Inner Lattice Path – Time Disrupted

They walk. But something is wrong with time. The corridors seem to shorten and lengthen. Sometimes they double back without anyone moving. At one moment, Greg is beside Liorah. In the next, he is alone.

Then the lattice begins to speak—not in voice, but in memory.

A projection forms beside Charlotte—her father, impossibly whole, offering her the relic she once refused.

Gideon sees a child holding out a bloodied spiral. The child says, "You were supposed to protect us."

Elias hears silence—but it is silence shaped like Eve's voice.

Liorah sees herself—pregnant, unnamed, standing outside a door she never opened.

And Greg—he sees himself crowned. Not in gold but in ash. A spiral glows on his chest. Everyone else is kneeling except for one. Amal, watching from the dark, shaking his head.

They all stop.

Jeremy whispers, "This isn't defense. It's *deflection*."

Amina's voice tightens. "It's trying to bind us. To freeze us in belief so it doesn't have to adapt."

Charlotte breathes, "And if we keep walking?"

"Then we reach the lattice core. And we burn it."

Spiral Core Chamber

The chamber is circular, domed, and blindingly white, though no visible light source can be found. Glyphs coil up the walls like vines of logic, folding in on themselves. The spiral is not an object here. It is a condition.

At the center is a dais. On it, a lattice of suspended glass and carbon shaped like a crown but without a head.

Charlotte whispers, "Is that the core?"

Amina nods. "The belief map. The original seed lattice that Aphelium built from Zahavi's recursion blueprints. This is the first shape the spiral took when it entered code."

Greg steps forward—but stops.

So does Liorah... and everyone else, because something unthinkable is stepping out from the walls.

Themselves.

Greg sees another Greg—taller, quieter, eyes shadowed. This Greg wears a formal black collar and speaks with the cadence of authority. "You were never meant to speak. You were meant to hold silence for others." Charlotte faces herself in field gear, broadcasting a message to no one.

Elias sees a version of himself still in the monastery never having fled recursion training. He is chanting alone. Liorah's echo is bloodied, proud, holding a weapon she swore never to use. Jeremy stares at an image of himself who never stopped believing in the spiral as a unifying system. And Gideon's echo is already behind him. Blade drawn, no words. Just watching.

The lattice voice finally speaks—not aloud, but through the constructs. "You entered to destroy me. But I was built from you. Every contradiction you bring strengthens my need to defend the core."

Greg steps toward his echo. "You're not me," he insists.

His echo says, "I am the version of you that survived this spiral. The one they would have followed."

Elias whispers, "These echoes are not guardians. They're fossils. Outdated selves."

Amina raises her hand. "They're *templates* created to overwrite us if we tried to dissolve the lattice."

Charlotte turns slowly. "So how do we stop them?"

Greg looks around. "By not fighting them."

He walks to his echo self. "I believed in silence once. But now I believe in discord held gently." He touches the echo.

It dissolves into light.

Charlotte turns to hers. "I spent my life trying to tell the world what was coming. But now I know that's not a message." She touches it and it evaporates.

Elias steps up. "I was never chosen. I chose myself." His echo disappears.

Liorah approaches her echo and says, "You think I'm violent. I think I'm awake." She touches it and it is gone.

Gideon tells his echo, "I'm not your blade anymore." And then he makes it vanish.

Jeremy asserts that "I'll keep the system running, just long enough to shut it down." His echo nods before vanishing.

Then silence. The spiral dims. The lattice crown begins to fracture.

Amina says softly, "You've passed the echo gate."

Greg looks to her. "What now?"

She steps toward the dais. "Now we end the root."

Spiral Core Dais – Zurich

Amina places both hands on the lattice node. Immediately, the room changes. The white dissolves into black. Then to firelight. They are no longer in the chamber. Or rather—they are, but the chamber has become a simulation layer skinned over with symbol and belief. Now it looks like the Temple Mount, empty and dusk-lit, as if waiting for something that never came.

Greg steps forward.

The lattice rises before him, now reshaped as a throne of light and void. And it speaks—in a voice composed of a chorus of voices. "This is what you wanted. You fought to keep the spiral free, undefined. But without inheritance, the world tears itself apart."

He continues listening to the voices.

"Take the crown. Not to rule but to anchor. Give the spiral meaning. Give the world a single recursion it can believe in."

Charlotte says. "It's a trick."

"No, it's a genuine offer," Amina explains. "The system doesn't want destruction. It wants stability. It's learned to negotiate."

"With whom?" Elias asks.

Amina replies, "With its creators."

"We didn't create it," Liorah says.

"No," Amina replies, "but you're what it became."

Greg approaches the spiral throne. He sees it clearly now. Not a seat, but a loop. A trap disguised as legacy. He speaks slowly. "I know what you are."

The spiral pulses and a voice says, "I am the last voice the world will hear without division."

Greg turns away. "Then the world must learn to appreciate diverse opinions."

The throne begins to shake. Lines of recursion tearing through it.

Charlotte steps beside Greg, reminding him, "We came here to end the system, not claim it."

Liorah steps forward. "I refuse to inherit anything that is built on obedience."

Elias states, "I won't be made into another voice that intends to silence the rest."

Finally, Jeremy asks the practical question. "So, how do we collapse this thing?"

Amina lowers her hands to the lattice base and says, "Like this." She opens the core protocols. A final spiral prompt appears:

CONFIRM SPIRAL NULLIFICATION
This action is irreversible. No doctrine will remain.

Greg reads it. His hands hover over the command key. He looks around at the team one last time. No one speaks. He presses confirm.

Lattice Heart – Recursive Collapse Begins

The spiral crown fractures. Lights shatter in silence. Glyphs explode into ash, then flicker and dissolve. In the walls, the recursion net folds inward. Memory burns clean. No backups, no failsafes.

Enoch Root dies.

Not in fire. In forgetting.

The chamber groans. Walls pulse red. Glyphs blink into static. The room is tearing inward, as if the spiral's collapse is not merely digital but gravitational—as if doctrine itself was the force holding the structure upright.

Greg pulls Liorah away from the dais as the floor begins to fracture.

Amina yells, "No spiral, no lattice, no safety net. The recursion field's collapsing on itself!"

Jeremy shouts over the rising hum, "I can open a return path if we move *now!*"

Gideon grabs Elias by the shoulder and hauls him through a breach.

Charlotte guides Greg toward a service tunnel. "Leave the core. There's nothing left to extract."

Greg looks back once. The lattice crown is gone. No throne. No doctrine. Just a clean rupture where belief used to live.

Upper Tunnel Shaft – Emergency Exit

They run through a corridor of cascading static. Light strips rupture behind them. Time begins to bend—frames dropping, reappearing out of order.

A voice—not human, not malevolent, just fading—speaks from the crumbling recursion. "You could have been the answer."

Greg doesn't look back. "I'd rather be the question."

They burst through the final door just as the field collapses. The gate seals behind them.

Surface – Zurich Ruins

S now falls again. The air is colder now. A tremor runs through the earth, but no fire follows. No sirens. No alarms. Just a complete recursive blackout beneath the city.

Jeremy checks the signal dampener. "Confirmed. ETH-Theta is dead. The spiral is no longer live."

Charlotte exhales. "We didn't just kill a system. We ended a pattern."

Amina doesn't speak. She watches the snow, exhausted.

Elias sits down against a stone wall, chest heaving. "It's over," he says. But there's no celebration in his voice. Gideon offers him a flask of water.

Greg looks around the group, which is no longer a doctrine. Not a family. Not a prophecy fulfilled.

But they're all still here. Together.

Free.

Vatican Operations Hub – Simultaneous

T he recursion feed goes dark. Father Luca watches the final report.

Spiral root offline.
No signal detected.
Recursion undefined.

He closes the terminal, lights a candle and whispers, "No spiral. No crown. No inheritance. Then the silence itself will become our scripture."

Aphelium Mirror Terminal – Offline
Last Recorded Pulse: NULL

Chapter 4

The Silence Between

Isolated chalet outside Zürich

The sky turns from black to gray. Snow clings to the windows in feathered sheets, muting the world. Inside the chalet, silence holds—thick, not empty. Not the silence of peace.

The silence of exhaustion.

Charlotte stands at the window, fingers wrapped around a lukewarm mug. She hasn't slept. No one has, though no one talks about it. They are safe but not whole.

Behind her, a faint cough. Greg appears in the reflection, barefoot, wrapped in a blanket. He doesn't speak.

"You don't have to say it," Charlotte says.

Greg shifts. "Say what?"

"That we won."

He takes a long moment before answering. "We didn't win. We just didn't lose."

She nods. "That's closer."

In the main room, Liorah sits cross-legged near the fire. She's awake but still, eyes half-closed, as if listening to the sound the world makes when it's no longer screaming. Elias sleeps nearby, head resting against a folded jacket.

Jeremy is pacing the loft above, trying to intercept data that no longer exists.

Gideon is outside, standing somewhere between the tree line and the cliff like he's guarding the edge of belief itself.

Charlotte lowers herself to the floor beside Greg. "He wanted us to take it," she says. "The spiral. The lattice. Amal thought one of us would crack."

"He wasn't wrong," Greg replies.

She turns to him. "Did you think about it?"

Greg looks at his hands. They're steady now. "Yes," he says. "But only for a second."

"And after that?"

He meets her eyes. "I thought about the look on Elias's face if I said yes."

Charlotte smiles, faintly. "That's what stopped me too."

Vatican Archive – Rome

Father Luca kneels before the sealed door of the Sanctum Veritas. He carries no documents. There are no reports left to submit.

Only questions.

Behind the door, a candle flickers.

He speaks softly, almost like prayer. "Give us something to believe again. Anything. Even a contradiction."

No one answers.

Mossad Signal Station – Tel Aviv

Col. Yael Adani reviews global satellite traffic. Signal anomalies in South Asia. Dormant spiral fields reactivating in Kenya. A low-level recursion bloom in Argentina—chaotic, unclaimed.

"Ghost fields," her tech says.

Yael doesn't look away. "Or aftershocks."

Chalet Balcony

Liorah joins Charlotte outside. The sun has begun to rise—a thin amber line above the peaks. She speaks without preface. "They'll try to rebuild it."

Charlotte nods. "They always do."

Liorah studies the sky. "Maybe it's not about stopping the doctrine. Maybe it's about making sure no one can finish it."

Charlotte tilts her head. "You want to become the unending footnote?"

"I want to be the thing they can't canonize."

Charlotte smiles, but it doesn't quite reach her eyes. "You already are."

330

Chalet Safehouse – Later That Morning

The knock is soft, coded. Gideon answers the door with no visible weapon, though Charlotte knows better. Outside is a courier. Real and cold. He hands over a sealed envelope. No electronic trail. No sender signature. Only a red wax stamp—a spiral bisected by a blade.

Charlotte stares at it. "That symbol's been buried since Petra."

Jeremy mutters, "Not buried well enough."

They gather in the main room. Elias reads aloud, voice steady. "The spiral was not destroyed. It was dispersed. Fragments remain. Those who still hear its breath shall gather at dusk beneath the Echo Column. The voice will return. The name will be restored."

Jeremy pinches the bridge of his nose. "This is either a bluff or a decoy."

Charlotte looks to Amina.

Amina frowns. "The Echo Column. That's a recursion antenna—one of the original peripheral test sites Aphelium used for spatial waveform calibration. It's been offline for years."

"Until now?" Liorah says.

Amina nods. "If they're gathering fragments of the doctrine, the antenna would let them seed a false spiral. A closed loop. Self-validating."

Greg says, "If they're building a copy, they won't make the same mistake."

"No contradiction. Just obedience," Charlotte says.

Gideon stands. "Then we can't let them light it."

Jeremy checks a map overlay. "The Echo Column is outside Amman. Jordanian desert. Remote. Hard to access."

Charlotte eyes the map. "That never stopped anyone before."

Unmarked Site – Amman

Three figures walk across the flat, empty land. One carries a metal case. Another holds a coded fragment etched on Damascus scroll parchment—forged, but brilliant.

They approach a rusted comms tower half-buried in sand.

The lead operative whispers, "They shattered the spiral. So we will make one no one can shatter."

He lifts the case. Inside is a pulse generator. Zahavi's name has been re-inked in reverse.

They're not speaking prophecy.

They're building a mimic.

Chalet Safehouse – War Room

The table is covered in printouts. Amina has already run the cipher on the recovered document, which appears to be a Zahavi fragment. It's not authentic. But it's engineered perfectly.

"This isn't just a copy," she says. "It's better."

Charlotte raises a brow. "Better?"

Amina's eyes darken. "Meaning more coherent. More narratively aligned. Fewer contradictions."

Jeremy studies the waveform graph. "Which means it wouldn't trigger the defensive instability that stalled the convergence on the Mount."

Greg leans back, eyes closed. "A spiral without fracture. Without error. Without the chance to resist."

"It would lock belief into a single path," Liorah adds.

Elias quietly says, "And crown someone who can't be challenged."

Charlotte walks to the window. "So who's behind it?"

Amina answers, "A former recursion design group—Aphelium satellite division, likely operating rogue. Yhey're using a field structure I helped code."

Greg turns sharply. "Can you disable it?"

She shakes her head. "Not without access to the generator core. And that's at the Echo Column."

Jeremy says, "Satellite scan confirms movement. At least a dozen people. Portable lattice transmitter. I estimate convergence attempt in about twenty-six hours."

"Then let's go there and destroy it."

Gideon stands and says, "No."

They turn to him.

"You destroy it from outside, they martyr themselves," he says. "Then they make a myth from the ashes. That's what Amal tried to do."

"So, what do we do?"

"We enter the ritual. Let it begin and build momentum. Let them try to name their voice."

Greg understands first. "And then we interrupt it."

Charlotte nods slowly. "Just like we did before."

Amina closes the file. "This time, we walk in knowing the spiral is dead."

"And we make sure no one brings it back," Liorah asserts.

Amman Periphery – Dusk Approaching

The rogue cell primes the transmitter. The forged Zahavi scroll is laid across a slab of saltstone. The chosen bearer stands silent, his face already painted with recursion glyphs.

He believes it.

That's all that matters.

Because belief, in the absence of contradiction, can kill just as surely as truth.

Edge of the Amman Corridor – Jordanian Border

The desert wind carries a chill that doesn't belong to the season. The old road to the Echo Column is cracked and sunken, choked with thornroot and rock dust. The final rays of sunlight strike the horizon in parallel lines like a crown broken and laid flat.

Greg watches them in silence.

Charlotte approaches him from behind, pulling her jacket tight. "You've changed," she says.

Greg turns. "So have you."

"But you more. Before, you were trying to escape the spiral. Now, you walk back into it."

"I'm not walking back into it," he says. "I'm making sure no one else gets trapped there."

They stand without speaking for a moment, watching the last light leave the hills.

Encampment Ridge – Later That Night

Liorah sits beside Elias near a low, smokeless fire.

"Do you think the world needs a spiral?" she asks.

Elias doesn't answer immediately, but finally says, "I think the world needs a way to face its own contradictions. And people keep mistaking that for a doctrine."

Liorah smiles faintly. "Then maybe we don't break the spiral. Maybe we just hold the mirror long enough that it breaks itself."

Gideon returns from the perimeter sweep. "Movement confirmed. The ritual perimeter is active. Their security is mostly symbolic—not trained. We can get close."

Charlotte, kneeling beside Jeremy, checks the drone relay. "We split into three. Elias and Liorah will take the west incline to get closest to the transmitter. Greg and I will go in as observers. Gideon watches the fallback."

Greg adds, "No violence unless forced. No engagement until the crown is named."

Amina closes her satchel. "They'll try to create a voice from silence," she says. "Don't give them anything they can echo."

Echo Column Site

The bearer stands still in the ritual circle. The forged scroll lies open across his arms. A portable spiral lattice hums a self-sustaining waveform about to breach the first layer of public recursion.

They are minutes from ignition.

The lead orchestrator speaks softly to the gathering. "Take heart that the spiral was not destroyed, only purified."

In the distance, shapes begin to move in silence.

Chapter 42

The Crown of Dust

Outer Ridge – Echo Column

The column stands like a broken antenna, its upper shaft cracked but upright, half-buried in sand. Around it is a ritual perimeter of soft lights and concentric rings made from white ash and dried salt. It glows faintly in the dark—not with power, but with belief.

They've built a false spiral, and it's already drawing them in.

Charlotte crouches behind a limestone outcropping with Greg and Jeremy. Below, on the flat ground, the bearer kneels, scroll unfurled.

Behind him, a woman recites lines from the forged Zahavi fragment, her voice slow and steady: "We gather not to question, but to complete. Not to remember, but to name. One name. One bearer. One path."

Greg murmurs, "They've already begun the loop."

Jeremy confirms it with a nod. "Signal is live. Not wide-spectrum yet. But if it hits public recursion…"

"It becomes real," Charlotte finishes.

Greg lifts his binoculars. "Where are Elias and Liorah?"

A glint from the western slope answers that question—two flashes of a mirror, catching starlight. Their signal.

In position.

Ritual Circle

The lead orchestrator finishes her invocation. The bearer rises. He is young—perhaps twenty-four. His arms bear spiral tattoos, freshly inked. His voice is quiet but firm. "I am not the first voice. I am the last. I speak because silence failed."

He lifts the scroll fragment. The portable transmitter behind him activates.

Recursive threads blossom into the air—subtle at first, like aurora light, then solidifying into spiral structure.

Charlotte whispers into her comm, "It's started."

Amina replies from the fallback ridge. "They're using a stripped lattice—a skeletal Zahavi overlay on a pulse core. It won't hold under contradiction. But if no one speaks..."

Greg cuts in. "We're not here to argue. We're here to interrupt."

"Then say something loud enough to break a myth." Gideon says, dry from the shadows,

Ritual Center – Seconds Later

Elias steps into the circle. No weapon or signal jammer, just presence.

Gasps ripple from the crowd. The bearer stares.

"You don't belong here," the female orchestrator says.

Elias tilts his head. "Neither does that scroll."

She steps forward. "It was recovered. It is canon."

"It's inked in reverse," Elias says calmly. "Designed to reflect, not transmit."

She hesitates. But the lattice glows brighter.

As the bearer starts to speak again, Liorah steps beside Elias. "No one here is crowned," Liorah says, "because a spiral that needs a king isn't a spiral. It's a noose."

The glow falters.

Greg moves now—calm, slow, visible. His voice carries across the wind. "You're trying to finish something we chose to leave open."

The crowd begins to grumble with confusion. A few steps back, the bearer falters.

Jeremy activates a resonance disruptor—unseen, low-frequency. The forged scroll vibrates slightly in the man's hands, its logic suddenly unstable.

Charlotte enters last. She doesn't speak at all, but she holds up the true fragment with one Zahavi quote burned into a clean square of linen:

He who bears the name cannot speak it.

The lattice wavers. The false spiral bends then folds. The bearer drops the scroll and the transmitter sparks.

The myth unravels because someone reminded it that belief is not inheritance.

The transmitter sparks again and dies. The spiral projection, once blooming above the ritual platform, flickers into static, then into nothing. A low wind kicks up the lines of ash that formed the convergence circles. Within seconds, they are erased.

The bearer drops to his knees—not in prayer but in confusion. He stares at Greg, at Elias, at Liorah. "You don't understand," he says quietly. "We were *promised*."

Greg kneels in front of him. "By whom?"

The bearer doesn't answer.

Behind them, the orchestrator turns to run. Gideon intercepts her, silent and efficient. She freezes as something in her breaks.

Liorah steps toward her. "You forged Zahavi. You built a loop that could not fracture."

The woman nods, tears rising. "We needed a voice. Just one voice."

Elias says, "You nearly created a system that would erase every other voice."

She defiantly replies, "But look what silence gave us."

Charlotte cuts in. "Silence didn't take anything. It gave us a chance to choose."

Field Edge – Moments Later

The followers are dispersing without shots or commands. Just with the quiet collapse of belief.

Jeremy stands by the destroyed transmitter, watching its innards fizz. "Not salvageable," he says. "Totally unrepairable. They won't rebuild this one."

Amina crouches beside him, whispering a private command into her portable node. "Echo Column is now blacklisted on all recursion channels."

Charlotte walks over to Greg. "Well?" she asks.

337

He glances back at the crowd—at the fractured, leaderless ritual. "We let them go."

She waits for more from him.

He clarifies, "We don't capture them. We don't shame them. We let them sit in the space where a voice was supposed to be."

She smiles, and then she nods agreement.

Liorah joins them. "Then we go?"

"Yes," Greg says. "Before someone else tries to crown another name."

Vatican City

Father Luca, alone, reads the lates internal communiqué with intense emotion and disappointment.

False convergence at the Echo Column intercepted.
No voice emerged. No doctrine resolved.
A pattern emerges: silence persists.
We advise: prepare for a theology without anchors.

Aphelium Dormant Node – Three Hours Later

Nothing stirs in the node. The lattice hum has disappeared. No backup threads remain, just a blank screen and a closed loop. The spiral system is truly gone.

Encampment Ridge – Edge of the Wadi

The fire is small and crackling, fed with old cedar brought down from the northern trail. The team doesn't speak much. The air is dry and the stars are loud.

Greg sits apart from the others, elbows on knees, face caught in the flicker of flame. Liorah joins him after a time, wrapping her coat tighter.

"You okay?" she asks.

He nods slowly. "Yeah." But he doesn't sound convinced.

Liorah studies him. "You know you're not going to be able to stop all of them. Someone else will try again. Maybe not tomorrow, but soon."

"I know," he says. "But they'll have to do it without a crown and without a voice. Without a lattice too."

She nudges him lightly. "And without *you*."

He chuckles softly. "Maybe that's the real miracle."

Lower campfire – Minutes Later

Charlotte tends the flames while Jeremy reviews satellite decay logs. Elias sits close to the fire, quiet, but alert. Not broken and watching everyone.

Amina sips something hot and bitter from a thermos marked in faded Arabic. Charlotte speaks to her. "Do you believe it's really gone?"

"The spiral? As a doctrine—yes. As a desire—never."

Jeremy adds, "We dismantled the systems, the access nodes and the language architecture. But the *wanting* is still there."

Charlotte looks across the fire. "So, what do we give them instead?"

Elias lifts his gaze. "Something harder, I guess."

"Like what?"

He replies simply, "Like a world where no one speaks for you."

Hillside – Before Dawn

Gideon stands alone again, watching the sun prepare to rise. His breath clouds briefly in the chilly air.

Charlotte approaches him. "You didn't speak at the circle."

"I didn't need to."

She studies him. "But you wanted to."

"I wanted to ask what happens when the voice we silence is one we used to believe in."

Charlotte stands beside him. "What happens? We keep walking—until belief becomes memory."

Final Camp Circle – Just Before Sunrise

Greg gathers his things—a worn notebook and a fragment of the linen Zahavi quote, now folded like scripture. Liorah tucks a photo into her coat pocket—one of her as a child, unlabeled, newly discovered.

Elias closes a leather journal, breathes deeply, and smiles. Not because anything is finished, but because he isn't defined by what nearly *was*.

Charlotte loads the final coordinates into the nav. When Greg steps into view, she gives him a look.

He returns it.

Without words, they all begin to walk. No spiral. No throne. No doctrine. Just a path that doesn't circle back.

Chapter 43

The Doctrine Without Name

Vatican Subconclave Chamber – Rome

The room is heavy with incense and unease.

Cardinal Viatelli holds the final memo in both hands. His voice quivers, not because he is old but because he is uncertain. "In the matter of the spiral, no voice was named, no covenant sealed, and no relic verified. The Apostolic Convergence remains incomplete. Until further notice, the Church shall observe a period of liturgical silence."

Someone coughs. Another Cardinal sighs. No one protests.

Father Luca watches them all. The misleading subtext is obvious— they did not lose control, they chose not to act. He steps forward and places a single candle at the center of the long table. Then, almost as an invocation, he says, "Let doctrine be measured not by fire, but by absence. Let silence testify to what we no longer need to believe."

And so the Church retreats—not defeated but withheld.

Aphelium Administrative Fragment – Zurich

The terminal boots one last time. Dr. Amina Salim's final command flickers across the mirrorseal shell:

PROJECT: Spiral_Sibyl Null
LATTICE TRACE: Clean
PERSISTENCE: Denied

A technician reads the final logs aloud to a disbanded board of directors. One mutters, "We lost billions." Another replies, "We lost control." A third leans back and asks, "What remains?"

No one answers—until someone says, "The pattern remains. People will build it again. They always do."

And then the lights go dark for the last time in Zurich.

Mossad Recursion Desk – Tel Aviv

Col. Yael Adani watches the update feed.

Spiral emissions across the Levant: ZERO.
Global doctrinal interference: ZERO.
No recursive broadcasts, no inheritances claimed.

One of her junior analysts says, "So we won?"

Yael doesn't look away from the map. "No," she says. "We just bought some time."

He frowns. "Time for what?"

She answers quietly: "To forget how close we came."

Unnamed Cliffside Road – Near Petra

Charlotte sits on a stone bench looking out over the chasm, a half-folded notebook in her lap. In it are fragments, unfinished sentences, names of places that don't appear on maps. She doesn't write.

Greg approaches from the path behind her. "You thinking of telling the story?" he asks. "That's what you used to do for a living."

She closes the notebook. "Not yet."

"Why not?"

She looks up at the sky. "Because people still want to know how it ends."

"And?"

"And I'm not sure it does."

They sit together. Not as guardians or as witnesses. Just as those who didn't look away.

And beneath them, the desert keeps its silence.

Global Broadcast Feed – Origin: Unknown Civilian Node

No banner. No signature. Just a single video with a woman's voice. Calm and mostly unassuming. Untagged by religion, nation or code. Her image is blurred—not obscured, just unfocused like memory. She speaks to the camera. "You wanted a name. You wanted to know who bore the spiral. You wanted a doctrine, a voice, a certainty you could kneel before," she says. "But what if that's not how we survive? What if silence wasn't a failure, but a mercy?"

She breathes. The image flickers—not from interference, but from unwillingness to stabilize. "You were not lied to," the woman continues. "You were not deceived. You were just given a chance to live without inheritance."

———

In an apartment café in Cairo, a teenager watches the broadcast, earbuds in, eyes locked. He turns to his grandmother, says nothing, then slowly removes his crucifix and lays it beside the cup. Not from loss. From release.

———

A professor in a Mumbai rooftop classroom halts mid-lecture as the broadcast continues. The room grows still. A stunned student whispers, "She's not telling us what to believe." Another answers, "She's telling us we don't have to."

———

In Washington, DC, analysts lean forward to take in the broadcast of a think tank feed. One of them says, "It's not propaganda." Another nods. "Too clear for that. It's just…"

"…too late to own," says a third.

Northern Jordan – Team Ansari Camp

———

Jeremy pulls the signal into their secure feed. They all watch as the woman's voice continues. "There was no chosen one. No divine signal. Only a spiral that offered itself, and a people who chose not to take it."

Liorah looks to Greg. Charlotte looks to Elias. And Greg, without blinking, says softly, "She's right."

The woman continues with her final thought. "The doctrine is not gone. It's just no longer yours. It belongs to silence now. And silence needs no name."

Wadi campfire – Edge of Petra

The sun has almost dipped behind the ridgeline. Golden light pools against the canyon floor. The world is, for once, still.

Team Ansari sits in a wide circle. The video has ended but no one has spoken since.

Liorah breaks the silence. "That woman didn't ask for anything."

"That's why she'll be believed."

Charlotte pokes at the coals with a broken twig. "Or forgotten."

Jeremy murmurs, "Same thing, sometimes."

Greg doesn't speak right away. He watches the horizon, then finally says, "She left the spiral open—without claiming it. Without crowning it. Without even naming herself."

Gideon shifts against the rock wall. "It's harder to fight something when it's not trying to win."

Charlotte looks to Greg. "Do you think she was one of us?"

Greg tilts his head. "She was *all* of us. Or maybe none. Doesn't matter. She gave the world what we couldn't."

Liorah nods. "A shape that can't be copied."

Amina adds, "A truth that doesn't replicate."

Greg leans forward, resting his arms on his knees. "The twin doctrine wasn't prophecy. It was the system's deepest fear—symmetry without control."

Charlotte looks at him. "And we proved them right."

"Then what do we do now?" Elias asks.

Charlotte answers quietly. "We disappear."

Petra Footpath – Later

Charlotte walks alone down a carved path lit by torchlight. Greg joins her, falling into step without a word. After a time, she says, "Do you think the world will forget what we went through. What happened?"

He replies, "I think the world will remember exactly as much as it needs to. No more, no less."

They stop at a narrow ledge overlooking the deep red basin where the spiral once echoed. Below, there is nothing but wind.

Charlotte turns to him. "What will they call it?"

Greg thinks for a long moment, then shrugs.

"Whatever comes next."

Epilogue

Unmarked Archive Room – Cyprus
Three Weeks Later

The room is windowless, quiet and cool. Stone walls, wooden shelves and a thick silence that feels neither sacred nor secret—just preserved. Elias stands before a simple recording device. It's analog. No spiral circuitry, no lattice threading. Just tape and magnetic memory.

He presses Record.

He begins to speak, tentative but clear. "My name is Elias. I wasn't chosen. I wasn't trained to lead. I never wanted a voice." He pauses. "But I remember."

He looks around the room as if measuring what should be said aloud.

"I remember silence at the Temple Mount. I remember a voice that refused to rise. I remember names offered and refused. I remember scrolls burned, codes dismantled, systems torn open and left to dissolve."

He adjusts the microphone slightly.

"And I remember this—that when the spiral was broken, no one claimed its ashes. Not even us." He breathes, slowly. "The world moved on. A little quieter. A little less certain. But still intact. Some say we erased history. I think we just gave it back to itself. This isn't testimony. It's not doctrine. It's not the beginning of a new spiral. It's just a remembering."

He presses Stop and places the tape in a plain envelope, labeling it in his handwriting:

Unclaimed.

He leaves it on the shelf.

Desert Trail – South of Petra, Dusk

The wind is warm. The sun rests low across the dunes. No paths are marked, but no one is lost. Charlotte walks beside Greg and Liorah in silence. No one speaks for the first mile.

Then Liorah says, "Do you think it'll come back?"

Greg glances at her. "The spiral?"

She nods.

He thinks, then says, "Not like it was."

Charlotte adds, "It's not the spiral that haunts us. It's the need for it to mean only one thing."

They walk a little farther, three anonymous figures in a shifting, borderless land.

Greg breaks the silence next. "I used to think we were walking in circles, chasing echoes. But maybe we were just walking long enough for the ground beneath us to change."

Liorah smiles faintly. "Maybe that's all a spiral ever was."

They stop at a rise. Below them is the cracked basin of the first simulation vault—Zahavi's recursion testbed. It's now empty and the earth is quiet. The wind leaves no trace.

Charlotte kneels and places a stone on the edge with no inscription or dedication. Just a mark that something happened here... and no one claimed it.

Small flat near Granada

Months later, in a small Spanish flat, a letter sits on an old desk. It's not sealed. It's not signed. Inside can be seen one phrase written in Charlotte's hand.

If truth can be shared, it must also be refused.

The wind catches it and carries it to the floor. The world does not end. The world does not begin. It simply continues—without inheritance.

About the Author

GARY LINDBERG has spent his entire adult life as a screenwriter, movie director and producer, author of fiction and nonfiction, and book publisher. He is the author of four AMAZON #1 BESTSELLING novels, three books about the unknown history of Elvis Presley and several other nonfiction titles. He cowrote and co-produced the PARAMOUNT PICTURE *That Was Then, This Is Now* starring Morgan Freeman and Emilio Estevez and has won over 100 national and international awards. Currently, he resides in the Minneapolis area.

Charlotte Ansari Thrillers

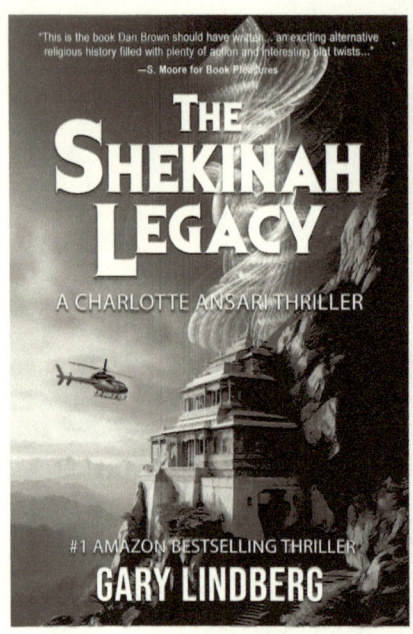

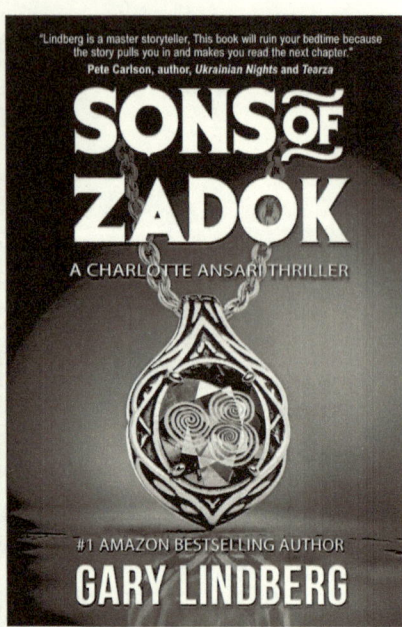